WHITE SUGAR, BROWN SUGAR

A story of two boys and a friendship that defied the odds of race and time.

MICHAEL A. PYLE

WHITE SUGAR, BROWN SUGAR
by
Michael A. Pyle
Published by:
Armstrong Media Group, LLC
1655 N. Clyde Morris Blvd., Suite 1
Daytona Beach, FL 32117
armstrongmediagroup@gmail.com

Copyright 2012-Armstrong Media Group, LLC
2023, revised reprint

This book is dedicated to everybody who ever suffered racial or other discrimination, everybody who ever suffered from alcohol or drug dependence or addiction, including those who died, those who overcame it, those who never overcame it or have not yet overcome it, those who utilized AA or NA, successfully or not, those who work as counselors or other treatment specialists for drug, alcohol, delinquency, anti-recidivism or similar treatment organizations, and those who work in hospice and other end-of-life assistance organizations.

PROLOGUE

"I never expected to still be alive at the old age of thirty-nine," the white man said.

The black man sitting in the rocking chair to his left put a glass to his lips and took a sip. He looked at the white man, eyes smiling, and, emphasizing a black dialect that wasn't his speech pattern anymore, "Ah shore didn't think I'd be sittin' heah on the docks a yo fancy white folks club, sippin' a soft drink and rockin'."

Hearing a baseball being smacked by a bat at the nearby ballpark, David "Jude" Armstrong said, "With my dad gone, it's probably the last time I'll be here." He took a sip from a glass of club soda with lime.

"Lansing was a great man," Roosevelt Harris said. "I'd never have survived if it wasn't for him."

"He liked you better than he liked me, Roosevelt."

"Naw, Jude. Your dad loved you, in his way. He was just a gruff old guy."

A cabin cruiser edged into a slip. Its wake slapped the pilings beneath the dock.

Jude's son Mark approached, carrying a fishing pole, followed by Roosevelt's son, Tad. "Dad." Mark pointed to the coquina stone wall on the other side of the basin and said, "Can we go fish over there?"

"Me too?" Tad asked, looking at his father.

The two men glanced at each other, like a couple of referees making sure they were in accord, and both nodded. The boys ran down the dock.

"Do you worry about your kids getting caught up in what we did?" Roosevelt asked.

"You know it, especially when it comes to Kim. She's more like me and my mom.

"We were lucky." Jude's wife, Joyce, and Roosevelt's wife, Gloria, came out of the yacht club with Kim. Kim leaned on Jude's leg. Gloria laid a hand on Roosevelt's shoulder.

Jude said, "You know, I can look right over there, across the water, and I can see you, the age of Tad, fishing with your parents, your aunt, and your mom."

"And I can picture you right here, looking just like Mark, walking along with your cast net, watching the water. And your dad working on his boat."

They were both silent again for a while. Finally, Roosevelt said, "Well it's been quite a journey, thirtysomething years, ending with five of the longest days in my life. I'll never get over these last days with your dad."

"I won't either."

PART I

Early 1960s

Chapter 1

ROOSEVELT HARRIS SAT in the back seat of the old Buick between his mama and his aunt as his grandfather, Papa, came to a stop. The dusty car heaved as he shifted into reverse. Breathing heavily, Papa turned and looked back. His gray eyebrows sprouted from dark brown ridges, and wiry, gray hair rose above his deeply wrinkled forehead. Roosevelt's grandmother, Nana, leaned out the passenger window and pointed with gnarled fingers as they crept toward the curb. Five cane poles stretched from the top of the dashboard through the middle of the front seat and out the back window on the left side, where his mama sat.

Roosevelt glanced at his mama and smiled, glad she'd come back home. Fishing wasn't the same without her.

Ahead stood a dock with a sign saying HRYC. It led to a sprawling white wooden building, capped with a faded red tin roof and perched above the water on thick wooden stilts. Fancy white folk came and went, stood around talking or tended to their large boats.

Slightly behind the car, a white boy walked along the wall with a cast net. He was about Roosevelt's age, eleven. He usually fished on the HRYC docks.

The white boy glanced over at them, and then returned his gaze to the still water. While walking slowly along the wall, he draped part of the net over one arm, spread out the rest with his other hand, and stuck a sinker between his teeth. He stopped and flung the net. It twirled in neat circles like a lasso and plopped onto the water. He pulled the string to close it, yanked it up, and dropped several thrashing mullets into a bucket.

Shifting into park, Papa looked out the window at the white boy and muttered under his breath, "Dat ain' right."

As the family climbed out of the car, Auntie Barbara said, "Dat white boy takin' all da fish. What he need all dem fish fo?" Then, raising her voice, she said, "Hey, you. Get outa heah."

The white boy looked up and stopped. Nana and Mama positioned themselves in their usual fishing spots along the wall on Beach Street, legs dangling over the wall, and tips of poles close to the water. Papa sat on an upturned milk crate. Roosevelt walked along the wall toward where the boy stood and dropped his line into the murky water.

David "Jude" Armstrong had been fishing on the Halifax River Yacht Club docks when he'd noticed the swirling evidence of a school of mullet on the streetside of the basin. He recognized the Negro family as they emerged from the creaking old car. The Negro boy walked toward him. He was thin, with tight, curly, reddish hair cropped short. He wore beat-up jeans and a blue, wrinkled T-shirt. His dark skin showed through holes in the fabric of his dirty sneakers.

While the skinny lady and the old woman fished silently, the lady on the wall yelled and waved her arms and then propped her hands on her hips. He couldn't hear what she was saying.

Jude would have to pass the family to get back to the yacht club. He poured some water from the bucket and draped the net partially over it to hide the fish.

As Jude walked toward Beach Street, the Negro boy hooked a mullet and yanked the pole back. The mullet almost struck Jude in the face. He ducked. The boy looked at him, white eyes peering from chocolate-colored skin. "Did I hitcha?"

"Uh-uh." Then he said, "How do ya catch mullet on a hook?"

The Negro boy smiled, pulled a piece of bread out of the pocket of his ragged jeans, pinched off a small chunk and rolled it into a ball. He popped it into his mouth, wet it with spit and stuck it on a tiny hook. He held up the baited hook, then swung the pole around and dropped the tip to just above the water.

Roosevelt pointed at the white boy's net. "Where ya get dat net?"

The white boy looked at him through bright blue eyes and grinned. His hair was light brown, streaked with blond, and his tan face was dotted with freckles. "My dad." His flabby belly hung slightly over the waistband of his shorts, which were all he wore.

"How much it cost?"

"I don't know. About five or ten dollars, I guess."

The old colored man called from the other wall and motioned with his hand. "Roos'velt, come on over heah."

Roosevelt shrugged his shoulders and looked sheepishly at Jude. The boys walked together. Jude glanced down to be sure the net obscured the fish in the bucket. Roosevelt stopped near the old man and baited his hook.

As the white boy continued down the sidewalk toward the fancy white folks' docks, with his net slung over his shoulder, Papa said, "Don' be goin' roun' da white boy. He not yo kind." He shook his head. "Fishin' spose ta be peaceful. Time ta use yo mind, talk with yo family, and the Lord will let a fish bite ever now and again. What dat boy done ain't right."

"Yessuh," Roosevelt answered.

The sun sizzled. Jude walked down the weather-beaten dock, to where his dad tinkered on his boat.

His dad hopped onto the dock and said, "Son, do you realize what you're doing? That family comes here to fish, probably to catch dinner. They do it as a family. Your net is fine for getting bait fish. But not to raid the basin. Don't do that again." His dad rarely used his name, but if he had, he would call him "David."

Being scolded by his dad always shook him up. Jude didn't get what the big deal was. He looked over at the wall, where Roosevelt and the family sat, poles hanging over the water, occasionally tossing a pole backward when they had a bite. He glanced back at his dad and shrugged. "Okay."

Jude's mother staggered toward them with a man named Duke. Puffing on a cigarette through her black cigarette holder, she tossed a strand of reddish-brown hair off her forehead. Duke held a glass of whiskey in one hand and an unfiltered Camel in the other. His dark brown hair was greased back. On overnight boating trips, Duke would go from boat to boat at dawn banging on boat tops and yelling, "It's Bloody Mary time." Shaking his head and frowning, Jude's dad would proclaim, "That man's not yacht club material."

Jude's father stared at the two. His mother was wearing her stupid sunglasses, with gold-colored leaves sticking up around the tops of the frames like rays of the sun. When she'd bought them, she'd announced, "It's gold filigree."

Duke motioned toward Roosevelt and his family, fishing peacefully on the wall. "Those niggers supposed to be fishing over there?"

Jude's father shot him a look. "We don't use that kind of language."

"Ought to stay across the tracks," Duke said.

Jude's father shook his head and grimaced.

Jude's mother swayed slightly. "I'm going to the house to pick up the scrapbook so I can show the pictures from the Commodore's Ball." Her voice was hoarse and her words heavy.

Jude wasn't sure when things had changed between his parents, but his dad frequently seemed grumpy and his mom distant and disinterested. Their frequent arguments were always followed by awkward silence. His mom came to the yacht club during the day more often than before but spent her time with men like Duke who drank a lot.

"I'll be back in a few. Duke's running me over to the house," his mom said, taking another drag on her cigarette. "In his new MG." She smiled, oblivious to her husband's glare, turned and stumbled away. Duke set his glass on a piling, flicked his cigarette butt into the water, smirked at Jude's dad and followed.

His dad was speechless. Jude walked down the dock, stabbed by anxiety.

* * * * * * *

Jude rubbed the head of Sooty, the fluffy, jet-black Persian cat purring and swishing back and forth at his feet, whipping her tail against his knee as she turned.

"What are you doing?" he whispered, though nobody would have heard since it was five in the morning. She gazed at him through penetrating green eyes. Kellie, his pet Sheltie, joined them in the hallway.

Jude descended the inside stairs to the garage, accompanied by Sooty and Kellie. He crept through the garage in darkness, flicked on a light switch, pulled up the heavy wooden door and pushed his bike outside into the morning hush. Car tires hummed across the metal grate of the drawbridge over the Halifax River to the south, and then clackety-clacked along the concrete sections of the bridge. The bridge joined Silver Beach Avenue on the east side to Orange Avenue, which ran from the west end of the bridge, past the baseball stadium, the fire station just north of the yacht club, and then on past the railroad tracks and into the Negro section.

Jude often crossed the tracks with his mother when taking Pearl Mae to her small, tan, concrete-block house. Pearl Mae was a young colored woman who'd worked at the Armstrong house for as long as Jude could remember. Jude's dad was helping her pay for college.

He loved early morning, alone. Sooty trounced off after a palmetto bug on the driveway, swatted it and backed away, her back arched.

The air hung on him warm and sticky. He leapt onto his bike and trudged up the steep hill of the driveway as the chain clanged lightly against the chain guard. Birds chirped in the darkness. A dog barked. At the top of the driveway, the pavement crested and dropped steeply toward the street; he flew down the hill, his hair blowing back and the wind echoing in his ears. Rounding the turn onto the sidewalk, he heard the waves pounding at the beach, a few blocks away.

As he pedaled, he planned his day. It was already 5:15. There was an awful lot to do before school. The papers were thin on Tuesdays, unlike Thursdays, when folding the extra sections of advertisements required another half hour, and sometimes he couldn't jam the entire batch into the canvas bag at one time. A police car cruised slowly eastward toward the beach as he passed Broadway.

As he neared his father's law office, where he had an outside room just for folding papers, a garbage truck stopped next to a group of dented tin garbage cans, brakes squeaking in the still air. A young colored man hung on the back of the truck. He had dark skin, richer and blacker than any Jude had ever seen. He bounded off the truck, lifted a can with one hand and threw it into the hopper.

The only colored people he'd had contact with were Roosevelt and his family, Blackie, who worked in the kitchen at the yacht club, Pearl Mae, and Grover, who mowed the Armstrong's lawn once a week. He'd seen Pearl Mae's son before but hadn't talked to him. The man yanked the can from the hopper and threw it back against the two empty cans standing on the sidewalk. They clanged together, and one rolled into the gutter, reverberating the sound of metal on concrete. Mrs. Baker's dog howled.

One time some years ago, Jude had used the word "nigger" in his father's presence. His father had turned to him, furious, and said, "That is a terrible, hateful word and is absolutely forbidden in this household."

Jude knew that colored people weren't allowed on the beachside of the river unless they were working, usually solitary older men, on beat-up bicycles, towing lawnmowers, with tangled, rusted metal rakes and shears attached with twine. Negroes lived to the west of the railroad tracks that ran parallel to the river. They could freely travel east of the railroad tracks to the west bank of the river, and onto the west side of the bridge. But they couldn't cross the bridge unless they met some exception. He had no idea why.

His bundle of papers waited outside his little room. He reached into the off-white canvas bag hanging between his handlebars, with big red letters saying Daytona Beach Morning Journal/Evening News, pulled out his wire cutters and snipped the wire around the bundle. He pulled off the handwritten notes from Circulation—two new customers, one hold for a week, and one drop.

He opened the door to his folding room, pulled the string that switched on the bare overhead light bulb, sat on the wooden step and started rolling. A cockroach scurried by.

He folded and snapped rubber bands on the papers, while scanning the front page. President Lyndon Johnson's picture was on the front page, but he gave up on the article after a moment. He pulled out the local section and saw a picture of Dr. Lee Steward on the front page, standing proudly next to an eight-foot sailfish he'd caught on White Lady III last weekend. White Lady III was the Armstrong family's 26-foot Chris Craft, and Jude saw himself in the background of the photo, hosing down the deck. Jude knew Dr. Steward as Uncle Lee. He wasn't really his uncle, but he had to call all close family friends uncle or aunt so and so.

A week ago, the front page contained an article about a bunch of Negroes causing a big ruckus in St. Augustine by trying to enter a white diner. They were arrested. Every day since then the paper had a story about demonstrations; first the Negroes, then white people, and in some cases both. Today the paper said white people were marching into the colored neighborhoods. Some preacher named Martin Luther King was being held in jail in Jacksonville so he could testify at some hearings. Jude knew from his father that a hearing was when a lawyer argued about something in front of a judge. He only came across words like segregation and integration while sitting here scanning the paper, or once in a while from Walter Cronkite. He finished wrapping the papers—only twelve minutes—good time.

He jumped on his bike, dropped a paper on Mrs. Wilcox's front walk and bopped one against the screen at old man Cochran's apartment. The sun's first rays were just peeking over houses to the east. He crossed Halifax Avenue for the river houses and zoomed down a long, dark driveway, his heart pounding, thinking of whoever or whatever could be hiding in the bushes. He flopped a paper on the front porch of a creaky old wooden house and rolled over the grass and to the next house. He veered to avoid an armadillo lumbering along a walkway, but it skittered off.

He ran the locations and spellings for this morning's geography test through his mind. He wished it would be multiple-choice questions. But Mrs. Longdon always said, "If you know it, you know it. You don't need me giving you hints."

The other part of his route took him around the area where the winos and bums hung out at night. He zipped down Main Street toward the ocean, dropping papers at doors leading to street-level shops and upstairs residences. The bright orange sun hung under the coquina walkway connecting the boardwalk to the pier. The stench of old garbage and stale alcohol was strong. Rats milled about near garbage cans.

Since it was only 6:30, he rode home on the beach's hard-packed sand. A few wispy clouds floated high in the sky. The waves loomed clear and blue and crashed hard. White foam rushed toward the shore and then slid back into the sea. Seagulls pecked in the sand and chased tiny fish around in shallow pools left behind by the retreating water. A few people strolled on the sand.

Arriving home, he sped down his driveway and skidded to a stop in front of the garage. Upstairs, his mother sat at the table with a cup of coffee and a cigarette. It didn't seem like she was fixing breakfast today.

* * * * * * *

Jude sat toward the front of class holding his hand over the right side of his face, trying to avoid Melissa Bretz's gaze.

"Did you study?" she whispered.

He glanced over at her. She smiled, blushed, and shifted her gaze, thank goodness.

Danny Jones smiled at Jude and then at the floor. Jude had tried to make friends with Danny, but Danny's family was very poor. One day Bill Olson had said, "Him and his family live like a bunch a niggers." Jude was shocked, but he never talked much to Danny after that. He was ashamed for not saying anything but didn't want to be teased for playing with a poor boy.

Mrs. Longdon entered, clapping her hands. "Everybody in your place. Right now!" Jude was already sitting quietly in his seat.

Some of the louder kids lingered, talking and horsing around, until she raised her voice.

At recess, the boys played kickball. As always, Jude was among the last to get on a team. When he missed a kick, John glared at him and said, "Useless." Jude hated sports. His parents forced him to play baseball, just like they forced him to play piano. He dreaded every baseball practice and every game. He felt like such a klutz in his gray uniform, "Bricklayers and Tile Setters" emblazoned on the back in red, his huge red hat saying BL & TS. Most of the other boys played as though they'd been born with a ball in their hands.

The geography test was fill-in-the-blank. He couldn't remember how to spell Czechoslovakia to save his life. They exchanged papers for grading, and he got a ninety-one.

After school, Jude realized other kids were going to Jack Pierce's house. Jude had hung around with him when they were younger, but now Jack was popular. He wondered what it was that caused the other kids to want to hang around with Jack. Jude's father was a lawyer. Jack's just owned a plumbing business. It was probably because Jack wore blue jeans to school and played sports. Jude didn't like watching kids making plans, so he went home.

* * * * * * *

Jude plunked the black and white keys of the piano, producing an awkward rendition of "Camp Town Races." His teacher said, "Marvelous, my lad," as ashes dropped onto the keys from the cigarette that bobbed up and down in his mouth.

Jude knew it wasn't marvelous. He couldn't follow the beat. His mother would make a big production of having him play for the crowd at parties. The guests' faces confirmed that they'd be happy not to hear him.

Pearl Mae was in the basement, ironing and humming along with some Negro preacher hollering on the radio beside her. The radio was turned way down, but he could still hear yes suhs and dass rights in the background. "How my boy doin'?" she asked, not missing a hum. "Did you do good at school today?"

"I'm okay. School was okay."

"I hear you done real good on your repo't card."

"Yes ma'am." He liked Pearl Mae. Her skin was the color of coffee ice cream. She liked to tell him she used to bathe him when he was a baby. That was embarrassing.

Jude walked down to the river and onto the floating dock in front of his house. He found two crabs in the trap, but they were jammed with the orange spongy stuff that meant they were pregnant, so he tossed them back.

He pushed his wooden pram, a small heavy sailboat with a squared bow, off the sandy beach and into the dark water. He paddled away from shore, not bothering to put the weighty cloth sail up. Just past the oyster bar, which was about four feet under at the moment, he dropped the paddle in the bottom of the pram, lay back and shut his eyes. The water lapped quietly against the bottom. The crack of a bat smacking a baseball carried over from the practice field across the river, where Jude would stand in the baking sun hoping to avoid a ball. A fish splashed nearby.

Jude thought of the school kids messing around at Jack's. He wondered again about why he didn't fit in. Suddenly he realized it was almost five o'clock. He needed to get going. He paddled to the shore and took off for his evening paper route.

* * * * * * *

When Jude returned home, his dad was sitting in front of Walter Cronkite, tossing down salted peanuts and savoring a Schlitz in a frosted mug. "How's my boy?" he asked without looking at Jude.

"Okay." He looked out the window at the shore. He sat down, but after a few minutes decided not to interrupt his father's news watching.

His mother's mood seemed better. She put dinner on the table—broiled mackerel, smashed potatoes, salad, and spinach. He hated spinach but would drown it with vinegar.

"Soup's on," she said, not to anybody in particular.

At dinner, his dad turned to him. "David, the light was on this morning in your room at the office."

Jude looked away to avoid the stare. His stomach became an instant knot. His mind raced back. "I was sure I'd turned it off," he said.

"I hope not to hear of that again."

Jude quivered. His father's stare burned a hole through him.

"Yes sir," came out all shaky and high. His sister glanced at him and looked back at her plate. His mother ate silently.

After dinner, lying in bed, he felt almost sick to his stomach. Tears began to break through his tightly sealed eyelids. Kellie plopped her face onto his bed and whimpered. She understood. He reached over and put his arms around her furry neck. She

licked his cheek. He'd be sure to keep his room at the office
absolutely perfect and lawyer-like.

* * * * * * *

Roosevelt awoke confused, frightened by the sound of things
banging in another room.

"You fuckin' ho," a man yelled.

"Fuck you," Mama answered.

Nana shuffled in, pushing the door closed behind her.
Roosevelt looked across the room and realized that his mama
hadn't slept in her bed.

"Roosevelt. You needs to be gettin' up now fer school." He
looked at her for an explanation. Her puffy dark brown cheeks
wiggled when she talked. "Don't you worry none. He leavin' now."
She stroked his cheek.

His mother yelled, "I dint fuckin' take yo stash. Get the fuck
out." The front door slammed, vibrating the windows in the
bedroom.

Nana smiled. "Let's get goin' baby." She leaned down and
pulled him to her. "It'll be awright."

The gritty sand ground under his feet on the linoleum floor.
Mama was in the only bathroom. He went back to his room to get
dressed. He found a T-shirt that wasn't too wrinkled and pulled on
some pants. He slipped his shoes on with no socks.

Mama came out of the bathroom all funny like she got when
she was about to get herself in trouble. Her words dragged out,
"There my boy. How's it goin'?" She went to hug him, but he didn't
hug back. She rubbed her hand across her nose, down her face and
then to her wrist. "Baby whassa matta? Y'eat yo breakfus yet?" He
didn't feel like eating. He knew it wasn't going to be all right.

Walking to school in the hot, still air, he passed small wooden
houses surrounded by dry dirt and weeds.

He stopped at Mr. Washington's house, where the old man
was raking dried leaves into a pile, leaving tracks on brown dirt.
"How yo mama, Roos'velt?"

"Doin' fine. You ain' goin' cross da rivah taday?"

"Naw. Flat." He pointed to a flat tire on the rear of his bicycle,
hooked up to pull a lawnmower stacked with two rakes and a hoe.

Rufus skidded up on his bike. "Ulysses done stab Ben last
night."

"Huh? You seen it?"

"Yeah, was goin' inta da sto'." He pointed. "Ulysses stood ova there by the do'. Ben come up. They bof smile at each other and nod. Then Ben put out his hand to shake and Ulysses run a knife in 'im. Pull it out and walk off. Ben stood dare looking real surprised."

"I ain' never seen nobody die," Roosevelt said.

"I ain't neitha. Dint seem like much. He just kind of move down to da ground real slow like. Dat was it."

Roosevelt shuddered. They walked to class.

Sweat was pouring down Mrs. Jefferson's forehead. The other students were talking, horsing around and making loud, rude comments about some girl out in the playground. The bell rang, and Mrs. Jefferson blew her whistle. It always took several long blows before anybody paid any attention. The students moved slowly toward their seats.

History was about the Freedom Train and Abraham Lincoln. Sudie answered a question, "the Emaciation Proclamation."

Mrs. Jefferson laughed and said, "Emancipation, but that ain't far off the truth." Nobody seemed to know what was funny. Roosevelt sure didn't.

A bald white man wearing a wrinkled brown suit came into the classroom and sat in the back. Mrs. Jefferson stammered. That wasn't like her. She probably didn't run across too many white people either. With the mysterious white man spying on them, the class was quieter and better behaved than usual.

As they left class, Regina said, "You know dey gonna put us and crackas in da same school someday."

"You nuts," Willie Bob answered.

* * * * * * *

At lunch Roosevelt sat, minding his own business. A big kid named Punch came up, leaned down and said, "Bastard." Roosevelt looked up at his sneering jiggly cheeked face. "You know what a bastard is, doncha?" Punch asked. "You is a bastard," he continued "'cause you ain' got no papa and yo mama don't even know who was yo papa."

Roosevelt had never been in a fight. He knew he was supposed to say they should meet at the old Esso Station on the corner of Orange and Campbell. But he'd rather get out of it without looking like a sissy. A small crowd was gathering, including a couple of girls.

"I do know who my papa be," Roosevelt lied. "They plenty a folk what don't live together. Ain' nothin'."

"Yo mama a ho," Punch replied. "Ax anyone."

Roosevelt felt his entire body become tight and tingly. The crowd and voices became distant. Leaping through the air, he struck Punch's throat with one fist and grabbed his ear with the other. Punch fell backward and landed with a thud. Roosevelt grabbed Punch's face with his hands and sat hard on his chest. Punch's eyes widened, and he made a choking sound. Somebody said, "Yo Roos'velt, let 'im go." But Roosevelt didn't want to. Punch tried to talk, so Roosevelt released his hold, but Punch couldn't get it out. Blood gushed from his lip.

This should teach everybody. Nobody'd better talk about his mama again. He'd taken down the biggest bully of the school.

Roosevelt walked home slowly, kicking the dry dust and wondering what Mama was doing. She wouldn't be home for dinner and probably not for a few days. She had the look real bad this morning. He felt a tear forming and shook his head to make it disappear. He was cool and tough and had just taken care of Punch like nobody ever had. He could not be seen blubbering like a baby.

He passed the lot where the old men and "da nevah-worked," as Auntie Barbara called them, played cards, drank wine and told stories. The toothless one had just finished telling some kind of story and let out a happy whooping noise. The fat one was roaring so loud he about fell off the tree stump.

Younger men stood by the shade tree. One handed something small to another and they all looked around suspiciously. He didn't see his mama anywhere around. Roosevelt knew they were selling dope. Roosevelt would never do dope. His Nana and Auntie Barbara said dope caused his mama the trouble she was always in. Roosevelt took a seat on the bench outside Wimpy's Bar and Grill. A couple of the old ladies from church greeted him.

How could he make his mama stop? Could he act better? No matter how she promised, there'd come a time when she'd start anyway. Then, she'd be mean and far away.

As he got up to leave, Rufus came up. "You beat the shit outa Punch, man!" he said grinning real big. "Nobody eva done dat befo. Gimme five, man."

They slapped each other's hands.

If Punch heard a bunch of kids saying Roosevelt had beat him up, he'd take care of Roosevelt real good.

* * * * * * *

At home, Roosevelt pulled out materials for a report on the Incas he had to write by Monday. He liked to do things right away. He needed a little help with something he'd read. His mama could help him, but she wouldn't come home. His grandparents would struggle through it with him, but they couldn't read well enough. He didn't want to ask Auntie Barbara.

At the table, Nana said the blessing. She passed the mashed potatoes, greens, and pork chops around, sighing and humming to herself, not looking up. Papa looked concerned but said nothing. Roosevelt found the pork chops tasteless and hard to swallow. A fly buzzed around, dropped to the table and then zipped off again.

Roosevelt heard a car pull up. His chest quivered and his stomach churned. But then the screen door opened with a squeak and Auntie Barbara walked in, letting the door slam, wood on wood.

She leaned and kissed her mother on the cheek. "Good evenin', Mama." She leaned down to Papa and put her arms around his neck. "Good evenin', Papa." Rubbing her hands on Roosevelt's shoulders, she said, "How my favorite nephew doin'?" Then she stopped and looked around the table. "Oh. Ya'll ain' heard nothin' from her, huh?" She shrugged her shoulders and bobbed her head from side to side. Then she turned her gaze to Roosevelt with the look of "poor chil', what's gonna become a him."

"I knew it was too good to last. I knowed it two weeks ago." Her voice became higher and louder as she continued. "What'd I say when she didn't feel like goin' to church? I said loud and clear that she was headin' down dat road again. She was on her way back to the clutches of Satan hisself. Didn't I say dat? And now where she be? She leave her young boy all alone. You think she'd even take the time to be sure her poor young chil' got home from school all right."

"Let me get you a plate," said Nana, trying to slow her down, but it was too late.

"I'll tell you what that good fer nothin' dope fiend is out there doin'. Want me to 'splain?"

"No thank you," said Papa. He got her attention and motioned with his head and eyes at Roosevelt. She looked at Roosevelt like she didn't even know he was there. Roosevelt was fighting back the urge to break out crying.

"Oh, I'm sorry, you poor little chil'. You poor, poor chil'."

"Barbara," her father said sternly. "That's enough. Sit down and eat."

"May I be excused?" Roosevelt felt his voice squeak.

"Yes chil'," Nana whispered and smiled understandingly.

* * * * * * *

On a Saturday, Jude and his dad carried equipment down the dock of the yacht club and hopped aboard the White Lady III. Uncle Lee nodded toward a man with a large, protruding belly and said, "David, this is Mr. Griswold." Uncle Lee always called Jude "David," because that's what David's own dad called him. It was interesting since Jude's dad was a David too, but went by his middle name, "Lansing." David figured his dad didn't approve of the name his mom had chosen. Griswold smeared suntan lotion on his forehead and ignored Jude.

Uncle Lee cranked the engine. White Lady III awoke with a rumble, exhaled smoke, and purred, spilling water out the two rear exhaust pipes, as she bobbed lightly on the water.

Jude cast off and hopped aboard at midships. White Lady III slid out of her slip and cut through the calm water, the color of smoked glass. Uncle Lee guided her south at the main channel and pressed down on the throttle. The engine roared. The bow rose gracefully. Huge wake built up behind and then became smaller as she planed.

Jude's father fell into a seat next to him and wired ballyhoo on large hooks, grunting from time to time. Jude watched the water churn behind the boat as South Bridge shrank from sight. They passed small boats with fishermen casting nets. Uncle Lee didn't slow down, but the wake was quite small at 2700 rpm. On tiny boats that rocked from side to side, fishermen stood peering into the water, unconcerned. One managed to throw his net in a perfect circle at the height of the wake assault.

Mr. Griswold sat on the transom and chugged a beer. He emitted a loud burp. Jude's father looked at him with disgust. Mr. Griswold reached down and scratched his butt, not the least bit concerned by the Armstrong look. Jude knew the word going through his father's head— "Barbarian."

Jude went below, and Uncle Lee let him take the wheel. Jude could handle the boat as well as any of them. He had sea legs more sure than most of the adult guests who came along.

Jude sounded three long blasts of the horn to get the Dunlawton Bridge to open and throttled her down slowly. He steered perfectly through the draw. Once through the draw, he throttled her back up as they passed Guana Island—a haven for hundreds of white sea birds, who deposited a great amount of smelly bird crap.

Griswold stood next to Uncle Lee, and said, "That nigger, Jackie Robinson, who the fuck's he think he is. Now he got himself a job announcing for ABC. He's still writing letters to presidents. First it was Nixon, then Kennedy, now Johnson. Saying all this shit about Selma and all." He shook his head.

Jude glanced around for his father. This conversation wouldn't make him happy. His dad stood on the rear deck, puffing on a cigarette. He had on his seaman's face. He looked completely at peace, enjoying the smoke and living the life he loved, away from work and problems.

Uncle Lee answered, "I saw Jackie play that first time here in Daytona. He had some spunk. He's a hall of famer. People listen to him."

"So what. He's got no right gettin' into politics," Griswold said, waving his beer with one hand and cigarette with the other.

Jude took her around the last buoy before the mouth of the inlet and headed out, climbing large waves and dipping straight down beyond the crest.

His dad stood beside him. The route they'd taken two weeks ago now looked sandy and foamy. "The channel's moved. Head that way." Jude veered to starboard but was broadsided by two quick waves. "Let me take it," his dad said, sliding Jude out of the seat.

He flicked his cigarette into the ocean and settled in. He adjusted the speed regularly as he maneuvered the rolling waves. The engine rumble increased each time the props came out of the water. He steered to the left almost to the red buoy. A wave hit the boat off the starboard side and splashed in over the sides, soaking Mr. Griswold, who looked a bit pale. Jude walked with no problem over the wet deck to the stern to pick up a chart that had fallen.

Once they'd cleared the bell buoy, the breakers turned to rolling waves. The boat crossed a line of foam where the dark water of the river met the bright, turquoise water of the sea.

Griswold slipped and Uncle Lee caught him. Then Griswold vomited, and as Uncle Lee tried to avoid the puke, Griswold slipped out of his hands and crashed to the deck. Uncle Lee leaned over the side, scooped up a bucketful of seawater, and dumped it on the prone Griswold.

After the mess had been cleaned up, Uncle Lee let out the fishing lines, two straight out off the stern and two on outriggers. The ballyhoo occasionally popped over wave crests. Jude went to the galley and fixed a sardine sandwich on rye for his dad and ham and cheese for the others. He delivered a sandwich and a Schlitz to each, including Griswold. Jude climbed to the flying bridge, where he drank a Mountain Dew and downed his cheese sandwich before the cheese melted and the bread got toasted. A couple of seagulls floated above, eyeing his food.

For more than an hour, the boat bobbed on the undulating swells without a strike. The coast was out of sight now, like a string of fuzz. Jude had been lulled into a light sleep, but he was startled awake when the reel to the starboard stern screamed. Uncle Lee ran to it and tightened down the drag, trying to sit and yank the pole all at the same time. He got the butt of the pole into the stabilizer and began working—pulling the pole back and reeling as he lowered it again. As the fish neared the boat, it went first to one side and then to the other, revealing the shiny side of a bonito, about two and a half feet long. Griswold snagged it behind the gills with a gaff and flopped it onto the clean wooden deck. It jumped around until Uncle Lee freed it from the hook and threw it into the ice chest.

When the second strike hit, Uncle Lee grabbed the rod, set the hook and sat Jude down with it. Jude leaned back and reeled, then lowered the pole and rested. After about five minutes, the fish neared the boat and Jude's dad reached over the side with the gaff and pulled in a good-sized mackerel. Jude's muscles ached, but it was worth it.

Jude's dad mussed his hair and said, "Good job, my boy." Jude felt a tingle. It wasn't very often that his father touched him or gave him a compliment. It meant a lot. All the adults had a beer to celebrate the second fish.

There were only two more strikes. Griswold managed to get one close but lost it by pulling too hard and yanking the hook out of the fish's mouth.

As they cruised back up the river, Griswold and Uncle Lee staggered and slurred their words. Griswold loudly told a story about "a nigger girl."

Jude's father shot daggers with his eyes and proclaimed, "That's enough. We don't talk like that on White Lady."

* * * * * * *

Dressed in her Sunday best, Nana came in and said, "Time ta get up, Roosevelt." He glanced at Mama's bed, knowing before he even saw it that she hadn't been home. "Breakfas'll be on the table in a minute, Baby. Come along now. Papa done clean yo church shoes last night."

He sat up slowly. Church was okay. But it wasn't the same without Mama. A couple of weeks ago when Mama hadn't wanted to go to church, Auntie Barbara had started in on the Satan and Hell business. She was like a machine; once she was cranked you couldn't stop her. Only Papa knew where her off-switch was. Mama said once, "If you figure I'm goin' to hell anyway, then I might as well go out having a good goddamn time." But Auntie Barbara couldn't listen while she was on one of her tirades. She just kept on like nobody else was talking.

As he put on his blue church suit, the aroma of fried eggs, sausage, and homemade biscuits floated in.

At the table, he had trouble getting the food down. He hoped Mama wasn't in jail, hurt, or dead. Thoughts of her behind bars surrounded by a bunch of screaming women shuffled through his mind. He dismissed them, but he pictured her lying in a hospital bed.

"Baby doll, you need to eat up. You just pushin' the food around on yo plate, honey." Nana dried her hands on her apron, leaned over his chair, and engulfed him in a hug. "You got nothin' to worry about. Yo mama be comin' 'roun presently."

Auntie Barbara walked in. Roosevelt saw Nana give her the "shut yo mouth chile" look. Auntie Barbara got the hint.

* * * * * *

The white brick AME Church stood proudly above its steep concrete steps on the corner of Campbell Street and Loomis. Punch climbed the steps with his mother and brother. He wasn't dressed like a bully today.

It was roasting inside the church. Auntie Barbara led the way down to the third row from the front, nodding and smiling at just about every row. Nana followed her closely and nodded at a few people too, but she was not the politician that Auntie Barbara was. Papa lumbered along behind, rocking from side to side on his old legs. They all slid down the pew, with Roosevelt following Papa. Just as he sat, another family followed him into the pew led by his classmate, Missy, who sat right next to him, smiling and wiggling.

"Mornin', Roosevelt," she whispered softly.

He wasn't about to encourage her by answering. He just shot an evil eye at Auntie Barbara for sticking him in the pew where Missy could always be found. He would never hear the end of this. An usher squeezed another old fat lady into the left side of the pew, pushing Missy right against him. He could feel her body move as she breathed, and could smell her hair, her breath, and her clean clothes. He felt her eyes on him. He felt on fire. Sweat formed on his forehead. He knew Punch and everybody would be snickering.

The choir started up. The organist banged wildly on the keys. The congregation moved in unison. Pastor Brown suddenly appeared, and stood, eyes closed, his face proud and determined, facing heaven as though captivated. As the choir wound down, Pastor Brown moved behind the pulpit with hands raised high.

"Do you feel the spirit?" he exclaimed loudly. "Has it entered your very soul, brothas and sistas? The magnificent harmony of the choir's voices enlightens the soul. Can you feel the Lord God's presence?"

There were a lot of "Yes suhs" and "I feel its" with every question and comment. Though he hadn't said anything yet, Auntie Barbara seemed near rapture and ready to faint dead away. Finally, when the pastor had reached his peak, the choir was near heaven, and the congregation was worn out and weak, it was time to end. When Missy moved away from him, he was wet with perspiration. Walking ahead of his family, he spotted Punch waiting. He paused, but then figured Punch wouldn't lay one on him in front of everybody.

"Hey, lovah boy," Punch said loud enough that everybody could hear it. Then he whispered, "Dat ho Missy look so happy leaning on yo strong shoulders. I wonder if she done heard dose lies bout you fight good. Oughta show 'em what you really fight like."

Punch kicked Roosevelt's left foot. Roosevelt stumbled forward, and his face struck Mrs. Jackson's ample, soft rear end. Punch roared with laughter, and came close, breathing all over him. Punch whispered, "Tomorrow at da gas station. Just you and me. You a dead motha fucka."

* * * * * * *

When the family got home, Roosevelt rushed straight to his room. No sign of Mama. She loved drugs and men more than she loved him. That was for sure. Just like Auntie Barbara said. He pushed his face deep into his musty pillow and wished he could go away. A feather poked his nose. His stomach felt like it was flipping around. His throat felt tight. He just wanted to cry and cry, but it did no good.

Nana called him for lunch. He dried his face on his pillowcase, got up, and went to the kitchen.

His grandparents and Auntie Barbara had already sat and were devouring fried chicken. He took his seat quietly and struggled to get some food down.

After lunch, Roosevelt sat on the swinging wooden bench on the front porch with Papa. Papa pulled him close and put his arm on his shoulder. "You a good boy. Yo mama, she allus been like dis. She love you. She really do. Dose drugs make people do funny things. Don' you never let me catch you doin' no drugs. They's bad." He shook his huge head slowly and twitched his lips. "Yo mama be home soon. I sure a dat."

Roosevelt fought back the tears that tried to break through, saying to himself, "I ain't gonna cry."

Auntie Barbara came out on the porch. "So here be da men folk. We was wonderin' where ya'll took off to."

Roosevelt's gut tightened. His muscles tensed. He wanted to get away before she got started. "Scuse me, Papa."

He walked along the dirt tire tracks toward the garage to get his fishing gear ready. He wanted to extend his line so he could get a better lift. He slipped past the heavy wooden door, which had been jammed open for a year or so. Sunlight shone through dirty, cracked windows and the open door. He moved slowly into the dark, musty garage, brushing away spider webs. He found his cane pole and the new line and took it outside. The shiny, dark brown pole was strong and had a good spring. He sat on the ground and worked on it, biting the line with his teeth.

At the river, the family, less Mama, fished at the usual spot. By the end of the afternoon, Roosevelt had snagged six of the fourteen mullets in the bucket. Papa and Roosevelt walked over to the entrance dock that led out to the white folks' club. A faucet could be reached from the wall, so they didn't have to trespass on the dock. Papa could gut a fish so fast it seemed like he had some special vacuum cleaner in his knife.

As they were finishing up, the white boy who fished with the net rolled up on his bike, nodded to Roosevelt, and rode down the dock, fender jangling as it banged across the boards.

Chapter 2

WHILE NANA COOKED, Roosevelt finished some arithmetic homework at the kitchen table. The sound of spattering oil and the aroma of fresh fish cooking made his mouth water. The phone rang and Roosevelt jumped up, thinking it was Mama. "Hello."

"Who speakin' there. Dat young Roosevelt? My man! Wha's happenin?"

"Yessuh," he answered weakly. He didn't know what to say to Uncle Theodore. Usually there was some warning when he called—an operator would announce the call and ask if they'd accept the charges. This time he snuck right through. It was the first time he'd done that in a long time, ever since he got sent up to the state prison at Raiford. "You wanna speak ta Nana?"

"Yes, my man. I'll be seein' you soon enough. We gonna have some good times. Gonna go fishin'. How yo mama?"

"Just a minute. Heah Nana come." He dropped the receiver and ran to the kitchen for Nana. "Uncle Theodore on the phone."

She shook her head slowly, with the determined face she showed when Uncle Theodore called, and walked to the phone.

"Hello . . . Did Roosevelt accept the charges? . . . Huh? . . . You wha'? . . . How?" She looked confused and unhappy. "We gonna have ta talk 'bout dis . . . When? Call back tomorra. I be talkin' to yo papa . . . Yes. I love you too, son." She placed the receiver on the cradle and sat looking at it.

Auntie Barbara entered, but came to an abrupt halt, alarmed. "Whassa matta Mama? Who call?"

"Yo brotha, Theodore. Been released early. Want ta come home to stay for a while."

"He no good. You know dat, Mama. Can't be trusted no how. You can't let him stay heah." She shook her head as she presented her case.

"Seem dif'rent somehow. Talked calmer than I evah knowed him to." Nana tapped the phone with her big hand. "Promised me he was gonna stay off the stuff dis time. Say his life all change." Nana shook her head slowly. "I jus' don' know."

Barbara put her hands on her hips. "He done promise ta stay off the stuff a hunerd times. Don't mean nothin'. He a con just tryin' ta get you all choked up. And he did, didn't he?" She got rolling in her preaching speech and moving around the room. "He know exactly what he doin'. Gone come down heah and live fo free, set hisself up some dope dealin' and maybe a lady or two ta work the streets for him. He'll act all good till he get on his feet and then so long family."

Roosevelt saw a tear roll down Nana's face. Papa walked in as Auntie Barbara continued.

"Whassa matta?" he asked, looking back and forth from Auntie Barbara to Nana, and then to Roosevelt. "Who call?"

"That good-fer-nothin' son a yours done got free and wanna come on home where it be safe and he can use ya'll. He wanna see zactly what he can get away with. Givin' Mama all this peace and love talk to throw her off guard. You gotta..."

"Hush, Barbara," Papa said. Then he looked at Nana. "Tell me what he said."

"He got free early, on good behavior. Say his life change so much even the warden done notice it and recommend early parole. Talk so peaceful and serene like I almost wouldn't a knowed 'im. I took him serious. I tol' him ta call back tomorrow so's we could talk about it first."

Papa moved smoothly over to where Nana leaned on the back of the couch, put his arm on her shoulder and gently moved her toward their bedroom, out of Barbara's and Roosevelt's presence.

When they finally sat down to eat, Papa's stern look kept the conversation down. Nana was quiet. Even Auntie Barbara said no more about Uncle Theodore. The fish wasn't as good as it had smelled.

Roosevelt sat on his bed looking out the window at the steamy afternoon nothingness. The phone rang. Nana answered and moaned, "Oh Lawd. I cain' take much mo." Roosevelt's throat tightened. He ran to the kitchen.

"What is it?" his grandfather asked.

"My baby. It's Anne. She in jail," Nana wailed.

"Mama?"

"Yo Mama in big trouble."

"What happen?" Papa asked.

"Drugs. She got pick up with heroin."

Roosevelt was stunned, but thankful Auntie Barbara had left the room.

"Where she be?" asked Papa.

"Out to the County Jail. Been there a day. Said she was afraid to call. Ax to talk to Roosevelt, but the operator ax fo mo change and the phone went dead. I sorry baby." She pulled Roosevelt close and squeezed his shoulders against her belly. A big wet tear dropped onto his head. "Trouble, trouble, trouble," she said.

Roosevelt sat on the sandy wooden steps of the porch. A light wind pushed the dust around in the yard. He felt confused and tired. Nana made it sound like Mama was going to be away for a while.

A rat burst from the garage of the house next door, raced across the yard and slipped under the house. Roosevelt tapped his foot and ran a church song through his head, fighting back the urge to cry. It would be okay if Mama could just come home. Papa lumbered out onto the porch, the old planks creaking under his weight. "What're ya doin' boy?"

"Nothin'. Jus' sittin'."

"Worried 'bout yo mama?"

Roosevelt nodded, humming the church song, trying to keep it all in.

"Oncet ya get started with drugs, dey grab on ta ya. Dey don' let go."

Auntie Barbara turned off the street and parked. Dust swirled as she got out. "Oh Lawd," Papa said. "I ain't in da mood ta discuss dis wif yo aunt. Talk 'bout fishin'."

"Can I get me a cast net like dat white boy got?"

Papa put his hand over his face. "Ain't fair ta catch fish like dat. Dey ain' got a chance with dat heavy net falling on top of 'em."

Auntie Barbara marched to the steps. "How could you be talkin' 'bout fishin' at a time like this? Didn't you hear what happen'? Roosevelt mama in jail. I said it before and I'll say it again . . ."

"Please don' say it again," said Papa quietly.

She was disarmed for only a couple of seconds and then lit in with, "I told ya she was into the drugs again. As clear as day. Don' care nothin' 'bout . . ."

"Barbara, use some sense, girl," Papa said loudly.

Roosevelt felt the attack. She was talking about his mama, not some lost soul she wanted to yank into church against her will. Roosevelt crunched a bug under his shoe and ground it into the dirt.

Barbara huffed inside and banged things around. Soon the tempo and tones of her voice grew to a crescendo. Roosevelt could almost picture Nana opening her mouth to get in a word from time to time, only to be shut down by the motor mouth.

"Yo aunt a bit outspoken." Roosevelt didn't look up. "Yo mama gonna be all right. We gonna go down when she see the judge. He'll see she a good woman, a good mama, and her family love her. Then he'll prob'ly let her come on home."

A tense quiet at dinner made Roosevelt's stomach so tight it was hard to get a bite down.

Just as they finished and Auntie Barbara stood to carry things to the kitchen, there was a knock on the wooden screen door. The spring creaked, and a voice called, "There my sistah Barb'ra. Good to see yo face."

She didn't answer, but her footsteps stopped sounding on the wood floor.

"Ain't I gonna get a hug or nothin'?" Then, after a long pause, "I ain' never seen you speechless befo'. Act like ya seen a ghost or somethin'. Just li'l ol' me."

By then, Nana had struggled to her feet. As she neared the hallway, Uncle Theodore rounded the corner, smiling as big as could be. He and Nana hugged silently.

Papa stared at him for a moment, then stuck out his hand to shake. "Lookin' good, my boy," the old man said.

Uncle Theodore came around and yanked Roosevelt out of his seat to hug him. "Boy, how you done grown. And good lookin' too. What grade you in now?"

"Goin' inta seventh, junior high."

"Like school? Doin' good?"

Roosevelt was surprised that Uncle Theodore even asked that much about his life. He'd never shown any interest in him before. He looked up. "I do okay."

"That's my man." His uncle rubbed his shoulder and walked around the table.

Nana eyed him suspiciously.

He noticed it and smiled. "I know you find it hard to believe, Mama, but you'll see I'm different now. My life done change. Don' worry, Mama. I don' want nothin'."

Auntie Barbara opened her mouth, but Papa's stare kept her quiet. "What you plan to do, son?" asked Papa.

"Been studyin' a little inside. Got my GED. Maybe can get a better job this time. Like ta go on ta school."

Papa nodded. Roosevelt watched as Uncle Theodore sat there smiling, not the nervous, anxious schemer he once was. He seemed in no hurry. He seemed perfectly content just to sit there with his family.

"Where Anne?" he asked finally. Roosevelt looked down. Everybody was quiet. "What? Where she at?" He looked alarmed.

"Right where you just done left," began Auntie Barbara. "And for leadin' a life just like you. Anne been out..."

Papa dropped his fist on the table and stared her down.

"What she get in trouble for?" Uncle Theodore asked quietly.

"Drugs," answered Nana.

"What kind? Usin' or sellin'? She already been sentenced?"

Auntie Barbara cocked her head. "Yo favorite—heroin, brown sugar from Mexico, or perhaps yo other favorite—white sugar from China. What dif'rence it make?"

"The type of drug affects the sentence. Was she sellin'?"

"Don' think so," said Papa. "Got court on Thursday. We don' know nothin' really."

"Maybe she needed this," said Uncle Theodore.

"Maybe my baby needed to go to jail? What kind of rubbish you talkin' son?" Nana asked, her voice rising.

He smiled, still looking calm as could be. "It take what it take to change a life, Mama. Babyin' don' do it. She gotta get down and out. Where there ain' no hope. Then a person be ready to let the force in."

"Force," said Barbara, raising her eyebrows.

"Allah."

"What's that? Ain' that the Muslim stuff? Oh Lord," cried Nana.

"Yes, Mama, according to the prophet, Elijah Muhammad."

Watching Nana and Auntie Barbara's wide eyes, Papa said, "Let's talk 'bout somethin' else. Theo, ya think you can fix up your old bike for Roosevelt? The boy ain' got no bike."

"Be more'n happy to give it a try Papa. Anythin' I can do for my nephew." He grinned. "Sure feels good to be home with ya'll. I'm a mighty lucky man. Lucky to be alive. Lucky to be with my family, feelin' good, and no urge to take a drink or get high. A beautiful day. Let's sit on the porch and enjoy the night air. I ain' been able ta do that for a long time now." He stood, put an arm around Roosevelt's shoulder and got them all out on the porch.

* * * * * * *

Roosevelt floated in and out of sleep, worrying, and looking across the room at Mama's neatly made bed and then out the window. He didn't feel like getting up.

The door opened a crack and Uncle Theodore, white teeth shining, peeked in. "How's my boy? Got somethin' ta show ya outside."

What was he up to? The only time he ever paid attention to Roosevelt before was to act as an alibi or to snatch a few dollars from Nana's purse. "Come on boy. Day's slippin' by. It's beautiful outside. First day of yo summer vacation. Second day of my freedom. Let's enjoy it."

Roosevelt went to the bathroom to pee and brush his teeth.

As he came out, Nana strolled by humming. "Mornin', Grandson," she said. "I saved you some breakfus for when you come back in."

Uncle Theodore appeared by the door beckoning him with the big smile. Roosevelt followed him to the garage, where Uncle Theodore, with great flourish, whipped off a piece of canvas and displayed Uncle Theodore's own bicycle, now with the handlebars straightened and the rust sanded off, the chain slick and wet with fresh oil, the seat lowered, the fenders straightened and painted with a red stripe, and the tires inflated. "Papa say my boy need a bike." His smile was so wide that Roosevelt thought his cheeks would break. "Ride it, come on." Roosevelt stood speechless, staring at the bike. Uncle Theodore moved the bike forward and backward, trying to tempt him. "You know how?"

Roosevelt shook his head no.

"No problem my boy. Let's go getcha somethin' ta eat so you'll have energy ta ride. I can show ya."

Uncle Theodore put his arm over his shoulders and led him to the house. He poured some milk for both of them, put some butter and honey on the fresh biscuits Nana had made, and sat with him while he ate.

Nana offered Uncle Theodore some coffee, but he shook it off. "My body's a temple, Mama. Don' drink it no mo." She rolled her eyes but seemed to almost smile.

Afterward, Uncle Theodore held the bike up by the handlebars and said, "Mount it from the left and put yo feet on the pedals." He walked backward holding the bike. "Feel the balance. Lean a little to the left. Whoa, not so far. Now just a little to the right." He stopped, stood on Roosevelt's left and walked him forward. Trotting alongside, he said, "Pedal." Roosevelt picked up speed. "I'm gonna let go just a bit. I'll catch ya if ya start ta fall. Keep peddlin'." Roosevelt wasn't sure when he was holding and when he wasn't, but Uncle Theodore kept up the pace, with his hands hovering near the bike as Roosevelt pedaled down the street. "You got it, my man. You bet. Now slow down easy, by puttin' the pedal back a little, and stop." He was holding on again.

He held Roosevelt's arms to support him as he started up from a stand, and then trotted alongside again, holding his hands slightly away from the boy's shoulders. Then, he ran slightly ahead of Roosevelt, raising his arms like a bird in flight to show how he could make a turn. After Roosevelt had succeeded on his own for a few more blocks and turns, they stopped at Pearson's Grocery, got a couple of bottles of YooHoo and sat on a bench.

A man came up. "Dat you blood?" he asked Uncle Theodore. "'S hap'nin?"

"You." They shook hands, thumbs up, and then went knuckle to knuckle.

"When'd ya get out?'"

"Thursday."

He sat next to Uncle Theodore and spoke real low.

Uncle Theodore kept smiling and said "Got another way now. Don' do that stuff no mo."

The man's jaw dropped. He looked at Roosevelt, and said, "Oh, I know, ya gotta watch the kid."

"I meant it."

"Cool, man. I'm flush. You know where ta find me." He shook Uncle Theodore's hand again, with two or three different steps, and was gone.

* * * * * * *

In the evening, Roosevelt was bone tired. He was taking a bath when Papa rapped on the door. "Yo mama on da phone, Roosevelt." Roosevelt threw a towel around him and ran to the phone, almost slipping on wet feet as he hit the wood floor of the living room.

Nana looked concerned as she handed him the receiver.

"Mama," he said weakly.

"How my baby?"

"When you comin' home?"

"Can't right now, Rosy. Sorry I ain' call ya. Jus want you to know I love you."

"I love you too, Mama," he said trying to control his voice. He couldn't control the tears.

"I'll be home soon as I can, and I'll nevah take off again. Nevah. Papa and Nana gonna bring ya ta court. You won't cry none, will ya? They won't dress me up nice. I don' look too good."

"I'll go, Mama."

There was a lot of racket in the background, the sounds of women yelling, laughing, and arguing. "I gotta go, baby. My time up. I love you. Bye."

"Bye, Mama." He put the receiver down slowly, feeling the other family members focusing on his face. He turned and walked toward his room.

* * * * * * *

One afternoon in July, Jude's friend Billy Howell called. "Wanna spend the night on the island?"

Jude knew he meant the little island, sometimes called Ratte Island, slightly off Beach Street between the Broadway Bridge and the Main Street Bridge, across from the Buick dealership. After getting permission from his mom, Jude rushed around packing his mess kit, sleeping bag, flashlight, food and drinks. He pulled the heavy wooden rowboat, green with bare areas of fiberglass showing in several spots, down the shore to the water. He ran up to the house, lugged the red gas tank down the hill, and placed it in the boat. Billy rattled down the grass hill on his bike, dropped it on the ground and slung his sleeping bag and knapsack into the boat. Together, they pushed the boat out into the water. Jude dropped the weather-beaten green six-horse Johnson, pumped the gas, and yanked on the cord. On the second yank it roared to life. Jude allowed it to warm up for a couple of seconds, down-throttled, and flipped it into forward. He increased the speed slowly until it was at full throttle, had risen to maximum plane, and dropped back down to skim across the water. The orange sun had descended and tinted the blue sky orange. In the channel, the lightly dancing chop slapped the hull. A pelican stood guard on top of a channel marker as they neared the island.

Jude throttled down and veered to port to avoid it. As they neared shore, he twisted the handle all the way, slammed the gear into neutral, lifted the engine, and skidded up the off-white sandy beach. Tiny sand crabs and fiddler crabs scurried into their holes.

"Dogs," Billy said, pointing to fresh tracks in the white sand. "That's okay," Jude answered. "So long as there's no bums."

They walked around the island looking for evidence of dogs and people. Near the shore, they found a low shelter made of old pieces of plywood, tied together with twine.

"Think somebody's in there?" Billy whispered.

Jude shrugged his shoulders, crept toward the opening in the front of the shelter and peeked in. "It's empty."

Billy kneeled and examined the black cinders and wood remnants of a fire. "It's cold." He slid his hand across the dirt, checking for tracks. Finally, he shook his head. "I don't see anything fresh." They walked back to the boat to get their gear.

They set up the olive-green canvas pup tent. Numerous slits had been sewn together and holes patched with tape. They unrolled their sleeping bags, laid them inside and lit a fire. The sun was starting to set.

They sat near the fire and talked. Billy asked, "Your parents always get along?"

Jude looked at him and shrugged.

"My father left last night," Billy continued. "My mom threw him out."

"Why?"

"I don' know. My mom was screaming at him. He didn't say a word that I could hear. All I heard from him was the front door banging shut and tires squealing."

Billy's eyes were bright and watery. Jude tried to think of something to say. He wasn't comfortable discussing feelings. And he wouldn't want to do anything to make Billy think he was queer. He just sat there quietly and hoped his presence was enough. After a long silence, Billy asked, "Your parents ever have a fight like that?"

"They fight. But usually when my mom's mad, she just doesn't speak to him for a few days. I never know what to do. It seems so strange. He just looks sad, like he doesn't understand. She gets over it after a while."

Billy sighed. "Mine used to fight a lot, but after a while they usually got all kissy and would be fine in the morning. I wish I knew what he did this time."

Jude forced himself to say, "Don't worry. She'll let him come back."

Jude wondered if that's where his parents were heading. Sometimes they seemed so mean to each other. The look in their eyes said it all. But he convinced himself that things were more stable now.

* * * * * * *

One Sunday morning, Roosevelt picked at his breakfast. Uncle Theodore encouraged him to eat and said Roosevelt's mama needed to spend some time in jail to get her head on straight. "It take what it take, Roosevelt."

Nana and Papa were getting ready for church. "Come on Roosevelt and Theodore. Get dress."

"Uh, Mama, I ain' goin'," Uncle Theodore said.

"What you mean you ain' goin'? This family go ta church togetha."

"I'm Muslim, Mama."

She turned her smoldering eyes to Roosevelt. "Get dress Roosevelt." He went to his room to dress.

Roosevelt could hear the commotion as Auntie Barbara arrived in the kitchen and learned that Uncle Theodore wouldn't go to church.

Uncle Theodore said, "I am sorry to not go along with yo wishes Mama. I respect you and your church. But I have a new life now. I have already prayed to Mecca this morning, which is my belief. Please respect it as I respect your beliefs. I won't try to change you."

Auntie Barbara spent the ride to church covering the subject, even suggesting that by the time they got home, the heathen would probably be long gone, with all their belongings.

Papa said, "I see a change in that boy—long overdue—long overdue. If bein' a Muslim done change dat boy, I say it's a wonderful thing."

Auntie Barbara stared at him, mouth open. "I cain' believe what I'm hearin'. It's blasphemy. Blasphemy. Thou shalt not honor false gods. There is only one God, and he be heah in the AME Church."

After lunch, Uncle Theodore tried to encourage the family to go
fishing but couldn't get them interested. "How 'bout if you and me go,
Roosevelt?"

"Blasphemer," hollered Auntie Barbara. "You want to put
those poison thoughts into Roosevelt head. He don' need ta hear
none a dat."

"I promise I won't discuss religion with him."

Papa nodded his approval. Uncle Theodore walked, carrying
the poles. Roosevelt rode the bike, holding the bucket full of gear
over the handlebars. They went to a new place north of the
Broadway Bridge. They sat on the wall across the narrow waterway
from an island.

After about an hour, two white boys wearing shorts, but no
shoes or shirts, walked down the bank of the island and dumped
camping equipment into a wooden rowboat with a motor on the
back. Roosevelt recognized one of them as the boy who fished with
a net at the yacht club. The two boys pushed the boat off the bank
and jumped in. Net Boy started the boat and steered past Roosevelt
and Uncle Theodore. Net Boy and Roosevelt nodded and waved
at each other.

As soon as the boat was past the fishermen, it took off fast and
was gone. Roosevelt felt a nibble and hooked another mullet.

"What's a Muslim?" Roosevelt asked.

"I tole yo Grandmama we wouldn't talk about dat."

"I just wanna know."

"Well, it's a religion. We follow the same God, but he has a
different name, Allah. He the Black man's God. Lot a people
in prison follow Allah. And people in other countries follow him
too. When you accept Him and follow the principles, yo life go
real smooth. No stress. Everythin' okay."

"You mean he a Negro?"

"You got dat right."

Roosevelt couldn't picture a Negro God. Would he look like
Papa? Like Uncle Theodore? Like the principal at school? He'd
always imagined God as a wise old white man with white hair, like
George Washington. One or the other had to be right. There was
no way that some people could see him as George Washington and
others could see him as an old Negro man.

"I ain' nevah heard of a Negro God," he said quietly.

"Who you think gave our ancestors the picture of God here in this country? The white man. It ain't the same God your ancestors had in Africa."

Africa? Where did that come from? This talk was getting very complicated for Roosevelt. Nana was probably right. They shouldn't be talking about this. "Can we go now?"

They stood and gathered their gear to go home.

"Did you enjoy fishin' today?" Uncle Theodore asked, grinning.

"Thanks. It was fun, Uncle."

* * * * * * *

On a Thursday morning, Jude rushed through his route, and zipped over the South Bridge to the yacht club.

He bounded aboard White Lady III, which was waiting for him. Approaching the channel, Uncle Lee gave three long blasts on the horn and the bridge began to open. Uncle Lee turned to the north and passed through the draw; he pushed the throttle down smoothly as they passed Jude's house on the shore to the right. After passing Ratte Island and all the bridges, the water turned darker, the waterway narrowed, and small, uninhabited islands appeared on the port side. Eventually, they arrived at the weathered bridge with rock-carved lions perched over the water in St. Augustine.

Jude's father steered into the channel of the yacht basin. The engine putted slowly as they neared the dock. He revved and down-throttled, threw it into forward and reverse, and docked. Jude's father sipped a Schlitz, while Uncle Lee chugged one.

* * * * * * *

In the restaurant overlooking the basin, Uncle Lee ordered one beer after the other. He called the waitress "Babe."

She smiled and winked at Jude's father. Jude's dad didn't smile back, but looked at Jude seriously and shook his head.

"We could take you for a boat ride when you get off," said Uncle Lee.

"Thanks honey, but I gotta get home to my man."

"He's a lucky man," Uncle Lee responded, stifling a smelly burp.

As she walked into the kitchen, Jude's father said, "Can't you at least act civilized when we are with you? It's embarrassing."

Uncle Lee ignored him and looked at Jude. "She's pretty hot, huh?"

Jude's father stood abruptly, flipped a ten-dollar bill onto the table and ushered Jude up and out of the restaurant, leaving Uncle

Lee and his beer at the table. As they moved down the dock, Jude glanced back. Uncle Lee sat, smiling, smoking a cigarette, and drinking.

Jude's father said, "That's no way for a physician to act."

* * * * * * *

"Put on yo Sunday best Roosevelt," Nana said. She was all gussied up. Papa came out, stuffed into a coat and sporting a short, wide tie. Auntie Barbara and Uncle Theodore joined them, and Papa drove to the courthouse.

The large courtroom was packed, mostly with fidgety Negro families, dressed in church clothes. The few white families sat huddled together on the right. Papa excused the family, and they slid down the wooden bench toward the left wall.

A deputy slammed a door open and stood with his hand on a holstered revolver. Five Negro men and two white men, handcuffed to each other and dressed in grey flannel shirts and pants with Volusia County Jail printed on the shirts, shuffled along the worn wooden floor in a haphazard line. Some smiled or nodded toward the public area.

A white woman in a green sheriff's uniform walked in pulling handcuffs that attached Mama and another Negro woman. Mama half smiled across the room. She seemed to light up when she spotted them.

Several white men dressed in suits occupied two large tables crowded with books, briefcases, and papers. From time to time, one or two would walk across to the opposite table and whisper. Others would take papers to a grey-haired white woman who sat in the front facing the crowd, and they would whisper. Roosevelt scraped his hard-soled shoes on the floor until Auntie Barbara elbowed him.

The bones in Mama's face stood out. Her sad, apprehensive eyes darted back and forth from one table to the other.

An old man in the corner yelled, "All rise. The court of the Honorable Uriel Thornhill is now in session. All who have business here draw near." A silver-haired white man cloaked in a black robe marched in and sat abruptly. He reviewed some papers in a file and said something to the grey-haired woman. She handed a file to a man standing next to her. He called a name, and the male deputy escorted a handcuffed white man to the front.

Roosevelt watched as one man after the other, both white and Negro, faced the man in the black robe. They all looked sheepish. Not one was set free. In every case, a man from the tables would make a request to the judge, and the judge would say no.

The man who called names said, "Anne Harris." The lady deputy escorted her up. The judge said, "Possession of heroin. Here you are again." He shook his head and frowned. "How do you plead, Miz Harris?"

A man with no hair got up from the table and stood with her. "Not guilty," he said.

"Bond is set at ten thousand dollars."

"Judge, we respectfully request that your honor take into account the fact that the defendant has ties to the community and family members in the courtroom . . ."

"Denied."

"Judge, she can't possibly make . . ."

"Next case," the judge yelled, slamming the file across the high desk to the old woman.

Mama shot a confused look at the bald man. He shrugged and whispered something to her. She looked across the room, like a frightened child, to where Roosevelt was sitting, as the lady sheriff grabbed her arm and led her away. Roosevelt felt a sensation he'd never experienced, like a huge lead weight pressed down on his chest. His entire insides hurt. He shook as he tried not to cry. Nana and Auntie Barbara wailed. As they stood, Auntie Barbara started in, "I told you he wouldn't be wantin' to listen to nothin' . . ."

"Hush up," said Papa.

* * * * * * *

After leaving the Intracoastal Waterway in Jacksonville and taking a picturesque cruise around the horn and down the St. John's River, Jude, his dad, and Uncle Lee arrived at the Armstrong family cottage in Astor.

The next morning, Jude gulped down some cereal and strolled down to the river. He baited a line and dropped it into the water. A couple of new cottages and docks dotted the water line to the south. A small boat passed by, motor humming, creating dark swells that rolled like twisted mirrors toward shore.

The men puttered around the cottage and in the boat all day. Uncle Lee downed two or three beers for every one Jude's father drank. By evening, Uncle Lee was swaying back and forth and repeating old stories with a deeper drawl than usual.

Finally, his eyes started to rise into his eyelids, and he lay on the couch, not to move again for the rest of the night.

Jude's dad fixed himself a cup of coffee, motioned to Jude to follow and strolled down to the dock.

His dad seemed to want to talk, but was silent a long time, shifting his weight and making throat noises. He lit a cigarette, drew in deeply, and let it escape through narrowed lips. Finally, he managed, "Enjoy the trip over?"

"Sure."

"Your Uncle Lee tends to overindulge." He sighed aloud.

Jude nodded.

More silence.

"Think I work too hard, or am not home enough?"

Jude wasn't sure what to say. He was hardly ever around, but he was authority. Jude didn't want to say, "Yeah, you're a terrible father and I feel abandoned."

He finally answered, "You're around pretty much. We do things, just like now."

"Your mother doesn't understand that my profession requires long hours and community involvement." He stopped talking and looked up, where a few bright stars shone in the otherwise jet-black sky.

If Jude answered honestly, his father would first put on a hurt face, and then become angry. Then he would delve into a lengthy description of how much time he actually did spend with Jude, all the fishing and boat trips, and on and on.

"Well," his father continued. "Aren't we sitting here, talking man to man under the rich and beautiful sky? Isn't this the life?"

"Yes, Dad."

"Son," he began again quietly. "I, well, I . . . uh . . . do love you."

Oh God. Now what? Jude struggled but managed to get it out. "I love you too, Dad."

* * * * * * *

Uncle Theodore darted around preparing to go fishing. He said to the sulking Roosevelt, "My man, your mourning days have come to an end. Get yo lazy black behind out of bed."

Roosevelt looked up at his insanely smiling face and had to laugh.

"Dat's my man. Yo mama gonna be free when Allah . . . I mean when the good Lord say so. You gonna see. It gonna be good for her."

At the wall on Beach Street, Roosevelt looked across at the fancy white folks club, thinking how much money white folks must have. Only a few Blacks he knew had money. One guy his mother knew wore boots with thick high heels, bellbottoms with huge flares, ruffled baggy shirts and gold chains. When his fancied-up yellow Cadillac turned the corner, people flocked to him.

The funeral director and doctor had the nicest houses west of the railroad tracks. They didn't dress like the men in Roosevelt's neighborhood. They'd greet each other grandly, shaking hands with one or two simple up-and-down motions. One would put his arm around the shoulder of another and talk. Sometimes, they'd laugh. At other times, they'd talk in earnest about the state of the world, NAACP, or politics. They didn't speak like the loud, loose, animated men of the streets around Roosevelt's house.

Auntie Barbara called the doctor an "Uncle Tom." She said, "He oughta be proud to be a Negro, and not be actin' like a cracka."

Roosevelt landed another mullet. Uncle Theodore hollered, "Roosevelt pullin' 'em in."

Nana smiled at him and nudged Papa. Uncle Theodore grinned. Roosevelt hoped next time Mama would be with them.

* * * * * * *

In the evening, the phone rang. Uncle Theodore picked it up. "Hi sis. How things?"

After a short silence, he said, "You need to work on your attitude, Sis. Are any sistahs inta Mohammad in there?"

And after another silence he said, "Muslim."

Later, he said, "It would do ya good, sis."

He handed Nana the receiver. "Hi, baby. Any news on when you'll be free?"

She said, "Um-hum" a few times, while shaking her head from side to side. "Yo lawyer think that the bes' thing? . . . Well, he know best, I s'pose."

She handed the phone to Roosevelt. "Hi Mama," he said quietly.

"I'm changin' my plea to guilty and tryin' for a plea bargain."

"Wha's that mean?"

"Nana can explain. How my baby?"

"Okay. When ya comin' home?"

"I don' know, Rosy," she answered, her voice fading into the noise of metal crashing and clanging.

"Time," yelled a deep voice in the background.

"I gotta go, Rosy. You take care a yo'self. I love you."

He went into the kitchen and asked Nana, "What she gonna do?" "Befo' she said she wasn't guilty. Lawyer say she should say she done it and make a deal. Say she goin' to stay in jail a while no matta what and might as well try to make it better. I don' know about that. I just don' know." She wiped away a tear from her dark brown cheek and pulled Roosevelt's head against her.

Chapter 3

ONE MORNING, Jude was startled awake by a thumping sound from his parents' room. Sooty flew off his bed and scampered across the floor. He heard angry, muffled voices, but couldn't make out the words. The loud thump sounded again. His mother screamed, "You tried to hit me."

"Don't be ridiculous," his father answered.

His mother's voice became muffled again. He felt shaky and scared, not wanting to hear, yet wanting to know what was going on. He heard footsteps stamp down the hall, then his mother's soft sobbing. Jude let go and cried too, quietly, so she wouldn't know he'd heard.

Kellie moved next to the bed, dropped her smiley face on the sheet and wagged her tail. Sooty returned and lay at the foot of the bed. Jude petted Kellie's head and rubbed Sooty's plump, furry belly with his foot. He couldn't go back to sleep.

At five, he got up and quietly moved down the hall. He found his father on the couch in the living room, surrounded by several Life magazines, all torn to shreds.

The quiet house didn't seem a peaceful place this morning.

* * * * * * *

Several weeks after the last time, the Harris family sat again in the courtroom.

The judge said, "I understand you have a plea change, Miz Harris."

The same bald man as last time stood at her side and offered, "Your honor, we have reached a plea agreement with the prosecution."

The judge looked at the other table. "What's the deal, Mister White?"

A young, nervous white man with blondish hair combed back off his forehead, dressed in a blue pinstriped suit, rose. "Hundred twenty days, less time served."

"How long has she already served?" asked the judge in a simple, businesslike voice.

"Forty-five days."

"Is that the deal?" the judge asked the bald man.

"Yes, your honor."

The judge looked at Mama. "Ms. Harris, do you understand that by changing your plea and entering into a plea agreement, you're waiving your right to trial, accepting a conviction, and agreeing to serve another seventy-five days in county jail."

She nodded slightly.

"The court approves the plea agreement, accepts the change in plea to guilty, and sentences the defendant to one hundred twenty days in the County Jail, less time served." He smashed the wooden gavel on the desk, stood and floated out of the room.

Mama turned and smiled as she was led from the courtroom.

Roosevelt waved and made an effort to smile, while trying to calculate how many months that was, and when she'd be home again.

* * * * * * *

Jude and his sister Jenny had spent the night in the middle of Mosquito Lagoon on the White Lady III with their dad. As they drove down the driveway to their home, they noticed several cars in the driveway. Their dad looked at Jude and grimaced. They climbed the stairs and entered the Florida room. A cloud of smoke hovered over the table. Their mother sat at the head of the table, Jude's dad's seat, a cigarette in her hand and a frosted mug of beer in front of her. Duke, the man from the yacht club, sat to her left, shuffling cards. A cigarette hung from his mouth. A glass of something like dirty water sat in front of him. Mrs. Howell, the mother of Jude's friend Billy, lifted her tired eyes and gave a silly grin. Another man Jude hadn't seen before sat in the other chair.

Jude's father stood at attention at the end of the table. Then he stomped off to the bedroom. Jude went into his own room.

His mother came down the hallway. In a thick, throaty voice, she said to his father, "Get your things and go, please."

He didn't answer. Jude could hear things being slung about. Then he heard heavy, unusual laughter from the Florida room, similar to Uncle Lee's laugh before he'd pass out.

His father entered the room, looking sad and bewildered. "I'll call you in a couple of days," he said.

Jude lay in bed. Duke appeared at his door. "Come on, boy. We just cooked up some burgers like you've never had before."

In the kitchen, the guests happily got things out of the refrigerator, threw food onto plates and staggered to and fro as though battling rough seas.

Duke put some kind of orange sauce on a burger and gave it to Jude, saying, "You've never had anything like this before."

Jude and Jenny sat at the coffee table, while the inebriated adults sat at the dinner table with fresh beers and burgers. Jude had to admit that the new and unusual taste was great. Jenny asked him to scrape the sauce off hers, which he did.

Those at the table whooped with delight as they stuffed their faces. They all had sauce on their noses, cheeks, chins or all three. As soon as they'd finished, they lit up cigarettes and Duke dealt some cards to the mystery man and himself.

Jude went into his parents' bedroom and called Billy, who seemed sullen and quiet.

"Somethin' the matter?" Jude asked.

"My mom's out drunk somewhere."

Jude wasn't sure whether he should say so, but he said, "She's here."

"What's she doing?"

"I don't know. Playing cards. Havin' dinner."

"Oh, great. I had a sandwich because she didn't leave anything."

"My mom threw my dad out, too."

"I thought everything was fine there."

"Everything's very strange."

As Jude walked back through the living room, the room that had always been reserved for special occasions and special guests, Duke wove his way from the Florida room and flopped onto the couch. He set his glass on the bare marble table, held a lit cigarette above an ashtray on the couch, dropped his head back and snored.

The mystery man and Billy's mom left. Then Jude's mom went into the living room, dropped on the couch, leaned against Duke and passed out. Jude cringed.

Jude ushered his sister away and helped her brush her teeth and dress for bed. Then, he looked up a 1924 S Mercury Dime and a 1918 Buffalo nickel he'd found in his newspaper route collection money and put them in Blue Books. Although he should practice piano, his mother and Duke were sleeping right there. She wouldn't even realize that he didn't practice.

* * * * * * *

Roosevelt fought to get his breakfast down. Uncle Theodore said, "Your body need nourishment." He put his arm around Roosevelt's shoulder. "It's a loud and scary place. Remember, you there to see yo Mama and give her support. Don't let the surroundings keep you from yo mission. She need you."

Roosevelt nodded. He wasn't sure how to greet her.

The trip to the county jail in Deland was a long, boring ride west on U.S. 92; the thumpity-thump of the tires on the concrete panels made him sleepy. He remembered how weak Mama's face looked at the last hearing.

In Deland, Papa slowed, lowered his window and stuck his hand out to signal a turn. After a couple more turns, he stopped in front of a brick building with a sign in front saying Volusia County Jail.

Two guards stood near the door. Roosevelt looked up the brick wall at tiny windows high above the parking lot, protected by bars. On the roof, at the rear of the building, he saw a heavy fence with barbed wire rolled along the top.

Inside, Papa announced that the family was there to see Miss Anne Harris.

Unusual people sat on benches in the open, cold, cement-floored room. There were long-haired, skinny and sickly white people, Eva, a Negro woman who hung around the parking lot at Campbell and Washington, and a number of other unruly Negro and white people.

Everything seemed so hard, confusing and unpleasant. A man grabbed the top of Eva's hair and pulled it.

"Ah, God damn it," hollered Eva. "What da fuck you doin' my hair motha' fucka'."

"You ain' no woman," he snickered. "You got a dick, dontcha? Or d'ya cut it off?"

"Oh Lawd," said Nana, shaking her head and turning away.

The man reached for Eva's crotch as another reached for her breasts. They pulled their hands away hurriedly, laughing hysterically. They gave each other five. Eva was livid.

Finally, the family was ushered through a heavy metal door with bars. Then they were led into a large room and asked to sit at a table facing a glass partition with a small hole to speak through.

A large woman in a uniform sat in the corner scowling. Mama walked in with an exaggerated strut, like one leg was part wooden or something. She blew a kiss through the little hole as she sat. No hugs.

Looking at Roosevelt, she said, "How you doin'?"

"Okay," he answered, shrugging his shoulders.

"Miss me?"

"Yes'm."

"I'll be comin' home soon, baby."

She turned to Papa and Nana. "How you all doin'? Everythin' okay at home? How Theodore be?"

Papa nodded and answered, "Ever'thin' all right. Somethin' almost magical happen' ta Theodore. Ain't like never befo'. Got a calmness 'bout him."

"What happen?"

"Don' know. Say it's 'cause he Muslim now."

"Don' talk such nonsense," butted in Nana. "We here to visit with Anne."

They talked about her lawyer's advice. Roosevelt looked around at the bare room. The sound of metal on metal and loud voices intruded from the jail area every time the thick metal door opened.

Roosevelt studied Mama's face. Her eyes looked sad, but her face wasn't so thin now. As Papa described Roosevelt's fishing success, she smiled and looked at him affectionately.

"Can't wait ta get outa heah," she said. "Hate dis place. I'll stay clean dis time. I swear."

"Harris," hollered the white woman. "Time."

Mama stood and shut her eyes. "Thank you for comin' ta see me. Please come again. Roosevelt, imagine a hug from me. I love all of you."

She turned and was ushered away. The door slammed shut behind her with a thud. Roosevelt felt tears roll down his cheeks.

* * * * * * *

Roosevelt sat next to Uncle Theodore on a bench at Wimpy's. Uncle Theodore asked, "Ever been to the beach?"

"No. I didn't think we was allowed across the river."

"Didn't used ta be. But even now, people all suspicious when they see a Negro ova there. Only one part a the beach we can go. You ain' never seen nothin' like it. Water all salty. Rollin' waves."

Roosevelt could hardly imagine. "Can we go sometime?"

"Sho."

His uncle was cool. He loved his grandfather, but Uncle Theodore was younger and understood some of the same things that Roosevelt did.

"Why'd you go ta prison?" Roosevelt asked.

"From livin' wrong. It was all my own doin'. But I learned a lot dis time. Helped me change course. Thanks to Allah."

Roosevelt didn't understand this Allah stuff and what Mohammad had to do with it, but Uncle Theodore was no longer the mean, scheming, treacherous man he used to be.

As they left, Roosevelt noticed his friend Rufus sprawled on the dirt, leaning against the building, with his eyes closed.

"Rufus? You awright?"

Rufus looked up. His head bobbed like that of a sick dog. His eyelids drooped. He rubbed his hand over his face and scratched furiously under his nose. Roosevelt recognized the hand action from when his mama was doing heroin.

"Rufus!" he yelled into his ears. Rufus struggled to open his eyes. His pupils were pinpoints. That confirmed it. Roosevelt felt sick to his stomach.

* * * * * * *

One evening at a boring yacht club event, some boys Jude knew strolled by. "We're going to the ball park," Gary Nathan said.

Jude followed.

Audience chatter emanated from the park where the Daytona minor league team was playing. Jude and the three boys stood on the street corner outside the stadium, just behind home plate, waiting for foul balls to come over the wall. A couple of Negro boys stood on the street along the first base line and a couple more waited outside the third base line, which was beside a thin waterway.

A loud crack sounded from home plate. A ball rose in the sky near the first base side, dropped onto the pavement, and was caught on the third bounce by a Negro boy.

Jude and his group stayed behind home plate. The next ball came over the first base area and hit a car on the round right front fender before being grabbed by the same Negro boy.

Later, another went over the third base line and the Negro boys on that side ran for it, but it bounced into the water that ran along the back of City Island. A Negro boy jumped into the water. He returned with the ball, having managed not to get cut up on the oysters, and sold it to a spectator through a gap in the fence.

The next foul came over home plate and bounced across the street. A yacht club boy stopped to wait for a car to pass.

As Roosevelt ran toward the bouncing ball, he noticed the four white boys, all blond and tanned, wearing nice shorts and buttoned shirts. Only as he arrived at the curb did he realize one was Net Boy.

Jude recognized Roosevelt, just as Gary grabbed the ball and said, "This is our spot, nigger."

Jude was horrified to hear the word he'd been taught never to say. He turned and walked directly away and returned to the club.

Roosevelt had never been called a nigger to his face before. As Net Boy walked away alone, a Negro boy turned toward the third base line and muttered under his breath, "Fuckin' crackas oughta be inside da stadium. They gots plenty a green ta buy a damn ticket."

PART II

Mid-1960s

Chapter 4

JUDE LEANED AGAINST THE TRUNK of a tree while his friend Billy and another kid named Greg Dexter lit cigarettes. Greg sang, "Winston tastes good like a cigarette should," as gray smoke enveloped his face.

"Wow, look at those knockers," said Greg, pointing to a photo in the Playboy Jude had snuck out of the yacht club men's room.

Jude imagined rubbing his hands over the girl's plump, round butt.

"I could beat off to that," Greg said.

Jude felt a stirring in his pants. He changed position to hide it. He guessed beating off had something to do with that.

Greg lit another cigarette from the butt of the first. He looked at Jude. "Don't tell me you don't smoke."

Jude shrugged. "I have," he lied.

Greg glanced at Billy and rolled his eyes.

Jude wanted Greg to think he was cool. "Gimme one."

Greg smirked, handed him a cigarette and held up his lit Zippo. Jude took in some smoke and let it out.

"You're not inhaling. Do it like this." Greg took some all the way in and let it out slowly.

Jude sucked in smoke and coughed. After a few more deep draws, he started to feel queasy. He stubbed it out and tried to get the world back in order.

"Wanna sniff glue tomorrow?" Billy asked, looking at Jude.

Oh no! Something else Greg and Billy had already experienced. Jude didn't know what it even meant.

"Well?" asked Greg.

Jude nodded, said "Okay," got up and went inside.

His mother and Duke sat at the table playing Gin Rummy, each sipping a glass of whiskey and water, with mostly melted ice cubes.

The house was filthy now that his dad had stopped paying Pearl Mae to clean it.

Duke snapped up and slammed down cards, becoming impatient whenever Jude's mother took more than a couple of seconds to act. "Make your play," he'd say. Then, he snatched every card she dropped, moved something in his hand and dropped a card. Very soon, he said "Gin," and laid out his hand.

When she got up to make dinner, Duke looked at Jude. "Wanna play?"

As Duke dealt him a hand, he explained. "Start the play by discarding the extra card."

Jude dropped a two on the discard pile.

"What're you doing getting rid of a low card this early?" hollered Duke. "Get rid of the high cards with no matches."

Jude got rid of a king next, and Duke grabbed it. In a moment, Duke roared, "Gin."

By the seventh hand, Duke's head bobbed, and his hands had slowed. He closed one eye when arranging his cards. Smoke rose into his nose and eyes from a cigarette clenched between his teeth. Although Jude knew he had the advantage, he was thrilled when he ginned on Duke. Duke stared at him through blurry eyes, got up, stumbled to the formerly fancy, reserved-for-special guests, living room couch, and passed out.

* * * * * * *

Jude, Billy, and Greg pedaled to the toy store. "Testor's glue, I presume," the owner said with a smile.

"Yeah, two big ones," said Greg. The boys plopped change on the counter.

They raced back to Greg's house. When they arrived, Greg squirted some glue into three small bags, handed them out, and put his bag over his face. Jude copied Greg. He breathed slowly at first, wondering what would happen. Greg's bag filled and collapsed rapidly. In a few minutes Greg sat heavily on the ground, closed his eyes and lay back. The bag fell next to him. He smiled. Billy lowered his bag and stood, staggering, pointing here and there and laughing.

Jude continued to sniff. The world began to look different. The sky had taken on a different hue. The trees transformed into living beings and moved angrily. The ground rolled.

Still on the ground, Greg picked up his bag again. Billy fell to the ground, laughing.

Jude's body felt numb, rubbery, unreal. He felt no pain, no feeling—like he was floating. Jude dropped his bag, stood and tried to walk, but his feet weren't right. After a couple of steps, he fell to the ground.

Giggling, he picked up the bag and sniffed more. The enjoyable oddness extended to new vistas. Billy's face looked like a rubbery fun-house image. Jude rested and sniffed, over and over, each time reaching a fresh plateau.

* * * * * * *

Roosevelt awoke to his Nana's voice in his ear. "Honey. I sorry, honey, ta tell ya dis. Papa done pass on."

"Huh?" He struggled to understand.

"Yo grandpapa. He dead. Passed on in his sleep." She pulled him up and hugged him, sobbing slightly.

"Mama know?"

"No, uh-uh. I'll try ta get word ta her."

Roosevelt sat at the kitchen table, stunned, as Nana called the Public Defender. "Sir, I believe there must be a way fo her ta come ta da funeral. Her Daddy dead. She need ta say good-bye." She waited for a few moments, and then said, "It don't sound like you really care." Then after some more silence she said, "All right then, so set a hearing."

She hung up, a determined look on her face, and called somebody else. She explained the situation again. "I know ma'am. The P.D. done tol' me he gonna file a petition, but I don't think he gonna. I can file it if you just tell me how." She was silent. "Ma'am, ain' there no way ta get dis in front a da judge?" She shook her head, looking at the floor.

* * * * * * *

There were a lot of fancy clothes at the funeral. Mama wasn't there.

Missy had changed. She had perky breasts and strutted to show them. She looked cool and a little sexy. She grinned at Roosevelt and turned away.

The smell of mothballs filled the air. Old people whispered to each other. Roosevelt watched Missy. Now that she looked so good, she wouldn't look at him. She used to just love him so much it made him sick. After the service, she came down the receiving line, hugged him and said she was sorry.

Cleve Broxton, two grades ahead of Roosevelt, came up. "Missy, you look mmmm-mmmm in dat get-up."

She smiled and looked him over good. "Got some reefah?" she whispered.

"You know it suga'. C'mon. Let's do some."

Roosevelt stood dumbfounded as she walked away to do whatever he really didn't want to imagine.

Reefer seemed to be a door opener that he might just have to learn about.

* * * * * * *

Rufus stopped over in the afternoon. "Just come ova ta pay my respects." They shook hands. He looked a lot better than he had on the ground outside Wimpy's.

"Listen man," Roosevelt said, "You ain' doin' dat stuff no mo', is ya?"

"Naw, man. Just a little smoke. Wanna do a reefah?" He pulled a thin white hand-rolled cigarette from his pocket.

"Sho," said Roosevelt like it was old hat. There was nothing wrong with that.

In the woods behind Roosevelt's house, Rufus whipped out a lighter and got it going, took a couple of heavy hits and then handed it to Roosevelt. Rufus said, "Ya gotta hold it in, man." Roosevelt took his second hit, held it, then let it out slowly. When they'd finished, Roosevelt tried to keep his eyelids up.

"Let's go get some Colt 45. It go real good with the high."

Roosevelt didn't hesitate. If this feeling could be better, he'd try it. Rufus got somebody to buy them a quart. In the dirt parking lot behind the store, Rufus took a long swig and handed it to Roosevelt. He tilted it up and took a swallow of the strong, bitter stuff. He fought back the urge to spit it out. Each swallow after that was easier. He almost liked the taste by the time they finished the bottle. They stood and walked again.

A girl of about thirteen, tall and very dark, came from a side street. Rufus nodded at her.

"'S' hap'nin?" she asked.

"You," Rufus said.

She smiled. He smiled. Roosevelt swayed back and forth. Her small pointy breasts showed through her thin top. He imagined Missy's.

"Wanna toke?" Rufus slapped his shirt pocket suggestively. She smiled again, "You got dat right."

She walked between them into the woods. They sat in a stand of trees, and Rufus lit up. As they smoked, she laughed and rubbed her shoulders against first Rufus and then Roosevelt. Rufus slid a hand right up the outside of her shirt and began massaging. She rested her head back and sighed. "Oh baby."

Rufus motioned with his eyes to the other breast. Roosevelt reached for it, gingerly, half expecting to have his hand swatted away. She didn't flinch. He swore she even moved it toward him. He felt himself bulge at the inside of his pants leg. Rufus started mouthing a breast through the shirt, so Roosevelt did too. Rufus slid his head down, bit the bottom of the T-shirt and pulled it up to reveal the see-through bra.

Roosevelt's heart pounded. He'd never before seen this much of a woman so close. Rufus unhooked the bra and the two of them sucked like crazy. It tasted sweet and bitter at the same time, a little sweaty, a little salty. He pinched the nipple beneath his lips and tongue. She thrust her pelvis.

Rufus unzipped her shorts and yanked them down. Roosevelt kept suction on the breast while watching the mound through her thin panties, bouncing up and down. He could hardly stand it.

Rufus yanked his own pants and underwear off. He got above her and she led him in. Roosevelt had never seen another guy's hard before. Roosevelt sucked one breast while massaging the other. She was going absolutely wild. Rufus humped and bounced for a short time and then got off.

She sat up suddenly and grabbed at the snap of Roosevelt's pants. In an instant, she had his pants and underwear off. She rolled back over on her back and led him in.

As Rufus sucked a breast, she sighed loudly. Roosevelt thrust until he exploded. As he shrank, he felt comfortable and rested. What a wonderful thing this reefer was. He had to have some for Missy.

* * * * * * *

Junior high was a real drag. In class, Jude was petrified to be called on. Between classes, he'd scramble to his locker, cram books that weighed a ton into the little rusty area and search for what he needed for the next class. Bigger kids would jostle and push him. In elementary school, at least there were younger kids, so he wasn't the shortest in the school. Now, he was a runt. He didn't belong.

Fourth period was the worst—Gym. Showering was required. Most of the boys already had at least a small tuft of curly black hair down there, but he had none. His looked like a bare baby bird.

Every evening he prayed for hair. It was the first thing he checked every morning. God wasn't listening.

He'd sneak to the sink, splash water on his face and head, yank off his shorts and shirt, but not his underwear, wrap a towel around his waist, and sit.

* * * * * * *

Roosevelt bought a nickel bag of reefer. Rufus taught him how to roll a joint, and they smoked one. Then he walked to Missy's house. She opened the door and gave him the once over. Her curves showed through the thin dress.

Roosevelt couldn't get any words out. Suddenly, his visit seemed so silly and embarrassing. Finally, he asked, "How ya doin' Missy?"

"Fine."

"Whacha doin' taday?"

"Nothin'".

Two sentences he'd managed to get out, and no response worth anything. He continued. "Wanna go for a walk?"

"Why?"

Jesus. She wasn't going to make this easy. He squeezed one of the joints in his shirt pocket so she could see its outline.

Her eyes lit up. "Roosevelt Harris. Didn't think you'd be comin' heah with reefah. Get yo' ass in heah."

"Ain't no one home?"

She shook her head no, grinning wickedly.

She led him straight to her bedroom. She opened the curtains so they could blow the smoke out. When the joint was gone, they sat in silence, her eyes gazing outside and his darting back and forth from her, the outside, and the furniture.

"What you thinkin' boy?"

He shrugged. She peered into his eyes. He was embarrassed. He felt himself moving. Her eyes roved down and fixed on the movement in his pants. She smiled. Then she slowly reached over like she was going to actually grab it, but instead put her fingers all around the bulge like a hovering spider. Grab it, grab it, he begged silently. She began moving her hands all over his body, his legs, his stomach, his chest, under his shirt, and every time she would approach, her hands would suddenly take a detour and tease around it, sometimes lightly touching him through his jeans with a fleeting glance of a finger.

Suddenly she leaned down and bit his nipple through his shirt. She moved her body over him and swayed back and forth, her pussy within inches of the swelling in his pants. He thought he might go mad.

She pulled his T-shirt over his head, dropped it on the floor and tongued his chest and stomach.

"You like this?" she asked.

He nodded and grunted. He could say no more.

She moved off him and perched on all fours, staring at his crotch like a cat after a trapped lizard. Abruptly she lunged and surrounded the bulge with her lips, gumming it through the pants, growling like a cheetah. He squealed. He began fumbling around, trying to reach the bottom of her dress, but it was out of reach. She mounted his belly. Her panties were wet. He pulled her dress over her head, revealing a dark, taught stomach and two small breasts. He did what he'd learned with Rufus and the girl in the woods, and went for her breasts with his mouth, manipulating the nipple with fervor. She rubbed her wetness back and forth on his belly. He'd had enough. It was time. Now or never.

He rolled her over quickly and yanked down her panties, revealing a slight patch of hair. He yanked off his own shorts and entered her. She was very active, much more so than the girl in the woods. In a few minutes she screamed, "Yes. Yes. Now. Now!!!" He didn't know what she meant but thrust harder and erupted.

Marijuana had come through again. It was his friend.

* * * * * * *

Several days after Jude's first beer, and only a week or so after first sniffing glue, Greg announced that his sister, Linda, had some speed.

Jude arrived at Greg's after his evening route. Greg's sister had a beautiful face, straight blond hair and twinkling eyes. At sixteen, she was two years older than Greg, three years older than Jude and Billy. She called Billy her cute little teddy bear and hugged him, pulling his head into her breasts.

Greg's bedroom was in the basement, with its own door to the outside. She said to Billy, "You're first. Come on," and she led him into the bathroom, saying, "Give me a sign if Mom comes down."

A couple of minutes later, Billy came out of the bathroom holding his arm up at the elbow, wild-eyed. The tiny pupils had shrunk to nothing. He zipped here and there saying, "Wow. Wow.

Whew. Man!" Linda hugged him from behind, as Greg went into the bathroom.

Jude entered the bathroom and found Greg holding a syringe, full of yellow fluid, pointing at the ceiling. He flicked the side of the barrel with his finger, causing a bubble of air to rise. Then he tapped the plunger, and a tiny stream of the yellow fluid squirted out of the needle.

Jude hadn't realized doing speed meant taking a shot. He hated shots. But if he chickened out now, he'd never hear the end of it. In the mirror, he saw Linda behind him, grinning.

Linda held the upper part of his right arm above the elbow. "Clench your fist a couple of times," she whispered. He did. Greg studied his arm, then aimed the point at a vein. Greg's jaws clenched as he ground his teeth wildly.

Jude looked away. This was awful. How stupid he was to be doing this just so these kids would think he was cool. He wanted to call it off. He felt the prick of the needle and watched it enter. Greg pulled the plunger back. Some of Jude's blood flowed into the barrel, tingeing the yellow substance pink. Jude thought he would faint. Then Greg pushed the plunger in and pulled it back again, drawing blood back in. Jude felt his heart pick up speed. His body began feeling numb. His brain crackled like the time he'd eaten a spoonful of horseradish. Zoooom. He was going in high speed. He sat down. He stood up. He walked around. He looked in the mirror. He was another person. Man, what a rush!!!

They stayed up all night, talking, and listening to music Jude had never heard before. At four in the morning, Greg and Billy went with him to do his paper route. Greg didn't have a route anymore because it wasn't cool. He sold nickel bags of pot instead. The three boys rolled the papers in remarkable time. Then they zipped through the route, wearing down as they finished.

Back at the house, they passed out. At three in the afternoon, Jude awoke groggy and out of sorts. They sniffed some glue and he felt better.

* * * * * * *

Roosevelt knocked on the door of Missy's house. Her little brother opened the door and looked him up and down.

"Yo. Missy heah?"

"Uh, uh. Done gone off wif Donald."

Damn it. Who'd she think she was? "Who Donald?"

The boy shrugged his shoulders.

Roosevelt was pissed. She should've known he'd show up to get her high. She should be waiting for him.

He wandered to the store and found an adult to buy him a quart of malt liquor. He went to the rear of the parking lot and sat on the ground behind the abandoned car. He lit a reefer and opened the quart. How could Missy have gone off with another guy? The malt liquor numbed his limbs. What a relaxing feeling. He was at peace. That whore Missy wasn't gonna ruin his day by fucking around on him. After a while, he leaned against the car and nodded off.

When he awoke, the sun was setting. He had to get home. He stood slowly, his legs wobbly, and staggered across the parking lot.

Rufus lay on the ground in front of the store curled up like a little baby, in a puddle of his own puke. Roosevelt himself almost puked at the sight. With every step pounding in his head, Roosevelt struggled to get home.

Nana took one look at him and said, "Oh boy. You comin' down wif somethin'. You look awful." She led him to his bedroom. She left and returned and coaxed him to eat chicken soup. He felt queasy. He couldn't stand the smell of the soup.

* * * * * * *

In the morning, Nana hovered over him. He felt so awful. As she left, Uncle Theodore came in and stood above him. "Whassup, nephew?"

Roosevelt groaned.

"Look to me like you done drunk somethin' what didn't agree with you. You reek of alcohol. And here yo' Nana think you got the flu. Since when you drink?" Uncle Theodore continued. "You only thirteen. Tha's a little young ta be doin' that. I'm disappointed. This ain' good. The best thing about it is you got sick and feel awful. That's what it'll do to ya."

Roosevelt could have punched him. Just like he said that Roosevelt's mama belonged in jail, now he was saying that he was pleased Roosevelt was sick. The son of a bitch.

* * * * * * *

Later, when nobody was home, Roosevelt walked back down to the parking lot behind the store. The man who'd bought him the beer, a light-skinned Negro with reddish hair and freckles, grinned. "You look like shit."

Roosevelt nodded.

"Hair a da dog," continued the man.

"Huh?"

The man smiled, "What you need is da hair a da dog that done bitcha. If you feel bad in da mornin', drink mo'."

It didn't sound good. The man entered the store and returned with a Budweiser Tall Boy. Roosevelt sipped. After a while, he began to experience the pleasant feeling he'd felt before. The headache left, but not the queasiness in his stomach.

Returning home, he found Nana. "Chil'. Whatchu doin' out? You sick."

"I feelin' betta, Nana."

"You look a little better, I guess, but you need ta lie down fo da rest a da day."

* * * * * * *

Jude sniffed glue or shot speed at Greg's house daily. On Thursday night, Linda called to say she was bringing a surprise, but would need thirty dollars. The boys scraped it together.

Linda walked in unsteadily, with an odd, crooked smile. Her hair was greasy and her pupils huge. She plunked three tiny purple pills on the dresser and grinned. "LSD—acid—purple microdot."

Jude wasn't sure whether his friends had done it before. He wondered when the needle would come out.

But this time, Linda said, "Well, eat 'em."

Jude popped one in his mouth and chewed. It felt and tasted chalky, and a little sweet. He paced around, waiting for it to work. After a while, the room began swirling with colors, shapes, tints, and hues. It hummed and cooed. Faces became distorted and discolored. His stomach tightened into a rock, and he felt a strange tasting mucous in his throat.

As he turned his head, the furniture trailed across the room in slow motion. His body was not his. He glanced at himself in a mirror on the wall; his face was out of shape and mutating. His eyes were bright, but his pupils covered almost all the blue.

Whoosh. Greg waved a hand in front of him. It left a tracer in the air. "Far out, huh?" Then he waved two hands in opposite directions. Jude was mesmerized. Linda laughed. She leapt on top of Billy and kissed and mauled him.

Greg put on a 45 record he'd gotten. "Hey, listen. The Beatles did this; it's not on an album."

The song began, "Hey Jude, don't make it bad. Take a sad song and make it better."

Jude wondered what it meant. It continued, "Hey Jude, don't be afraid. You were made to go out and get her. The minute you let her under your skin, then you begin to make it better."

Every time the Beatles said, "Hey Jude," Greg and Billy yelled it, and pointed at him.

"What's it about," Jude asked.

"I dunno," said Greg. "But let it under your skin and make it feel better sure sounds like shooting up to me."

Linda said, "You know what your name means? In the Catholic Church, it's the patron saint of lost causes."

Everybody laughed. Billy said, "I doubt if you're a saint, but I think you're a lost cause."

"I thought it meant Jew," Billy said. "Are you a Jew?"

"It only meant that in German, during the Nazi era. I'm named after an uncle—my mom's brother."

After listening to music and talking for a long time, they tried to sleep. The hallucinations in sight and sound remained strong. Jude tossed and turned, hearing noises from the others in the room. At about three, Billy complained that he needed to get some sleep. Linda said she had an answer for that and pulled out three yellow capsules. "Yellow jackets," she said. "Downers."

They each popped a couple. Two hours later, they were still awake but more messed up. Jude struggled to his feet to do his route. Greg joined him. Billy was lying in a bed, fully dressed, entangled with Linda.

The hallucinations had changed to slower-moving traces. It was difficult to escape the room on rubbery legs.

Outside, in the early morning light, the world was dull, moving in slow motion. Trying to make his flaccid legs pedal uphill, Jude almost fell over.

Rolling the papers took forever. Jude was sleepy and alert at the same time. The hallucinations kept changing. Traces rolled slowly this way and that. He kept snapping his fingers with rubber bands.

Trying to mount the bike loaded with papers, Jude fell and landed on the concrete, scraping his knee. He and Greg laughed as Greg pulled him off the ground. Neither could steer a straight line.

Eventually, they finished the route and returned to Greg's house. As they entered, Greg's mother was in the room, saying, "I can't believe this. How old is this boy? You know better than this. My God! I just can't believe you'd do such a thing."

Noticing Greg and Jude, she said, "Look at you. You look terrible."

"I see trouble, trouble," she hollered, as she chased Linda up the stairs.

* * * * * * *

Roosevelt had been drinking and smoking reefer for days, sometimes skipping school and hanging out at Rufus' house.

Before class on Friday, Roosevelt met Rufus in the woods behind school. Rufus jammed the butt of a joint between the ends of a bobby pin, lit it, and after it burned for a moment, blew it out. He pushed a mountain of smoke under Roosevelt's nose. "Breathe in, man, deep . . . shotgun," he said.

Roosevelt's nose tingled. His brain burned. Rufus handed him a bottle of Mad Dog 20/20. Roosevelt gulped the dark red wine and passed it back. After a while, numb and floating, Roosevelt followed Rufus through the brush and onto school grounds.

As they swaggered into the building, Missy came up, smiled and said, "'S hapnin?"

"You, baby," said Roosevelt.

"Whyn't ya bring some reefah for me?"

Roosevelt looked at Rufus. Rufus slid him a reefer and walked off.

"Come on," Roosevelt whispered to Missy.

She grinned brightly and giggled. They stooped through a hole in the chain link fence near the gym and sat on the ground in the trees. As he stoked up the joint, she stroked him through his pants. She took a hit, continuing the massage. By the time they finished the joint, she had his pants down. Then, they were both undressed. At that moment, he was convinced that he was the one for her and she for him. She always came back.

Soon they were on the ground. Her whimpers were interrupted by the rustle of footsteps on brittle leaves. Before he could react, Mr. Lincoln, the principal, stood above them.

"Get dressed," he said and turned his back.

He marched them across the rear playground toward the office.

In the office, an old woman took Missy into one room, and the principal ushered Roosevelt into another. He scraped a chair across the wooden floor and straddled it backward, his arms over the back of the chair. After an endless silence, he said, "I'm going to have to call your parents."

Roosevelt remained silent. The bastard would have a little trouble finding anyone claiming to be his father. He wouldn't be able to find Mama either.

Nana would be so hurt. Mama too. Auntie Barbara wouldn't shut up for a week, while Uncle Theodore would be full of logical and deep advice.

Why should he be punished for getting high, missing a class, and getting it on with Missy? What was the big deal? But Roosevelt couldn't bring himself to plead for mercy. He just stared at the floor. He'd become irritated at the basset-hound face staring at him.

"Do you regret your actions, young man?"

Roosevelt shrugged his shoulders again. He did. Sure he did. He regretted getting caught more than he regretted almost anything he could think of. He hadn't even finished. Fuck this guy. He was the one who should regret interrupting.

"I've had it. I'm calling your parents." He marched from the room.

A half-hour later, he returned, followed by the stern but concerned face of Nana.

"Child," she said almost blubbering. "What has got into you?" She wiped a tear with a Kleenex she'd pulled from inside her shirt sleeve. "I done the best I could raisin' you. And this is what you do?" She shook her head slowly, her eyes red and sad.

Roosevelt thought his heart would break. The son-of-a-bitch had made Nana sad.

"I'm thinking of expelling him, Ma'am. He's not the least bit remorseful."

"You mean foreva?"

"Either that or a lengthy suspension. I can't have this type of activity," the bastard continued. "Drugs and sex on school grounds."

"Oh Roosevelt," sighed Nana sadly. "Please suh. He need school. We'll work with him. His Mama ain' at home, like I told ya."

Roosevelt sat glumly, eyes down.

The old man sighed and shook his head. "I'll give him one more chance if you promise to work with him. Young man, we'll see you back here in one week, fifteen minutes before class starts. Think about this during your week off. One more chance."

"Thank you suh. Thank you. You won't regret it," Nana whimpered. "He a good boy."

* * * * * * *

Jude stood in the white-and-black checkered bathroom of Krystal, a hamburger joint near Main Street, and dropped a tab of orange barrel. It was his fifth time in two weeks doing acid. He'd found a new heaven. It cost fifteen dollars a tab. He only made enough for two tabs a week from his paper route.

He'd just made his first direct buy from a dealer. He'd approached a twenty-year-old named Nick in the parking lot of Krystal, cleared his throat and said, "You got any acid?" Nick walked cool, talked cool, and was loved by girls.

Nick stared him up and down in silence. Jude felt as though he were standing there frozen in time. He feared Nick would insult him and laugh at him at any moment.

Finally, Nick growled, "Ten minutes, behind McDonald's," and turned to walk away.

Ten minutes later, they stood in the dark among the ruins of an old coquina building. Jude handed him fifteen crumpled one-dollar bills. Nick stuck them into his shirt pocket and started to walk away without handing anything over.

Jude almost called after him, alarmed, but then Nick turned his head and said, "Over there."

Jude zipped to a pillar, found a small round piece of aluminum foil, and snatched it up. What a great way to deal! Nick was a genius. He'd never get busted.

* * * * * * *

Inside Krystal, Jude sat alone at a booth overlooking the parking lot as the trip arrived gradually. His throat tightened. The now-familiar mucous clumped in his throat. Sounds of dishes clanging behind the counter and spatulas slapping on the metal grill echoed and intensified. The greasy smell of tiny burgers, grilled onions and fries permeated the air. A woman walked past—*woosh*! He lost himself in the trail following the woman like a comet. The hallucinations were more colorful and the patterns more pronounced than any he'd experienced so far.

He was in another world. His reflection in the glass showed eyes stuck wide open. He couldn't put a normal face on no matter how he tried. As Nick walked toward the car, he looked up, nodded and shot a peace sign over his shoulder. Cool. Here he was, just turned fourteen, being acknowledged by one of the coolest dealers around, and right in front of the crowd in the parking lot. This was the best, the very best. He lit a cigarette.

Woosh. Something large and gray was beside him. He looked up, into the stone face of the cop who protected the Krystal from wild kids. The kids called him Superman. "What're you doing, kid?"

"Whadda you mean?" he choked. "Um, I'm drinking a Coke."

The cop studied his face. Jude looked down to hide his eyes. The cop's huge, black, shiny shoes stood on the checkered tile floor. The tiny tile squares bounced up and down, back and forth.

"Kid," the voice resonated. "What are you on?"

Horrified, Jude looked up at the huge, stony face and back at the floor.

"Get out of here, kid," the cop ordered.

Jude stood slowly, Coke in hand, and with all his might tried to walk straight toward the door, as sounds, shades, and imaginary wind inside the room swayed him back and forth. He reached for the door too soon, stabbing at nothingness, but finally reached it and was outside.

He crossed Ocean Avenue and headed toward the ocean pier. As he began the long trek toward the building in the middle, the boards seemed to creak under his feet. A sign over the entrance to the pier bar said "Allman Joys."

He stopped at midpoint in a steady breeze that blew his hair over his face. All along the beach, tiny lights of motels sparkled and pulsated.

He imagined the people dancing inside. He'd been to a dance once. He'd felt more uncomfortable there than any place he'd ever been. It was even worse than a baseball practice or game. Everybody else seemed to know exactly what to do. Kids talked, danced and enjoyed themselves. Jude stood in the corner watching, petrified. He couldn't imagine where they'd learned how.

A strong gust of wind came up and he rode in his mind on the long guitar riff of bluesy, southern rock and roll. It had a flavor and visual hallucinations—stars, Zs, zigzags, in living color.

Waves crashed below, leaving white frothy foam dancing in the moonlight.

He loved LSD. This is the way he liked the world, not quite normal—different colored, different patterned, where sounds and visual images all played together as a moving orchestra. He saw himself sitting in the booth overlooking the parking lot, seeing the king of LSD dealers shooting him a peace sign and a knowing glance.

This was heaven.

* * * * * * *

Roosevelt didn't want to disrespect Nana. She meant well. She just didn't understand. Uncle Theodore got on his nerves even more.

Lying on his bed, Roosevelt remembered the last time with Missy—if only they'd finished before old man Lincoln showed up and spoiled it. He hadn't had any reefer in three days.

It was boring and hot. Nana had gone out. The rear screen door slammed behind him as he bounded out and along the wooden porch, through dusty yards and wooded areas to the corner. As always, old men sat on milk crates and creaky, twisted aluminum chairs under the sparse shade of a lone tree behind the store, trash strewn all about.

A dealer named Tom stood, munching on a toothpick. Roosevelt stopped in front of Tom and cleared his throat. "Got any reefer?" His voice sounded far off and girl-like.

Tom gave him a serious once over. "You Anne's boy, ain't ya. How she doin'? When she gettin' out?"

"She okay. Should be comin' home soon. Don' know zackly when. I need to buy some reefer."

"You ever smoke reefah befo?"

"Uh-huh. I got 'spended from school and I ain't got nothin' ta do. I need ta get a buzz on."

Tom smiled bigger than life, reached into his pocket and pulled out two rolled reefers. He handed them to Roosevelt.

"How much?"

"A gift. Go get yo buzz on."

Roosevelt hurried home, lit one up behind the garage and got good and high. Just as he finished it, he heard the old car pull into the driveway. He peered around the wooden garage door. When Nana stepped inside, he ran, leapt through the window without touching the sill, and rolled onto his bed. He was lying there looking bored and breathing carefully when she opened the door to check on him.

Chapter 5

JUDE WALKED TO SCHOOL now that he was in junior high. Only lamers rode bikes. He wanted to be cool. One morning, some eighth graders sat on a wall across from the school smoking cigarettes.

One of them was a kid named Benny, one of the coolest kids in school. He was older than Jude, had long hair, and broke school rules. As Jude passed, Benny said, "Hey, kid, got a light?"

Jude snapped open his Zippo and lit Benny's cigarette. Then he pulled a Winston from his own pack and lit up too. He sucked smoke up his nose, using the French-smoking technique he'd learned from Greg.

"Like to get ahold of some a that purple barrel," one of the boys was saying to another.

"Who's got any?" asked another boy.

Suddenly the boys turned to stare at Jude. "What're ya standin' there for kid?"

How surprised they'd be to know he could buy from Nick. He said, "I dropped a tab last night. It was heavy."

The other boys glanced at each other, snickered and guffawed. "You little dick. You don' even know what it is."

"Acid. Do it all the time. Purple microdot. Orange barrel. Whatever."

"Where ya get it?"

"I buy it."

"He's fuckin' with us," said Benny.

Jude said, "Want me to get you a tab? Fifteen bucks."

"Oh right," Benny giggled, elbowing one of his friends. "I'm gonna give this dickhead fifteen dollars. What do I look like?"

"I'll get a tab if you bring the money for it on Monday."

"Sure dickhead."

"If you're not gonna have the money I'm not getting it."

"Okay. You bring it and I'll have the money."

Well, they knew who he was now. They may think he's just a dickhead today, but on Monday it would all be different. He snuffed his smoke, lit another and walked toward the school without acknowledging the older boys again.

In English class, they were diagramming sentences. He sat behind a hot girl named Janet. Whenever she moved her head, her long blond hair flowed like silk across her shoulders. Her profile was delicious. She turned to say something to the girl next to her and caught Jude staring. He looked away, but it was too late. Janet made a face and rolled her eyes. He felt his face turn red. She seemed to enjoy his shame all the more and made eyes at Mary so she would look at him too. There was nothing he could do but sit there and sweat.

* * * * * * *

On Friday, the last school day of Roosevelt's suspension, the family bustled around preparing to drive to the county jail to pick up Mama. Uncle Theodore, all done up with a light brown suit, rushed in excitedly and helped Roosevelt put on a tie, like Papa used to do.

Nana sat in the front of the car, sniffling from time to time. "Family gonna be all together again," she said.

Auntie Barbara was quiet for a while, but then, started, "I sure hope Sistah Anne done realize' the error of her ways. She gotta stay 'way from dat dope. Stay clean away from it. Ain' nothin' but bad news. Nothin'. How many times she done been down dis road . . ."

"Barbara," Uncle Theodore stated firmly from the driver's seat, just like Papa would have. "That's enough."

She was quiet for a moment, almost humming her thoughts, and then, "Well, you know what I's talkin' 'bout. Drugs are the scourge of the earth. She know good and well . . ."

"BARBARA!" Uncle Theodore bellowed, almost turning all the way around in his seat.

"Bad news, they are," she managed to get in.

At the jail, they waited at least forty-five minutes. The huge metal door opened many times. Then a tough-looking guard led her through. Framed by dark wrinkled lids, Mama's eyes sparkled. The guard walked her straight to the desk, did something with some documents and turned away, leaving Mama standing alone. She turned slowly toward her family. Roosevelt ran ahead of the group and hugged her. Her tears fell on his neck.

* * * * * * *

The first morning after Mama returned, Roosevelt dressed quietly so as not to wake her.

She rolled over. "How's it goin' in school, Baby? Anythin' new?"

He shook his head no. Nana hadn't told her about his suspension.

"You done growed since I seen ya."

She was paying attention to him. That was a good sign.

She yawned loudly. "How good this bed feel! Cain't tell ya how good it is ta be home. Missed ya a lot, Roosevelt."

"I missed you too, Mama. I gotta get ta school."

He crept over and kissed her on the cheek. She grabbed him and hugged him until he thought he would be crushed. She let go. "Run along. Don't be late."

The morning was bright and fresh. At school, he sauntered down the hallway.

Missy stood in front of her locker. He walked up to her. "'S hap'nin?"

"You," she whispered sweetly.

All right. He was still in. She looked luscious. Her lips were moist and her hair bobbed in long curls over her forehead.

"Got anythin'?" she whispered.

"Uh-uh." The thought of toking on a reefer excited him. Thinking of Missy lying naked in the leaves aroused him. But the image of Mr. Lincoln's big ugly face standing over them replaced the thought and ruined it.

"Gotta get ta class," he said and turned away. He glanced back and caught her looking at him.

* * * * * * *

After school, Mama sat with him, smiling with a spacey, happy look, but not quite as bad as Uncle Theodore. He wasn't used to seeing her calm. He wasn't used to seeing her at all.

Uncle Theodore came in, patted Roosevelt on the shoulder and leaned down to hug Mama. She looked at him like he was from outer space.

He said, "Ain't it a beautiful day?"

She looked at Roosevelt and smiled. "Yeah, s'pose it is."

Now this was weird. Usually, nobody paid any attention, and now he had these two sitting here smiling at him.

"You know the dif'rence 'tween adjective clauses and adverbial clauses?" he asked, looking first at his uncle and then Mama. Uncle Theodore dropped his eyes to the table.

He looked at Mama. She said, "Roos'velt, you needs ta do yo own school work."

"Let's go fishin'," said Uncle Theodore eagerly.

"Fishin'?" answered Mama. "That's one good thing 'bout bein' in jail. Didn' have to do no fishin'."

"We has a good time fishin', don' we, Roosevelt? C'mon with us. Please."

She smiled again, showing her bright teeth. Boy, she looked good. "I'll come along ta watch. Ya'll do the fishin'."

They parked on Beach Street opposite Ratte Island.

As they fished, Mama strolled back and forth on the wall, tossing little stones into the water.

Roosevelt said, "She's gonna scare off the fish."

"Shhh," whispered Uncle Theodore. "Don't matter none. Just good for her ta be outta da house. Look at her. She enjoyin' herself."

She turned off the wall and skipped across the grass, stopping to pick a wildflower and sniff it.

Roosevelt hooked a fish. His mother said, "Look at da size a dat 'un, Roosevelt."

Sure, Mama, he thought. Well, if she was going to spend time with him, she could lie all she wanted. He couldn't remember a time EVER when she was so open, so loving, so here, really here. She didn't have half her mind on running off someplace or another.

Mama leaned on a skinny palm tree behind them. "You sure diff'rent, Theodore. What happen' to ya?"

"Turn' my life 'round."

"How?"

"You ain' never heard nothin' of Muslims in prison?"

"That's Aye-Rab shit, ain' it?"

"It's a long story, and Mama don't like me talkin' about it in front of Roosevelt."

"They was one girl in the cell block talked a little 'bout it. Everybody done tol' her ta shut up. There was some Aye-Rab girl in there too and ever'body said they ought to kneel down together. I stayed out of it and away from that bitch."

Uncle Theodore grinned. "If you wanna learn about it, I'll be happy ta teach ya. The euphoria you experiencing now is gonna pass and you gonna be let down. Now's da time ta prepare yo'self."

Her face showed she was turning off. Uncle Theodore smiled. "When you ready, if you ready, let me know."

* * * * * * *

Jude looked at the clock—5:30—quarter to six. Mornings were getting harder and harder. At ten till, he forced himself up. He dragged himself out the bedroom door. On his way to his mother's bathroom, he stopped abruptly. He saw a shadow—a person—ughh. A son-of-a-bitch with no clothes on was kneeling on the floor, with his head buried between the spread legs of Jude's naked mother, who lay on her back snoring, her boobs draped to each side of her chest.

Bile reached the top of Jude's throat. He fought it back. Jesus. Who was this mother fucker? He imagined Duke staggering back here to take a leak and catching this view. Funny. It appeared the guy couldn't stay awake either.

Outside, he walked his bike up the steep driveway. Though he weighed less than ninety pounds now, he felt heavy. Reaching his dad's office and his packet of papers, he dropped the bike and collapsed on the steps. The local section contained an article about kids arrested for selling LSD. Jude scanned the kids' names. He didn't recognize any. There was an article about Martin Luther King and a march being held somewhere. He wasn't interested.

He wanted to get to school in time to sell the acid to Benny in front of the others. He struggled up one street and down the next, not getting off his bike or backtracking when he didn't throw a paper quite on the mark. Close enough.

Mrs. Patterson yelled through the door, "My paper was wet yesterday." Screw her. His legs ached.

At home, he found the man he'd seen earlier, now sleeping soundly in a sitting position on the Florida room couch. Duke was on the living room couch. His mother was in bed, under the sheet. Her bedroom reeked of whiskey and smoke. He got to feeling nothing, as usual.

He cleaned up and rode his bike back to his dad's office. He'd have been late if he walked all the way to school, but he wouldn't be caught dead showing up at school on a bicycle.

As Jude walked toward the school, Benny said, "Hey, fuckhead, you get my acid?"

Jude pulled the aluminum-foil-wrapped tab from his pocket and held it out.

"Lemme see what's in there," Benny said.

Jude unwrapped the foil and showed the tiny blue tab. Benny's eyes bugged out. The others crowded around.

He eyed Jude suspiciously. "How do I know it's real?"

"You've never seen acid before?"

"Uh, sure."

Jude was sure this was a first for Benny. Jude was giving him an education.

"Well, thanks," said Benny holding out his hand. "I'll bring the money tomorrow—ten bucks, right?"

Jude closed his fist. "Fifteen bucks. Bring the money and I give you the tab."

"How do I know it's good?"

Jude shook his head. Benny wasn't his idol anymore. "You're pathetic," he said under his breath. He dropped the tab back into his pocket and walked to class. He heard some of the boys razzing Benny.

Jude stopped at his locker, in an open alcove on the second floor. If Benny was mad enough about the put-down, he might turn Jude in. He shouldn't keep the tab on him or in his locker. It was so little he could put it almost anywhere and nobody would find it.

Janet and Mary swished by. He stopped to inhale Janet's draft and imagine what was under her plaid skirt.

Glancing around, he opened the empty locker of a student who'd moved away and stuck the tab in the crook of the front right corner.

In history class, there was a test. He answered Abraham Lincoln to one question because he'd heard the name mentioned during the week. He tried to copy an answer from Ernest, the scientific type. The little shit hunched over his paper. Jude filled in ten out of thirty blanks, unsure of any of the answers.

He could see his father holding the wretched report card in his hands, stern eyes burning through him. A deep empty sensation burned in the pit of his stomach. Stupid fill-in-the-blank test. You shouldn't have to know such details as long as you could pick them out of a list.

* * * * * * *

While he folded papers that afternoon, a lady opened the door to his little room. "Your father wishes to see you," she said.

What could be worse? What did he know? Jude followed her stiff form down the hall, the old wooden floor creaking under the carpet. She ushered him into the office where his father was leaning back, telephone in hand, with a thoughtful, authoritative expression on his face. He said final words into the receiver and placed it on the cradle.

He turned toward Jude, narrowed his intense eyes, and said, "Shut the door."

Jude closed the door and crept across the room, past the brick fireplace and oak credenza, to the stiff leather chair in front of the desk. His father stared. Jude quivered and looked down.

"When did you take up smoking?"

He guessed he meant cigarettes. How'd he know that? Jude stammered, "Uh, I don't know."

"I saw you on the street. I'm disappointed."

Jude nodded.

"How are your grades?"

"Okay, I guess."

"How are things at home?"

"Okay."

"I hear there's a lot of drinking going on there."

Jude shrugged.

"Well, is there?"

Jude didn't like all that happened in the house, but he loved his freedom. It would be crazy to give his father any ammunition. "Not much. Things are fine."

"Are you studying?"

"Yeah."

"Yes, sir," his father commanded.

"Yes, sir."

"Are you and Jenny eating well?"

"Yes, sir."

"I'm considering seeking custody, to provide a more stable environment."

What an awful thought. Be careful. "Why?" his voice trembled.

"I don't think you're being raised properly."

"Things are good." Well, they were good for his new lifestyle. His sister was doing okay.

Jude flashed on the naked man with his head in his mother's crotch. He shuddered and tried to get the image out of his mind.

"Well, I'm watching. Your grades. Your smoking. Don't disappoint me."

Jude nodded. Wouldn't the old man be thrilled to know he had two tabs of acid in his pocket? He had to get out of there.

He struggled through the route and arrived home exhausted. He reviewed coins after dinner. He used to love the artwork on the Peace Dollar. Now, it was boring.

* * * * * * *

Jude dropped a tab of acid at one in the morning, figuring he'd have an interesting night, and he'd still be tripping on his morning route, and maybe even at school. As it came on, he lay in the dark watching patterns on the ceiling. Then he stood, opened the window wide and enjoyed the river breeze. An eerie, echoing sound traveled on the air from cars crossing the bridge. He liked tripping alone. Nobody took anything away from it.

He decided to go outside. He crept down the hill and sat on the floating dock. The slight waves pitter-pattered against the Styrofoam float supporting the dock. Larger waves sprayed up between the boards. Occasionally, a small fish would jump and hit the water with a splash that echoed weirdly up to the sky and back.

Whoosh. A pelican flew close overhead and perched on a piling. Sparkling stars danced on a rich, deep, blackboard. He tried to pick out the big dipper. He used to gaze at constellations with his telescope. But that was when he and his mother were interested in things other than being loaded.

LSD took him to the perfect place. He was on a trip and was right here. He was in his own mind with wonderful sights and sounds. He could get started on a thought and go anywhere. His body was sometimes his and sometimes not. The cool living air blew right through him.

He imagined meeting Janet in the hall at school. Wait, it wasn't possible to be alone in the hall. Well, maybe if they both had to stay after for something.

He approaches her nonchalantly.

"Hi Jude," she says. She swings her head. Her hair sways around her shoulder and partially across her face. She moves closer to him. He reaches for her hand and pulls her to him. She meets him with her mouth open. He hugs her and slowly moves his hands down to her round butt. Perfect. She pushes against him, and he can feel himself growing.

Splash. A pelican hit the water. White water frothed to the stars.

He tried to get back to Janet. Now, back to the hallway. Approach again. He couldn't get her face in the picture. He tried to remember her butt again. No good. One day he would fuck a girl for real.

* * * * * * *

Roosevelt, his mama, and Uncle Theodore sat at the kitchen table. Roosevelt studied geography. The others chatted.

Auntie Barbara strutted into the kitchen, poured water into a flowered coffee cup and sighed loudly. "So, the two of you gonna find yourselves some work? Quit hangin' 'round doin' nothin'. Just soakin' Mama. I said it before, and I'll say it again . . ."

Roosevelt's mama and Uncle Theodore looked at each other and rolled their eyes simultaneously.

"Well, what ya'll gonna do?" She banged her cup on the table. Nana trudged into the room. "Barbara, that's enough."

"I ain' gonna sit idly by watchin' 'em freeload off ya. Sittin' 'round talkin' 'bout Malcolm X like he some sort a god. Talkin' 'bout religions what ain' Christianity."

"Sis," began Uncle Theodore slowly, deliberately, "I been lookin' fo work. I expect ta have somethin' soon." He radiated calm. "Now, Anne ain' ready. Give her time. Takes time ta . . ."

"Ya'll just lazy," Barbara interrupted shrilly. "Ya'll use all this mumbo jumbo 'bout bein' sick. Ya'll took drugs 'cause you wanted to. It's on you. Don' drag me an Mama into yo lazy drug abusin'. . ."

"Barbara," interjected Nana quietly. "When I want 'em to help out, I'll say so. Please, Barbara, let it be."

"You don' see nothin'. . ."

"Das enough, Barbara, I mean it," she said more forcefully.

Auntie Barbara stood, slammed her cup on the counter and stormed from the room.

"Mama, we can move out if you want," Roosevelt's mama whispered under her breath.

Nana shook her head deliberately. "Take what time ya'll need." A huge tear rolled down her cheek. Uncle Theodore and Mama stood and hugged her.

A peace remained in the room after Auntie Barbara's storm went with her.

* * * * * * *

Jude stood in the bathroom; his gaunt, drawn, and darkly hollow-eyed face startled him. He wet a face cloth and washed under his eyes, unsure whether the dark rings were newspaper print or lifestyle. It didn't seem to help.

He dressed hurriedly and grabbed the tab he'd bought for Benny.

Benny and his gang sat on the wall, puffing cigarettes. Benny spotted him and hushed his followers. Jude approached slowly and casually, still partly off earth. He set the tab on a ledge as he walked up.

Benny asked, "Got my acid?"

"Sure. Gimme the money."

Benny held up a ten and a five, and Jude snatched it.

"Well?" asked Benny impatiently.

"There," Jude pointed with his face to the tiny tin foil wrapped tab of acid.

Benny rushed over and nabbed it, opening the foil slightly to inspect.

Jude strutted proudly across the street and through the door.

* * * * * * *

On a Saturday morning, Uncle Theodore rallied the family to go fishing by the yacht club. Mama was not so eager and bright-eyed as when she'd first come home, but she was still Mama. Auntie Barbara grudgingly agreed to go along. Everyone moved in slow motion, loading cane poles and other necessities into the old car.

At the river, Roosevelt walked along the seawall where the white boy had shown him his cast net. He dropped his line into the water.

Roosevelt thought he smelled reefer. Damn. Smelled just like it. He sniffed hard and looked back at his family. He glanced all around and then heard voices, white boys. Smoke wafted up from the bushes.

"You dumb fuck," one of them said. "You think that bitch would even look at you?"

"I can get her anytime I want."

Several boys laughed.

"Here, shotgun."

Somebody coughed. Four boys rounded the hedge, glassy-eyed and unsteady. One was Net Boy, older, taller and skinnier than the last time he'd seen him.

Roosevelt stood wide-eyed right in their path.

One said, "You spyin' on us, nigger?"

"Leave him alone, and don't call him that," answered Net Boy, grabbing the other boy's arm.

"Why, what's he to you, yer brother?"

The other boys laughed.

As they passed, Net Boy turned his head and grinned, red eyes peering through thin slits. A boy pretended he was going to throw Net Boy into the water, almost falling in himself. Auntie Barbara shook her head and scowled as they passed.

Jude was happy he'd gotten these shitheads away without teasing Roosevelt more. He figured Roosevelt was probably impressed seeing Jude loaded on grass.

Chapter 6

ROOSEVELT SPRAWLED ON THE COUCH leaning on Mama, who calmly ran her fingers over his hair as she spoke. "You gettin' ta be a great fisherman, Rosy."

"Mama, please don' call me dat."

"I always used ta call ya dat. You got like a reddish glow to yo hair."

"It's a girl's name."

She smiled and rubbed his shoulder. "You like Theodore a lot dontcha."

"Yea."

"Shore is dif'rent now."

Roosevelt nodded. He sure was.

"Don' you never let me hear you doin' no drugs Roosevelt." she sighed. "Ain' nothin' but trouble."

"I know Mama."

He felt the warmth of her arm through both their clothes. He couldn't remember when he'd sat like this with her. She began humming a gospel song he vaguely recognized. Something else unheard of. She was a different person—not quite as much as Theodore—but she now seemed perfectly content just to be sitting, saying nothing, scheming nothing, just sitting.

"Ain' heard ya talk 'bout Missy lately. You seen her?"

Roosevelt shrugged.

"She a nice girl. Has a sparkle in the eye. And sweet. She still sweet on you Rosy?"

"Ain' seen her in a while."

"Ya'll ain' had sex, is ya?"

"Mama!"

"Well, ya know it can cause problems."

"Mama."

"Gonorrhea, syph, babies."

Roosevelt looked away.

"Look Rosy—er—Roosevelt. Ya don' hafta talk 'bout it wif me. Just be careful."

She was boring in on him with her eyes. He could feel his cheeks hot as fire. He couldn't find any place to look.

"Maybe you'd like ta talk 'bout this wif Uncle Theodore. He know all 'bout this kind a stuff."

This was getting as bad as listening to Auntie Barbara on her soap box. She was still looking into him.

He stood suddenly.

"Where ya goin'?"

"Out, Mama." He marched straight out of the room.

Mama remained quiet and peaceful on the couch.

* * * * * * *

At the corner, Tom leaned against a concrete pillar under the overhanging brown stucco roof, a toothpick bobbing up and down between his teeth.

Tom nodded. "'S hap'nin', my man?"

Roosevelt shrugged.

"How yo mama?"

"Okay."

"Wanna toke?" he asked, showing a small joint.

"C'mon."

Tom shuffled toward the back parking lot, motioning with his head for Roosevelt to follow. As they rounded the abandoned car, Tom lit it, took a long toke, and handed it to Roosevelt. Roosevelt sucked the smoke in and held it. Instant calm.

Tom said, "Y'ever toot?"

"What?"

"Snort, you know, coke?"

All the memories of Mama taking off flooded back. He saw her staggering around the kitchen, rubbing her nose and face, looking disinterested, slurring her words, not caring about him. "No. Uh-uh."

Tom went into the store and returned with a quart bottle of malt liquor. He took a deep swig and handed the bottle to Roosevelt, who tipped his head back and poured several swallows down his throat.

"Reefer was good," Roosevelt said. His head tingled in the back. He struggled to keep his heavy eyelids up.

"Had hash in it." Tom answered, taking another swig.

Roosevelt had no idea what hash was. But he knew he was far beyond where he'd been before.

Roosevelt sat on the ground leaning against the side of the building. Tom grinned down at him. His gold front tooth glittered in the sunlight.

A wobbly brown car rolled up. A light-skinned man motioned to Tom. Tom strutted to the car and leaned in, checked his watch, nodded at the grinning occupants of the car and returned to his post. The car pulled away.

Roosevelt took a swig from the warming malt liquor. They smoked another joint. He felt like he was floating. The ground swirled and flipped.

"Say 'Hey' to yo Mama," Tom said as he swayed across the parking lot.

Dizziness hit Roosevelt hard. His mouth filled with saliva. He staggered behind the abandoned car and sat heavily on the ground, lying back and rolling to his side. The ground came up at him continually like the seats on a Ferris wheel. He tried closing one eye, then the other, and then both. That was worse. He opened both eyes and sat up. His stomach churned. He spit the continual flow of saliva on the ground. Finally, he fell back to the ground face up. Vomit seeped out like mud from a weak geyser and rolled down his face. His throat burned. He forced himself onto his side again. His ribs heaved as though they'd burst. Eventually, the flow subsided. The vomit caked onto the side of his head as he lay on the hot, dry, gray dirt.

Roosevelt awakened and lay still. Crickets chirped. Stars shone through the branches of the tree overhead. He tried to understand where he was. His body ached. His throat burned. The side of his face was gooey and heavy with caked dirt. He stood on wobbly legs and moved slowly across the parking lot, sickening himself with his own putrid stench. Afraid he'd vomit again, he stopped to lean against the wall of the store.

A tan Chevrolet turned into the dirt parking lot and stopped. Two white teenagers glanced around. What could white boys be doing here? Tom swaggered toward the car, holding his right hand at his side, fist closed. He leaned into the passenger window and reached in with his right hand. He withdrew it holding rolled green bills between his fingers. He dropped the cash into his front pants pocket.

As the car careened around the rear of the store and disappeared, Tom said, "Damn, man. You nasty. Whew. You been back there pukin' ever since I left you?"

Roosevelt nodded meekly.

"Wanna do some more?"

Roosevelt shook his head no.

"You'll feel better."

Roosevelt's stomach flipped.

"C'mon. I got somethin'll make ya feel better."

"What?"

"Toot. Make ya feel better."

He pulled Roosevelt away from the wall and walked him by the arm to the old car. He creaked open the door and kneeled on the ground next to the passenger seat. He poured some white powder onto a small mirror and carved it with a razor blade. He rolled a twenty-dollar bill into a long cylinder and showed Roosevelt what to do.

Roosevelt hesitated. This was it. This was the thing he'd said he'd never do. But coke had never been Mama's problem.

He needed to go home and make it through the evening. This could help. It would be only this once. He took a deep snort into each nostril and stood waiting for the effect. Soon, the sick feeling was gone. He felt alert.

"Now, go wash yo' fuckin' face. You look like shit. You smell like shit. Whooo."

Roosevelt zipped across the parking lot, his legs working perfectly. The stench of the bathroom was worse than his vomit-caked clothes and skin. He held his breath, leaned over the grime-stained sink and splashed water on his face. He glanced at the dark, fuzzy mirror. He moved his head from side to side to see around the distortions caused by a long crack. His skin glowed. The whites of his eyes shone.

Man, he felt great. He'd missed dinner for sure. They'd be wondering where he was. He was going to hear some shit. He hoped Mama wouldn't recognize the coke appearance. He cleaned up as much as he could and walked back out into the stifling evening air.

His brain sizzled as he ambled down Campbell Street toward home. He thought of Missy and wished she'd show up and do him right now. Man, she was something else. This toot was something else too. How great it'd be to do them together—he and Missy both snorting some toot and then fucking like crazy. He felt electricity in his pants.

He slowed down as he approached the house, to collect his thoughts and calm down. He opened the front door too hard and then tried to catch it before it slammed into the wall. His mama, Auntie Barbara, Nana and Uncle Theodore, all approached him urgently, looking at him too intently.

"Where you been child?" asked Auntie Barbara.

"We been so worried," said Mama.

"You look sickly baby," offered Nana.

He glanced from face to face. Uncle Theodore moved close, breathing in deeply. Roosevelt tried to hold his breath.

"Oh, man," Uncle Theodore said, grimacing and shaking his head.

"What?" asked Auntie Barbara and Mama in unison.

"Reeks of puke, reefer, and alcohol."

"Oh Lawdy," hollered Auntie Barbara. "Another one. What dis family coming to? Who gave you dis stuff?" She pointed at Roosevelt's mama and said, "You a bad influence."

Roosevelt's head was swimming. He tried to concentrate on the high and wipe out all the talk and staring. But it was getting in.

"Rosy. You doin' drugs?" Mama asked.

"Jus' some smoke, Mama."

"It's all bad son." She shook her head sadly.

Auntie Barbara started on another tirade.

Uncle Theodore took Roosevelt by the arm and led him outside. "Roosevelt, my man. I know you done more than reefer tonight. You got two people right here that been through it all. Don' think 'cause we still alive that it's cool. Ain't cool at all. I know I cain't tell you nothin' you don' wanna hear. Just please think about what yo Mama and I been through. You don't have to."

The lecture drug on. His uncle was trying too hard, pausing and gathering his thoughts. Roosevelt's mind wandered to the vision of Tom slicing up the small mounds of cocaine on the mirror.

* * * * * * *

One day after school, Jude stopped at Greg's. Billy and Greg were sitting on the bed in Greg's room doing a joint.

Linda zipped into the room and plopped on the bed, leaning against Billy. "You guys know Nick, don't you? Oh yeah, little Jude here buys from him."

"Yeah, what about him?"

"OD'd. They found him in his van."

Billy said, "Fuck. On what?"

She shrugged.

Jude didn't want to ask what OD meant.

Linda said, "Guys got any money?"

"For what?" asked Greg.

"Speed. Desoxyn."

"How could you shoot up knowing that Nick died from dope?" Billy asked.

Jude tried to control his shock.

"Well, listen, pansy-ass queer," said Greg. "This is speed. You can't OD on an upper. It makes you up, not down. Get it?"

"You can overamp," offered Billy.

"Ever heard of it happening? It's just part of that crap they feed you, like 'Reefer Madness'."

They all laughed at that one. The movie tried to make marijuana look like it could cause somebody to go nuts. It was all bullshit. When they'd shown it in class, the goody-two-shoes kids were scared to death. Jude and his friends had laughed and snickered through the whole thing.

Linda returned, dropped several small yellow pills into a spoon, drew some water into a syringe, and dribbled it into the spoon. "Who's got a lighter?" Three were lit at once.

She moved the spoon around over one lighter until the liquid was bright yellow and almost boiling. She drew the liquid into the syringe.

"Hold my arm baby doll," she cooed to Billy. She sat on the toilet lid. Popping the needle into her vein, she drew back. A trace of blood entered the barrel, tingeing the yellow fluid. Then she pushed the plunger in.

Leaving the needle hanging for a moment, she pulled her T-shirt up and pulled Billy's face toward it, saying, "Suck my tittie."

Jude had never been in the presence of a naked breast, other than his mother's, which he hadn't wanted to see. Billy's head bobbed as he slurped. She moaned.

Jude felt his heart race. He felt movement in his pants. Linda pulled the syringe out and placed it on the sink.

Then she glanced at Jude and smiled. "Come here Jude." He took two steps closer; she groped him through his pants. He groaned. He'd never been touched like this, had never had an erection in public, and didn't want to. He felt it stiffening. She stopped.

"Your face is red, Jude. Don't you get much action?" He didn't answer. He watched her deep brown eyes and her thin, appealing lips. She kept moving her hand up and down the outside of his jeans, as Billy kept sucking. Jude stood, speechless.

He never knew what she wanted with Billy. He definitely looked a lot older than Jude. Jude hadn't changed a bit since he was twelve. He came up to about her breasts. He weighed less than a hundred pounds to Billy's one-thirty or so.

She tired of the breast sucking, knocked Billy's head away with her forearm, and too quickly hid the forbidden mound beneath her T-shirt.

"Want me to shoot you up?" she asked Jude.

He nodded. Then she yanked the plunger out of the glass barrel, wiped some spit around the rubber gasket and stuck the plunger back in. She cupped her hand under the faucet, and when water pooled, held the barrel of the syringe above the palm of her hand and drew water in.

As she plunged the speed into him, warmth traveled up his arm. His head became numb. His ears rang. The feeling of ecstasy and exhilaration came on like a jet fighter swooping down into the sea. This was it.

Linda put the syringe down and groped his jeans again. "Ahah. Just as I suspected," she grinned. "It's gone."

Chapter 7

JUDE SHOWED UP AT GREG'S HOUSE and knocked at the exterior door to his room. Linda opened it.

"Well, what a nice surprise. I was just thinking I need a little action, and here's the little virgin boy to satisfy me."

Jude gulped.

"Come on, let's do a doobie."

She grabbed his arm, pulled him into the room, took a joint from her purse, and lit it. On the second toke, she turned the joint around, with the lit part inside her mouth, held Jude's head in her hands and blew the smoke into his open mouth.

As soon as the joint was done, she was on him, kissing him wildly and digging her tongue into his mouth. She pulled his T-shirt over his head and dropped it to the floor. She began kissing his stomach and trying to suck and bite his nipples but couldn't get hold of one. She unbuckled and unzipped his pants. He didn't know what to do, what to feel. No girl had ever touched him before or seen him naked. She yanked his pants down, catching him roughly with the underwear strap.

"Oh, poor baby, let me kiss it and make it better," she said, and moved down on him, kissing above his scant pubic hair, then to the side of his thighs, and then engulfing him in her mouth. He felt a sensation he'd never felt while awake, although he had a vague recollection of it from wet dreams.

He started concentrating on his paper route. Who was after Mr. Cochran? How many holds were there? He couldn't think of anything else.

Then, Linda turned and sat, sucking him into her warmth. As soon as she started moving, he felt like he was going to explode, and he did. She continued moving back and forth wildly. The sensation changed, becoming uncomfortable. He started thinking of the dangers of VD, what would happen if Greg or one of his parents walked in, how fast she was going, that Billy was the one she really wanted, that she'd probably done this with him.

Soon, it slopped out.

She tried to bring it back to life. "Goddammit," she said finally. "You took me there and left me."

She got up and dressed. As she marched out, she said, "You need to work on your action. I'd still call you a virgin. That little bit of nonsense doesn't even count as a fuck."

He groaned and covered his face with his hands.

* * * * * * *

Roosevelt loped down Campbell Street. Rufus leaned against the wall in front of the store tapping his rattlesnake-hide boot on the dusty windowsill.

"'S hap'nin' dude?" Rufus asked. He looked healthy. "Buy some smack?"

"Smack?"

"You know, smack! Scag, man, heroin."

"You still doin' that shit, Rufus?"

"Blade."

"Huh?"

"Go by Blade now, not Rufus," Rufus answered. "You ain' done scag yet?"

Roosevelt shook his head. He sat on the wall.

An olive-green Impala turned the corner and stopped. The driver had very dark skin, a thin, chiseled face, and a tall afro. He leaned across to the passenger window and motioned for Blade to approach. At first, Blade didn't move. The driver remained in his leaning position. The passenger sat gawking, a gold tooth gleaming in his mouth.

Eventually, Blade made his trek across the sidewalk. He reached a cupped hand into the car and pulled it out. As the car moved away, Blade sauntered back to the wall and retook his position. He removed a roll of twenties, tens and fives from his pocket and flicked through them as though shuffling a deck of cards.

Blade went behind the store. A beat-up white hearse turned the corner and stopped in front of Roosevelt. A white dude with long hair and a scraggly beard rolled down the passenger window. "Hey dude. Got anythin'?" Roosevelt shook his head.

"Where can we cop some scag man?"

"Hang on," Roosevelt said. He walked behind the building and said to Blade, "Some white dudes in a big ol' funeral car wanna cop some."

Blade smiled. "Wanna deal it to 'em?"

"Uh-Uh," Roosevelt said, shaking his head.

As they walked toward the front, Blade said, "Always make 'em wait. Dat's da power. Ya don' need dem. Dey needs you."

Blade bebopped ever so slowly toward the corner and put another bounce in his step as he rounded it. He nodded at the men in the car and took his place on the ledge.

"Hey, you got the smack?" the man asked, slurring his words slightly.

"Na. Ain' got none."

Roosevelt glanced at him, surprised.

"Who's holdin'?" the man asked.

Blade shrugged.

The men drove away.

"I b'lieve those honkie motha fuckers were narcs."

"How you know?"

"Dey talk strange. Dey look like some kind a fuckin' hippies. Dopers don' look like dat. Jus' didn't feel right. Now, if someone who ain't a narc come up ta you, an' you sell to 'em, give you a buck a bag."

"What's a bag?" Roosevelt asked. Blade pulled a paper bag from his pocket and poured a number of tiny rectangles of aluminum foil on the table. "Each a dem's a bag—ten bucks each."

"For dat little thing?" Roosevelt asked.

"Lots a power in one a dem bags."

* * * * * * *

Jude was perched on the coquina rock wall in front of the cemetery on Main Street, kicking the wall with the heel of his bare feet. Across the street at the Boot Hill Saloon, a biker pumped his Harley, as others looked on.

Billy flung himself up on the wall. "Can't find any."

"Shit. What about Schmidt? Ain't he on the street?"

Billy shook his head.

"Got all this fuckin' cash and can't do anythin' with it. There's got to be some speed around somewhere."

Billy shrugged. "Wanna do some scag?"

"What's that?" Jude asked, embarrassed one more time for not being cool.

"Junk, you know, smack, heroin."

He shrugged, "Sure, why not."

They bounced down from the wall and jumped in Jude's old car. They crossed South Bridge. They passed the baseball practice field, turned south on Beach Street, passed the yacht club, and turned west on Bellevue. Across the tracks looked the same as it had when Jude was a kid—tiny wooden houses, postage-stamp sized, barren and dusty yards, and decrepit cars.

At Campbell Street, Billy said, "Turn the corner here, and go slow."

Jude turned the corner and slowed in front of a food store, with dusty, stained signs hanging behind dingy windows. Two Negroes sat on the dirt-caked windowsill.

"Stop," said Billy.

Billy signaled. The guys on the sill didn't move.

Jude tried to discern their attitude. Then he recognized Roosevelt. He flashed on the conversation they'd had long ago, the embarrassing racial episode at the ballpark, and the time Roosevelt had found him smoking reefer in the bushes. Roosevelt was scrawnier than before.

Finally, the other boy stood and approached the car. "Whatchu lookin' at fools?" he drawled.

"Lookin' to score," answered Billy.

"You da man?"

Billy shook his head no. "Just wanna buy some smack."

"Ain' seen ya'll 'roun' heah befo'."

Billy's Adam's apple bobbed. "We ain' narcs or nothin'."

Blade turned to Roosevelt. "Whatchu think, Roos'velt? Dese guys cool? Ever seen 'em befo'?"

Roosevelt nodded and pointed at Net Boy with his chin.

"You know this fucker?" Blade asked Roosevelt, pointing at Net Boy. "He a cop?"

Roosevelt shook his head.

"Ever see him high?"

Roosevelt nodded.

"Ask 'em how many." Blade said to Roosevelt.

Roosevelt looked at Blade. Blade shrugged and pointed toward the car with his head.

"Whatchu want?" Roosevelt asked.

"Three bags."

Blade stood and motioned for Roosevelt to follow him around back. He handed Roosevelt three bags. "Five bucks fo you if ya do da deal."

Jude fidgeted, moving forward in his seat, trying to see around the side of the building.

Billy said, "Where'd the fuckers go? Move up."

Jude edged the car forward as Roosevelt sauntered around the corner, approached the car and leaned in. "Thirty dolla'." Jude peeled off three tens and handed them to him. Roosevelt dropped the bags and smiled slightly.

"Yer name's Roosevelt, ain't it?" asked Jude. "Uh huh?" Roosevelt held a hand out to shake.

"Jude," responded Jude, extending his hand across Billy and shaking, thumbs upright.

"Catch ya around," said Jude. He pulled away and drove off slowly down the street.

* * * * * * *

They rushed into Billy's bedroom through the back door. He reached under his mattress and yanked out a soup spoon, singed on the bottom and still containing crusty brown remnants of its last use. Jude turned on the stereo and plopped the needle on Frank Zappa and the Mothers of Invention. Billy grabbed a water glass from his bookshelf, dumped the water into the sink and refilled it from the tap. He carefully unfastened the corners of a tiny rectangular aluminum foil package and poured the dark brown sugar look-alike into the spoon. He squirted water on top and swirled it all around with the top of the plunger.

The Mothers sang, "And they had a swimming pool." A good LSD song.

A cigarette dangled from Jude's lips as he held the lighter under the spoon. When it began to bubble like thick molasses, Billy drew the dark liquid into the syringe.

"Hold me off," he said, and Jude grabbed his upper arm with two hands.

He jabbed the needle into the vein in the crook of his arm and registered. Jude removed his hands, and Billy pushed the plunger in, withdrew it three-quarters of the way and pushed in again. "Ah, it's good," he moaned under his breath.

He handed the works to Jude and flopped on his back onto the soiled bed sheets. Jude drew some water into the barrel and squirted the slightly stained water through a hole in the window screen. He drew some more water in and squirted it on Billy's face.

"Fucker," moaned Billy.

Jude fixed up as Billy had done. He drew the liquid into the syringe. He wound a belt around his upper arm, twisted it back and held the middle between his teeth.

He pushed the needle against his vein. "This thing's like a fuckin' nail."

He tapped harder and finally it jammed through the skin and into the vein. He pulled back to register, let the belt fall from his teeth and shook it loose. Then he slowly pushed the plunger in. The feeling came on like a deadening, heavy weight. He let out a single hum and relaxed. He dropped on the bed and closed his eyes. This was it. This was the way he wanted to be all the time. Total peace and tranquility.

* * * * * * *

Roosevelt had a regular deal going to sell for Blade. Jude showed up one day wanting to score. Roosevelt said, "Let's talk some business."

"Business?"

"Yeah, lis'en. Any more white dudes like you like ta do dis shit? How's about I make product available to you, so you can deal across the river?"

"How much?"

"You sell twenty bags, I give 'em ta you fo eight dollahs a bag. That's a hun'red sixty for the bunch. You make forty dollahs. Then you don't hafta buy yer own."

Jude nodded slowly. Sounded good. Then he'd have the power. "Okay, but you can't fuck with me like you like to. We need to have an arrangement for me to cop. No power show."

"Whatchu talkin' 'bout? I treat you good. Hey I's offerin' you the deal, ain' I?"

Jude laughed. "Yeah."

* * * * * * *

Jude was standing on the corner of Main Street one afternoon, after having sold almost all of his stash. Melissa Bretz turned the corner. "Hey, Jude."

She'd changed. Her face had slimmed down, her breasts had filled out, and suddenly her body was something to look at. "I hear you sell smack. I want some."

"Y'ever done it?"

"I'd like to."

"Got a place to go?"

"Sure, my parents are at work."

They hurried in silence toward her house. Jude shivered with anticipation. He was wondering whether he'd have sex with her, and at the same time dreading it. He hadn't tried sex again since the fiasco with Linda.

They entered the small, fifties-style house and went straight to the dining room table. He produced a syringe and matches, and asked her for a large spoon.

She looked afraid, surprised.

"What's the matter? You said you wanted to get high, right?"

"Yeah, but I didn't think it would be with a needle."

"You can snort it if you want. You don' hafta shoot it."

She nodded. He dumped half a bag onto a piece of notebook paper on the table, rolled a dollar bill into a tight cylinder, and gave it to her. She inhaled deeply. At the same time, he finished his ritual, crossed his legs over his wrist in order to raise the vein, and injected.

A few minutes later, she said, "I like the feeling a lot."

He lay back on the couch. Her face was above him now, close. Her blondish hair brushed back and forth across his face. He could see the shape of her small breast and erect nipples through the cloth. They kissed slowly. He enjoyed every slurp, every movement of the intertwined and mutating tongues.

He kneaded the cheeks of her butt like a cat playing with a blanket. He felt incredibly aroused, but that this time he could last. He slipped her top over her head. He sucked a strawberry-colored nipple. She moved against him.

"Ooooh," she cooed. Her voice almost got him out of control. He couldn't believe they were here, doing drugs together, sharing drugs, time, talk, saliva, trust.

They removed each other's clothes. They explored each other with their mouths. Then he entered her. She met his moves and gyrated gracefully and exuberantly.

Increasing his speed, he was relieved that he didn't feel the urge that he had last time. She continued to move in concert with him. After a while, she screamed and wrapped him in her legs. But he continued to thrust, and she continued to respond. He had no inclination to have an orgasm, but he felt utter satisfaction.

"My parents'll be home within an hour. We've gotta go."

So, his first sexual experience hadn't been successful. This made up for it all. This was heaven.

"I always loved you, Jude Armstrong. But I never dreamed you had this to offer. Holy shit. Holy shit. I should a done this before."

Jude knew now that heroin had something else powerful to offer besides euphoria itself.

* * * * * * *

Roosevelt woke up to find Mama wearing a dress. It wasn't Sunday. "What's goin' on. Somebody die?"

"Gonna find me a job."

"Where?"

"Old South. They's lookin' fo a salad prep lady. Reckon I can do dat."

The family often ate at Old South Plantation Buffet and knew most of the wait staff and cooks.

As he ate pancakes made by Nana, Uncle Theodore came in and sat. "How's my man? You avoidin' that stuff?"

"Yeah," he lied, studying his plate.

Uncle Theodore looked across the kitchen at Nana and whispered to Roosevelt, "You know every drug leads to another."

Roosevelt nodded.

Nana set a second glass of milk in front of him and said, "You need to put some weight on, child."

Outside, he got his stash to sell and sauntered down Campbell Street. He started thinking maybe he should try Missy again. He had coke, and smack too. He'd heard of a speedball, where you mixed them together. That would certainly outdo whatever she'd been doing.

She answered the door in a long, beat-up T-shirt, looking sleepy and disinterested.

"Got somethin' fo ya."

"Whatchu talkin' 'bout?"

"Coke baby."

"Ain' nothin' better."

"Might be somethin' better. How's 'bout white sugah and brown sugah together? Coke and smack . . . Speedball. Make you speedy and relaxed, and they kicks in at diff'rent times."

Her eyes lit up. She opened the door wider. "Come on in my man."

He pulled out his cap, tweezers, fit, coke and scag, and dumped it all on the table. He poured coke into the cap, and then a bag and a half of smack on top. He got a cup of water from the kitchen, drew up and squirted onto the combined powders, making a light brown mixture, and burned it. The sizzling quinine and combined drugs produced a powerful smell. He pulled up a dose for her.

"I ain' never shot befo'."

He took her arm, told her to hold herself off, and inserted the needle perfectly into the vein in the cleft of her arm. He drew back, pushed in, drew back again, and plunged in again. Her eyes rolled back.

"Oh my fucking God," she sighed, in a faraway voice. She slumped backward on the bed. "Oh sweet Jesus."

"Jesus didn't do this for ya baby," Roosevelt said as he busily prepared his own dose. He injected it and enjoyed the same effect.

They lay side by side on the bed for a few minutes. Then they got naked and did it for a long time.

When he finally stopped and collapsed, she said, "Oh my God. I ain' never had it like that. Thank you fo the drugs, and thank for doin' me like dat. You welcome heah any fuckin' time you want."

* * * * * * *

Just like every Friday night since their parents' separation, Jude and Jenny had to spend a boring evening with their father.

As their father drove down Main Street, Jude sat in the front seat, horrified that somebody would see him.

"You're about due for a haircut, young man."

Jude knew that was coming. In a few weeks, Principal Sanders would be measuring the hair at the top of his ears, the top of his collar and on his forehead. But for now, he was enjoying sweeping or shaking the bangs back out of his eyes.

At the restaurant, Antonio, the owner, rumbled around like a bustling old grandmother as he seated them at their reserved table. A bottle of wine, a glass and a plate of provolone cheese waited. Jude loved the cheese.

As usual, Jude ordered Italian salad and lasagna. He could never finish. He always took home the leftovers. He could toke a little pot, warm up the lasagna, and every flake of basil and tomato sauce would come alive again.

"Duke's been spending a lot of time at the house, hasn't he?" began Jude's father.

"I guess," Jude answered, shrugging.

Jenny studied the spaghetti she was twirling with her fork and big spoon.

"I think I should have custody of you two."

God, again. Jude needed to stop this; it would mess up his life. He liked being able to smoke in the house and play gin with Duke.

"It's not like that," Jude said.

Jenny kept eating.

"You look sallow, emaciated; your hair is disgusting, and your mother is oblivious."

Jude stared at the wall, and put on a disinterested, pissed-off face, hoping to stop the inquiry.

"Jenny, would you like to come and live with your father?"

She glanced up, looked back at her food, and shrugged. "I don't know," she said under her breath.

Their father frowned and drained the last of the wine from his glass.

* * * * * * *

Back in the car, Jude's father drove toward their grandparents' house. They entered the homey old house where they'd spent every holiday since Jude had been born, the wooden, screen door on the slanted porch slamming behind them. The heavy glass and wood front door stood open, and *Grand-mère* and *Grand-père* sat in their chairs, *Grand-mère* sipping port wine and *Grand-père* toking his big brown cigar. *Grand-mère* struggled out of her chair and scurried over to kiss each child on both cheeks.

"Come 'ere," said *Grand-père* from his seat, beckoning to Jenny. She scrunched up her nose but walked to him. He pulled her into his seat. "Come here, boy," he said, beckoning to Jude. He hugged him, with his familiar, awful, slimy, ashy cigar bobbing in his mouth.

"Can I get you something to eat—some dessert," asked *Grand-mère*.

"No, thanks. We ate," said Jude.

She looked him over. "You look like you could use some more."

"Look at this hair," *Grand-père* said twirling some of Jude's hair. "You look like a girl. When are you going to cut this?"

* * * * * * *

Roosevelt lit a smoke and waited for Blade, who was supposed to have arrived an hour before. The son-of-a-bitch was making him wait, and he was now going to be late for his meeting with Jude. He puffed and stewed.

Eventually, he went to the shack behind the store and shot up the last of his stash. He'd been doing very well, and his star dealer, Jude, was beating out all his other dealers. Jude was the only one who sold in honkie town, and that kept a bunch of whites from venturing across the railroad tracks. Too many of them got ripped off or worse when they came over. They didn't know who was a real dealer. They could do a successful deal with Roosevelt one day, and the next day they'd beckon somebody else. It was like the dumb honkies thought all Blacks were the same person.

He eventually decided to walk down Campbell Street toward Blade's house. He came upon Tom, who stopped in front of him. "Blade OD'd."

"Wha'?"

"He dead; overdose. The motha didn't even know da power of his own shit."

"Fuck," responded Roosevelt, looking at the ground.

"His supplier, Eugene, wanna see me and you; need to get his product out. He say he want us to take ovah for Blade."

"Nice a you to not fuck me ova'."

Tom smiled, his tall, lanky body swaying in the sun, and his huge dirty-looking Afro bobbing above his dark, lined face. "Ya know I would if I could. But the fuckah ax fo you directly. Say' you got the honkie trade. C'mon."

As they trudged along the dusty streets, past beat-up, neglected wooden houses, a few concrete-block ones, and barren yards, Roosevelt wondered whether he knew Eugene. The name didn't seem familiar. They arrived at the South Street projects, a group of two-story, low-cost apartments with concrete-block walls and jalousie windows. Broken-down cars sat idle among playing kids. Tom stopped and rapped on a door.

The jalousie opened slightly, and a deep, older voice said, "Who dat?"

"Tom and Red," Tom answered.

"Wha's dis Red shit?" asked Roosevelt.

"Das what he call you," Tom answered.

Roosevelt decided he'd accept the name. It was better than the "Rosy" his mama liked to call him. A few locks clicked and the door opened. He guessed he'd seen the man around before. He was not at all what Roosevelt was expecting. He had to be over fifty, his huge belly pushed the waist of his pants down to the bottom of his gut. "C'mon in."

He opened the door to a normal-looking living room, a black leather couch and matching chairs, a glass coffee table, and on the other side, a glass dining room table with metal-based chairs. On the table lay scales and several large plastic bags with hundreds of already-prepared aluminum-foil-wrapped dope bags. He motioned for them to sit at the table.

"Listen, I know you two were the street for my man Blade, that dumb fuck. I hope ya got better sense. You do the dope, but in moderation. Moderation, my men. If you get yo'selves strung out, you can't sell my shit no mo. If ya do too much, den you get sloppy, and ya get greedy. Ya start cuttin' bags, doin' shit like dat. And dat ain' gonna fly. And if you fuck me, or if I find out you fuck a customer by cuttin' a bag," he whipped out a large switch blade, which clicked easily into open position, "I cut yo fuckin' guts out."

He scooped a bit of smack out of a large open container, poured it into a soup spoon, and did the same into two more spoons. He produced three glass syringes with tiny points, and a glass of water. Each busied himself with his own ritualistic method.

"Now then," he began, businesslike, "I gives ya a hundred bags at a time. That's a thousand dolla' street. You both should go through dat in 'bout fo o five days. You never call me. You never use my name. When you out, you come back here and knock on da door. You never talk to anybody else who might be here 'bout why you here. If my bitch or kids or anybody else here, you don' say nothin' 'bout drugs till you see dat we talkin' drugs o' doin' drugs. I gots fam'ly don' know nothin' 'bout dis enterprise. Got it?"

The two nodded.

"You gives me six hundred dolla', and I gives you a hundred mo' bags. There be room in there fo you to cut a deal wif a street dealer, or you can sell yo'self on da street, whatever you want. But don' go cuttin' prices. It's ten dolla' a bag to the user. Ya got it?"

Red and Tom nodded anxiously. Eugene lit a cigarette, and Red did too. This was cool.

He handed each a baggie with a hundred bags. "Remember. You fuck me, I cut yo ass up."

PART III

Late 1960s-1970s

Chapter 8

AS THEY'D OFTEN DONE when they were kids, Jude, Greg, and Billy took the boat to Ratte Island to spend the night. Jude had loaded his thick, canvas army tent, a few beat-up sleeping bags, food, beer, cooking and eating gear, and plenty of drugs and paraphernalia.

At the island, they removed their supplies. A boat idled up to shore and two guys and a girl got out and approached. "Who the fuck's that?" Jude whispered.

"Jay, Thumper, and Marie," said Greg. "I told 'em to come."

"Fuck," Jude muttered. He wasn't sure where they'd come from. They'd suddenly just appeared on Main Street in the past couple of weeks. He didn't trust them.

During the evening, Jude and Greg shot heroin inside the tent, out of view of the strangers. Jude refused to sell to them. But Greg was dealing for Jude, so he sold them some. Jude remained concerned because he didn't see them shoot up. The group sat around the fire eating hot dogs, drinking beer, and telling drug stories.

Later, Jude rowed the boat across the slip of water to the shore by Beach Street. He pulled up onto the muddy, oyster-shelled bank and climbed the wall. Roosevelt was waiting for him. Jude purchased a new supply.

"'S happ'nin' dude?" Red asked.

"Partyin'."

"Whatcha got out there?"

"Reefer, beer, smack. Some friends. Wanna come out?" Jude almost hesitated as soon as he had suggested it. He didn't really want to share his supplier with his dealers. He could get cut out. Besides that, although they bought drugs in "nigger town" as some of them called it, or "across the tracks," as Jude called it, he wasn't sure they'd want to hang out with a Black. "Yeah, man, I wouldn't mind tokin' a bit."

As they got into the boat, Jude said, "Don't let on you're my supplier. And there's two guys and a girl I don't know and I'm not sure about. So be careful." Jude paddled to the other side.

Around the fire, the others were doing a joint. Jude watched the three newcomers to see if they were inhaling. But it was too dark to tell.

"This is Roosevelt," Jude announced.

"Red," corrected Red.

"Hey, Red," said Billy, shaking hands, "Billy. We've met on Campbell Street." Red nodded.

They drank beer, smoked reefer, hung out, nodded out, talked and wandered around. Jude lay on the sand, looking up at the stars, hearing the group talking, laughing, coughing, and carrying on in front of the fire.

Jude heard a car horn on shore. It sounded like a Volkswagen. Beep, beep, beep. What the fuck? Now what? He glanced through the trees toward shore and saw headlights flashing. Goddamn it. Just advertise.

He pulled himself to his feet and went to the campfire. "Did ya'll tell anyone else we were gonna be here?"

"My sister," Greg said.

"All right!" Billy said, smiling. "Let's go get her."

"Jesus Christ. I guess I'll hafta get her just to shut her up," said Jude.

He and Billy walked to the shore, climbed into the boat and rowed across. At the shore, Jude said, "Can you shut up? You tryin' ta get us busted?"

She stood swaying on the muddy bank below the wall. Streetlights lit her grinning, wasted face. Her eyes were slits. "Hi boyzh," she slurred. "Thanksh for comin' to pick a girl up." She put her arms around Billy's neck and started making out with him, at the same time groping Jude's crotch. Jude backed away and pushed the boat into the water. She pulled Billy's pants down to his knees and pulled him to the boat by his growing dick. The bottom of his pants drug across the mud. Stumbling like a prisoner in leg chains, Billy flopped into the boat and fell onto a bench. Linda started sucking him.

Before long, she tired of Billy and turned to Jude. Something moist in her hair touched his face. He turned away in horror, afraid it was from Billy. "I am sho fuckin' loaded," she said, "sho fuckin' tired," and she slumped on Jude.

He tried to push her off. He kicked Billy's leg, "Hey, fuckhead, get her off me."

Suddenly she wretched and barfed all over him, warm, sour and chunky.

"Awe, fuck," he said. "Goddamn it. What's this shit? I come here for a peaceful high on my favorite island, and I got two assholes passed out, and cum and puke on me. Jesus fucking Christ." He lurched and dropped her into the bottom of the boat, laying her head on a boat cushion.

At shore, he got out of the boat, scooped dirty, smelly river water in his cupped hands, and cleaned himself the best he could.

At the campfire, Greg said, "Where's my sister?"

"Totally, totally loaded. I don't know what she's doing, but she's fucked up. Her and Billy are passed out in the boat." He didn't bother to mention that neither had pants on.

"She had a bag of yellow jackets this morning," said Greg.

"What's that?" asked Thumper.

"Nembutol—barbs—you know, downers."

Jude said, "No wonder she's so fucked up. She puked all over me."

"Is she okay?" asked Marie, a look of genuine concern on her face.

"I guess," he answered.

"Maybe I should go check on her," she said as she stood and walked toward the bank. Greg stood too.

"Greg. She and Billy aren't exactly dressed," said Jude. Greg sat back down.

Marie returned, guiding Linda, who was stumbling in a stupor, pigeon-toed, eyes fluttering and eyeballs rolling. Fortunately, her corduroy pants were on and zipped most of the way up. Marie helped Linda into Jude's tent. Jude heard Marie say "shit." Then he heard a thump, and he knew Linda had hit the ground.

* * * * * * *

Sometime during the night, Jude and Red went inside the tent to do some dope. After getting off, Jude shut his eyes and floated, so peacefully, rocking like a boat on water. He was thinking that scag in combination with reefer and beer gave a new rounded, smoother edge, a new lower level to his intoxication.

At some point, he awoke to see Red and Linda talking over a lit match, apparently doing some smack.

Later he awoke when Linda kicked him as she yelled, "Oh my God, oh my God." He opened one eye to see Billy on top of her, right next to him. Greg staggered in to see what the commotion was. His jaw dropped, and he staggered back out.

Jude awoke early to do his paper route. He did a fix, to clear his head. Greg was lying next to him. He went to the boat, and found Billy lying in the sand, with puke caked on his face and in his hair. Jude leaned close to him to be sure he was breathing.

Beneath a bush, he saw a pair of white legs, toes down, inside a pair of dark legs, toes up. He tip-toed closer. Linda lay naked on top of Red. Smelly puke was everywhere.

He checked Red's pulse and found it. He checked Linda's and did not. Shit! He checked again in her neck—nothing. He leaned down and put his ear on her back. Nothing. "God fucking damn it," he exclaimed in a loud whisper. "Fuck!" He rolled her off of Red.

"Red, goddammit. Wake the fuck up. Red!" he whispered loudly. Red looked up, blinking.

"She's fucking dead. She fucking OD'd," Jude exclaimed in a loud whisper. "What the fuck are we gonna do?"

"What? Jesus Christ. You sure?" Red asked, pushing her still body. With his ear in front of her face, he exclaimed, "Oh fuck. Oh fuck."

"What do we do with her?"

Red sat stunned. "I dunno. I dunno. Oh my fuckin' God. She was so active, fuckin' my goddamn brains out."

Jude felt all electric, jiggly, panicked inside. "What do we do?"

"I don't fuckin' know," Red exclaimed. Tears ran down his face. "Roll her into the water? Like maybe she drowned."

"Oh, sure. Greg knows she was here."

"Don't do none of us no good ta have 'em find 'er here. We gotta get rid of her. Let's put 'er in her car an' take her to a park. Leave her on a bench like they did wif Blade."

"Where's her keys?" Jude said. He picked up her jeans and checked the pockets.

"Never saw 'em; maybe she left 'em in the car."

"Come on," Jude pleaded. "Help me get her in the boat." Jude grabbed under her armpits and tried to lift her. Her once luscious breasts sagged and flopped like bread dough.

Red tried to lift her feet. "Heavy," he said. "Let's each grab an arm and drag her into da boat." They pulled her across the sand, her once fine ass bumping over oyster shells, sticks, and other debris.

"Okay" said Red, "Lift 'er up so 'er ass is on the side and set her in." They picked her up, as still and heavy as a rolled carpet. She fell into the boat. Bam. Her legs hung off the side. They struggled to fold them into the boat.

They reached the other shore and dragged her up the wall, banging her against the rocks, trying desperately to avoid damaging her further, trying to keep her dead limbs and floppy head under control.

At the top of the wall, they laid her on her back. Her breasts draped to the sides. She smelled of puke and worse. Her skin looked gray in the rising morning sun. "Hurry up. Let's go," said Jude.

Jude was startled by running footsteps on the wall behind him. A marked police car and an unmarked car bounced over the curb and skidded across the grass from two directions, raising dirt and dust. Jude froze. Red turned to run.

Jude felt the barrel of a gun to his temple. "Move and I'll blow your fuckin' brains out, kid." Jude felt a sudden urge to piss, and before he could stop it, warmth poured down his legs.

A man kicked him from behind, saying "Spread eagle, doper." On the ground with a heavy knee in his back, he saw two more men in jeans and T-shirts paddle his boat to the island. They pulled guns and ran into the bushes.

Red got about five steps before he was tackled. The cop sat with an elbow on the back of his neck, and a knee in his lower back. His face was ground into the dirty grass. "Now we got your nigger ass," the man said, chuckling. "And your little white buddy."

Red was lifted from behind, his arms almost pulled from their sockets, and thrown onto the trunk of a car, the hollow metal sounding as he thumped upon it. "Any weapons or needles?"

Red didn't answer.

Hands went through his pockets. The cop pulled his syringe and cooker out of one pocket, and bags of scag out of another. "Hah," exclaimed the cop, as he slammed the evidence onto the trunk of the car.

"Hey, look at this," somebody called. "White doper pissed his pants." All the cops laughed.

* * * * * * *

At the police station, Jude was shoved into a cell with metal bars, a tile floor, tapered to a drain in the center, and an aluminum toilet and sink. Red was pushed into a cell across the hall, and a little while later, Greg and Billy were thrown into another. He noticed that Marie, Jay, and Thumper did not arrive.

Jude lay on the thin-mattressed cot looking at the ceiling, fighting back tears. One of the cops from the bust opened the cell door and motioned for him to exit. The cop ushered him into a room and pushed him to a metal chair at a table. Then the cop returned with another man, and they straddled chairs opposite him.

"So, little son-of-a-lawyer, we've been watching you. We were gonna get you for dealing, but now you really fucked up." He laughed. "So, let's talk. First, though, look at this sheet, and we'll read along, like a class at school . . . Ahem, you have the right to remain silent. You have the right to an attorney. If you cannot afford an attorney, one will be . . ."

Jude felt panic coming on. This was serious.

"Who gave the chick the dope? Who shot her up?"

"She was loaded on barbs when she arrived. She didn't get high with us," Jude responded, gulping.

"That's bullshit. She had fresh tracks."

"I don' know. I didn't give her anything, and I didn't see her do anything," he said, trying to enunciate more clearly than usual.

"How do you know Roosevelt Harris?"

Jude shrugged. "I've known him for years, from fishing around Beach Street."

"He's supplying you, right?"

"What do you mean?"

"He's your drug connection. He supplies you and you deal."

"I don't deal."

"Bullshit. Talk to us about Rufus Coolidge."

"I don't recognize that name," Jude answered, trying to remember if he really did or not.

"His body was left in the park, right across the street from here. The cop pointed west to the park bounded by Orange Avenue, Volusia, and Nova. Is that where you were taking the chick?"

"We were taking Linda to a hospital," Jude answered, squeaky-voiced.

"Well, we're gonna charge you with murder two, possession of alcohol, marijuana, heroin, dealing heroin, and anything else we can think of. How does that sound?"

"Murder? I didn't kill anyone," Jude gulped, feeling tears well up in his eyes.

"Felony murder's easy to prove, because we just gotta show you were committing one of the felonies we got you on, and she died as a result. All we gotta have is possession of heroin for that. Oh, and we have the weapon—a used syringe. And we did find you trying to conceal her body."

Jude blinked, shocked. He imagined his mother drinking herself into a stupor, his father glaring at him, hurt, defeated, betrayed, and embarrassed for himself. This was really serious.

"How long's Roosevelt Harris been your supplier?"

Jude didn't answer.

"Come on, dammit. Answer. How long? What's your deal? Who's behind him?"

Jude shook his head, and the tears reached his mouth, tasting salty and bitter.

"Come on. If you level with us, it'll be easier on you. You know Harris is going to sell you down the river."

Jude looked down, petrified. The man to his right banged his fist on the desk. "Answer us, you fuckin' dope fiend. You're never gonna get out of prison."

The man to his left put his hand on Jude's forearm. "Hey man, we can really do a lot for you if you just cooperate. Help us out, and we'll help you out, man."

Jude felt it coming, and tried in vain to stop it, but suddenly he was blubbering like a baby, tears streaming down his face, his chest quivering with fear and shame. "I don't know. I don't know," he cried, and put his head down on the table.

The man to his right lifted his head by his hair. "You killed that girl, just the same as if you'd stabbed 'er with a knife. It was your drugs that killed her. And if you don't turn on Harris, he'll send you up."

"Look," offered the more peaceful one again. "We know you get your dope from Harris, and we know he got his from Coolidge, until Coolidge died a couple of days ago. We know who they both got theirs from."

"Well," Jude said, trying not to sound like a smart ass, "you know more than I do."

"Just give us a statement that you get yours from Harris; that's all we need."

"I'd like a lawyer please," Jude requested, with a shaky voice.

"Your daddy'll tell you it's better to cooperate. To get your charges reduced. But, if you don't wanna cooperate, that's your loss." He rapped his knuckles on the metal table and stood.

They pushed him into another small room, with a table and a phone. They closed the door. Jude began to cry again. He wondered whether they would be able to hear when he called. What time was it? Ten a.m. His father would be at work. He dialed the number and asked for his father.

His father picked up, breathless, "What's the matter?"

"Dad," he whimpered, "I'm in real trouble. I asked for a lawyer, so they'd stop."

"Where are you?"

"Police station. I've been arrested," he sobbed.

"For what?" His father's voice came stern, concerned, angry, and perplexed, all at once.

"A lot of things." Jude fought to control his sobs.

"David, what are the charges? I need to know."

"Possession and dealing in heroin, possession of alcohol and marijuana and . . . murder," he managed.

"What are you telling me? I . . . I. Oh my God. Oh dear God. How could this be? I should've taken action sooner." His voice trailed off. "All right, I'll be right there." His voice sounded subdued and sad.

Jude felt very, very sorry for having hurt his father. He'd never expected his fun little jaunt to lead to anything like this.

* * * * * * *

Back in his cell, he looked at Red across the hall. "You tell 'em anythin'?" Red whispered.

Jude shook his head no, mouthing back, "I swear." Then Jude whispered, "Tell 'em we weren't gonna dump Linda's body. We were takin' her to a hospital."

Red nodded.

Two cops took Red down the hall. Billy and Greg watched, their faces and clothes streaked with mud and dirt, their hair tousled, and their faces drawn.

When Red was gone, Greg asked, "Jude, what happened?"

"You don't know?"

He shook his head no.

"Your sister OD'd, and we were taking her across the water to report it, when they busted us."

Greg blinked. "Whadaya mean, 'OD'd?' Is she all right?"

"No, man, like dead. And their blamin' it on Red and me. I swear, you know she was loaded when she got there, and I didn't give 'er anything."

"Fuck!" exclaimed Greg. "She's fucking dead? Oh my God." He sat heavily on his cot, holding his head. Tears streamed.

Billy sat on his own cot, open-mouthed and stunned.

Jude's father entered the open area with another man and handed papers to the uniformed man at the desk. The man studied the papers, stood and went to another room, leaving the two men at the desk. His face haggard and lined, Jude's father glanced around the cellblock.

The cop opened Jude's cell. "You've been released by order of Judge Bennett, into the custody of your father. You are ordered to appear tomorrow morning at eight a.m. for arraignment at the city court. Do you understand?"

Jude nodded. Greg called out, "Mr. Armstrong, can you help us too? Can you get us out a here?"

Mr. Armstrong sent them both a sidelong, disgusted glance and marched out of the cellblock, following his smelly, long-haired, scrawny flesh and blood.

* * * * * * *

Red sat across from two white men in a room with an aluminum table and hard chairs.

"Your buddy, Armstrong, already gave us the low-down. We just need you to confirm a few things."

Red stared at the man.

"Armstrong says you're his supplier. You used to get your drugs from Rufus Coolidge, who goes—er—went, by the name of Blade. You were with Blade when he OD'd last week, and you and somebody else took him to the park across the street from here for an eternal nap. Then you moved into his position in the organization."

Red swallowed, trying to picture whether Jude would really say any of this, and if he hadn't, how the cops knew what they knew. Jude didn't know Blade's real name. Nobody could say Red was there when Blade died, or had moved his body, because he wasn't. "You arrived last night to supply Armstrong, and he invited you to the island. We had it under surveillance, so we saw your little meeting." The man stared at him. "Okay so far? We got it right?"

Red just stared back.

"All right, then. Miss Dexter was already high when she got there but had slept off whatever she had in her. Then you injected her with heroin so you could get a little white pussy. Then, while you were bangin' her, she kicked off."

"So, then you and Armstrong decided to dispose of the body, in the same manner you did yer buddy, Blade, but we showed up and ruined your plans."

The other man asked, "What would you like to confirm or deny about this description?"

"I din't shoot her up with nothin'. She came on to me, woke me up. Say she wanna try it wif a black man 'cause she ain' never done dat befo. We was doin' it on the beach, and she relaxed after a while, an' I was real high so I just kinda relaxed too, and I guess I nodded off. I didn't have no idea she was gone, man. No idea at all. I didn't give her nothin'."

He looked at both men, who sneered back.

"An' I didn't have nothin' ta do with Blade kickin' off. I don' know nothin' 'bout how he got where he was found."

"Okay, smart guy, we found an awful lot of heroin and cash in your pockets and on the island. We know you supplied Armstrong."

Red shook his head.

"Only thing we don't know is who supplies you. We can reduce the charge on the girl's death to murder two instead of murder one if you tell us who your supplier is."

"Murder? Whatchu talkin' 'bout? I dint kill nobody," Red answered, stunned, feeling blood rise to his face and his pulse quicken.

"That's right, boy. Murder. You killed that girl with the drugs you gave her, and we can prove it."

"I didn't sir. I didn't kill nobody."

"Listen, she died right on top a your black ass. We got no problem proving you were with 'er when she died. We even got it on camera."

"We was just havin' sex. She was already loaded, man, and she was havin' sex wif everyone."

"Are you gonna tell us who your supplier is?" the gruffer man asked again.

"I wanna lawyer. I ain' talkin' no mo'."

"Okay, boy. You're going down just 'cause you won't tell us the truth. How stupid can you be?"

Tears welled up in his eyes. He looked down. He was sure Jude hadn't given him up. He wasn't going to cop out on anyone to save his own ass. It wasn't the noble thing to do.

* * * * * * *

The old courtroom was packed with people when Jude walked in, flanked on one side by his stoic father and on the other by his lawyer, marching briskly down the aisle, their hard shoes clacking on the wooden floor. They entered the enclosed area and scraped chairs noisily on the floor as they sat, one on either side of him.

All the spectators sat behind the little railing. Greg's parents sat behind Jude, sniffling and sobbing. Jude couldn't imagine how they felt, having lost a daughter and having their son here too. Billy's mother sat behind, a Kleenex to her nose. A door opened to the right, and eleven prisoners, two Negro females and six Negro males, and then Greg, Billy, and Red, all dressed in gray jumpsuits, ambled in, chains scraping on the floor. They were shackled at their wrists and ankles, and all were connected to each other. Greg and Billy were both red faced; tears streamed down their cheeks. They glanced in Jude's direction, then at their parents behind Jude.

Roosevelt felt that the guards were picking on him. "He's just like his mama, Anne Harris, the nigger, whore junkie—fruit a the tree," one said, and they laughed. Roosevelt believed they pushed him more forcefully, chained him more roughly and treated him like a slave.

They dragged him into the courtroom. He was pissed to see fucking Jude dressed in his Sunday best at a table protected by two white men in suits. Son-of-a-bitch. Maybe he had sold him out. His rich lawyer daddy took care of him.

The chains connecting the prisoners were disconnected so they could be called individually to march to the front. Guards stood with hands on holstered guns. Others held rifles.

Jude watched as prisoners were called to the front and then returned to the bench with the others.

A white man, dressed in a rumpled gray suit, stood up and spoke for all the prisoners. He obviously was a lawyer but didn't seem to know anything about his clients. The first prisoner was charged with grand theft, and the second with possession of drugs. The judge heard their not guilty pleas, and gave an amount of bail.

Then Billy was ordered to stand. He clanked his way to the spot. The same man stood beside him. The two whispered something to each other. The judge said, "William Howell, you are charged with possession of alcohol by a minor, possession of marijuana, possession of heroin with intent to sell, and manslaughter. How do you plead?"

"My client pleads not guilty, your honor."

"Mr. Howell, how old are you?" the judge bellowed.

"Sixteen."

"Do you have a parent in the courtroom?" Billy nodded to his left.

"Ma'am, please approach. Where's his father?"

"Uh, he's not around, sir." She glanced at Jude's father, who avoided her look.

"If I release him to you, will you be able to keep him home?"

"Yes, sir."

"You are released to the custody of your mother pending trial or other disposition. Next."

Red shuffled to the front. "Roosevelt Harris, you are charged with possession of alcohol by a minor, possession of marijuana, possession of heroin with intent to sell, trafficking in heroin, possession of paraphernalia and second-degree murder. How do you plead?"

"My client pleads not guilty," said the man.

"Are you Anne Harris' boy? Miz Harris, is that you over there? Please approach."

She approached with Uncle Theodore and Auntie Barbara. Auntie Barbara was sniffling loudly.

"Miz Harris, you're looking better than I've ever seen you. I hope that's a good sign for you. But it seems now that your lifestyle has resulted in the usual vicious cycle that we see time and time again. I want you to think carefully about how this boy has been brought up. I don't think it's safe to send him home with you."

"It's safe, yer honor," blubbered Auntie Barbara. "We takes special care a Roosevelt and we promise ta keep him out a trouble."

"Yes, sir, we will," added Uncle Theodore. Mama nodded.

"Theodore Harris. You are looking good too. I almost wouldn't have recognized you."

The judge shook his head. "These charges are very serious. The Information indicates that you, Roosevelt Harris, are a known high-level heroin dealer, that you distributed the drug and actually injected it into this woman, leading directly to her death, and that you attempted to dispose of her body after apparently practicing necrophilia with her."

Greg's mother sobbed.

"I believe you are an obvious flight risk and will continue the same practices unless I hold you over. Therefore, I remand you to the juvenile justice department for holding in a juvenile detention facility pending trial. At this time, I am not binding you over to an adult facility, although I could. Regarding the murder charge, the grand jury will convene next week. We'll address the other charges after the grand jury has determined whether the murder charges stand."

His mother trembled. As Red was ushered away, Uncle Theodore and Auntie Barbara led her from the courtroom.

Next came Jude. The same charges were read. "Mr. Armstrong. I am shocked and disturbed by these charges. When your father asked me to release you to his custody yesterday, I thought we were dealing with possession of drugs. I had not realized that you were a distributor, and I did not realize you had anything to do with this death. How do you plead?"

"Not guilty, your honor," his lawyer answered.

"Mr. Armstrong, the father. What can you tell me to convince me to continue to let him stay in your custody instead of locking him up?"

"Your honor, my wife and I have had marital difficulties, and have been separated for some time. I've been concerned about the safety of my son and daughter and, in fact, have drafted pleadings to have them removed to my custody. But this happened before I was able to complete it. I assure you that I will keep him in my home and will exercise total control over him until trial. I give you my word."

The judge looked thoughtful. He shook his head from side to side, furrowed his brow, and said, "David Jude Armstrong, I've known your father and your family for many, many years. I've seen you growing up around the yacht club. I am so extremely disappointed in what has occurred that I can hardly put it into words." Jude felt like rubber. This didn't sound good.

"I am going to honor your father's request. You follow his orders absolutely. I do not wish to see you in here on any other charges. And if you fail in any way to honor this trust, I will lock you up, perhaps in the adult facility. Believe you me, at the age of fifteen, as little as you are, you do not want to be there." He rapped the wooden hammer on the desk, and Jude was ushered out rapidly, while Greg's mother and father looked at him aghast, hatred and tears in their eyes.

* * * * * * *

Jude prepared for the first day of the new school year in the extra bedroom of his father's tiny apartment. He now shared a bedroom with his sister. They'd left most of their belongings and all their pets behind. He waited for his father to exit the only bathroom.

Jude had lost his job, for missing the route twice on the infamous day, and because of the charges, which were published by his employer. That first morning after Linda had died, he'd been jolted to hear his name on the radio and see the newspaper headline: "Prominent Lawyer's Son and Others Charged in Drug Death of Girl."

He hadn't expected his name to show up in the paper, being that he was only fifteen, but there it was, a three-page article with a teaser on the first page, filled with photos of everybody—high school yearbook photos of the white boys and Linda and a mug shot of Red. The article also contained a map showing the location of all the action, a photo of the park where Blade's body had been found, photos of Ratte Island and the strip of water between it and Beach Street, Linda's and Red's cars, Jude's boat, the remains of the fire they'd set between the tents, and dark, grainy surveillance photos of Jude and Red in the boat and on the shore with Linda's body. The article went into the history of Jude's family as founding fathers of the city. Then, it addressed an alleged disparity of justice based upon racial issues, pointing out that the only Negro, Roosevelt Harris, remained in custody, while the rest had been freed.

Jude had not had any mind-altering substance since the awful night, three weeks ago. At school he felt stares, whispers, excitement, and disgust from students; he felt sighs and shame-on-you's from parents and administrators. But nobody asked or said anything about it.

He came across Greg in algebra class and sat next to him. Greg looked up at him, with basset hound eyes, and looked down again, shaking his head. Billy also seemed to keep his distance. There was a strained unspoken discomfort among the three, and there seemed to be no use discussing it now.

At noon the first day, the principal called the three in for a meeting with himself and other administrators, to be sure that it was understood that they would be expelled if there was any indication whatsoever that they were using, possessing or selling drugs, and they could still be expelled even if they behaved, depending on the outcome of the court action.

* * * * * * *

In lock-up, Red tried his best to look tough and nonchalant, cool and distant. Most kids were about his age. The other kids seemed to almost hold him in awe. None had charges as serious as his. Some wanted to know what it was like to have sex with a white girl, what it was like to have sex on heroin, how much money he was making, whether he'd just screwed her to death and things like that.

He was scared and bored—scared that somebody would try to hurt him or get him into trouble. Old Eugene must be mighty pissed about all the product he lost in the bust. But hopefully he'd also realized that nobody came for him because Red had kept his mouth shut, as promised.

This was the area with the highest level of security in the facility—for serious offenders, who would probably end up in prison someday. After a month, he was allowed to see his family on Wednesday and Sunday evenings.

He hated to use the commode out in the open—on display. His stomach was grinding again, like it did so much, so he sat on the cold aluminum can, prison pants down to his knees, trying to look nonchalant, listening to people mouthing off to each other and to the guards.

And he was angry that he'd been singled out because of his race and that Jude, Greg and Billy didn't seem to be serving any time. It was so unfair. He didn't really blame Jude. He knew it wasn't his fault, but then again, the white son-of-a-bitch with the rich, powerful family had escaped and left him alone.

Chapter 9

JUDE ARRIVED AT THE BACK DOOR of his new afternoon job, the Old South Plantation Buffet. Two waiters sat on upturned plastic containers smoking cigarettes. Jude nodded to them. They looked at Jude but didn't speak. Being white in this business made him the minority. Out of twenty or so employees on duty at any time, including the ten or so waiters, the only whites would be the manager, maybe a salad worker or a baker, maybe a line server or two, a dishwasher or two, and Jude. The Negroes were friendly to him, but they had their own relationships.

Jude passed the door of the large bathroom with lockers, which would be full of waiters and cooks, whooping and carrying on, talking of sports and other things known to them and foreign to Jude. He entered the smaller bathroom, the one that only white men, including the managers, used, so it was peaceful and non-threatening. In front of the mirror, he adjusted his dumb paper hat, shaped like that worn by an army private, and tied his white apron over his uniform of white cloth pants and a thin, white, button-up shirt.

He unlocked the storeroom and flung the screen enclosure halfway up. There were six requests under the window—a half pound of rice and two pounds of turkey stuffing for the kitchen, a pound of carrots and a half pound of Greek peppers for the salad area, and the leftover roast beef from yesterday for the kitchen, along with about thirty large green peppers for stuffed green peppers.

He put the products for the main kitchen on the metal countertop under the window. Then he took the requested supplies to the bakery and salad areas. He passed the pot scrubber, a large dark black man named Tough, who he understood had been a high school football star. "Hey now," Jude said as he passed.

"Wha's happ'nin'," Tough said in his deep voice.

The main kitchen staff was busy. One cut green peppers, another ground left-over roast beef and steak. Ben, the chef, wearing a pressed and starched chef's hat, seasoned a round of roast beef. Sylvester, the short order cook, wore his chef's hat beret style, flopping down on one side; he flipped burgers and steaks on the griddle.

In the salad area, Anne, a thirty-something or forty-something black woman with light chocolate skin and freckles, was slicing cukes. She glanced up at him. "Jude. How you doin'?"

"Good. Need some help?"

"Sure, wanna cut me some a dem carrots?"

"Okay, what're they for?"

"Carrot salad; whatchu think? We gonna have somethin' original 'roun' heah?"

After he'd cut the carrots, he went to the serving line, and emptied what was left in the clean dish rack. He stacked the sterile white plates into the areas below the counter. He pushed the empty dish cart into the dishwashing area at the other end of the counter on the way back to the storeroom to get the rest of the evening orders out.

Two white teenagers were preparing the dishwashing area.

"Wha's happ'nin'?" Jude asked.

"Hey man. We're goin' out back to do a doobie at break. Wanna come?"

"No thanks, man," he said, wandering away. He hadn't touched a thing since the night Linda had died, about eleven months ago. The thought of drugs turned him off. He thought of Linda often, her beautiful blond hair, her sly devilish eyes, her succulent lips, her beautiful breasts and butt. God, she'd been cool. What a disaster that whole mess had been. He got queasy remembering the attempts to conceal her dead, flaccid body. Gotta get to work.

The regular storeroom man, Luther, had left him a list of chores. Clean twenty pounds of potatoes, sweep and mop the floors, fill up the containers, rearrange the salad refrigerator. Luther went nuts if things were out of order. Jude grabbed a box of potatoes and lugged it out to the peeling machine. He dumped potatoes into the top of the container and turned on the faucet, so water flowed over the potatoes from above. When he flicked on the machine, the potatoes rumbled along over the uneven, rough-textured belt surrounding the bottom and sides of the cylinder. In five minutes, they would all be clean from the rough rinsing. As each batch was ready, he removed them to a large barrel in the fridge filled with cold, salted water.

Sylvester came back, slammed a request on the countertop and pounded until Jude came out and saw him. Jude retrieved five sirloin steaks from the meat fridge and flopped them onto the counter.

Mr. Roberts entered and walked around, analyzing the counters, the ridges under the screen enclosure, the floor, and everything else for dust, dirt, and evidence of vermin. Jude filled up barrels of powder, flour, corn meal, and sugar, as required by the list. With a large knife, he cut a flour bag, and watched the white powder fall, as always thinking of how much heroin or cocaine that would be. Any kind of powder, especially brown sugar, got his gut churning. He could taste it in his mind.

"Jude, baby, I done run out a raisins," Anne said from behind. He scooped some up, dumped them into a small paper bag, and registered on the huge graph-like purchase sheet that they would need more.

"Thanks honey," she said and swished away.

As he mopped the floor, the dishwashers walked in unsteadily, with their eyes at half-mast. Nothin' but trouble, Jude told himself. Keep telling yourself that. Nothin' but trouble.

* * * * * * *

Red carried his tray to a table where several from his hood were sitting, munching, talking shit. He slid in and slurped sticky spaghetti.

"Red, man, tomorrow you free from this honkie hell hole. I speck you ta be jabbin' some scag wifin a hour a leavin' here, dude; you know what I'm talkin' 'bout?"

"Yeah, man, do some fo me too," another kid said, grinning. Red smiled. He almost didn't believe he was getting out.

"An' he gonna get some pussy! Man, I could do dat. You be thinkin' a me."

"I ain' gonna think 'bout you when I dippin' my wick, and you better not be thinkin' bout me neither."

They all hooted.

The eleven-month lock-up hadn't been too bad. He'd worked on his basketball game, built up some muscle, learned some stuff in school, stayed clean, and avoided trouble. He knew if he got locked up again, it'd be real jail, with real guards, and real rapists. He reorganized his few belongings.

Delan showed up at his door looking for his roommate, Foghat, the stupid white dude who couldn't keep his hands off his dick at all. Red said, "Where you think he is, in the bathroom beatin' that thing to death. But should be kind a interesting 'cause he done run outa hand cream and Carver done give 'im some menthol shit. His dick must be on fire by now."

The kid laughed and headed toward the bathroom.

Red went down the hall for his last Narcotics Anonymous meeting at this facility. Ten kids sat in metal chairs around a large folding table. Two older white men from the outside conducted the meeting.

Several inmates shared. A kid talked about a dispute he'd had with his father. A kid described pouring smack into a cooker, cooking it up, drawing it up and shooting it. Red squirmed. It happened in every meeting. He could imagine sticking the needle in, registering, booting it, feeling euphoria. Pulling out of the memories, he looked around to see if it was affecting anyone else.

A man turned to Red. "I understand you're getting out tomorrow, Roosevelt."

Red nodded.

"Do you have a meeting schedule?"

Red shook his head no.

"I don't really know if you consider this all a bunch of shit. You haven't shared much. But I hope you've gotten something from these meetings. If you want to stay clean and sober, the only way is to adopt these principles—follow the twelve steps—come to these rooms and share."

He kept babbling. How did he think he, an old honkie who never did a real drug, could give advice to Red? Red had never bought any of this shit. He just tried to keep quiet and look interested. He wouldn't go to these stupid meetings on the outside unless he had to.

"So, whadaya say, Roosevelt, will you come to that noon meeting next week?"

Red hadn't been listening, so he didn't know when or where. He nodded.

They all stood, took each other's hand, and said the Lord's Prayer, the only part of the meeting that Red found soothing and useful.

In the evening, inmates wished him well, joking about drugs and sex. None suggested he attend N.A. meetings or stay clean.

He lay awake most of the night, both excited and hesitant. What would happen? Would Missy fuck him? Would he want to get high, and if he did, would he? What would it be like at home? The memory of his last sexual encounter came to him. That Linda had gone for him, had told him she'd never had a black man, had asked him to give her more drugs, had taken the drugs and the sex willingly and excitedly, and then had died right on him, leaving dried vomit and a sour stench as the final memory, her limp, heavy body pushing him into the sand.

* * * * * * *

After arriving home, Red walked to Old South to see his mama. He arrived at the back door. A black man with a chef's hat was smoking a cigarette.

Roosevelt asked, "Anne Harris heah?"

"Sho. She inside, in da salad area, straight on through and on da right."

At the salad area, Mama stood, facing away from him, breaking pieces of lettuce into a large metal bowl. She was talking to a white dude, who was chopping a pile of onions.

"You better watch out fo dose dudes," she was saying. "Dey bad news, baby. Dey gettin' high 'round heah all da time. Sneakin' out back. Dey think nobody know, but dey wrong. Dey on da way down. Damn, dem onions makin' me cry ova heah. Thanks for doin' dat."

"They only smoke reefer far as I know," the white guy said.

"Don' matta," she said.

Red said, "Mama?"

She dropped the lettuce, turned, said, "My baby," and hugged him.

The white dude turned and looked. His eyes bulged. "Fuckin' Red. Dude. Whatchu doin' out?"

Red recognized the voice, but the short-haired, straight-looking, cracker didn't look like skinny, doper Jude.

"No shit, man. Dat you Jude? Look at chu. Look like you own dis place." They stood looking at each other, not sure what was cool—to hug, to shake, or not to touch at all. After a long pause, Jude extended his hand, thumb up, and they shook, each also grasping the clasped hands with his other hand. "Damn man, you reek," said Red, laughing.

Red's mother looked from Roosevelt to Jude, concerned. "I don' even believe dis. You da one got Roosevelt in trouble. You neva got no time."

Red came to his defense. "Mama, he didn't do nothin'. It was my problem and my fault. Forget it, Mama."

* * * * * * *

Roosevelt sat at the kitchen table with the family, a plate of fried mullet, roasted potatoes, and greens in front of him.

His mother was quiet. Roosevelt hoped she was okay. She was working. Uncle Theodore looked worried.

Auntie Barbara, munching on a large mouthful of food, said, "I don' like dat Ol' South Plantation ya'll workin' at." She chewed some more, getting revved up. "It's a racist, discriminatin' place. Wanna keep de black man down."

Uncle Theodore rolled his eyes upwards. Nobody else spoke. Roosevelt tried to get some food down before it got too wild.

"I mean it," she continued. "Da white folk do nice white folk jobs. De black folk do da slave work. Standin' at the end a da line waiting fo the white folk like slaves. Like slaves, I say. It ain' right. An' they don't make nothin'. What do they get fo carryin' dat tray? A dime? Dat's just fittin'."

"My job ain' a slave job," answered Mama. "An' Roosevelt's ain' neither. The men what wait tables ain' hurt none. Dey get paid mighty well. Dem dimes and quarters add up."

"Dey's dressed like monkeys. You should get out a that place," Barbara argued.

"What you do at yo job, honey?" Nana asked Roosevelt. "Tell me 'bout it."

"Nothin' much. Wash dishes. Funny how that food can go out smellin' good and smell so bad half hour later."

Auntie Barbara said, "Only black folk work back there, don' dey?"

"Naw, I been workin' wif a white boy. Ain' been no other black boys back there."

"That's just 'cause dat ain' close 'nough ta slave work. Dey ain' got nobody else." She slammed a fork full of food into her mouth.

Uncle Theodore said, "I knows a bunch a brothers what works at Old South as waiters, and I ain' never heard a one of 'em complain."

Nana said, "Anne, honey, you mighty quiet tonight. You feelin' all right?"

"Yeah, Mama. I fine. Just tired. Dat's all."

Auntie Barbara studied her. "Look at me. You lookin' down, studyin' yo food. That's a bad sign. I know you. A bad omen. Whatchu thinkin' 'bout?" Barbara dropped her fork. "Dis ain' good. Look at her."

Finally, Mama looked at her. "Shut up, goddammit Sissy. Just shut up." She looked at her mother. "Sorry Mama. I dint mean ta swear."

Roosevelt hadn't heard Mama call Auntie Barbara "Sissy" for a long time.

Uncle Theodore put an arm on Anne's shoulder and asked, "Anne, you ready now fo me ta splain how I found peace in my life?"

"Theo," she said, "I don' want to hear yo Muslim peace bullshit," and she walked away, saying "Sorry, Mama."

* * * * * * *

One day, after Red had been promoted to assistant fry cook, Mr. Roberts stopped him on the way in. "Roosevelt, your mother's late."

Red shook his head, trying to look disinterested.

"Can you call and see what's keeping her?"

Red rinsed his hands. As he walked toward the office, Mama slammed open the metal back door and strutted up the hall, saying, "Sorry I's late, suh."

As she passed by, she wiped her hand across her nose.

Red knew from her face that she was loaded on smack. He asked, "Need some help?"

"Hey, baby. Sho. Could use some." She handed him some lettuce to clean and chop.

They worked without talking. From time to time, Red strolled to his own area to check the heat of the oil. He seasoned the mackerel with paprika and garlic salt and dunked the trout in a seasoned mixture of flour and water. Jude brought a lump of butter from the storeroom and placed it in the cooler.

"Jude . . . favor?"

Jude shrugged. Red pointed at the shrimp. Jude nodded. He set up an aluminum bowl with batter for the cleaned shrimp and a plastic bag for the shells. Deftly slipping his right thumb under the first three or four sections, lifting them back, then releasing the last sections, and ripping the shell off just above the tail section, Jude went through fifteen pounds in no time.

Jude took a bag of tomatoes to Anne and returned to the kitchen. He asked Red, "Your Mom do scag, man? Sure acts like it."

Red shrugged, looked down, and half nodded agreement. "Damn, man, and I thought my mom was wild," he laughed. Red didn't smile.

* * * * * * *

A few days later, Mr. Roberts called Red into the office. "What's going on with your mother, Roosevelt?" the asshole asked, his hands folded together like a tent. "Something's changed in her attitude, her work habit . . . when she even shows up."

Red shrugged. "I don' know."

"Have you seen her?"

Red shook his head, no.

"Well, Roosevelt, I'd be happy to help if there was something I could do, but she's just hurting herself, and hurting everybody here. People have to chip in to do her work. That's not right."

Red didn't answer.

"All right, Roosevelt, tell her if she doesn't straighten up, she's out of here." The old fart stood up, adjusted his pants, and waited for Red to exit.

After work, Red walked down to the corner. He didn't see Mama. Tom sat on the windowsill.

"'S happ'nin'?" Tom drawled.

"I thought you was inside."

"Got out last week."

Red nodded.

"Ready ta do some business again bro'?" Tom asked, flicking the butt of his cigarette off into the evening sky.

Red shrugged.

"Eugene say he'll do da same deal as befo'."

Red hesitated. The beauty of the potential high clouded his mind. He tried to recall the problems heroin had caused him, the death of Linda, Mama's problems. He convinced himself that it was okay.

Red and Tom got their supplies. Red stopped by his hiding place to retrieve his works, and hurriedly returned to work, hoping Jude would still be there cleaning up. His car was in the back parking lot, all alone. Red banged on the back door loudly several times. Finally, he heard, "Who is it?" muffled through the heavy metal door.

"Red."

Jude let him in. "What the fuck, man?"

"Got any money? I got some smack."

Jude stood frozen. His stomach churned and his heartbeat quickened. There was no hesitation. All he wanted to do was feel the rush. He reached into his pocket and pulled out a ten.

They went to the counter where Jude put outgoing products and fixed up. Within seconds, Jude was hit with the familiar, relaxing, soothing, surrealistic impact. "Oh, fuck," he managed, hearing his own voice, low, hoarse and far away. Everything was so peaceful, smooth, perfect.

Jude mopped in slow motion as Red sat on the counter smoking a cigarette. "How much you get?" asked Jude.

"Ten bags. Got eight left. Gotta sell 'em."

"I can sell half," Jude offered, and Red gave him half.

They were back in business and back in the high, just like that.

* * * * * * *

On a Saturday afternoon, Jude, Billy and Greg smoked a joint and drank warm Busch beer in Billy's car. Then they went inside Peabody Auditorium for their high school graduation ceremony. Jude donned his long red robe and stood in the hot back room, watching his classmates buzz around chatting with each other, dreaming of the future, and talking of college. He envied the ease with which they communicated. He felt alone, unusual, and unaccepted. But at least he was high.

* * * * * * *

Red rapped on the door of Eugene's place to pick up his supply. He heard stirring inside. A woman's voice, which sounded a lot like Mama's, said, "Don' let 'im in. Goddamn it Eugene. Just don' answer."

Eugene opened the door, and Red caught a glimpse of Mama moving to the back room. "That's my mama ain' it?"

"Donchu worry 'bout her, man. Let's do business." He pulled out a large baggy and dropped wrapped bags onto the table.

Red moved to the open door to the bedroom. "Mama?"

"Goddamn it, Roosevelt. What da fuck you doin' heah? Goddamn it to hell. An' you gettin' strung out too. I gots 'nough problems with this shit. Don' need no other junkie in da fam'ly." A tear rolled down her cheek.

"And you, you fuck," she said, pointing at Eugene. "How could you get my son ta dealin'?" She marched to the gray, torn cloth couch and plopped down, holding her face in her hands and bawling.

Red hesitated, and then handed Eugene cash. Eugene counted out twenty bags and placed them into a plastic baggie.

As his mama slumped on the couch Red approached, leaned down, and kissed her on the cheek. "'S okay, Mama," he said.

She looked up, wiped a tear away, and said, "Don' wind up like yo mama."

* * * * * * *

On Main Street one evening, without his supply, Jude said to Billy, "Know who's got some smack?"

"Naw, man. I can get Dilaudid."

"What's that?"

"Synthetic morphine. Need a scrip ta get it. Wanna try some?"

"What's it cost?"

"Ten bucks a pill. Like a bag."

They walked a few blocks south of Main Street. Billy knocked on the door of an old, two-story green plaster house. A teenage girl Jude recognized from school opened the door and let them in. Jude followed Billy to a bedroom. Billy showed Jude how to drop the Dilaudid into the spoon, pour water in, and stir it around a little with the top of the plunger. It dissolved as he moved it.

"Don't hafta cook it?" Jude asked.

Billy shrugged. "Doesn't really need it."

The brand-new needle slid right in. The rush hit hard. Different taste—different deadening feeling—but the same euphoria. He sat there with the needle in his arm, dumbfounded. "Great. Very clean," he managed.

When they walked out, an old man, about fifty or sixty, bald, with a weathered, wrinkled face, confronted them. "What's this? goddammit," he said to Billy. "I told you not to bring anybody here."

Walking back to Main Street, Jude said, "Who was the old guy?"

"Hank. My supplier."

Jude was shocked. "The guy looked like anybody's father."

"Well, you know Melinda, who let us in? He's her father."

* * * * * * *

Red sat on the windowsill, stewing. Eugene hadn't answered the door. Red didn't want to tell his customers he had nothing. After all, Red was the man. He was the one with the power. Nobody could supply smack like Red could. Heads would turn when he walked into a room. And now, just like that, he was nobody.

Was Eugene just showing him the power trip? Could he have OD'd? Or been busted? Was he screwing some bitch? And then suddenly Red flashed on Eugene with Mama. No. He lit a cigarette and inhaled hard.

Armstrong's old station wagon creaked around the corner and stopped. Jude flicked a smoke out the passenger side and motioned to him.

Red walked slowly to the car, not eager to admit he wasn't holding.

"What's happ'nin', bro'?" Jude asked cheerily.

Red shrugged.

"Got some scag, man?" Jude asked.

Red shook his head dejectedly.

"When you gonna have somethin'?"

Red shook his head.

"Hey, ever do Dilaudid?" Jude asked.

"Whassat?"

"It's a pill, like smack. Dissolves in water. Ya shoot it just like smack. No quinine smell or taste. It'll do you good, man."

"How much?"

"Ten bucks a pill. Same's a bag."

Red handed cash through the window.

Jude drove to the house he'd visited with Billy. His classmate, Melinda, opened the door. He glanced her up and down. Her small breasts showed through her T-shirt.

Saying, "Dad'll be back in a minute," she motioned to the tiny, hard-looking plastic couch.

The door opened and Hank walked in, stopped and gawked at Jude. "What the hell you want?"

"Can I buy from you?"

"Goddam it," the old man replied, looking at Melinda. "What the hell you think this is?" He ushered Jude into a bedroom.

He slammed the door behind them, glaring at Jude. "Listen you little fuck. Don't you ever talk about drugs in front of my daughter or tell anybody anything about drugs in this house. Got it?"

The crow's feet around the man's eyes gave the impression he was smiling. But Jude got the picture that he was pissed.

As they did the deal, Hank said, "I need a ride tomorrow to get a supply. I'll split the pills I get with you."

Jude gulped. "How many you getting?"

"I never know. Prob'ly forty or so." Jude calculated twenty pills for free. If he shot five, he'd still make a hundred and fifty dollars.

"Be here at seven a.m. Don't be late."

Then Jude remembered that he had to work. Well, he'd call in. This could work out much better. He'd make more than he made in two weeks at the restaurant. And he'd get high.

Jude nodded. "I'll be here."

* * * * * * *

Red was about to give up on Jude. He'd imagined every possible situation—that Jude had been busted, that he'd ripped him off, that he'd OD'd. He fumed and worried, smoked another cigarette, looked at his watch, and waited. He loved to make his customers wait, but he didn't like it done to him.

Jude finally rolled around the corner. The car rocked to a slow stop. Cigarette bobbing in his mouth, he said, "Got a place ta get off?"

"How many you got? I got customers waiting in the projects."

"I got some extra, if I can go with you."

Red hesitated. He'd never seen a cracker in the hood other than right on this corner. At the same time, he could get there much faster in the car, and he wanted to get off. He got in the car.

Red directed him. They parked in front of an apartment. Red knocked on the door. The door opened slightly. "Who dis?" a boy with a deep black face asked.

"The dealer," Red answered.

The boy gave Jude the once over, and then backed away, opening the door. Three other boys sat in the dark room, staring at him. Nobody moved or talked.

Red said, "Dis dude got a new drug, like smack, but straight from a legal drug store."

"Wha's it called?" one asked.

"Dilaudid. D's," offered Jude. "I'll fix up a dose for me an' Red so ya'll can see."

They gave him a spoon and a glass of water. He removed a syringe from his sock, dropped the tiny pill into the spoon, dribbled water into it, stirred it around and drew it up.

Red got off. His eyes fluttered. He sighed. "Shit, man. Dis shit's gooood."

Jude fixed up a dose for each of the others. He felt like some great white missionary taking a new belief to a faraway land. He had the ultimate power. He was the teacher. They looked up to him. Then he got off and they vegetated on the uncomfortable furniture.

"Where da hell you get dis shit, man?" asked one boy.

"Across the river."

"Can you get mo'?" asked another.

"Tomorrow, I'll have a bunch," he said, hoping he was telling the truth.

"Will ya come back?"

"Ya'll need ta talk ta Red, here. He's yer dealer."

Chapter 10

AT 7 A.M., AS INSTRUCTED, Jude tapped lightly at the door to Hank's apartment. Hank opened the door, looking happy with his smiley eyes. Carrying a medical bag, he looked like a country doctor going to visit a sick patient. He tottered to the car and stopped short.

"Jesus. I didn't know you had such a beat-up, old car." The old man started walking slowly again. "Oh well. Can I drive?" he asked.

Jude shrugged and got in the passenger seat.

The old man cranked up the car and jammed the stiff old transmission into place. "This car ain' gonna do for long if you're gonna be my new ride."

Jude was surprised. He hadn't thought the man had a regular job in mind.

Without saying a word, the old man crossed the river at the Main Street Bridge, and headed north on U.S. 1, driving the speed limit, holding the steering wheel tightly. On I-95, Jude smoked and watched the road. This was an adventure.

Jude tried to make small talk a few times, but never got much response. He tried to picture where they were going and what they were going to do.

Hank exited the highway and drove along a quiet two-lane highway. In a small town, he parked in front of a building with a sign saying Randall Schwimmer, M.D. on the door. Jude looked at him, surprised. "Is this guy the dealer?"

"In a way. I have a doctor's appointment."

"What?" Jude thought. "I brought him here for a doctor's appointment?" The old man walked into the office. Jude sat, stunned. For the next hour or so, Jude grew impatient. In the sweltering heat, he smoked cigarettes, searched for radio stations, unsuccessfully, played some Traffic on his portable eight-track tape player and walked around the parking lot. Two hours after entering,

Hank strolled toward the car with an eerie, uncharacteristically enthusiastic grin on his face. He got in, still smiling, backed the car out, drove slowly down the street, reached into his shirt pocket and handed Jude a small white piece of paper. At the top was Dr. Schwimmer's name and information. In the middle, he saw some scribble in which he made out the number 40, something like "bid" and a long word starting with a D. He tried to make it out, and then realized that it said "Dilaudid."

The old man smiled. "He's one of my many suppliers. You can be my ride, but only if you get a new car."

"How am I gonna get a new car?"

"You better figure it out. Make some money with yer pills, and do it quick, 'cause I'm used to nice cars." Hank pulled into a shopping center and stopped in front of a drugstore. He grabbed the prescription and went in. Jude smoked a cigarette, anxiously, imagining the high. Then Hank emerged, smiling even more. He drove a few blocks, turned down a secluded street, and pulled into an area of weeds behind a large tree.

Jude asked, "Why do these doctors write scrips for you? You pay 'em or what?"

Hank turned off the car, opened his medical bag, and handed Jude a set of works. "I got a bad heart."

The two of them proceeded with their own rituals.

"I don' get it."

"This is a common drug to treat angina. I always have two scrips, but I only fill one. The other is nitro; they give that for angina."

"What's angina?"

"Heart pain. Chest pain. If you got heart disease, you get this pain, and you can get a scrip easy. I tell 'em I've just moved to town, show 'em scrips for nitro and Dilaudid from another town, and tell I'm out a pills and need new scrips. I act real dumb like I don't know what it is. And they write it every time. Then I go back about once a month to get a new scrip. That's why I have doctors all over the state. We're goin' to another now on the way back."

Jude was off before Hank was finished preparing his mixture. Jude cleaned out his works and nodded off, floating on a cloud.

* * * * * * *

Red was peeling shrimp when Jude arrived at work. Jude walked to the salad area.

Anne looked up smiling. "Hey, Jude. Can ya get me some radishes, sweetie?"

She looked straight, and cheerful. He decided not to tell her what he had. Later he told Red. Red's eyes widened. "How many ya got, man?"

"Fifteen for you to deal,"

"Deal, man," Red responded.

Jude dropped Red off near the projects. Red walked past Blade's apartment, still dark and abandoned, and knocked at the door of Blood's crib. His customers were waiting.

"Yo. Whassup?" asked a girl named Tawana, slim and hot looking, her dark skin glowing. "C'mon in. You got da stuff?"

Red smiled. "Now whatchu think? You doubt my talent? Huh?" He rubbed his pelvic area against her jutty ass as he passed.

"Ooh, baby," she smiled and giggled.

He dealt five of the pills and did one himself. They shared the two needles, two cookers, and one lighter. One would squirt the blood out of a syringe a couple of times, and then the next would fix up. As they got off, they stumbled to the couch or the bed, groaned, moaned, and sighed. "Fuck," said Wooster. "Dis shit's killer. Makes dat brown sugar look just like sugar. D's da thing, man."

* * * * * * *

One evening, Jude convinced Red to shoot some D's with him. Jude drove toward the bridge and headed across. "What da fuck you doin', man? I cain' go 'cross da bridge. Slow the fuck down befo' we gets stopped."

"Ain' been a law against Blacks coming over here in years."

"Don't know nobody ever crossed the bridge 'ceptin' Uncle Theodore, an' he was workin'."

At his house, Jude took Red in through the garage and up the cellar stairs. Mom and whoever was slobbering around the table might say something about Red being Black. But just as Jude opened the door, Duke staggered around the corner in the hallway. Duke almost gasped. Jude decided it was best to take Red to say hello.

His mom and Billy's sat with drooping eyes and wasted faces.

"Hey, sweetie," his mom said, pulling him down to her and landing a wet kiss on his face. Then she looked, surprised, and almost smiling, and asked, "Who's zhish?"

"Red. We work together," Jude said, embarrassed just as soon as he said it that he was making an excuse for being with a Black.

The group nodded but remained in their stupor.

Red was surprised to see Jude greeting a cat and dog. They were nothing like those in his neighborhood. The house was huge. Jude's bedroom was larger than Red's grandma's entire living room, kitchen and dining room together.

Jude locked the door, pulled out works for both of them and set a pill for each on the desk. They both got off. Jude put Steve Miller on the stereo and collapsed on his bed. Red flopped onto the other bed.

Red wanted to live just like this one day. Maybe he'd have to sell drugs to get this much money, but he'd do it. Maybe he'd even live on this side of the river.

A thud sounded in the hall, followed by a larger, deeper thud. Red was afraid, but Jude stood nonchalantly and wandered across the long room to the door.

Jude opened the door and looked down to find Duke sitting on the floor, leaning against the wall, a smoke in one hand and a half-spilled drink in the other.

"'S up, Duke?" he asked.

"Losh my balance. I'm okay." Jude helped him up.

Red leaned on the door jamb, watching the sad, comical spectacle. This is some strange house, he thought.

* * * * * * *

A few weeks later, Jude bought a brand-new '71 Toyota Celica. His dad co-signed the loan. The loan payment was less than half a day's take. The next morning, Hank almost skipped out of the house, swinging his doctor's bag, and smiling like a child on Christmas morning. Hank jumped into the driver's seat, adjusted mirrors and his seat, pulled some slick, plastic, wrap-around sunglasses out of his bag and admired himself in the mirror, grinning from ear to ear. He cranked the car up, shifted into first, and revved the engine. Then he zoomed the accelerator, pulled the clutch, and squealed off down the street, shifting forcefully through the gears.

For once, Hank talked as he cruised on the highway. "My Uncle Stan was a race car driver on the old beach course," he said. "I always wanted to be a driver."

Jude glanced over at Hank's serious, yet still smiling, face. "Where we goin'?"

"Mount Dora. And it's time for you to do some work."

"Like what?"

"To get your own scrip."

"How?"

"Fake a kidney stone."

"Huh?"

"You don' even know what a kidney stone is? You ever get one and you'll sure know what it is and you'll never forget. You build up this stuff like a fuckin' rock in your kidneys, and it hurts like a mother. When it's comin' out, you bleed out of your dick and you scream like a woman havin' a baby."

Jude cringed and crossed his legs. "How the hell am I supposed to fake that?"

"Tell the lady at the desk you got this terrible pain, and kinda point to the back of your midsection, and say yer peein' blood. You'll always get in without an appointment with that blood-in-the-pee story. Then you look like you're in a lot of pain—whine; lean over; hold your back. Take a syringe with you. If they ask you to pee, draw some blood outta your arm, and spray it in the urine sample."

Jude was flabbergasted. It all sounded too complicated. What if the doctor asked him something he couldn't answer? What if he saw through him? Would he get arrested or something?

"I mean it," the old bastard said. "You gonna earn your keep today, or I'm gonna reduce your take."

Jude was pissed. He'd bought the new car just because the old man had demanded it, and now he was changing the deal.

A few minutes later, Hank pulled up to a doctor's office. Jude stuck his works into his sock. "You go to Dr. Allen and I'll go to Henderson," he directed, pointing in two different directions.

"Fuck," Jude muttered under his breath. He went in. At the desk, a lady dressed in a white nurse's outfit glanced up at him. "Yes?"

"I don't have an appointment, but I really need to see a doctor," he whined.

"What's the trouble," she asked, looking unsympathetic.

"I don't know. I got a lot a pain—like here," he explained, pointing to the rear middle of his back. He glanced at the reception area, and whispered, "And when I go to the bathroom, there's blood."

She gave him a look, perhaps suspicious, perhaps hateful, perhaps arrogant. He wasn't sure. "All right," she said after a while. "I suppose the doctor can see you. Have a seat."

He had a seat, and worried. He wondered whether he could pee if required to. He'd only had a glass of orange juice. From time to time, he fidgeted and made a face as though in pain.

After a while, a nurse escorted him into a room. He explained his symptoms again. She wrote some notes, took his pulse, and checked his blood pressure and temperature. He couldn't tell what she was thinking. She handed him a cup for a urine sample and directed him to the bathroom. Inside, he pulled out the syringe, withdrew blood from his arm and squirted it into the urine sample, hoping it created the right hue. He swirled the mixture together.

He limped back to the room, carrying the concoction, and set it on the counter. In a few minutes, the doctor entered and picked up his chart. He motioned for Jude to stand, and he pushed in various places around the front and back of his torso. Jude winced and grunted in fake pain as the doctor pushed on the area where Hank had told him to complain.

The doctor asked him whether he had pain when he urinated and he answered that it did hurt somewhat, but that the main pain was in his back. The doctor lifted the concoction and viewed the orange tinge.

"There's not much we can do. You'll pass the stone eventually. All we can do is keep you comfortable."

"What can you give me?" Jude asked. He hesitated for a moment, and then decided to try by just asking, and trying to mispronounce it a bit. "I've heard that dalawda, or something like that, works okay."

"Dilaudid. That's a Class A narcotic. I'll give you fifteen fours," he said, surprising Jude so much he wasn't sure how to respond. All Jude knew was fours, but he'd heard that they also came in weaker strengths of 3, 2 or 1. The way the doctor said "4s" seemed so casual it was like he knew exactly what Jude was up to, but didn't care.

The doctor quickly scribbled out the scrip, handed it to Jude and slipped out without another word. "Yes!" Jude said to himself, smiling.

In the car, Hank said, "We should go to different pharmacies," as he pulled into a parking space in a shopping center. Pointing to a chain pharmacy, he said, "You go to that one. I'll go to a small drug store around the corner."

Jude asked, "How many pills you get?"

Hank hesitated, and Jude knew he wanted to lie to him. "Thirty," he answered. Jude wanted to see the scrip, but didn't want to piss Hank off, so he could only take his word for it.

Within twenty minutes, they were parked in a secluded area doing their traditional procedures, which was followed by the familiar, deadening, heavy peace as the drug infiltrated their systems.

* * * * * * *

Red met Jude in the back parking lot of Old South on a mutual break and received ten pills to sell.

"I'm thinkin' a quittin' work," Red said.

"Me too."

"Can make a whole bunch mo' sellin' dope," Red continued.

Jude nodded.

* * * * * * *

After work, Red strolled to Robert's apartment. Tawana opened the door. Wooster, Robert and others sat at a table on which syringes and spoons were lined up like military planes on a runway awaiting action. Red quickly doled out a pill to each and collected crumpled bills. Everybody got off.

He sat on the couch like a king, with Tawana leaning on him and rubbing his leg. He was the D man.

Tawana kissed him. He enjoyed her full, luscious lips. A knock sounded at the door. Mama and Uncle Theodore peered through the window. Mama'd been clean for months now, and his uncle much longer.

"Fuck," he whispered and flew out of his seat, almost knocking Tawana to the floor. He glanced at the table, but the array of debris was all over the place.

Wooster opened the door. Mama stormed toward him, shooting a spiteful glance at Tawana, who was trying to regain her balance. "What the hell you doin' Roos'velt," she demanded. "Donchu know how bad drugs done fucked up my life? You tryin' ta go down the same road?"

Uncle Theodore appeared calm but moved slowly around the room. "Who's da dealer heah?" he asked, looking from one to the other. Everybody looked around, uncertainly. "Who?" he demanded. Somebody apparently gazed at Red, and Uncle Theodore got in his face. "You better not be da one sellin' dis shit, Roosevelt."

Red looked away.

Mama grabbed Roosevelt's arm and pulled him toward the door. He glanced back at the shocked people, embarrassed, feeling all his power and cool melting away. Tawana looked at him in disbelief—no more admiration—as his mommy dragged him away like a misbehaving little boy. He could kill them for ruining him like this.

Mama glared at him. "I just don' get it. Ain' chu seen da grief I been through? Donchu understand how strong dope is? Nobody can fight it forevah, no matter how strong you think you be." She hesitated for a minute. "Talk to 'im, Theo."

Uncle Theodore nodded but didn't say anything. Roosevelt's gut was tight with anticipation. His uncle was cool, and he would talk to Red like a brother, not crazy like Mama, or insane like his aunt.

Uncle Theodore pulled into the driveway. Nana was rocking on the porch, her big face solemn. She stood slowly and went inside. He hoped his aunt wasn't home.

Mama went inside, letting the screen door slap the frame behind her. Uncle Theodore motioned to a chair on the porch and sat next to him. He sighed heavily, trying to prepare for the serious talk.

"Roos'velt. You know, I started out innocently enough, just like you, but little by little the drug takes over. First, a little harmless weed. Then a little white powder. But it was smack what did me in. Dint happen right away. Took some months before I was stuck to it. But then, I was in trouble. An' I would do anythin'—anythin' at all to get well when the sickness would come. I hope you ain' experienced it—an' I hope you never hafta, but when you hooked, 's a bitch. I mean, 's like the worst sickness you eva felt. You gotta stop while you can, bro." He put his hand on Red's shoulder.

Red was almost moved for a moment. Here was a man who loved him—who knew what he was talking about. But Red couldn't believe it could be so bad. Hell, Uncle seemed just fine now.

"Roos'velt," his uncle continued. I know what yer thinkin'. You're thinkin' I'm fine, so it can't be that bad—ain' you thinkin' that?" he chuckled.

Red smiled and nodded.

"Believe me. I was ruined. I found Allah, and that's the only reason I'm here today. But befo' that, I got busted for breakin' into a store. I needed the money. I'd a done anythin'. An' those first days in da county jail, sick, sick, sick, were the worst days of my life. I was pukin'. I was shittin' pure hot burnin' liquid. I was shakin'. I was convulsin'. An' nobody gave a damn. First time I ever 'member prayin'. I prayed and prayed. I prayed ta God ta save me—ta relieve me of the sickness. I got through it. But it was a bitch." He leaned back and crossed his legs. "You lisnin' ta me?" he asked, tapping Red on the arm.

Red nodded.

"I ain' gonna bore you wif talking 'bout religion—talkin' 'bout da Muslim religion. Right now, you still got the chance ta just stop. Just don' do it no mo. 'S dangerous. So very, very dangerous." He shook his head. "Can you stop, Roosevelt?"

"I guess," Roosevelt answered meekly.

Mama came back out. "How's it goin' wif my boys," she asked. She sat down next to him and put her arms around his neck. "Y' know I love ya, Roosevelt. Only reason I'm after you is dat I care. An' I know 'zactly what dope'll do to ya. Yo uncle clean. I's clean. We just don' wanna see you havin' ta go through it. You don' hafta learn da way we did. Be smart, honey. Just be smart." She hugged him tightly and kissed the back of his neck.

This was getting hard. Mama, who'd been too busy getting high for years to show him any affection—any emotion—was seriously concerned for him. And she surely knew. He craved getting high sometimes when he knew it was available, but he just couldn't imagine a physical need for the drug.

"Ya, know," Uncle Theodore chimed in again, "not only is da drug itself bad news, but if ya'll sharin' fits, can spread diseases—like hep, man. All kinds a stuff in one dude's system, can be really bad in anotha's."

Red nodded. This was getting boring.

"I don' wanna hear you hangin' wif any dose people 'gain, Roos'velt, okay? An' who da girl?"

Red shrugged. "Tawana," he answered.

"Who her parents be?" Mama asked.

"Don' know."

"Well, stay 'way from her too."

Not for a minute, Red thought.

* * * * * *

"Are you dealin' in nigger town?" Hank asked Jude, leaning back in his seat, his sunglasses perched on his nose, zooming up and down the hills of the Ocala National Forest.

"Uh-uh."

"They got their dope. We got ours. You shouldn't be dealin' with niggers. Those sons-a-bitches do all kinds a shit to us when we try to buy over there. They make us wait. They steal our money. They cut the bags. They think we're fuckin' stupid."

This guy was older than Jude's father. But he talked like a hood. Jude flicked his smoke out the open window. He'd never pictured Hank buying scag. Although Jude had heard the word "nigger" many times, and he'd probably even used it before his father's speeches about the evils of racism, he just couldn't stand hearing this old fuck referring to his friends that way. He didn't feel like a privileged white boy. He felt a connection. Then he thought how stupid that was. He didn't know anything about Red's feelings, or his life. Red would be offended if Jude tried to say he had any understanding of Black life. He'd seen Red's family's tiny beat-up house. Then he chuckled to himself, thinking that Hank's little apartment wasn't much better.

"Hey, you listening? If you don't stop, our deal is off," the old man insisted.

Jude almost laughed out loud. He knew how to get his own scrips, thanks to Hank. He'd scored every time. He usually only got ten to fifteen pills, whereas Hank usually got from twenty-five to forty, but still he could cop his own and not share them with Hank. Hank needed his car anyway, and he wouldn't want to go back down to an old, unattractive car when he'd fallen in love with driving the Celica. Jude didn't intend for a moment to obey the old fart.

In Ocala, they went to separate doctor's offices on opposite sides of the square in the center of downtown. Jude got a scrip for twenty. When he emerged, he didn't see Hank or the car, but did notice a sign saying DRUGS down the street. He strolled down the barren sidewalk in the late morning sun, dragging the heels of his Dingo boots. The boots were perfect in this redneck town, where most of the vehicles parked around the square were pickup trucks with bales of hay in the back and gun racks on the rear window. His long hair and bell-bottom jeans weren't exactly right here, though.

Inside the store, he made his way on the worn wooden floor past dusty, stock-filled shelves to the rear, where the pharmacist worked high above the common folk, reminding him of the elevation of a judge or royalty. Actually, he thought it fit well, because there was nothing more powerful than what this profession had to offer. He handed the scrip up to the balding, beak-nosed man, who examined him over reading glasses perched on the end of his nose. Jude knew he looked scruffy, with the wisp of a goatee he was attempting to grow, his wavy flowing hair, and his ragged jeans. But the man began working without comment.

When he returned to the car, Hank wasn't there, which both pleased and concerned him. He saw a diner across the green and headed toward it.

He went straight to the restroom. He dropped a pill directly into the barrel of his syringe, crushing it somewhat with the plunger, and then drew up tap water cupped in his palm. He shook the syringe, to dissolve the pill. He stashed four more pills in his cigarette pack. Finally, he decided it was dissolved enough, and that his warm blood would dissolve the balance, so he jabbed it into the crook of his arm as he stood in front of the mirror, drew back, pushed in, drew back, and plunged in again. He watched his face relax and soften, as he felt the deadening fluid flow through his veins.

He cleaned the works, took a piss, lit a cigarette, and walked back through the diner to the outside. Hank was driving slowly down the street away from him and turned left toward the other side of the green. As Jude made his way across the green, Hank turned again, searching. When Hank saw him, he accelerated wildly, screeched the tires as he turned around, zoomed up behind him, and skidded to a stop.

"What the fuck are you doin'? Where the fuck have you been?"

"I had ta piss," Jude answered. "And I filled my scrip."

"Get in the fucking car," Hank ordered angrily. "God damn it. How many pills ya get?"

"Ten," Jude lied.

"Only ten? Why'd he give ya only ten? You better not be holdin' out on me. I don't want you fillin' a scrip without my seein' it next time. An' that's the drug store I was gonna use."

"Okay," Jude responded. "Then you can show me your scrips too."

"Are you sayin' I'm lyin'?"

Jude nodded.

"Son-of-a-bitch," Hank muttered as he drove along toward a chain drug store.

"Let me see the scrip," Jude demanded.

Hank said, "No," and got out.

Chapter 11

RED STOOD ON THE CORNER, waiting for Eugene. Red needed to re-up, so he could get product to his dealers. He checked his watch. Late. He didn't dig Eugene making him wait like a poor, miserable, cracker junkie. He paced, and smoked, and stood and fumed. Finally, after looking at his watch dozens of times, and scanning the street for the yellow Cadillac, he decided to go to Eugene's house. He no longer lived in the projects.

Red's friend Willis sat in a chair next to his taxicab, drinking a malt liquor and toking on a joint. "Yo, Willis," Red hollered. "Run me up da road."

"Where to?" Willis asked, letting a rumbling belch escape.

Not wanting Willis to know where he was going, he said, "I'll direct ya."

Willis trotted to the car on rickety legs. "You da boss, bro'," he said, smiling, revealing brown teeth separated by gaping holes.

Red directed Willis to the neighborhood, north of Volusia and west of Nova, near the community college. "Pull over at that store," he said.

"What da fuck you doin' there. We gots stores in our part a town. You don' hafta come out heah." Willis shook his head, bewildered.

"Listen, Willis, I gotta do something. Can ya come on back an' get me, say in uh forty-five minutes?"

"You payin' fo da down time?"

"Sho. Here's what I owe ya now. You can even go do another fare if ya get one. Just come back here in about fo'ty-five, an' if I ain' here, ya better wait on me."

Old Willis nodded his head. "Yes, sir, boss," he giggled.

Red wandered around until he was sure Willis was gone. Then he walked to the house. He didn't know why Eugene liked to live out here like a goddam minority.

He found the Cadillac parked beside the house. Eugene's crib was a weather-worn brown wooden house, with a wobbly wooden porch, out of place in the neighborhood, since most had been replaced with little concrete-block houses, and little concrete porches. He sprang up the steps, walked over the hollow-sounding floor, and rapped on the door. He stuck his ear to the door, straining to hear. Nothing. He banged a little louder and put his ear close again. "Eugene," he hollered, cupping his mouth near the glass. He thought he heard something, faint, so faint he wasn't sure. "Eugene," he yelled again. And he heard something again.

He heard a muffled sound that he could barely tell was human, but it had to be Eugene. He tried the door. Locked. He walked along the porch, peering into the two other windows into the living room, but couldn't see anything. He stepped off the porch and walked along the side of the house, checking each window he came to, and calling Eugene's name. Finally, he was at the bathroom. He couldn't see through the opaque jalousie window. He got up really close and called Eugene again.

"Help me, goddam it," Eugene wailed. "Go to da back door." His voice trailed off.

Red ran to the back door, flung it open and entered. He ran down the little hall and stopped at the bathroom. There were legs, dressed in long pants, shoes and socks, hanging over the edge of the bathtub. "Eugene?"

"Help me," he slurred.

The handle of a large knife protruded out of Eugene's gut, high in the rib cage area. A glass syringe half full of blood stuck out of his right arm. Red cringed at the sight but crept closer. The bottom of the bathtub looked something like a vat of dried red wine.

"What da fuck happen?" Red whispered.

"Dey rip me off. Dey stab me. Dey inject me wif product. Thank God dey did dat, 'cause at least it don't hurt dat bad."

"Who?"

"Dat Jerome motha fucka and some a his gang. Dey took da dope. Dey ripped my ass off. I ain' never been ripped off befo'. I ain' neva had nobody enter my castle and threaten me wif harm. And do me harm." His voice trailed off, ending in a groan.

"I need ta call you an ambulance," Red told him.

"Not yet; first, ya gotta listen ta me," he whispered, his voice beginning to rasp. "I was s'posed ta leave tonight to get a delivery. Ya hear? Da product's waitin'. You gotta go get it."

"Where?"

"Louisiana, outside New Orleans."

"What?" he asked, astonished. "How da fuck am I gonna get there?"

"I don' give a shit how you get there, ceptin' you ain' takin' my car. But you can take a greyhound, you can hitch a ride. You gotta get it."

"Oh yeah," Red laughed. "Old Red's dumb enough to come back hitchhiking wif his pockets full of heroin. Is black folk even allowed ta travel like dat?"

"Shut up and go to da kitchen. Open da drawer ta da left a da icebox. Dare a envelope wif some papers inside. Bring it." He struggled more and more to get his breath. His belly and the protruding knife handle moved up and down.

Red walked into the kitchen. Dirty dishes, glasses, and silverware were stacked in the sink and on the counter. A brown envelope stuffed with papers was in the drawer. He snatched it and returned. "Why'ntcha pull de goddam knife out?"

"I scared. I think I'll just leave it there like a stopper, till the ambulance get here."

He snatched the envelope from Red. "You fuck me on dis and you'll have a knife just like dis up yo' ass, ya hear?" He groaned. "Heah fo grand. Heah da directions. Ya go ta dis town, at dis corner, ta da phone boof. Ya call dis number, and ya wait. Da man come down an' exchange da money fo da dope. You drag yo ass back ta Daytona, and we back in business. Got it?"

Red nodded. This wasn't mule work. This was the actual buy. This was the big time. He was doing what Eugene only trusted himself to do. He was going to make his own connection in case Eugene ever couldn't do it. "Who I meetin'?" he asked.

"Don' you worry. You just tell 'em right away on da phone dat I's laid up an' I sent you. Tell 'em you my cousin. Tell 'em dey can call me if dey got questions."

Red imagined that the deal would be done following some elaborate, complicated procedure. The suppliers would drive big fancy Cadillacs, dressed to the nines. They'd talk. Have great comradery. They'd know he was cool. Red was the man they could deal with any time that Eugene wasn't up to it.

Eugene had closed his eyes, and through a heavy grimace, he added, "Now go on and call me an ambulance. It hurts like a motha. Get this goddam needle outa my arm first. Throw it away."

Red did as he was told and left. He walked around the block several times waiting to see that an ambulance arrived. He'd tried to explain how serious the injury appeared. He was surprised it took so long, and that even when they arrived, the lights weren't flashing. They pulled into the driveway, leisurely strolled up the stairs, rapped on the door, and finally went inside. He wondered whether they knew Eugene was Black, knew he was a dealer, or just treated everybody this way.

* * * * * * *

At seven in the morning, Jude knocked impatiently at Hank's door. Finally, Melinda opened the door.

"Dad's not here," she said matter-of-factly. "He's in the hospital."

He looked at her. Her angular face and pouty lips were enticing. "Huh?"

"Said he didn't get his medicine yesterday. His chest hurt so he checked in."

"He coulda told me," Jude responded, confused and irritated.

She made an "I don't really give a shit" face and closed the door. Now what? Should he try to go by himself? Hank was lying up in his hospital room, eating a great breakfast, getting Dilaudid by IV. Son-of-a-bitch.

He drove to Red's corner and was surprised to find him out so early.

Red said. "Got anythin'?"

"Ain' got nothin'. You?"

"Uh-uh," Red answered shaking his head. "Wha's up wif da ol' dude?"

Jude shrugged. "What's up with yours?"

"Got fucked up last night. Listen, I need a ride."

"Where?"

"Road trip." Red had never been farther than Deland. He was afraid. He'd heard horror stories of Blacks being harassed in southern states.

"How far," asked Jude, yawning, "and when?"

"Louisiana. Right now."

"What? Why? You got dope lined up there?"

"You might say dat." Red smiled evilly.

"What da fuck you got goin' on?" Jude asked, very interested. "C'm'on. Spill it."

"Eugene s'posed ta leave ta score. But he in the hospital. He gave me da money an' tol' me ta go and get it. He say it take 'bout ten hours ta get there." Red grinned.

"Holy shit. Hell yeah. Let's go."

Chapter 12

IN A HALF HOUR, they were on the road. They traveled on highways, along small country roads, past little towns, small cities, homes and farms. The world zipped by. Wind blew through the open windows.

They'd done their last stash. In the afternoon, Jude's throat felt swollen and full of phlegm. Hank had told him that was the first sign of withdrawal. He couldn't possibly be hooked. It had only been a few weeks.

Red said, "Wish we had some stuff." His arms and legs ached with a crawling, tingly, and nasty discomfort. "I feel like I'm gettin' a goddam cold," Red said, drawing the phlegm up forcefully into his mouth and letting a hocker fly out the window. "Ugh, shit. I ain' goddam jonesin', am I?" He rubbed his thighs and wrapped his arms around himself. "I ain' done that much."

Jude ached all over too. "How can we be strung out?" He shook his head. "You know, I never believed any of it. I never believed anybody got hooked. I thought it was just a story ta keep us clean."

"I know das right."

They arrived at six in the evening. Red made the call from the phone booth as instructed.

A deep, black voice answered. "Yeah."

"Dis Roosevelt Harris. Eugene done got sick. He sent me."

"Who dis is?" the man answered.

"Roosevelt Harris," he answered, trying to sound authoritative. "Eugene cousin. I mean, nephew."

"Who yo mama?"

Well, shit. Eugene didn't tell him who the family was. He said Mama's name. "Anne."

"Anne? I dint know Eugene had a sista name a Anne."

Red gulped. "I ain' sho they's officially brothah 'n sistah. You know, I don' zactly know da relationship."

The man hesitated for a long time. Finally, he said, "Wheah Eugene?"

"Someone stab him, an' stole his supply."

"You?"

Red hesitated. "Me? Like did I stab 'im? Hell, no. I done found 'im. I called da ambulance. He done give me da money and tol' me ta come out chear. I'm his main deala."

"Uh huh," the man answered, uninspired and unconvinced. "So, he jus' hand you a bunch a green and tell you to come on out ta Lou'siana fo 'im?"

"Uh . . . yeah."

"Awright. He give the directions to a park?"

"Uh huh."

"Be there at ten tonight. I gonna call Eugene. He home?"

"I dunno. He prob'ly ovah da hospital. Halifax."

"You alone?"

"No, white boy I deal wif brung me."

"White boy? A fuckin' cracka? Dat's mighty odd. Wha' kinda car ya'll ridin'?"

"Uh, a Toyota. Blue."

In the early evening, having nothing else to do, Red and Jude went to the designated drop zone. They sat on top of a beat-up, wooden picnic table and looked around. They smoked cigarettes, ached and worried, cleared their throats and spit sticky phlegm on the ground. They had the jitters. The sun dropped slowly, changing the look of the place, bringing on shadows. There was nothing much around—just a road and a stream—but no stores, no motels, no nothing. Just them and trees. They sat and sat.

Red lay back on the table and looked at his watch. "Nine thirty. Dis fucka betta show. I feelin' really fucked, man." He rolled around on the table with his arms wrapped around his chest.

Jude went off behind a tree and pissed. As he returned, four young black guys walked up, spread out like soldiers on patrol, inspecting the area.

One pushed Red's leg. He raised his head. "Huh?"

Jude came up slowly, unsure whether these guys were part of the transaction. They had to be.

"Got the cash?" one of the men asked.

Red hesitated, like he was trying to focus on them. "Who you?"

"Hey, I ax da questions. You got da green?"

Their faces were so dark that Jude couldn't make out any features. This was not the way either of them had pictured the exciting exchange of money for drugs.

"One a you was da one I talk to?" Red asked, his voice almost squeaking.

"Whatchu think? Da man gonna come on down to a public place ta see a fuck like you?" another one said.

Red was petrified. He'd been so hopeful that he was going to get the drugs to get well. This didn't seem right. It seemed like a shake down. He couldn't concentrate.

Jude felt very white, out-of-place and scared. If this was the deal, he didn't want to piss them off. But it didn't seem like the deal.

"When we see the money, you get the drugs," the first man demanded.

"The drugs here with you?" Jude asked, trying to sound self-assured.

"Don' ax questions like dat," demanded another man. "Dis our territory. You do it our way or split."

Jude looked at Red for a cue. Red stared back, wild-eyed and nervous. He didn't want to take a chance of losing Eugene's money. He wished Eugene had told him more. But he guessed if he brought the money out, he could still hold it till the drugs were in hand.

None of the guys looked strong. But at less than a hundred pounds, Jude wouldn't be any help. As for Red, he'd never fought a real fight with anybody. And they were both sick. Red turned and walked to the car, his stomach full of butterflies, reached under the seat and withdrew the paper bag. As he stood, he realized he'd been followed. He trudged back uphill and found Jude sitting on the table, surrounded.

Jude was just about certain now that this was not the deal. "How much product you sellin' us?" he asked.

"I told you to shut up," the first man said, sticking his dark face into Jude's.

"Dese guys ain' sellin'," he whispered to Red. "They're rippin' us off.

"They don't know who Eugene is. They don' know anything about the deal. They don' know whether yer here ta buy two bags or an ounce." He felt sick to his stomach, and something creeping through his intestines. He didn't know whether it was from fear and anger, withdrawals, or both, but he was going to blow chunks and hershey squirts soon.

Red was stunned, paralyzed with fear. He'd been screwed. Jude was right. These guys had no idea what they were buying. Now he had the money here and didn't know how to undo his stupid move. If these guys didn't kill him, Eugene or the jones that was taking over his body would. He felt like crying, puking, shitting, pissing. He didn't know what.

"Put the bag on da table," the first one ordered, pushing Red on the shoulder. Red clutched it against his gut. It was the last connection he had to peace and order.

One of them wrapped an arm around Jude's neck, the sharp bone of a forearm hitting his Adam's apple, and pushed what had to be a gun against his left temple. Another crammed a pistol into Red's gut.

"You like a bullet?"

Red felt tears stream down his face. He released the bag.

The man emptied the paper bag onto the table, and the four men hooted. "How much is zat?" one of them asked. "Jeeeezus."

"Holy fuckin' shit. We in da money," said another. "You suckers can come to our town any goddam time." He laughed uproariously. They all laughed, and split up the money, each tucking a packet away. "Lie down," demanded the first one. Jude didn't move fast enough. The gun struck the back of his head, and somebody tripped him. Suddenly he was face down.

Red lay down slowly, still trying to think of a way out of this hopeless mess. He wanted to undo everything. They'd fallen for it all like a couple of stupid chumps.

"Donchu get up fo half an hour. When you get up, you drive straight outta dis place. Go on back where ya'll came from, and don' come back." The others laughed.

One of them added, "You can come on back if you bring us a sco' like dis, any time." They all laughed again. "Any goddam time ya'll want."

They strolled casually down the hill, laughing, talking, leaving Red and Jude lying face down in the smelly dirt, in their shame and tears. Jude coughed, and choked, feeling the lumps and liquid come to his mouth—sour, nasty. He fought it back, but the fluid kept filling his mouth, and suddenly he wretched, puke spewing in the direction of Red, who responded, "Goddammit man, you stink. Jeeesus Christ. Cain' chu control yo'self,"

But just as he finished his sentence, his stomach erupted too, and he let go as well. "Uuughhh. Fuck," he said.

They lay on the ground for a long time, retching and puking, holding their stomachs and rubbing their arms and legs, their sickness seeming worse now that the possibility of dying a bloody and violent death had passed.

Finally, Jude tried to get up. His head throbbed, but the grinding in his intestines was more intense. Suddenly, he ran for the bushes, and he got his pants down just in time to spray runs all over the ground and bushes. "Oh God," he whispered to himself, "just get me through this. I'm so sorry I didn't believe in addiction. I'm so sorry for coming here. Help me." He writhed, feeling another wave of fluid erupt through his intestines. He fell to his side and lay there, his wet, burning ass hanging out, puking and shitting interminably, wanting to die.

The diarrhea hit Red too. He dragged himself to his feet thinking he had to pee, walked behind a tree and started, holding onto the tree for stability, but then he realized that his rectum was about to let go too, and he yanked his pants off and squatted. He hugged the tree, vomited and shit, and finally collapsed.

It was after three in the morning before Jude finally decided to try to get his body together. He grabbed leaves from bushes and tried to clean his ass, but it was all caked on like a paste. He couldn't see anything around him, but this place reeked. With the moonlight showing through the trees to guide him, he stumbled, with his pants around his ankles like a shackled prisoner, toward the stream. It smelled of sulfur. That was better than his odor. He grabbed a rock and leaned his ass into the water, but the rock moved, and he fell backward, hitting his spine on sharp, hard rocks. He cried out, but lay in the freezing water, feeling the shock of the cold hurt and numb his shivering body. Still lying on his back, he wet his hands and cleaned his face. His pants soaked water up like a wick.

Then Red stumbled down and cleaned himself up as much as possible, shivering and squealing every time he touched the freezing water to his body.

"Let's get out a here."

"God my ass is on fire," Jude said.

"I'm done with this shit," Red said.

"Whadaya mean, done?"

"Done. Done. This is it." He splashed water on his raw ass. "I'm worse than my mama. Anyway, I'll be dead as soon as I get home and Eugene find out."

Chapter 13

AS JUDE DROVE BACK the way they'd come, Red threw up out the window. Every mile or so, Jude pulled off to puke. They ached from the hair on their heads to the tips of their toes. Their skin crawled. The fluid flowing from their throats and asses burned.

"I ain' never felt so fuckin' bad in my life," Red commented, shivering. "I'm goddam freezin'. Cain't stop shiverin'."

Jude's teeth chattered. "We gotta get some dope. I think we're gonna have convulsions soon. I can't believe we gotta go through this in a car."

Jude saw a store with a sign saying DRUGS and pulled over. "Whadaya think about breakin' in?" Jude asked.

"What? You crazy? We ain' neva done nothin' like dat." Red shook his head vehemently.

"I'm sick a bein' sick. I don't care what happens. I wanna get well," Jude answered.

"No fuckin' way," Red responded. "Jus' park someplace. Should be almost over."

Jude ignored him and parked. He walked to the back door. It was locked. He'd never done a break-in before, so he wasn't sure what to do. He glanced around for an alarm. He didn't know what to look for, but he didn't see anything. He pulled the screen out, broke the window with a rock and climbed in. He rifled through a cabinet, looking for Dilaudid or something similar. Nothing. He saw a heavy floor safe. Leaning down with his lighter to inspect it, he heard a noise.

Red had become impatient and exited the car. He'd pulled the screen back and stood looking through the broken window. "C'mon, man; let's get outta here," he whispered loudly.

Jude said, "Just a minute." He tossed things around, searching.

"Come on," Red said again, but immediately felt a gun at his back.

A voice with a heavy drawl said, "Yer under arrest, nigger. Get yer ass down on the ground." The screen slapped against the wall. The man pushed him to the ground and put a knee in the small of his back.

Another man said, "Where's the other one?"

"Inside, I reckon," the man answered.

Jude heard the voices. He ran to the rear door, yanked off the heavy brace, flipped the lock and shoved the door open. He scrambled to the car, hearing vague voices in the darkness behind him. "Where's fuckin' Red," he said out loud to nobody. He jumped in, started it, and took off.

Headlights followed quickly behind him, and he turned sharply down a street, seeing a dead-end sign after he turned. He zipped through the gears hoping there'd be some kind of out. When he reached the last house, he saw no escape, so he continued, first bouncing up the heavy, steep curb, and then continuing through the yard, bouncing over unknown and unseen objects. At the rear of the house, he turned to avoid a fence and an old car, and felt a sudden, extreme thud, that seemed like it was pulling the guts out of the bottom of the car. He lost control and the front right fender smashed into something hard. The car swerved again and fell into a hole. His head hit the windshield and the passenger door. He lost touch for only a second, and then tried to get out, but he was too disoriented. Before he could regain his senses, the headlights were next to him, and a man aimed a rifle through the broken window.

"Yer under arrest, doper," the man said in a deep southern accent.

Blood seeped into his eyes. His head and body throbbed. He was ordered out of the car. He crawled out the window backward. A small crowd, some in pajamas and robes, stared. The man yanked Jude's aching arms back, cuffed him, and pushed him rudely to a pickup truck.

Red was shoved into a small, concrete-floored cell, with bars separating it from adjoining cells. A white guy lay on the bunk in one cell. A middle-aged black man was in another. Red stood over the aluminum toilet and pissed, holding a wall for stability. He still felt shaky, and just as miserable as he had all day. He wretched and dry heaved. He lay on a cot, curled into a ball, and begged God to save him. He let a silent sob come on but was careful not to let anybody see or hear.

Outside the cell, a doctor examined the gash on Jude's forehead and the lumps on his head. "He needs a couple of stitches," he said to a guard.

"Won't it just hold?" the guard asked.

The man shook his head no, pulled out a black leather doctor's bag, and was done in five minutes. Jude felt so bad all over that it didn't even hurt.

Red and Jude continued to emit putrid gas and bile all during the very long night and day in the jail cell. Other prisoners had said, "These fuckers reek, man," and convinced the guards to move them.

"When will it fuckin' end?" Jude had asked out loud more than once. He'd actually begged God for relief, saying he was sorry, that he'd never do it again, that he'd start going to church and become a believer. All his oaths and promises were useless.

Red had also prayed and begged God to relieve the pain and agony. He received no miracle either, but he felt better asking. And he honestly intended to keep his promises. He was convinced that drugs were not the way. There was no glamour here. Mama'd gotten straight, and he couldn't even honor her by being straight himself. At one point, he pictured himself in church preaching at the pulpit. But then that was going too far. He just wanted to get well.

Silently, they ate beef stew in the evening, which probably wouldn't have been bad on a good day. But they both hoped they wouldn't be here long enough to eat another meal.

"Whatchu think gonna happen in da mornin'?" Red asked.

"I dunno," Jude answered. "I don't know if my father's done anything to get me out."

"Well, dat won't help me. He dint do nothin' fo me last time. Whether I get out or not, I ain' doin' dope no mo'," he said. "Dis ain' no way ta spend a life. I done begged God fo help, and promised him, and I ain' goin' back on my word."

Jude flashed back on the last time he'd shot up and got a little thrill. He'd made a promise to God too, but now he'd get high again in a second. He'd meant it when he said it, but he didn't mean it now. He didn't believe there was really a God anyway.

* * * * * * *

In the morning, they were awakened rudely by a guard with a Deputy Dawg face and a big gut. "Git yer sorry asses up. Ya'll got court."

They'd both been picturing court in their minds all night. Jude wondered whether his father would be here, and whether he would have found a criminal law attorney to get him out.

Red figured he'd be at the mercy of a white judge, white guards, and every other white face in the room. He expected nobody to support him—no black faces, and no hope.

Wearing their gray and black striped cloth jail jumpsuits, with ankle bracelets connecting their feet to each other, and handcuffs holding their hands behind them, they were ushered out the back door, across the street, into the stately courthouse, through barren hallways and empty rooms, and suddenly into a courtroom with twenty or more people, including staff, police, a few other prisoners, and some spectators.

Jude scanned the room quickly, finding his father; Reverend Rogers, the minister of his father's church; a lawyerly looking dude, and to his surprise, Red's mother, Anne, all sitting at a lawyers' table. All right, they were here in force. And it seemed that they were even together with Anne, which made him very proud, and pleased with his father.

Red looked for a black face, and almost collapsed when he saw Mama sitting proudly with a table of white suits, including old man Armstrong. What was this? Did the old bastard have a change of heart? Was he going to help?

Their chains clanged loudly, raking along the old hardwood floors, as they were directed to seats alongside the table full of their supporters. Deputy Dawg, his dumpy, red-lined cheeks quivering and shaking, dumped them into hard wooden chairs next to each other, still connected. Jude looked over at his father, but received a dark, disappointed, hurt scowl. Red glanced at Mama and saw a shimmer of hope.

The judge, enveloped in a black robe, perused the file, shaking his head disdainfully. He looked at the boys, and asked, "Is there somebody representing David Jude Armstrong, and Roosevelt Harris, both of whom are charged with multiple serious crimes?"

"Yes, sir," the guy to Jude's left said in a gravelly voice, as he stood at the table. "My name is J. Atworth Holcomb, and I'm from Daytona Beach, Florida, and I am representing both of these boys."

"I take it that you are not licensed to practice law in Louisiana. I'll ignore that for a few minutes, but you will have to associate with counsel appropriately licensed in this state. Are you aware of the charges, Mr. Holcomb? Have you had the opportunity to counsel with the boys?" He dropped the file on the desk.

"I have not had the opportunity to talk to them. We just arrived late last night."

The old judge smiled and shook his head. "Mr. Holcomb, these charges could put these boys away for many, many years. We've got 'em both for breakin' and ent'rin' with intent to commit a felony, possession of drug paraphernalia, possession of marijuana, burglary, and so on. And we got Armstrong for evading an officer of the law and resistin' arrest." He took a gulp of water and dropped the glass back on the hard wood loudly. He cleaned water off his mouth with the back of his hand. "I'm willing to give you fifteen minutes ta talk ta the boys, if you want."

The lawyer fumbled some papers and files, looking lost. "Judge, I wonder if we could discuss a proposed resolution before having to put on a defense?" He glanced around the courtroom nervously. "Is there a prosecuting attorney with whom I can discuss a possible deal?" He looked back up at the judge, who was peeling a banana.

"Mr. Holcomb, we don't have time for all that legal posturin' and nonsense around here. We don't do 'deals.' The prosecutin' attorney, as you call him, has another job, and he gen'rally doesn't have time to come here on routine matters like this. All we're gonna do today is take a plea and either sentence 'em, set a sentencin' hearing or a trial, if they're stupid enough to plead not guilty in my court." He took a bite of the banana and munched like an ape.

Jude, Red, Mr. Armstrong, Anne, and the minister glared at the lawyer, hoping for some action. He saw their stares, hesitated, and commenced. "Judge, since I cannot negotiate a plea with the state attorney, and since we are in open court at a hearing, at which these defendants are expected to enter a plea, and about which we seem to be able to learn nothing of the charges . . ."

"Now wait here just a minute, fella," the judge interrupted. "We got all the documents right chear. Would you like to read the affidavits of the arrestin' officers?"

"Your honor, not meaning any disrespect of your procedures, sir. . . My point was merely that we would like the opportunity to examine avenues that are available, and we don't . . ."

"You don't what Mr. Holcomb?" He shifted heavily. "You don't like the way we do things up here?"

The lawyer appeared defeated. His hands trembled, but a determination and great effort appeared to be stewing behind his pale forehead.

"Your honor, if I may, I would like to introduce some people to the court." He spoke quickly, maybe too quickly for the old southerner, but like a man on a mission to avoid being interrupted. "I have with me one parent of each boy, and a celebrated and well-respected minister who runs a drug rehabilitation center, and we were hoping . . ."

The judge interrupted again. "You were hoping what, sir? That I'd just let these two criminals, these two hopeless, delinquent, drug addicts leave my jail and go off to some cushy place probably nicer than a federal pen?" He shook his large head and chuckled to himself.

"Judge, there is hope for these boys, and I'm sure your county would be just as happy for Florida taxpayers to pay for their room and board over the next few years instead of having to support them. Now, if I may . . ."

The judge looked up, scowling. "Are you implyin' that a criminal in this county can get off the hook because our taxpayers are too cheap to pay the expense of keepin' 'em in jail? Because I resent that, and I'm sure the whole town, and in fact the whole county would be pretty perturbed about that notion."

"No judge—er—your honor," Holcomb struggled. "If the court pleases, we'd like to let Reverend Rogers tell the court of the possibilities for rehabilitation. He has a wonderful . . ."

"Mr. Holcomb, this is a hearing in a court of law, not a sermon in a church," the judge began, wagging his finger at the lawyer.

Fortunately, Reverend Rogers stood up behind the table, and began to talk with his soothing, matter-of-fact, down-to-earth way, with a hint of a southern accent. "Your honor," he began, "My name is Able Rogers. I am a minister of a church in Daytona, but before I was a minister, I was a drunk. An alcoholic. Bottom of the barrel."

Jude knew Mr. Rogers well. He was listening to him like he never had before. His southern accent and mannerisms were much like those of the people in this area. That was a good thing, he was sure.

"A couple a years ago, a friend and I, a friend who was in the same alcoholic boat as I, developed alcohol and drug rehabilitation centers in our county. We eventually received state and local financial backing, including donations of land and old army barracks by the county. Your honor, our drug rehabilitation center for young people has been very successful. While we can't save everybody, and it takes the individual to decide they need help, our program has helped plenty of youngsters just like these two. They are still within the age range to be in the center for youth."

Red was spellbound. It wasn't that the man's words were so moving in and of themselves, but he had a natural way of speaking. Everybody was attentive, even the judge, who hadn't even looked like he was going to interrupt. The judge sat pensively, his hand propping his chin, and said, "Go on."

And so the minister did. He explained how the program worked, that females and males were separated, that they had group and individual therapy, counselors, many of whom had some background in addiction, either from schooling or from hard experience, that they encouraged and assisted the youngsters in attending meetings of A.A. and N.A., that the courts in the area trusted the program and regularly bound people over for treatment instead of jail, and that the facilities were not cushy. The judge continued to listen.

"Your honor," he said, winding down, "these parents will tell you of their intention to support and assist their children. There are circumstances that have resulted in this delinquency, and we'd be happy to go into them if that is necessary. But the bottom line is that I know we can help put these two boys back on the straight and narrow. We can make them productive citizens. We will make them the kind of boys that you will never have to worry about seeing again, if we can just have a chance with them."

The judge sat silently, his mental gears obviously working hard.

Red wondered how Mama had gotten here, so far from home. Like Red, she'd never been anywhere before. She couldn't possibly have traveled all the way across several states with a car full of white men—could she? Would they actually have let her in the car? Where would she have sat? What could they have talked about?

"Reverend Rogers," began the judge. "You have impressed me with your description of this project. I'm not convinced that boys who would commit such crimes will become useful members of society. I cannot fathom how somebody who would intentionally poison their own bodies and commit such depraved acts could be turned around." He hesitated for a long, long time. "But I am willing to give it a try. I will release them to the custody of their parents and you, to take them directly to the center. How long is treatment?"

"Generally, your honor, it's three to six months."

"Very well, I'm withholding adjudication, sentencing them to six months in treatment, with early release possible if you convince me to do so, but if either of them does not complete it for any reason, or commits any crime, or is found to use any drug during that time, I will bring him back here and put him in my jail for a long, long time." He smiled, looked at Holcomb, and added, "And we won't mind feeding them if they are prisoners in our county."

He slammed his gavel down, and said to Deputy Dawg, "Unshackle and release the prisoners to the custody and control of Reverend Rogers and their parents. And I thank you, Reverend Rogers, and Mr. Armstrong, and is it Ms. Harris?" She nodded. "For taking the time, and making the effort, to come here and lend your support."

The heavy chains clanged to the floor. The handcuffs were removed and set on the table. Roosevelt turned to his mother, who hugged him, weeping openly. Jude walked toward his dad and the Reverend. The Reverend moved to his side and put an arm around his shoulder.

His father looked at him, stern as ever, and asked, "How's the car?" Typical question for Mr. Armstrong, Jude thought. No hug. No compassion. Well, he'd gotten him out.

The sorry lawyer packed his papers and books into a large briefcase, and the group moved slowly out of the courtroom as the judge began the inquisition of another prisoner.

* * * * * * *

Jude's car was impounded right across the street. Jude almost cried at the sight of it. The entire chassis was bent and twisted. The front, rear and sides were dented, muddy, scratched, and colorless. The front windows were broken. Jude saw the outline of his head in the windshield. He'd loved that car. He had great memories of traveling on the highway, of Hank pretending he was racing, of shooting so much Dilaudid, so many times. And now it lay twisted, leaking water and dark fluids.

They all piled into the leather seats of Mr. Armstrong's Continental. Red and his mother sat in the back. The lawyer sat to their left. Jude sat in the front between his father and Reverend Rogers. They headed back along the same highway that had led Jude and Red to the Promised Land, where they were going to score so big, be so cool and successful.

Now, neither felt normal, but it was hard to say what was physical and what was emotional.

At mid-morning, Mr. Armstrong pulled into a small gas station. An attendant, dressed in a greasy, cloth jumpsuit, with oily rags hanging from the pockets, filled the tank, checked the fluids and cleaned the windshield. After the white adults had gone to the toilets, Red and his mother went around the building.

After a while, when they didn't come back, Jude decided he needed to go too. He rounded the corner to the side of the building finding the two of them standing, arms around each other, staring at the signs—"White Men"; "White Women"—and an arrow pointing around the building, saying "Nigger Men" and "Nigger Women."

Tears streamed down their cheeks. Jude said, "Ignore those signs. Just go right on in. It's okay."

When they didn't move, he pushed them toward the white-only restrooms. He didn't know if the signs were still supposed to be honored or were just relics from the past, but the attendant didn't come around, so nobody knew where they went.

As Mr. Armstrong pulled back onto the highway, Anne began quizzing Roosevelt about how their unfortunate trip to New Orleans had come to pass.

The others listened quietly, all a little uncomfortable. "Who sent chu out to New Awlins?" she asked.

"Ma, I don' wanna talk 'bout it."

"Rosy, Honey, I know you was dealin' fo Eugene. When you last seen 'im?"

"Ma," he whined, trying to whisper.

"He dead," she said.

"Huh? Who dead?"

"Eugene. Died da otha night. Somebody done stab 'im. There he was. In da baftub wif a blade in his gut."

Red couldn't believe it. He must have died moments after Red had left. So the supplier in New Orleans couldn't reach him. One more death related to drugs. Thank God he was over it. He was glad he wouldn't have to explain how he'd lost Eugene's money, and then felt guilty for his lack of compassion.

Jude glanced back. That was the end of that supply.

In the evening, they stopped at a diner near the Interstate. As Mr. Armstrong and Reverend Rogers led the group inside, Roosevelt felt the stares of the white faces. The group sat at a booth large enough for all six. Glancing among the six misfits like she wasn't sure what to say, a waitress reluctantly delivered menus. Red could see his mama was struggling to mouth and sound out the words. He reviewed the menu with her, wondering how she'd managed to order a meal on the way up. Probably she'd chosen what somebody else ordered.

Reverend Rogers asked for them to bow their heads, and he said a very short, quiet, inconspicuous grace. Jude was uncomfortable with the public display of religion, but he complied.

"I can't tell you all how pleased I am that it turned out so well," Mr. Armstrong said after they'd ordered.

Holcomb looked sweaty and fidgety. He excused himself and went outside. Mr. Armstong and Reverend Rogers watched him go with apparent concern. Anne seemed relaxed and at peace with herself.

Reverend Rogers described the drug rehabilitation center, which he said was called The Bridge. Jude figured maybe there'd be some hot girls, and he'd get laid.

But then Reverend Rogers began describing the very strict rules and regulations, and the fact that violation would result in immediate removal, violation of the court order, and jail. Then it didn't sound as fun.

Red asked his mother, "How you all get togethah?"

She whispered, "Pearl Mae. 'Member her? Mr. Armstrong don't like to talk 'bout it, but he done put her through college, at Bethune Cookman. She call his office, and he answer."

Mr. Armstrong said, "Pearl Mae is a bright young woman. She's almost finished her degree in education." He hesitated. "I'm sorry it took her to introduce us. But I'm glad to be able to put this team together for both of you boys." He grimaced again when he looked toward Roosevelt. "I realized that you were the same boy who'd been involved in that dead-girl episode, and I was not about to help you then. I'm sorry to say it, but I blamed you for that. In fact, I considered just leaving Jude in New Orleans, figuring maybe jail would do him some good. But Pearl Mae and Anne here convinced me. And of course, I've known Reverend Rogers for years, so I thought of him. I've followed his success in the treatment of addiction, and I've been impressed."

Holcomb returned when the food was served. It seemed that everybody at the table noticed the smell of alcohol.

Anne looked at the Reverend. "Suh. I heah you say you an alcoholic, but you don' drink none. I don' get dat."

"I have the sickness of addiction to alcohol. If I take one drink, I can't stop. So I do not drink. I will never be able to drink safely."

"So you don' believe in alcohol?"

He looked around, and his eyes fell on Holcomb. "Alcohol, in and of itself, is not necessarily bad. There are plenty of people, in fact, the majority of people who are able to drink socially, occasionally, and suffer no great harm from it. But some people have a genetic makeup that makes drinking a disaster for them. It runs in families. It's not the same as drinking too much. It's the development of a craving for it."

"I knows what a cravin' is," she said. "Plenty a times I say I ain' gonna do drugs no mo. I'se dead set I ain' gonna do it. But den sumpin happen. 'S like a light switch turn on and make me gotta have it. Den I cain' stop it."

"I know zactly what yer talkin' 'bout," said Red.

"Me too," said Jude.

"I'm glad you brought this up Anne. This means you all know exactly what addiction is."

Jude laughed. "I know my dad isn't one. He can drink a beer one day. Three the next, and none the next. I've seen him open a beer and let it go to waste. He's the same way with cigarettes."

Everybody but Mr. Armstrong and Holcomb laughed. Holcomb looked puzzled, but nobody brought him into the conversation.

"A normal drinker doesn't think anything of leaving a drink untouched," the Reverend said.

After the meal, Jude and others ordered coffee. Reverend Rogers opened a small container and withdrew a tiny white pill that looked exactly like a Dilaudid. Jude felt his heart accelerate. Reverend Rogers saw his excitement and simply stated, "sugar substitute." Then Mr. Armstrong took a packet of another sugar substitute and poured it into his coffee. Again, Jude became entranced as the fine white powder entered the dark liquid. His stomach tightened, and he felt the familiar taste in his mouth that came right before getting off.

Red caught the mirage and glanced at Jude, but Red's attitude was different, because he'd made up his mind that drugs were out of his life now.

Chapter 14

JUDE AND ROOSEVELT spent six months in The Bridge. They honed their cooking skills, becoming the chefs for the facility. Roosevelt grasped sobriety, and even was the main speaker at graduation. Jude snuck out a few times to shoot heroin, barely avoided being thrown out, and graduated without grasping the program.

After graduating from The Bridge, Jude had returned to his mother's house of insanity and to his job at Old South. His father had gotten his mom out of the river house and into a smaller fifties-style house. His father still had custody of his sister. But as an adult, Jude chose to be in his mother's home.

One morning, he felt particularly weak as he tried to rise for work. He finally managed to drag himself from the bed and stumble to the bathroom. He stood in front of the toilet, but nothing came out. He was woozy, swaying back and forth. He sat on the edge of the bathtub and tried to regain his balance. He felt faint—thought he might puke. He collapsed into the cold, hard, empty bathtub. He lay there for a long time, telling himself that he had to get to work. He just had to. Finally, he dragged himself up again, continued to feel like shit, and collapsed again. He felt like maybe he had to pee, and maybe to do more. He'd never felt worse with any flu, with any heroin withdrawals, or with anything. He'd never felt more on the verge of a dreadful death. He felt like he weighed a thousand pounds.

He grabbed the faucet and pulled himself up, feeling the plumbing shake in the wall. He again stood above the toilet, and the pee started to come. He held the towel holder to his left and swayed. Then he saw what was dripping out and almost gasped. It was exactly the color of Coca-Cola. He'd never seen or heard of such a thing. He tried to imagine what he'd eaten or drunk that could have turned it this color. He collapsed back into the bathtub.

Eventually, he felt the urge to sit on the toilet, and dragged himself to the toilet again. He struggled and strained. Eventually, something came out. He felt no better. Then he decided to see what the toilet contained, and he shocked himself again. The few little turds floating in the water were as white as chalk. No, no no, he thought. Something was really the matter with him. He'd never heard of anybody shitting white.

He just had to go to work. He dressed in his standard uniform of white pants, white shirt, and black shoes. He didn't even feel like smoking a cigarette. He drove over the bridge and arrived at work. He wasn't sure he could get out of the car. But he did. He performed only a few light tasks before the weakness hit him again. He went to the back corner of the storeroom and lay on top of some flour and rice sacks. He had no choice. He couldn't get up.

After a while, Mr. Roberts stood above him, asking, "What the hell are you doing Armstrong?"

Jude looked at him. He had trouble keeping his head up. "Sick," he managed.

"You're not sick. You probably just did something you shouldn't have."

"I'm sick. I don't know. I can't describe it."

The man sneered at him. "I don't really care, Armstrong. Get out of my restaurant."

* * * * * * *

On Monday morning, Jude arose and drug himself to his doctor's office. The doctor was an old guy with a foreign accent so strong he couldn't even understand him. Jude had visited him once before when he was unable to pee properly, and the Doctor had said "GC. You got da GC." Jude had asked what GC was, and the doctor had responded matter-of-factly, "Gonorrhea clap. You know."

This time, he approached the receptionist and explained that he felt so bad he had to see the doctor.

The nurse said, "Oooh. Yellow eyes."

Jude hadn't realized that.

The doctor touched his abdomen once and diagnosed his condition. "Hep," he said.

"You got da hep."

"What do I do?"

"I dunno. Where you get this? How you get it?"

Jude pointed at the crook in his arm.

"Serum hep. No contagious. Six weeks bed rest." He marched from the room.

* * * * * * *

Roosevelt strolled with a purpose. He was on his way to a meeting, the best place to be. He thought of the people he'd see there. They were all white, but it didn't matter. He felt comfortable with this odd group of misfits. There was Allan, the old dude with a clanging set of dentures who stood in the back of the room and made the coffee. He always enjoyed listening to Bullard, the ex-con who wore his hair in a flattop and loved to shock people with his tales of the inside. And he could never picture the interior of the smoky building without thinking of sexy and sweet Tara. She was exotic and cool. She had the sweet sexy look of a Black, whether or not she really had any of that blood in her. She kind of sashayed around the room, floating above the ground, shooting her sultry smile and moving her round butt just right.

The smoky room he loved so much was the long, wooden-floored interior of an old house, gutted years ago for the purpose of holding these meetings. Although it had no separate rooms, it felt just like his grandmother's house. An old desk and creaky chair were perched on a homemade, carpeted platform at the front.

The leader of the group, chosen from meeting to meeting, would govern the meeting from the platform. Fifty or sixty cheap, aluminum chairs stood in three sections surrounding and facing the podium. The trademark was the cigarette smoke, so thick that sometimes it seemed you couldn't see the other side of the room. Whether Roosevelt smoked during a meeting or not, his clothes and hair would be impregnated when he left. He loved this place.

Before he started attending A.A. meetings, he'd managed to stay clean, or mostly so. He'd spent more time in church. He was clean, but unfulfilled and anxious. He missed being high. He longed to escape. A glimpse of a saccharin pill, any powdery substance, or even a lit match or lighter would start his gut grinding. He could no longer criticize Jude for those thoughts.

One warm, summer evening he'd sheepishly entered his first N.A. meeting on the second floor of an old church building near Bethune-Cookman College. Three black men, a white woman and a white man milled about. Roosevelt recognized the white guy from the streets. The woman, sickly, skinny and sallow-faced, hung on the white dude's arm.

From the moment he arrived, Roosevelt didn't feel comfortable. Just like the N.A. meetings he'd attended inside, it seemed necessary to brag about doing more drugs than anybody else, and to throw in something outrageous, like a battle with an armed cop, a death, a particularly potent strain of drugs or something like that.

The meeting had seemed serious enough, with the Twelve Steps read first, along with some other traditional proceedings. But every story delved into details of some kind of drug adventure. By the time the meeting was over, Roosevelt felt a craving that he hadn't felt in some time.

He'd attended N.A. for a while, not always feeling as negative as he had the first time. After all, he kind of liked bragging too. He'd told his own stories about Linda's death, his own time in prison and The Bridge, and the disastrous trip to New Orleans. But he felt unfulfilled.

After a meeting one day, he was shooting the bull with an older black man. The man said, "I knowed you comin' up. How yo mama, Anne?"

"She good."

"Listen, Roosevelt, y'evah been to a A.A. meetin'?"

"Uh-uh."

"'S all the same, I reckon," the old man drawled. "Ya get hooked on drugs er booze. Ain' much difference. They'z a bunch mo white folks at the A.A. meetin', but they cool."

"But what about the physical part, the sickness?" Roosevelt asked, thinking that kicking heroin had nothing in common with putting down a drink.

"Far as I know, a real drunk see some serious shit too. Anyways, don' matta, this one fella what useta come 'roun' say da same thin' you say. He dint like comin' roun' heah 'cause he alus wanted ta do some dope aftawards. He say he don' feel dat way at A.A."

So Roosevelt gave it a try. The first time he'd entered the A.A. room, he felt moved. Maybe it was that the room was so packed with cheerful, friendly people, hugging, smiling and chatting with each other. Maybe the presence of God was in the room. Although he was the only Black in the room, he didn't feel any bias against him. He felt comfortable. He felt accepted. Even by the rednecks. These people shook his hand, hugged him, talked to him, and treated him like anybody else.

He didn't speak for the first few A.A. meetings. He sat, watched and listened. Every meeting had a particular opening process, just like the N.A. meeting, and then the chair would announce a topic, and call on people to discuss it. People would raise their hands, or the speaker would call on people. The ones who had a knack for putting recovery into eloquent descriptions would speak every day. Others would be quiet. Roosevelt realized that people would generally describe themselves in one of three ways—following their name with "I'm an alcoholic," or "I'm an alcoholic and addict," or "I'm an addict."

A couple of old-timers didn't care for people referring to themselves as addicts. They felt that it was an A.A. meeting place, and the addicts had their own place to go. They were a little more tolerant with the alcoholic/addicts than they were with the pure addicts. Roosevelt understood how they felt. But he had no place else to go, and he was convinced by some with a history in this club to keep coming back and ignore the concerns of these few.

One day, a few weeks after he'd started attending, the chair said, "The topic today is 'Higher Power.' For you newcomers, the Twelve Steps say you should rely on a power greater than yourself, a Higher Power. We all know the word 'God' is not used."

Roosevelt had heard these discussions before. He cringed remembering his attempt to make spirituality a topic at The Bridge.

Here, some people would say something like, "I turned the problem over to my Higher Power, who I choose to call God." Others regularly talked about God, while some adamantly stated that they didn't need to believe in God as a God in order to succeed in A.A. Roosevelt understood that A.A. had been created to give alcoholics non-religious tools to save themselves. The founders had known that while some might eventually find God, using that word too much in any of the literature would have kept many from getting sober.

An older woman raised her hand, and said, "When I got sober, I turned my life over to God. I started going to church. Jesus picked me up."

Some squirmed in their seats. Some smirked. It seemed to him that she'd gone too far. Roosevelt did believe in God. He enjoyed church, and he felt something in his life, which he attributed to God stepping in to help him. But he also knew that some A.A. members were turned off by discussions of God and Jesus.

The next speaker was a crusty old bastard who never smiled. He always told his story from the depths, with sincerity. He announced, "My name is Harold and I'm an alcoholic. This ain' no church. Bill W. and the good doctor left the word 'God' out of the early steps on purpose. You ain' gotta accept no God or Jesus into your heart or into your left damn foot ta succeed here. What ya gotta do is what the Twelve Steps say. Ya gotta accept that yer a goddam drunk. That yer powerless over alcohol. Ya gotta make a decision to turn yer will over to a Higher Power, whatever in the hell that might be ta you. Ya gotta make amends. An' ya gotta help other drunks. That's it. That's all there is to it. If ya wanna have Jesus in yer heart, that's up to you, but you and Jesus just keep it to yerselves." He shot a look at the lady and lit a cigarette.

A boy shot his arm into the air and was recognized by the chair. "Hi, ya'll. My name's Jay and I'm an alcoholic/addict. I'm happy ta be sittin' here today in my right mind and with all my clothes on."

The room erupted in laughter.

"'Cause when I was usin', I'd sometimes find myself out of my mind and without any clothes on."

The laughter continued.

"Ya know, I don't care about all this God talk. Every time we get on this subject, there's this big controversy. We got newcomers here today. Don't confuse these folks with all this talk. Ma'am," he said, looking at a thirty-something woman who sat shaking all over, "you can forget all this shit. If you wanna get sober, this is the place ta do it. If you later decide yer Higher Power is God, that's fine. If you decide yer Higher Power is Harold over there, that's okay too. We don't give a shit what you choose. It can be cigarettes, coffee, this room, your cat, Harold over there, whatever. But this is the place to be."

The quivering woman, dressed in a flowered, red dress, glanced up through her dark greasy hair and smiled a bit. A middle-aged woman beside her stubbed her cigarette and put her arm around the newcomer.

"Let me tell you," Jay continued, "you may think that I couldn't have suffered much from alcohol, bein's I'm only seventeen. But I'm a real drunk. I started when I was thirteen. Once I found a chemical means of escape, I couldn't stop. I sniffed glue; I sniffed gasoline; I smoked pot; I used drugs; and I drank. And I couldn't stop. Once I'd start, I didn't know what would happen. The last time I drank, I was on a binge of vodka for days. I started drinking from a bottle I found at my grandparents' house. Then, I convinced somebody to buy me some. And I just kept drinkin'. I drank it with tomato juice. I drank it with orange juice. I drank it straight. Now that's some nasty shit."

People roared with laughter.

"I couldn't find any more, so I walked into a liquor store, grabbed a two-liter bottle, and ran out. The guy chased me down the street, and I ran through some yards, jumped some fences, and cut myself up. But I never dropped that bottle. As I was jumping one fence, I caught my pants leg on a piece of wire, and was hanging there upside down, hangin' on ta my Higher Power, which at the time I chose ta call Vodka."

The crowd laughed again.

"The guy was gettin' close, so I carefully set the bottle on the ground, undid my pants and wriggled out. Now underwear was not an important part of my life at the time, although I have subsequently discovered the virtues and benefits of wearing them."

The crowd roared with laughter continuously.

"So there I was prancing along with only a T-shirt and a big old bottle of Smirnoff, my white ass showing and my privates danglin', and I rounded a corner and ran right into Mr. Law. An' he didn't seem impressed with the body that God gave me."

The audience continued to reflect their enjoyment.

"Anyway, like I said, I'm just grateful to be in my right mind and fully clothed today, and to hopefully stay that way in the future, one day at a time, with the help of the people in these rooms." He winked at the newcomer facing him on the other side of the altar and picked up his Styrofoam coffee cup to take a sip.

The chair looked around the room for somebody willing to share. Roosevelt felt an urge to raise his hand, instantly willing and hesitant, not sure what would happen. But the force got the better of him and he found his hand in the air. The chair simply nodded in his direction, so he began, "My name Roos'velt, an' I'm an addict."

"Hey Roosevelt," the room responded.

"I'm sorry I can't say I'm an alcoholic, but I never really had the opportunity ta drink that much before dope did me in. I'm shore ya'll don' want me ta go on out there and find out for sure if I'm a drunk too."

"No, you're all right," somebody chimed in.

"Anyways," he began again, trying to use the grammar he'd been studying. "I'm havin' a little trouble makin' out all this Higher Power stuff. I was raised goin' to church. I kinda like bein' there. I kinda liked bein' there even at the worse a my druggin'. That is, I'm no atheist, but church didn't help me when it come to keepin' clean." He cleared his throat.

People were looking at him, some nodding, some smiling. But nobody was responding with "Mmhmm," "Oh yeah," "Yes sir," "Yes Lord," or anything like he was used to in church.

"All I know is when I'm in these rooms, I feel somethin'. I don' know if it's a Higher Power or what, but seeing all ya'll clean, sober and happy—yeah, that's the thing. Happy. Man, I feel good, and I feel like there's no reason to dope." He hesitated for a second and saw the newcomer watching him. "And every time I see a new person come in, lookin' so scared and beat down, and I see how they come around in a few weeks, I think that's part of the Higher Power too. That's all I know. This is where I'm s'posed to be."

Somebody started clapping, and then they all joined in. Somebody hooted, and somebody else yelled, "You go, Roos'velt." His heart pounded. He hadn't expected to say so much. He hadn't wanted to talk in front of this group of white people. But when he got ready to talk, he just didn't care. And it didn't appear that they cared either.

After the meeting, people he hadn't noticed before came up to him. They said, "I loved listenin' ta you share," or "Yer gettin' it man," or "I'm glad yer here." Roosevelt stood smiling, accepting hugs from white strangers, young and old, business types, and biker types. Everybody milled about chatting and hugging. A couple of more or less attractive young women approached, and he had to admit in his heart that he got a little extra excitement when he hugged them than he got hugging a toothless old man.

Then Tara was there, smiling at him, her green eyes gleaming through the smoky air. A dimple indented the light brown skin of her face. Her hair hung in ringlets around her face. "Hey, Roosevelt," she said, extending her hand, "I'm Tara, and I really liked listenin' ta you today." Her voice had a southern, soulful smoothness to it. He stood dumbfounded, clutching her hand and saying nothing. She moved forward, still holding his hand, and embraced him with her other arm, giving him a peck on the cheek. Then she stood back again, gazing at him, still smiling brightly. "Cat gotcher tongue?" she asked, giggling.

Now his heart pounded. All conversations going on around him were in some other world. He just kept holding her hand. Finally, embarrassed and worried that next time she'd avoid him like he was some pervert, he managed, "I'm happy to meet you, Tara. And thank you for the kind words."

He released her hand. He wanted to ask her to go someplace for coffee or something, to just sit and talk, but he knew he shouldn't. She wasn't approaching him for romance, and he wasn't supposed to be dating anybody, particularly not another member of the group, at least until he had some solid time under his belt. Soon, they casually turned their attention to other people and eventually made it out the door without speaking to each other further.

PART IV

1970s

Chapter 15

A FEW MONTHS LATER, Roosevelt sat in his seat in the crowded A.A. meeting room. Tara asked to be let into his row. The people to his left shifted their legs to let her by. The only empty seat on the row was next to him. Her beautiful round rump glided right by his nose. Her aroma was spellbinding. Oh, dear God, thank you for this. But just as quickly, guilt washed over him, and he silently apologized for thinking God would care about his profane thoughts.

He got up the nerve, and whispered, "How ya doin', Tara?"

She smiled beautifully, and whispered into his ear, her full moist lips brushing his earlobe, "Could be better, but I'm happy ta be here." She placed her hand on top of his and squeezed. He thought he would faint.

The meeting wasn't exciting, but having Tara next to him was. The regulars told their regular stories. Tara seemed quiet, but nervous. He felt her presence.

At the conclusion of the meeting, Roland was chosen to stand at the front and give out chips. He announced, "These are chips, which mark our road to recovery. If you're just coming in or are returning from the war zone where you tried to drink or drug again, pick up a white chip. If you have one month today of continuous sobriety, free from all drugs and alcohol, pick up a yellow chip. If you have ninety days of continuous sobriety, pick up a red chip. Blue is for six months of sobriety. And if you've made it for one year of sobriety, and I don't believe we have any celebrating today, you'll receive one of these solid gold, brass medallions, signifying that you've gotten your life back." He stopped for effect and glanced around the room.

Roosevelt heard Tara sniffle. He glanced over to see a tear rolling down her smooth café-au-lait colored skin. Oh, God, he thought. He wanted to comfort her.

"Is there anybody here today who wants to try our way of life or is returning from a bad experience?"

Tara stood and slid back by him. He was too shocked, too hurt and too concerned for her to think lustful thoughts. She slid to the front, as graceful as ever, a stream of tears flowing down each cheek. She took the chip and a bear hug from Roland to tremendous applause. She returned to her seat. Roosevelt grasped her hand. She squeezed back, and trembled.

A few more chips were handed out. Then they all stood to close with the Lord's Prayer. He held hands with Tara on one side and a young man on the other. During the prayer, he felt the power of the group and God himself flowing like electricity through him.

After the prayer, he felt refreshed. He felt stronger than ever, more capable of making it through another day clean and sober, a day at a time. He turned to Tara, and they hugged. Then, feeling concerned about how it might look, he turned away and greeted and hugged other people. She did too. He kept her in his sight.

When there was a lull, he escaped from his final conversation and returned to her. "Tara, would you like ta grab a cup a coffee, either in the back room or someplace else?"

She looked at him, stalled, and finally nodded. "Let's go someplace." They agreed on Denny's, the staple of A.A. post-meetings.

They sat in a booth and compared notes on their lives and their histories that led them to A.A. Roosevelt felt so close to her. He learned that her father was black, and her mother was from Central America. That was why she was exotic. He'd never met anybody who wasn't either black or white.

Roosevelt said, "I gotta say, Tara, sobriety's the greatest gift I evah received."

Tears welled up in her eyes.

"I'm sorry," he said. "I didn't mean ta getcha choked up again. Let's talk about sumpin else."

"No," she said, wiping her cheek with the back of her hand, "I'm sorry to have let you and everybody else down. I'd been clean over two years, and I don't know how I coulda been so stupid. I was sittin' on the couch in my friend Angela's house. There were a couple a people there. And this guy showed up and put a six-pack of Colt 45 tall boys in front of me on the coffee table. I was so startled, I just looked at 'em. And this feelin' came over me. I remembered the good times. Didn't even think of nothin' bad that had ever happened to me. I just said to myself, whoa girl, look at that. 'S party time. Time for some fun. I tell ya before I knew what'd happened, I'd downed two, and shared some smoke. And then I was really fucked. I been loaded now five days. All that clean time. Gone in a flash. There wasn't nothin' to stop me."

Roosevelt had some trouble getting all of this. He heard people talk like this in A.A., but he still thought that with some willpower, and a real God, if you decided you were finished with drinking, then you were.

"I'm glad yer back, Tara. I get inspiration from you."

She smiled. "Thanks. You're cool, Roosevelt. But what I did, isn't much for inspiration."

"No, really, it's good. Seeing somebody with clean time go out is the biggest lesson."

Roosevelt struggled, and asked, "Can we have coffee again?"

"Roosevelt, you're a newcomer. Right now, I am too. We'll hafta wait till we both got some clean time. Then, maybe, if you're good, we can." She smiled at him coyly. "All right?"

"Okay," Roosevelt agreed, nodding. "I'll wait."

"But," she said, still grinning, "I am going to a speaker's meeting tonight, and if ya happened ta be there, I'd shore be sittin' with you."

He felt his face light up. He nodded vigorously. "You got it."

They stood and embraced, maybe a little longer than an A.A. hug, and she gave him a peck on the cheek.

* * * * * * *

A new manager had rehired Jude at Old South. One morning, he was reviewing orders and stacking fish, meat, and vegetables in the window.

Roosevelt's mother leaned in the window and smiled, showing erratic and damaged teeth. "Hey Jude," she said. Wrinkles stood in the dark skin around her tiny eyes. "Listen, what time you get off?"

"Three."

"Me too." She looked down, and then at him. Then she spun her eyes around the room and then back at him again. "Jude. Can ya give me a ride somewheres?"

"Well, uh, yeah," he said, wondering why she was acting so nervous. "Gotta pick up a package in Tampa."

Feeling his gut begin to churn, he asked, "What kinda package?"

"Scag."

He thought his heart stopped. He visualized himself jabbing a needle into his arm, booting the plunger. He could almost feel the deadening intrusion of the drug in his system. "Whatchu talkin' 'bout, Anne?"

"I got a buddy, Jerome. He need a package pick up. Girl's gettin' married tamorrow, so he cain't go. He gonna give me some product if I get it."

"Sure Anne," he responded. "We gonna do some?"

"Hell, yeah," she said, laughing.

Leaving town, they stopped at Joe's Food Store and stocked up on cigarettes, Slim Jims, Coke and other goodies, and then headed west. As Jude cruised up and around the ramp from 92 onto I-4, he thought of the way old Hank always slammed through the gears with a grin on his weathered face.

They smoked cigarettes and chatted. They passed downtown Orlando within an hour and continued past the highway signs for Disney World, which had opened two years before. Jude wanted to go there someday.

Jude recollected traveling with Hank to doctors' offices at various exits they passed—shooting up in vacant lots, orange groves, woods and lakefronts—and he recalled the hapless cops following them around in various small towns and larger cities. That had been the life. He'd enjoyed making the cops look like fools, getting the doctors to give them drugs, obtaining cheap, legal drugs directly from drug stores, and the notoriety. Everybody in town knew they'd come to Main Street at night with a full supply.

He enjoyed the ride today because he loved being on the road. He searched for radio stations, finding few. He anticipated with fear and excitement the dull explosion of heroin in his veins.

After a long silence, Anne said, "Need ta stop an' see Roos'velt."

"Oh, yeah. He's over by Tampa, ain't he? How's he doin'?"

"Great. Straight. He be in Saint Petuhsburg." She smiled proudly.

Jude hadn't seen Red for a long time but had trouble imagining him straight.

At some point his mind turned to sex, like it always did. Jude ran through his memory bank, reviewing the sexual escapades in which he'd succeeded, had messed around so much he felt he'd succeeded, or had succeeded in his mind only. He thought of doing it with Anne, but she was too old.

They arrived in Tampa and followed the hand-scribbled directions to a small apartment house. They stood and stretched for a minute, lit cigarettes, and started for the stairs.

"Wait a minute," she said, stopping. "I ain' sho y'oughta come up. He be 'spectin' me alone."

"Anne," he said, queasy, "Don' fuck me now. I done drove ya all the way over here."

"Ain' gonna fuck you none. Jus' hang out heah a minute. I'll getcha invited up." She walked up the stairs.

He saw her knock. The door opened. She spoke for a minute. An older white guy's head popped out and shifted both ways. She went in.

Jude finished his cigarette and lit another from the butt. Before too long, she hung out the door and motioned for him to go up.

In the room, the scruffy white guy sat at a cheap kitchen table in the middle of the living room, working on some dope bags. Jude thought he'd have a stroke just looking at it.

"Dis Paul," she said, motioning. Paul looked up and almost nodded an acknowledgment.

Paul fixed up a syringe and handed it to Anne. Then he prepared two more. Soon the three of them were pushing and pulling the plungers, their eyes fluttering and rolling, all in utter spiritual silence.

Before long, they left the apartment, and outside Jude asked, "Ya get it?"

"Naw. Ain' got it tanight. Gotta come back tamorrow."

"Anne, shit. We gotta work tomorrow."

"Cain't. Gotta stay."

Jude worried about his job but was enjoying the high.

"Le's go see my baby," she said, her voice dragging.

* * * * * * *

Roosevelt was also working again for Old South, as an assistant manager-in-training.

He'd learned a lot working with the manager, Mr. Woszisky, a tall, white, balding man, with smiley eyes and hang-dog jowls.

He regularly attended meetings, read the Big Book of A.A., wrote letters to Tara and described his hopes and fears in his daily journal.

One day he delivered some bags of flour to the bakery area. The baker, an old, white man named Charles, was in a piss-ass mood.

"Coulda got that myself faster," Charles almost hissed.

Roosevelt fought to calm himself. Losing his serenity would only serve to burn a hole in his own gut, while not harming Charles one bit.

Wanting to cool off, he went into the walk-in cooler. He stood in the humid, cold air, looking around at rounds of roast beef wrapped in plastic, and trays of leftover meats to be used for a goulash, macaroni, spaghetti or stuffed peppers. He tried to decide what he would pick up if somebody came in. His anger was slowly replaced by guilt. Would he have been so pissed if a black man had said the same thing?

He said a little prayer in his head. "Lord," he said, "I know Charles didn't mean nothin'. Prob'ly just havin' a bad day. I turn him over to you. Amen." And he felt better. That was it. It was over.

He walked straight toward the bakery area. Old Charles was leaning against a large beater, which was manipulating some batter. Roosevelt just smiled and nodded. Charles regarded him silently.

Then the old man spoke. "Mr. Harris, I need a little yeast."

Roosevelt went back into the cooler, picked up the yeast, and delivered it promptly with a smile.

The man said, "Thank you."

Roosevelt said, "You're welcome," and moved on.

He went from station to station, helping, talking, getting supplies.

Later, Mr. Wo quietly asked him, "Did you have a run-in with Old Charles?"

"Well," said Roosevelt hesitantly, "We had a bit of an awkward moment, but it passed."

"I think he's drinking again."

"Huh?"

"I think he's fallen off the wagon, you know? He always gets real sullen and obnoxious when he starts drinking."

"So," Roosevelt said, "this isn't the first time." Roosevelt had been working very hard on his English grammar and diction.

"No, happens about once a year." Wo shook his head sorrowfully. "The old coot's in A.A., but he'll just up and decide one day he's gonna get a bottle, and that's it."

Roosevelt tried to grasp it. In the past, he wouldn't have believed that alcohol could so completely take over a life. But he'd heard and seen enough in A.A. rooms to understand that addiction to alcohol was real and devastating. He thought he understood something about the pain that the old man was suffering.

* * * * * * *

During the dinner rush, Roosevelt went to a secluded rear storage area looking for a box of coffee filters. When he flicked on the light, he heard a noise in the back. At the end of an aisle, he saw a shoe and a white-shirted belly.

"Who's down there," he called.

Silence.

He approached slowly. "Who's there?"

Roosevelt reached the end of the aisle, to find Old Charles, the baker, staring back at him nervously.

"Charles, what are you doin'?" Roosevelt asked.

"Nothin'," Charles answered, his eyes darting around.

Roosevelt eyed him up and down, looking for the shape of a bottle. He smelled alcohol.

"Where's the bottle, Charles," he asked, forcing himself to remain calm.

"What bottle? I ain' got no bottle."

"Charles, I can smell it on you."

The old man stared back at him. He looked both angry and sad. Roosevelt understood. He pictured himself sitting in the dark someplace jabbing a needle in his arm. It wasn't much different. The old man had an addiction. The old man was sick.

"Listen, Charles, I understand. I'd like to talk to you about this later. Get on back to your station before somebody realizes you're gone."

He backed up so Charles could escape. The old man shuffled up the aisle, subtly shifting the small plastic flask from his rear pocket into a front pocket, hidden by the apron.

Roosevelt stood in front of the coffee filters trying to regain his composure. "There but for the grace of God go I," he thought, repeating a slogan often heard in A.A. rooms.

The worst thing, though, was that for a split second in the storage room, or maybe longer, he himself had thought of the beauty of escape. He'd had a craving. And it scared the hell out of him. How could this sad situation make him feel like that—after all this time being clean?

* * * * * * *

At the end of Charles' shift, Roosevelt said, "Charles, could I meet you for a cup of coffee?"

Charles stopped cleaning the tabletop and turned to him. "Sir, please stay out of my business," he said under his breath.

"Charles, I understand."

"You don't understand a damn thing," Charles retorted and turned away.

Roosevelt stood for a few minutes. But he knew there was no use trying to convince an angry man who hadn't reached his bottom to consider anything.

Chapter 16

ONE AFTERNOON BETWEEN lunch and dinner, Roosevelt stood in the fry-cook station peeling shrimp.

Old Charles shuffled up. "Ya got visitors," he said, an odd, perplexed look on his face.

"Visitors?" Roosevelt asked, thinking of a district manager, a health inspector or other work-related visitor.

"They're drinkin' soft drinks, out in the dining room." Old Charles looked at him uneasily.

Roosevelt walked toward the front line, passed the empty food tables, and turned toward the dining room. Before he could adjust his eyes to the darkness, he heard a gravelly, heroin-induced, "Dare my baby." His stomach tensed. Not a nice surprise. He knew the sound of her speech.

Mama staggered toward him and lamely embraced him. "Look atchu. You look like a real man." She grabbed him by the shoulders and shook him. "Look a dis, Jude. Ain' 'e cute all dressed in his starched white shirt and little bow tie?" Roosevelt cringed again.

Jude be-bopped up, held out his hand, palm up, and said "Yo, dude, 's up?" His voice also had the deep, slow, gravely, failing tone of heroin in the system.

Jude thought Roosevelt looked like any boring old working stiff. His neck had thickened, his shoulders and chest had become broad. His hair was short. He still wore his silly clothes.

He didn't walk like a druggie. He walked like a businessman.

Roosevelt slapped Jude's open palm and turned his own over, not wishing to support this situation, but not wanting to be rude. He didn't want his employees to see them or hear them. Thank God Wo wasn't here. What could they want? He escorted them to the most private area of the dining room, far from the line and all doors to the kitchen. He sat, a dozen questions swirling through his mind.

The two staggered and swerved before falling like sacks of potatoes into their seats.

"Uh, whatcha'll doin' here?" he asked, trying not to sound negative.

"Nothin'. Jus' came ta see ya," Mama answered.

"Y'all came all the way just to see me? Somethin' the matta?" He felt himself sliding into low slang, but it just kept coming out that way.

"Naw, Rosy. Ain' nothin' da matta'," Mama said, rubbing her hand over her nose.

"I believe ya'll high, aincha?" he asked, smiling so they wouldn't know whether he'd approve of an honest answer or not.

The two looked at each other and then back at him. Mama answered, "Jes' done a li'l taste."

He nodded. "Bring it with ya, er ya get it heah?"

They considered each other again, and then she answered, "Heah."

"How'd ya find it?"

"Had a name an' address. Went an' scored."

"So," Roosevelt continued, feeling like a prosecutor, "Ya'll came all the way heah ta do one little hit?" He hesitated because he knew the next sentence was untrue. "Ain' dare some mo, like if I wanted ta do some?"

Again, they considered each other. "Well, yeah," she answered. "Tamorrow."

"Ain'cha goin' home today?"

"Uh, uh," Mama answered. "Gotta stay."

"Why?" he asked.

"Roosevelt," she said, matter-of-factly, "we need a place ta stay tanight. Can we stay to yo crib?"

Oh shit, he thought. This was all he needed. But how could he reject his mama and former best friend?

He finally consented. He ushered them out the front door so nobody else would see them. As they left, Jude whispered to him that he'd like him to call the Old South in Daytona to tell them some excuse as to why he was at an out-of-town store and wouldn't be at work tomorrow.

After struggling for a response, he said, "Jude, I jes' cain't do dat. You gonna hafta make yo' own excuses."

* * * * * * *

Jude and Anne went into the black area of town and found a soul food restaurant.

The restaurant was owned by Mama Flo. She greeted them, took their order, cooked the food and served it. They had a smorgasbord of greens, fried chicken, cornbread, and beans. It was great.

Halfway through the meal, Mama Flo stood beside the table, arms crossed over her protruding belly, or maybe her breasts—it was hard to see where one ended and the other began—, and asked, "Food all right?"

"Yes, ma'am," Jude answered, trying to swallow and nodding. "Food's great."

Anne smiled and mumbled something through stuffed cheeks.

"Where you all from?" Mama Flo asked. Her flabby cheeks jiggled like there was something in them.

"Daytona," Anne responded, clearing her mouth.

"Ya'll a long way from home. Whatcha'll doin' heah?"

"Came ta see my baby. My boy work over ta Old South."

"Oh," the old lady said, now smiling. She probably had just come to the conclusion that this was not a drug-induced, cradle-robbing, racially mixed-sex situation. "Das nice. What he do dare?"

"Assistant manager," Anne answered proudly.

"Well, das fine. Jes' fine," the old lady responded smiling. She cleaned her hands, grabbed some empty plates from the table, and made her way back into the small, open, homelike kitchen.

They paid cash, returned to where they would do a deal in the morning, and copped two more bags. They got off and then went to Roosevelt's.

* * * * * * *

Roosevelt wasn't at his apartment, so they stood on the balcony outside his apartment waiting and smoking, enjoying the evening and the drugs within them. She was happy. She would touch his arm, giggling, and put her head on his shoulder.

He kept thinking, this old lady's Red's mom. And my God she's old. Look at her. He wasn't sure if she was flirting or not, but he thought so. Would he do it? Well, maybe.

He started touching back, getting a little closer, trying to determine what was going to happen. He was inept. He never even understood whether a woman was interested, or it was in his own head. But little by little he convinced himself that he and Red's old lady were gonna do it. He was pleased that he was full of heroin, because that would help him to perform well and not explode like a school kid.

* * * * * * *

Roosevelt arrived. With a stern, no-nonsense look on his face, he nodded and said, "Mama."

Roosevelt started in on a lecture, saying he would not permit drugs or alcohol in his apartment. He'd forgotten where he came from. His jive talk from this afternoon was gone. Little did he know that drugs were within the people who were in his apartment, and therefore drugs were already in his apartment.

* * * * * * *

At first, Roosevelt was lost in a dream, rocking on the waves in a small sailboat, the boom banging back and forth. He'd lost his way in the dark. The boat rocked incessantly and noisily despite the rather calm water. He dreamily recalled the few times he'd been on a boat, always with his old friend Jude. He'd never actually been on a sailboat. But he accepted that he was on a boat now, and Jude was there, and then he was not. His dream continued and altered itself, leading him into rough water, and then into a narrow stream, and then into the desert observing a drill pumping oil, and finally into a room. Gradually, he began to question in his mind why the sound of the boom continued now that he was in a room, and no longer in the boat. He was tired, trying to wake up enough to figure it out.

Suddenly, his eyes burst open with a start. Goddammit. It was no dream, and no boat. It was the sound of people fucking, the incessant banging of a headboard against a wall. He'd heard his neighbors do that a few times in the months he'd lived here, but this was the wrong wall. This was the wall of the room where he'd allowed Mama to sleep. Oh my God, he thought. How could this be happening? His former best friend, a junkie, going to town on Mama in Roosevelt's own crib.

But then Mama was really the culprit here. He'd invited her in because she was his mama. She'd shown up high, getting higher. She'd brought Jude along. After all, he'd suffered because of her drug abuse and deserting him when he was young, she had the nerve to show up high and have sex with Jude, loudly, right here in his apartment.

He tried to go back to sleep. He tried thinking of tomorrow's duties and his goals. He tried and tried to block out the noise. After another dreadful half hour, he yanked on exercise clothes, drove to a parking lot next to the public beach, parked and walked briskly up the beach.

Chapter 17

ROOSEVELT WAS HELPING at the salad line when Wo called him to the office. Roosevelt was uneasy. Maybe Wo'd heard about Roosevelt's drug-addicted mother and friend showing up.

"Got a call from the home office," Wo said. "You're moving on."

Roosevelt wasn't sure whether that was good or bad. "Moving on?"

"Getting your own restaurant," Mr. Wo said with satisfaction. "I'm proud of you. You're the first who ever made it through the rigors here and went straight to managing your own store. You've done really well."

Wo went out to survey the line and work areas, leaving Roosevelt on the phone with the home office. He learned that he was going to management training for one month in New Orleans, and then he'd manage the Daytona restaurant.

He was elated. All his hard work was paying off. The executives acknowledged his value and worth. It apparently didn't matter that he was Black. He hoped it wasn't because he was Black.

Then he pictured the trip and stay in New Orleans. He didn't have good feelings about that place, where he and Jude had gone with high hopes of getting rich and high, and ended up getting robbed, arrested, stuck in jail and sentenced to rehab.

He cleaned up, counted the till and arranged everything for the following morning. He didn't tell anybody about the change. He wasn't sure what to say. Wo came up to him at the end of the evening. "So, what do you have to say for yourself?" He grasped Roosevelt's shoulders and squeezed, grinning.

"I'm very happy. I appreciate whatever you did or said."

At home, he cleaned up debris his Mama and Jude had left strewn about, and then went into the room he'd put Mama in. The sheets were bunched at the bottom of the bed. Cum stained the bare mattress. He was afraid he'd puke.

He got everything organized and clean and went to a late meeting. He wasn't in the mood to share. Afterward, he walked on the beach, for the second time in twenty-four hours, and the second time in months.

* * * * * * *

As Anne and Jude approached the Disney area west of Orlando, on their way home to deliver the product, she declared, "I wanna get off." Jude had been wanting to do a taste. It had been some hours since their last hit, and they had an ounce right here.

"Find a grocery store," she said.

"For what?"

"Gotta get some brown sugar ta cut dis shit a little," she responded, grinning, her tiny dark eyes almost sparkling with delight.

When they had the brown sugar, Jude checked into a Ramada Inn. The desk clerk seemed suspicious since it was just a little after noon. In the room, they wasted no time. The dope had been packed into a rubber. She scooped out a small amount of the rich, moist powder and replaced it with an equal amount of brown sugar. She doled out a small amount of their new personal stash into their two spoons.

As Jude pushed in the final boot, he worried that maybe it was too much. He swayed but couldn't steady himself. He collapsed on the bed. "Fuck," he said, hearing his voice echoing like it was in another room. He'd never been this loaded. For a second, he thought he'd puke.

Anne was lying on the bed on her back. Her eyes were closed. The syringe hung from her wrist. Jude worried that maybe she'd gone over. He nudged her. She groaned. They lay motionless for a while.

Eventually, they got it together enough to screw. Afterward, they decided to get high again. They continued the two activities throughout the day and night. From time to time, Jude worried about his job, and Jerome. But he didn't know Jerome, and Jerome didn't know him. He was home free. He could get high as long as he wanted. But Anne could be in trouble. "Oh well", he thought. She cut it. What could he do about it?

They changed motels twice in the next two days. Finally, they did the last of their stash and returned to Daytona. He dropped Anne off and went home.

* * * * * * *

As Roosevelt neared New Orleans to enter management training, he felt weak and beaten. On the way into the city, he'd seen the drugstore where his last trip here had ended so badly. Now he passed the hill where they'd waited in vain for the drugs to show and had kicked heroin for the first time. Anxiety rolled over him. He knew he shouldn't feel this way. It was that bottom that had led him to where he was today. He should be grateful. But that was hard. Very hard.

Although he loved traveling across the countryside of America, to see new places and vistas, to enjoy freedom, he feared racial discrimination. He never knew what to expect as a black man in a white world. Would he be looked down on, treated rudely, or maybe even threatened or assaulted? He always questioned his own behavior, worried that he may appear rude.

This morning, in fact, he'd stopped in a country store for gas and cigarettes. He parked in the self-serve lane, and walked inside to pay, like he always had to at home. He said, "Gonna fill up on pump 3," and held ten dollars in his hand.

The clerk, an old white woman, looked at him, with what seemed like fear. It pissed him off.

Then she said, "You didn't pump it yet."

"Figured I had to pay first," he said, waving the money.

"Well, you gonna pump the whole ten?"

"Don't know. I'm gonna fill it up."

"Just get on out there an' fill 'er up, and then come on back in."

"Yes, ma'am. Can I use yer facilities first?"

"Ain't workin'."

He muttered to himself out loud as he went back out to pump the gas. He was pissed. She'd obviously said that because he was black. How do you ever know what these honkies expect, he'd thought. He'd banged the levers and handles, exasperated by the nonrational rules and lack of rules.

Then he started second-guessing his own attitude. Maybe the restroom was actually out of order. She'd trusted him by telling him to pump before paying. By the time he finished pumping, he decided he owed the lady a tenth step—the tenth of twelve A.A. steps—an apology.

He tried to put on a smile as the screen door slapped closed behind him. The woman was puttering around, organizing packs of cigarettes. She didn't look up at him. He stood at the counter, wondering how to get her attention without causing more difficulty.

"Ma'am," he said finally. "Good mornin'. I pumped seven dollars. And I need a pack a Kools please." He smiled at her.

She glanced up, took his bill, rang up the sale, and started handing him change. He struggled to get the words out, but finally managed, "I apologize for bein' rude before."

"Ain' nothin' honey," she responded, surprising him. Honey? That was certainly a first. "You ain't from 'round here, are ya?"

"No'm. Goin' to New Orleans. I'm in management at Ol' South Plantation Buffet."

"I know Ol' South. There's one up ta La Grange. Good food."

He thanked her and turned to leave. "Listen," she said. "Ya need ta use the restroom, ya can use the ladies', long as ya lift the seat and then put it back down."

He smiled. "Thank you ma'am."

* * * * * * *

The diarrhea struck Jude in the middle of the night, several hours after the itchiness and crawling skin had started, and long after the lump in the throat had settled in. Then came the vomiting. He wretched and shit, until only bile came out of both ends. His ass and throat sizzled. His gut wrenched. He filled up the bathtub and lay in it, not sure if the water was hot or cold. Immersed in water, the feeling of his skin changed, but he wasn't sure if it was better or worse. Suddenly, he was very cold. His teeth began chattering. His bones hurt. He shivered violently. How'd he gotten so hooked so fast? Well, he'd done a quarter ounce in just the past few days.

At three a.m., he went snooping in his mother's medicine cabinets, pushing pill bottles and other contents around, trying to find something good to help him out. Eventually, he located a bottle of tranquilizers. He popped three. Half an hour later, he thought the relief wasn't coming fast enough, so he took three more. A while later, he took even more.

At some time, Jude awoke, groggy. Blurred faces hovered above him. Their mouths twisted slowly and odd sounds emitted. He couldn't make out what they were saying or who they were. He tried to talk. But his own mouth made the same far-away, burbling sounds they were making.

He realized he was in a hospital emergency room. He didn't know when or how he'd gotten here. He tried to lift his head but felt too weak and dizzy. He started gagging. The bile burned. Nothing came out. His intestines surged. His ass burned. He tried to swallow. His throat was killing him.

An impatient wispy man appeared above him, dressed in a white hospital coat. "Well, you've gotten yourself into quite a pickle," the man said.

"Huh?"

"You overdothed. We had to intubate you. How do you feel?"

"Like shit."

The man grinned. "You can either leave or admit yourthelf into the mental ward."

Jude collapsed again. He tossed and turned uncomfortably. Eventually, he was awake again. He signed the admission form to the mental ward.

* * * * * * *

Roosevelt drove to Old South to get his bearings for the following morning, checked into his room, and went out to find a restaurant for dinner. He was feeling great—on top of the world. Who would have dreamed that a successful young guy like him had ever suffered such humiliation and catastrophe in this city before. He entered a restaurant and stood to be seated. The hostess said she didn't have a seat for a single person available and asked whether he'd like to sit at the bar.

He said, "Sure," and climbed the couple of steps to the bar area.

He lit a cigarette and studied the menu. The bartender asked what she could get him. He glanced up, took in all the bottles around the bar, hesitated for a second, thinking of the things he'd learned in A.A. and, in the next second, convinced himself he was in A.A. only because it was a good way to deal with his drug problem. Alcohol had never been a problem for him.

He ordered a Budweiser. As he waited, he questioned himself about whether this was a good idea. But he'd already ordered it, would have only one, and should just enjoy it.

He ordered a steak and fries, feeling like he should also enjoy a meal of a little expense, to celebrate his new career. He'd arrived at the pinnacle of his career. He found himself smoking too many cigarettes while waiting for his meal.

The server, a not-so-bad-looking white girl, said, "I haven't seen you here before. What's your name?"

"Roosevelt. Yours?"

"Mary. Like a free drink because the food's late? Whatever you want."

He hesitated. Free drink. He didn't even know what he liked. "What do you suggest?"

"I got a drink for ya. Guarantee you'll love it." She turned and started pouring liquids into an aluminum container, threw in some ice cubes, capped it and shook. She poured it into a glass and, grinning, plopped it down in front of him.

He sipped it. It was amazing—a little sweet—smooth. It tasted nothing of alcohol. He sipped it slowly, more to be polite than for any other reason. He wanted to down it. Soon his steak came. It was exquisite.

Halfway through the meal, Mary brought him another of her special concoctions. By the time he finished the meal, he felt wonderful. His view of the world was altered. Everything was smooth, soft, and peaceful.

Mary approached, smiling, looking even better than she had before. "Another?" she asked.

He smiled back. He didn't want to leave yet. He wanted to see if something would happen. This was his night. And he might even get laid. He nodded.

Roosevelt stood from his barstool to go to the restroom. He felt a bit unsteady on his feet. The farther he walked, the more he felt in danger of collapsing. The walls swerved in and out. The floor was dark and distant. In front of the urinal, he held the pipes to steady himself. He thought he might puke.

He convinced himself that he was a man, and he wasn't going to get screwed by a little alcohol. This was nothing.

He splashed water on his face, trying to come back to life. After all, he had a bartender to attend to. He'd forgotten her name, and at this moment couldn't even remember what she looked like. But damn it, he was going to enjoy her. And he was going to spend his last free evening having a good time.

He eventually made it back to the bar and asked, "What time you get off?" He was embarrassed at how awkward, distant and slurred his words sounded in his head. He wasn't sure how they sounded to her.

"Eleven."

"Huh?"

"Didn't you ask what time I got off?" she asked looking at him oddly. "I said I get off at eleven." She dropped some glasses into the sink. "Are you feeling all right?"

"Yeah. Great. Can I have shum water, pleashe?" Damn. His words sounded funny again.

She set a glass in front of him and moved around the bar, organizing, putting things away, and preparing for the next day's business. He tried to check out her body, but even with one eye closed had trouble making out the form. Maybe this had been a mistake. Maybe he'd had one drink too many.

She approached him again. "Listen, if you'd like to get together after I get off, I can't be seen leaving with you. I'll meet you. How about the parking lot at the corner?" She looked at him for recognition. "Okay?"

He nodded.

With one eye closed, he drove to the parking lot. Fortunately, there were few cars out. He parked and waited. His stomach felt a bit rough. He belched. Oh nice, he thought. That could get him far. He felt bad. Very bad.

He stood up and leaned against the car, smoked a cigarette and waited. Being drunk wasn't really a lot of fun, he decided. He never felt bad like this on a little heroin. He finished his cigarette, flicked the butt away, and lay down on the back seat of his car. The world flipped over backward. He sat up. He put his feet on the ground outside the car and tried lying down again. How miserable he felt.

The next thing he knew, somebody was kicking his feet. This wasn't a very nice way for the girl to greet him. He sat up and said, "Hey."

A white, uniformed cop stood with his hand on his holstered gun. "Driver's license."

As he stood, the cop stood back threateningly. Another cop car arrived and sat back with a spotlight shining in his face. The cop took the license, leaned forward and sniffed.

"I do believe yer drunk, Mr. . . . ." he looked down at the license, "Mr. Roosevelt Harris. Drunk." He snickered. He stood back and continued, "and here you are operating a motor vehicle."

Roosevelt looked around, "I was in the back seat, sir," he said, motioning.

"Well, Mr. Roosevelt Harris, exactly how'd you get here?"

Roosevelt decided not to answer.

The cop made him walk the line. He staggered and swayed.

He decided to try for mercy. "Sir, I really wasn't drivin'. I know I cain' drive. I wasn't botherin' anybody. I was gonna meet a girl. Sir, I just got to town. I gotta work tomorrow. Can you please gimme a break sir?"

The cop walked back to the other car, leaving Roosevelt standing by his car. Then he returned. "You better walk to whereever yer goin', 'cause if I see ya driving, you're in jail."

"Thank you, sir," Roosevelt said, and walked off, struggling to put one foot in front of the other. He glanced at his watch. Two a.m. Either the girl hadn't shown up or had left him there asleep. An excellent way to spend his first night in New Orleans.

* * * * * * *

Two days after checking into the hospital, Jude was bored. Here he was with a bunch of loonies, most of whom babbled, wandered, and played stupid children's games. The nurses were bitches, and not a one was decent to look at. He got an idea to contact Billy and see if he could get him some dope. What would it hurt? If he had a little buzz on, the time in this wacko ward would go better. He didn't consider that this was a bad idea for more than a moment. He got a dime, went to the payphone, and called Billy. When he told Billy he needed some dope delivered to the nut house, Billy said, "Sure."

Before long, Jude had a quick visit, received the dope, already fixed up and in the syringe, in a sly shift as they shook hands goodbye, and was set to get high. He wandered nonchalantly toward his room. A nurse was dealing with an old man who liked to show his scrawny white behind to everybody. Jude went inside his room, shoving the door slightly closed behind him. He decided not to close it all the way, because it was against the rules and would certainly invite scrutiny.

He slid along the wall to the left, next to his bed, out of the view of the door, yanked the fit from his bathrobe pocket, and jammed it into his left vein. As always, he registered immediately, not needing to tie off. He was rushing before he even pumped it in, and he slowly pushed it forward. Before he could inject all the drug, the old nurse entered and looked his way. He let his arm hang by his side, so the bathrobe sleeve hung over the syringe, half full of dope and blood. The dope could wait, but the blood would coagulate soon, and render the syringe unusable and the drug ruined. He had put in enough to be high, but he needed the rest desperately.

"What are you doing?" she asked.

"Nothin'."

"Come on out now. Know you can't be in here alone."

He walked out, trying to swing his arm slowly, feeling the cloth pull the syringe from side to side. She was behind him, so he couldn't do anything. When he got to the main room, the old bitch went behind the counter of the nurse's station, so he turned down the west wing toward the payphone. When he reached the phone, he stood with his back to the nurse's station, put the phone on his left shoulder, reached for the syringe with his right hand, and jammed on the plunger. The needle seemed to clog, and he pushed harder. Then he pulled back on the plunger, but nothing happened. He struggled to pull up the sleeve enough to see what was happening. He could see a clot at the bottom of the barrel. He pushed one more time, and the barrel blew off the point, spreading blood and brown fluid all over his sleeve, arm, and floor. Naturally, the old bitch appeared right behind him. She snatched the back of his neck and pushed him rudely, causing him to bang his forehead on the dial. The crook of his arm hit something, jamming the needle. He winced, reached and pulled it out.

* * * * * * *

Roosevelt was well into his second afternoon in New Orleans when a staff person came to inform him that he had an urgent call. He stood with trepidation, wondering what could be wrong.

His mistake of two nights ago was in the past. He'd gone to a meeting, taken a white chip, and sworn never to make that mistake again. Drinking was an issue he could no longer ignore or justify.

He picked up the receiver and heard the voice of Uncle Theodore, which concerned him more. "Roosevelt," his uncle said solemnly.

"Yessir."

"I got some bad news Roos'velt." He paused for too long. "Yo Mama dead. OD'd."

Roosevelt held the receiver away from his head for a moment, looking at it like doing so would change the news. Then he pictured the awful night just days ago when she and Jude had spent a high and bawdy night at his house. That son-of-a-bitch Jude.

"What happened, Uncle? Where was she?" His voice sounded a little too calm, he thought.

"Cops found 'er in the woods. Used works next to 'er."

"Anybody with 'er?" Roosevelt wanted a cigarette but wasn't sure how that would be taken by the office staff.

"Uh-uh." Uncle Theodore cleared his throat. "Why you ax?"

Roosevelt didn't want to talk about drugs in the office. He tried to figure out what to say. "She came to my place the other day with Jude. Don't know why. Don't know what they were up to. But it wasn't right. I dunno. I think somebody oughta talk to Jude about what happened." His chest felt heavy. He needed to get home.

"How da we find Jude?"

Roosevelt told him to check with Old South, thinking he might still be found there, and also told him how to contact Jude's father, thinking that there was no reason for discretion, and he wasn't sure whether Jude was living at home or not. Other thoughts darted across his mind, like the funeral and the burial. He asked Uncle Theodore whether anything was planned, and promised to be home as soon as he could.

Within an hour, he was on the road home.

* * * * * * *

After being caught, Jude was taken to a room and interrogated by a committee, led by the chief psychiatrist. He was an annoying, persnickety, effeminate man, with an odd tic in his cheek that made it difficult to pay attention to the words. Jude kept waiting for the next odd little jerk of the man's skin. What he had to say was as annoying as his looks and manner. He criticized Jude for wasting their time and for wasting Jude's own time in seeking help when he didn't really want it.

"Why don't you just leave now and kill yourself with dope?" the man said, sneering. "We don't need people like you. You're not mentally ill. You're just a selfish hedonist."

Jude didn't know what a hedonist was. The old bitch of a nurse sat there with her flabby arms crossed on top of the huge mounds of breast. Ugh, he didn't even like thinking about those things as breasts. Her jaw was set.

"What do you want to do with your life?" the shrink asked.

Jude shrugged. "I dunno. Just wanna get clean?"

"You think you'll get clean from sneaking drugs in?"

Of course, he didn't. What an idiot. He just wanted to get a little high. He decided he should answer something. "I'm sorry about that. It was a bad idea."

"You have two choices," the little wiener sniveled. "You can leave and go blow your veins and your brain out until you're dead. Or you can stay here. But if you choose to stay here, it will not be in the open, relaxed Ward A. You will move to Ward B, which has much more restriction—locked doors, no privacy, no visitation. Do you understand? And if you mess up once, you will move on to Ward C, which is the highly restricted area. There, you will be in a locked individual cell with padded walls, just like the other insane people who are there."

Hmm. What a choice. But he did kind of want to get clean. And it would sure be nice to stay here, away from the problems of the outside. How bad could the B Ward be? Couldn't be worse than being in jail. It'd give him time to relax.

"Furthermore," the asshole continued, "you will attend group therapy. Of course, the other residents do not have drug or alcohol problems, but they exhibit evidence of psychoses, so you should have a lot in common. What's your decision?"

Jude looked around at the audience, all expectantly watching him. He wasn't in the mood to leave this nice, safe place today. "Ward B," he answered.

* * * * * * *

Roosevelt raced toward Daytona, wishing the whole time that he could know what his Uncle Theodore had learned about Jude. But he didn't want to waste time stopping at a payphone. So he just drove and drove, stopping only once for gas and to pee. He didn't eat. He was devastated, and guilt-ridden, although he kept telling himself that he had no reason to feel guilt. His usual enjoyment of cruising along the open roads of the state of Florida was gone. He spent the time reviewing in his mind everything that occurred when Mama and Jude had visited him. And he remembered all the times when he was young that Mama disappeared, reappeared, and suffered through her addiction. He'd never blamed her for abandoning him.

Then his mind turned to Nana, who must be suffering again, like she suffered over so many years. This was the ultimate. She didn't deserve this. Of course, she'd not only suffered through her daughter's addiction, but also Roosevelt's. At least he'd made her proud in the last couple of years. She was looking forward to visiting the restaurant that he'd be running soon.

And suddenly, he cringed to picture Auntie Barbara on her soapbox, telling poor Nana "I told you so". What good would that do? But of course, what good would telling Auntie Barbara to shut up do? None.

Eventually he arrived at Nana's, hoping Uncle Theodore would be there. Memories flooded through his mind, good and bad, as he made his way to the door.

Nana met him at the door, drying her hands on her apron. She smiled and hugged him. "There my little Roos'velt." She held him back by the shoulders, looking him up and down. "You a fine lookin' young man. I glad ya came home." She hesitated, with a dark cloud of sadness enveloping her face. "I'm so sorry 'bout yo mama."

Roosevelt thought that was a funny way to say it, since his mama was Nana's daughter too. But he understood. She'd probably written her daughter off for her own mental well-being long ago. They sat and talked.

"Nana. Know where Uncle Theo be?" he asked, thinking how funny it was that the grammatical construction had popped out. His words seemed to flow with his surroundings.

"He be comin' heah in jest a few," she answered.

They talked more. Roosevelt heard a car door slam. He rushed to the front door as Uncle Theodore bounded up the steps, all smiles. Uncle Theodore enveloped him in his arms. "So good ta see ya. So sorry 'bout yo mama."

"You find Jude?" Roosevelt asked, perhaps a little too eagerly.

"Yup. Ain' talked to 'im yet. He in da nut ward."

"Huh?"

"Hospital. OD'd on tranks."

Roosevelt couldn't help laughing. That's where the fucker belonged. "Ya think he know anythin'? When'd he go in da hospital?"

"Seem like shortly afta she passed. Could be he know sumpin. Don' know. His pa say he wanna go ta da hospital too. We s'poseta meet 'im in a couple a minutes."

* * * * * * *

Jude was playing checkers with a wacko. The son-of-a-bitch had already beat him twice. The old guy kept running his dried-up hands through his dirty hair and scaly, scabby scalp. Then he'd lick his fingers. Jude didn't even want to touch the checkers after that. The guy was out of it, but he knew where to send a checker piece. Having lost for the third time, Jude lit a cigarette and challenged him to another game.

The old guy was setting up the board again when this teenage girl, uglier and weirder than shit, came up and sat on the bench beside Jude. She was always coming on to him. It was disgusting. The girl just wasn't there at all. He didn't know why he was so offended about how she was after his flesh, like a mindless animal.

After all, he was much the same. He'd screw any girl, and he didn't care about much more than that. But this girl just grossed him out. She was sitting behind him, running her fingers over his back and then playing with the curls of his hair. She would approach his neck and ear with her mouth, and he would cringe.

He'd finally had enough of her molesting him and stood, in the middle of a game.

The old guy went crazy. "You can't quit in the middle of a game. You can't. You can't."

"Whyn'tcha play with yerself," Jude said, smiling.

The girl loved that line and glued herself to his side. He felt her braless breasts, nipples and all, against his arm, and was almost interested for a moment. Then he remembered her brainlessness and lost interest.

He was pushed aside, and thankfully apart from the girl, by another rushing man. "Uncle Walt. Uncle Walt. Uncle Walt," he babbled, smacking his lips at the same time with every repetition, as he rushed toward the little television in the corner. Another program was on, and he kept screaming the name of the "Uncle Walt Show" and jumping up and down. Jude went into his room to meditate. Why exactly had he decided it was better in here than outside?

* * * * * * *

Roosevelt and Uncle Theodore walked along the lengthy, sanitized hallway of the hospital toward the psych ward. As they exited the elevator, Roosevelt spotted Mr. Armstrong marching in the same direction. Roosevelt called to him. Mr. Armstrong spun around on his heels.

He extended his hand with a stiff smile. "Roosevelt," he said. He looked him up and down. "You look good Roosevelt. I mean that. You look like a man."

"Thank you, sir."

Roosevelt introduced his uncle. They walked together toward the counter.

A woman looked up from her paperwork, a perturbed expression on her face. "Yes?"

"Hello," Mr. Armstrong said, smiling. "We're here to see David Armstrong. I'm his father and these are his friends. We need to talk to him."

The lady looked down at the papers. "Sorry. You missed visiting hours."

"Ma'am. Excuse me," Mr. Armstrong continued. "This isn't really just a visit. We need to talk to him about something that is quite important."

"Well, excuse me, sir," she retorted, "but there are rules, and you're not seeing him."

"I'd like to see the chief psychiatrist or physician in charge, please," Mr. Armstrong demanded, pushing his fist down on the counter forcefully.

She glared at him, and then her eyes darted around him. Mr. Armstrong, Roosevelt, and Theodore turned to see two men Roosevelt knew were cops approaching.

"Well, well, well," one said, grinning. "We got us a lawyer, and two junkie drug dealers. What a fine group."

Roosevelt was pissed. He'd been clean for quite some time. Uncle Theodore had been clean for years, and Mr. Armstrong was an all-right white dude.

The cop leaned on the counter and smiled at the lady. "We gotta see one a yer fine residents," he snarled.

"What's the name," the lady asked.

Flicking his thumb at Mr. Armstrong, Roosevelt and Theodore as he spoke, he said, "Prob'ly the same kid these guys are here ta see. He was the last one to see Anne Harris alive."

Mr. Armstrong glanced quickly at Theodore, a concerned expression on his face.

The woman behind the counter permitted them all to enter. Roosevelt wondered how this would work. Anything Jude said could be used against him in court. He pulled Mr. Armstrong aside. "Sir, don' you think we should talk to 'im separate from the cops? He mighta committed a crime."

Mr. Armstrong cast a sorrowful look at him. "The truth is the truth. I'm not going to assist him in hiding anything. If he's guilty, we'll deal with it. No sugar coating."

* * * * * * *

Jude was lying on his bed reliving an imaginary sexual encounter with Janet, the girl from high school who would never have looked at him twice. He was somewhat aroused and was considering whether he could go into the bathroom to relieve himself. But didn't want the humiliation of being caught by an orderly, erection in hand.

Two male guards appeared in his room. One, a guy with an acne-scarred face and a crew cut, said, "You got company."

At first, he thought the visit could be something good. But then he remembered that visiting hours were over and much more restrictive than they were in Ward A.

Having two guards announce the visit was not a good sign. "Who is it?" he asked without rising from the bed. The evidence of his arousal had shriveled into nothingness.

"You'll see," the other one said, grabbing him by the arm and pulling him up. Jude was alarmed. If he resisted, would they straitjacket him? They did that here in Ward B.

They took him to the front door of the ward, went through all kinds of procedures with keys and electronic releases handled by the woman behind the glass, and pulled him to the open visitor area.

He worried that they may be taking him to jail, to electric shock therapy, or some other unpleasant experience. "Where you takin' me?" he whimpered as they dragged him across the floor, his feet moving slower and slower.

They came to a door. One grabbed the knob and flung it open. Jude was aghast at the sight, trying desperately to formulate in his mind how such an unusual group could have come together. There were two creepy asshole cops who had made his life miserable at various times. There was his father, giving him that irritating, hurt, stern and mistrustful face that he wore so perfectly. Then there was his former best friend, Roosevelt and his Uncle Theodore, looking at him with inquiring faces. Roosevelt looked like middle America in black. He was a traitor. What the fuck could these people want?

Roosevelt had felt trepidation waiting for Jude. He'd been his closest friend. They'd shared many great times. Jude looked beaten and drawn, standing like a ghost in his tan pajama-like nut-ward get-up. Fear and dirty brown waves of hair shadowed his gaunt face. His eyes darted from person to person.

"Armstrong," began the jerk of a cop named Cooper—his very voice reminding Jude of several previous uncomfortable experiences—we're here to find out what happened to Anne Harris."

Jude was confused. "Whadaya mean what happened to her?"

"When's the last time you saw her?" Cooper demanded.

"Uh . . . a few days ago. Why?" Jude tried to imagine why anybody cared. Had they busted her, and they were trying to pin something on him now?

"What day?" his father asked.

Jude tried to remember. He really didn't know. It was about two days before he checked into this mental ward. How long had he been here? "What day's today," he asked, feeling his voice quiver.

"Friday," said Roosevelt.

"You were with her last Thursday in Tampa. What happened after that?"

The audience stared Jude down. "Well, we left Tampa the day we left Roosevelt's place. We stayed some days in Orlando—different motels. Then, like a few days later, we came home. I brought her to her house and dropped her off."

Jude's father sighed loudly and shook his head despairingly. Roosevelt's head sagged, and he rested it on his hands. The cop stood and paced the room. "Tell us about the drugs you were doing in Orlando." He flopped onto the seat next to Jude and stared into his eyes. Jude could smell his nasty cologne, mixed with tobacco.

"A little smack."

"Where'd you get it?"

"Tampa."

"How much is a little?"

"I dunno. Anne had it."

"Where'd you get the money to buy it?"

"I dunno. Anne had it."

"Listen you little son-of-a-bitch," Cooper demanded, pounding his fist on the table, just missing Jude's forearm, "We want the truth. Now. How much money did you have? Where'd you get the money? How much heroin did you buy? Where'd you get it? How much was left when you dropped Anne off at her house? Did you get together again? Were you with her when she overdosed? Did you inject her? Was somebody out to get 'er?"

"Whadaya mean? Is she all right?" He glanced over at Roosevelt and realized his eyes were watering up. "What happened Roos'velt?"

Roosevelt turned away.

They all stared at him again. He figured Anne must be dead. Nobody had said it, but it had to be. Was she murdered or did she overdose? Maybe the dealer helped her to overdose. "I really don' know what happened. We went ta Tampa on accounta she had a deal. She was ta do a pick-up fer a supplier here. He was payin' her somethin', but I don' know how much or anythin'. We went to some dude's place and, at first, he didn't have the stuff, but the next day she did the deal."

He looked around. Nobody looked friendly or happy. "We started for home, and I think she expected to deliver and get her money. But she just said, 'Let's stop in Orlando, get a motel, and do a little more.'" He saw disgust and horror on his father's face. "So we got high for . . . I dunno . . . a few days, I guess. Then we came home. I dropped her at her house. I went home. That's it. I OD'd trying ta get clean and checked in here. I swear."

Roosevelt was beginning to feel sorry for Jude. He was sure that Jude didn't know anything. But he figured Mama'd probably mentioned the name.

"Jude," he said. "Listen man, did she say anythin' ta tell you who she was doin' it for? You know man. If she was sposta come in with a full load, and came with a half, or a buncha cut-up shit, who know what da dude'd do? Maybe he helped her ta OD."

"Okay, lemme think. She said he couldn't go himself, because . . . because . . . Damn. I know. She told me. Let's see. It wasn't cause he hadta work. It was somethin' kinda wholesome. Somethin' family. I dunno, he had ta attend somethin' of his family, and his family didn't know he was a dealer. Somethin' like that."

The cops kept bugging him for a name. Then they started bugging him about the dealer in Tampa. He was able to give them explicit directions on how to get to the guy's apartment. But they seemed much more interested in who she was copping the dope for.

Finally, he was worn out. Roosevelt's face and his father's seemed beat too. The cops looked as stupid as ever, but at least they were out of questions.

His father hadn't said almost anything. He certainly wasn't there to represent Jude. Why had he come anyway? Some kind of lawyer. Cooper called the guards back in, and they escorted him out by the arms.

Roosevelt sat, drained, sorry for his friend, and sorry for himself. He watched Jude shuffle out of the room, almost lost in the too-big outfit. His long, brown, wavy hair bounced over the collar. Roosevelt's mama had been a good person. She was cutting the guy's dope so much, that she probably had no idea how strong it was. At this point, all he wanted to do was say goodbye to Mama, take care of his family, and get back to work.

PART V

1980s–1990s

Chapter 18

IT HAD BEEN QUITE A WHILE since Roosevelt had slipped. Every time, he'd suffered tremendous guilt, so he would promptly attend a meeting, take his lumps, and pick up another white chip. Now, he was working on three years completely clean and sober.

He was manager at the Daytona Beach Old South, although it was rumored that he was in the running for the district manager position. His restaurant was the highest-grossing store in the entire southeast. He enjoyed his job. Many in management indicated that its success was solely attributable to his able leadership.

Roosevelt had married Tara five years ago. Their son, Thadeus, Tad for short, was now four. But the marriage hadn't worked, mostly because Tara couldn't or wouldn't stay clean, and Roosevelt just couldn't tolerate that. They were still friends and sometimes still wound up in bed together. Occasionally, when Roosevelt picked Tad up after a visitation with Tara, they'd communicate desire, make a date for the next day or another reasonable time, and enjoy each other. He wouldn't do it unless she was straight. He couldn't stand it if she wasn't.

Roosevelt was the custodial parent because everybody acknowledged that he was more stable. He'd coordinated a cohesive network of caregivers for Tad. Nana babysat often in the daytime, but she was starting to lose her sharpness. He'd never wanted Auntie Barbara to poison the young boy with her ideas. Uncle Theodore had a flexible schedule, so he helped out.

Roosevelt was at one of his favorite places, a basketball court. While most enthusiasts had spent a lifetime shooting hoops, Roosevelt's love of the game had come late, after he'd gotten straight. He'd shot a few hoops in his early life, but drugs and sex had been much more important to him. Now, he hadn't smoked cigarettes for a few years, avoided drugs and alcohol, and worked out religiously four days a week. His muscle tone was better than ever.

He was on the court outside the YMCA battling an old elementary school acquaintance, Horace, under the basket, as other players moved around the perimeter and in and out of the lane. His shoes scuffed the rough asphalt as he moved in and out, charged, reached, grabbed, pushed and pounded on his nemesis.

As Horace went for a shot, Roosevelt batted the ball away. One of Roosevelt's teammates, whom he hadn't known previously, grabbed the ball and dribbled wildly toward the other end of the court. Roosevelt sprinted and caught up, received the ball on a bounce from his teammate, went into the air for a dunk, was fouled, and tried to bang it in anyway. But the ball bounced off the rim loudly, echoing with the rubber-to-metal clang typical of an outdoor hoop.

"That was a foul," Roosevelt said, but nobody seemed to care. There were no referees in these games, so fouls were common and uncalled.

He worked and worked, sweating and feeling vibrant. He loved this sport. Finally, his team lost the game, but it didn't matter. The teammates acknowledged each other as they separated. Then Roosevelt and a couple of others went inside to clean up because the kids from the Police Athletic League would be arriving soon. Roosevelt coached kids the city police deemed in danger, many of whom hadn't ever really done anything bad, but lived in the projects or other high-danger areas. The kids would arrive by van, eager to learn the secrets of success in basketball.

* * * * * * *

Jude's father, Uncle Lee—the former big drinker—and another businessman named Griswold, the racist man who'd gone fishing with them when Jude was young, had purchased an abandoned restaurant and were trying to make a go of it. Jude had put together a conveyor-belt contraption that carried chicken through a smoky outdoor grill, and then through an open searing oven inside the kitchen, and then back out and in again. Although the device cooked the chicken perfectly, the owners seemed discouraged that his knowledge didn't seem to translate into a broader understanding of purchases, marketing and other necessary managerial attributes.

Griswold was still an asshole. He regularly said things to Jude that made him feel stupid and unappreciated. Lately, all three owners had been commenting that perhaps somebody with more experience in that line was needed, not to replace Jude, but to operate another important aspect of the business. Jude's father had first mentioned Roosevelt as a candidate for the position and had inquired of Jude as to his current job status. Griswold had made an ugly comment about his race, but Jude's father had put him in his place. Jude knew Roosevelt was still a manager for Old South, and quite successful. It was decided that Jude would make the first contact.

Jude had helped unload the delivery truck and stock items in the morning. The storeroom attendant at the new restaurant kept putting things in the wrong place and taking too much time unloading boxes and emptying bags instead of stacking and unloading the truck first. Jude found it all very aggravating and felt his lack of skill at explanation and leadership as he struggled to convince the idiot to do it his way.

Jude had two hours between shifts, and went to his favorite watering hole, Last Chance, to down a few beers and some pizza. He liked April, the waitress, who was about as ugly as sin, but there was something about her smile that attracted him. He would never admit that to anybody. He liked the place. He could get mellow very quickly with a pitcher of beer in front of him, sitting alone at the counter. In the middle of the afternoon, the girl was often the only company. They would chat and have a good time.

He figured Roosevelt would be a few blocks away playing basketball with his friends, and then would work with the kids. Jude wanted to catch him between the two events to discuss the opportunity. Jude found it humorous that Roosevelt had become such a straight, goody-two-shoes athlete.

As teenagers, they were too full of drugs and nicotine to do anything athletic. He didn't know whether Roosevelt had a natural talent for it, but he knew he didn't. He didn't even understand the game. But he'd often noticed, back when he and Red had roamed the projects and black town streets, that kids in the neighborhoods would spend countless hours dribbling, pushing, running and shooting that stupid rubber ball into the net-less metal rims.

Jude chugged the remainder of his pitcher of beer, ate a few more french fries, lit a cigarette, and told the girl he'd probably see her tomorrow. She smiled, showing some rather unappealing teeth, and said she hoped so.

Jude arrived in time to see Roosevelt defending some smaller black guy who was trying to approach the basket. Since Roosevelt had built up, he stood his ground and kept the guy from moving. Jude could make out the bulging veins of Roosevelt's biceps and thought what good use those veins would have been put to a few years ago.

Jude knew that Roosevelt would be going inside to coach kids. He'd heard that, besides the coaching, Roosevelt regularly participated in A.A. and N.A. meetings held inside juvenile detention centers, prisons, and rehab facilities. Apparently, Roosevelt was a welcome visitor with a lot to offer in those meetings.

Jude placed himself in the line between the outside courts and the door to the gym and intervened as Roosevelt approached. Jude felt a little out of place. They were a frightening-looking bunch. But after all, this was the parking lot of the YMCA, so he belonged here too.

Roosevelt seemed to slow down a step or two as he approached, his face showing surprise at seeing Jude leaning against the wall. "Yo, 's up?" he asked.

"Dude, yer a sweaty mothah."

Roosevelt laughed. "You ain' broke no sweat in a long time, I'd say."

The other guys entered the building. Roosevelt stood facing Jude. They'd seen each other a few times since Roosevelt's mom had died, and Jude had convinced him that he'd had nothing to do with it and was not with her when she OD'd. The cops had wondered whether it was a murder for a short while, but they soon tired of the theory. In their eyes, she was just a worthless black junkie. They'd probably figured it was good riddance.

Roosevelt took in the sight before him, the scrawny, sallow-skinned, boyish-faced Jude was still there, looking calm and relaxed. A bit of a gut had also developed, and his eyes were set back in a deep circle of constant exhaustion, with bags at the bottom. He wondered what this mess of a person wanted with him.

"Y'know my dad and some guys bought a closed restaurant building and developed a new place. The Roasted Oak Grill. It's doin' pretty good. They wanna expand. Make some more around here, and then go on like, ya know, McDonalds."

"Uh huh," Roosevelt answered, wondering what this had to do with him. The odor of beer wafted from Jude. "You drinkin' in the middle a the day?"

"Huh? Uh, well, sure. Jus' beer. Even you have a beer once in a while, doncha?"

"No sir. Beer is just like anythin' else. Do ya get a buzz from it?"

"Well, yeah, but it ain' nothin'."

Roosevelt rolled his eyes. "Okay, Jude. I need to get on inside. Whatcha need?"

"Well, the guys wanna know if you'd consider comin' ta work with us ta help get this thing goin'. They'd pay ya well. They'd give ya stock. Least that's what they told me ta tell ya."

Roosevelt was a little surprised. He didn't know anything about the restaurant. It apparently was a start-up—an individual restaurant owned by some guys who had no idea what they were doing. Roosevelt was well-established with a good company that provided plenty of benefits, and he was in line to move up even higher in the company very soon.

And then there was Jude. He'd considered Jude like a brother in the past, but he would never put his financial security within even distant influence of Jude. Here he was, half-sloshed in the middle of a weekday afternoon, and he'd be returning to do whatever he did in the restaurant. Whether that included using a hand-held or automatic cutting device or calculating money, it made Roosevelt cringe.

"Uh, thank you, Jude. And please tell your father I said thank you. But I'm very established with my job. I've got a great future with the company. I'm financially rewarded very well. And I just can't even think of why I'd leave that for an unknown."

"Shit. Wonchu even think 'bout it?"

"Just did. Thanks."

Roosevelt held his hand up to shake. Jude stood, staring at him blankly, dumbfounded, so Roosevelt just patted him on the shoulder and walked away.

Jude hadn't imagined the scene turning out this way. He'd pictured that Roosevelt would have immediate interest. That he'd have said he'd skip working out with the boys that day and go straight on back down to Jude's watering hole to down a few and talk about the prospects and the details. Then Jude would have presented him to his father and his partners like a hunter returning to his hungry tribe with a prize catch. Damn it.

* * * * * * *

In the locker room, Roosevelt showered and put on clean workout clothes. He wouldn't get sweaty working with the kids. He called the restaurant to make sure everything was under control. He would return by five, in plenty of time for the evening crowd. He had everything quite well organized, and he always had time for these outings. He had a young assistant manager, who was eager to learn and to continue the tradition. He was white, but he seemed genuinely to consider Roosevelt as simply a good manager with no thought as to his race.

*   *   *   *   *   *   *

Roosevelt left the locker room and found that a couple of the kids had arrived. Jackson was one of his favorites, because of his intelligence, constant smile, and true skill with the ball. Braxton was also present. He was sullen and angry. They lived in the same projects, with the same family life, yet Roosevelt marveled at their different personalities. The other boys arrived in the PAL van driven by one of the other coaches, and soon almost the whole team was present. Roosevelt kneeled in front of the group, talking about things like sportsmanship and attitude, watching their eyes wander and wishing he could say it better.

Then he did a defensive drill, having them hold their arms up, wave them around, and be so active as to throw the offense off. He knew how hard it was to wave one's arms in the air for a long time. And he knew how hard it was to do foot drills. He had to remind himself over and over that these were young boys, many of whom had little background in athletics and little contact with adult males, at least those of good character. They probably received little nutritional substance. And they were kids, just plain kids, wanting to have fun. This was not a job. Not school. And not home, for those whose home life was not great. It was their free time.

He put the ball into Braxton's hands as he spoke, mentioned something to Braxton about hanging on to the ball and not losing it, and at some point during the discussion, when he felt that Braxton was wandering somewhere else in his mind, Roosevelt subtly reached over and, with his fingers, popped the ball right out of Braxton's hands. The ball bounced across the floor and another player ran and grabbed it. Everybody laughed, and Braxton's eyes looked like they'd pop out.

"What's the lesson there?" Roosevelt asked.

"Hold the ball," said one kid.

"Protect it," said another.

"How you do dat?" Roosevelt asked, trying to speak in their lingo, even though it was no longer his.

"Put yo arms 'round it," another offered.

He told the boy to toss the ball to another. He showed the receiver how to turn briskly away from the others and hold the ball close to the ground, constantly moving and watching the others. Then, they did a dribbling drill with another player running alongside trying to steal. Later, they practiced shooting. Finally, he had them run, do sit-ups and stretch.

＾ ＾ ＾ ＾ ＾ ＾ ＾

On Tuesday, Roosevelt took his son Tad to the inlet for the afternoon. He had been promoted to District Manager, as he'd expected. The home office had granted him two weeks off between the two jobs.

Tad loved running in the sand and shallow water, chasing the seagulls, and just spinning in circles. It seemed unusual for people of his race and culture, but he didn't know any people in his community who had ever had the opportunity to enjoy it.

Later, after he begrudgingly dropped Tad off at Tara's home, he went to the juvenile detention center for an N.A. meeting. Before the meeting, a new white kid sat in the circle of chairs as others milled about, socializing. The kid had brown hair crammed behind his ears, rolling over his collar, and hanging like a curtain halfway over his eyes. His small mouth was set in a frown. He reminded Roosevelt of Jude as a kid in the drug rehab center, in height and weight, as well as posture and attitude.

"Hello," Roosevelt said, extending his hand. "Roosevelt."

The kid didn't look up and didn't offer his hand. He remained with his arms crossed over his chest, recumbent, with his ass off the chair and his neck resting on the back.

"You new here, or jus' new ta the meetin'?" Roosevelt asked.

Silence.

"Okay, then, I know you're new here, and they made ya come ta this meetin', an' you figure you don' belong here. You only did dope for fun, or to escape somethin'." Roosevelt didn't wait for an acknowledgment. He knew better than to expect that a few words would turn a kid around. "Anyway, jus' do me one little favor. You don' hafta like bein' here. You don' hafta acknowledge anythin'. Jus' listen, with an open mind, an' if ya feel like sayin' anythin', please say it." There was no reaction. He patted the boy on the shoulder. The boy cringed and shrunk away.

The meeting began, and one of the three black residents began. "Dreamed I was usin' las' night. It was so incredibly real that I woke up with a rush. An' I wanted the real thin' jus' so bad. Ya know, I been here hun'red ninety-two days now, an' I ain' never wanted ta get high like I do right now." He shook his head in dismay. "Goddamn, man. I crave somethin'. Somethin'."

The other adult in the room said, "A usin' dream ain' like a wet dream. Ya dream 'bout sex, an' ya think ya actually doin' it, an', well, ya wake up refreshed." The others nodded and smiled.

Somebody said, "Course ya might end up a little sticky an' wet, but at least y'ain' got no blue balls."

The group laughed.

The new kid was almost smiling, Roosevelt realized, but still looking down.

"But," the adult counselor continued, "A usin' dream doesn't result in release. You wake up needin' it, an' there's no natural release mechanism."

"I know das right," said one of the black residents.

"Man, I can get crazy jus' lookin' at artificial sweet'ner."

"Yo, dude," said another. "Ya got that powder in the pink packet—look like coke; ya got them little white pills—sakrin, ain't it—look jus' like D's, man; an' ya got the friggin' brown sugar—look jus' like smack. Ya know man?"

The new guy cracked a smile. Feeling a little uncomfortable, Roosevelt joined in the laughter. It was hard to know when to stop trying to make the comparisons real before you got your own craving going.

"Okay," Roosevelt said. "Now that yer gettin' everybody blue balls of another sort, let's talk 'bout how ta make the cravin' go away."

As he looked around for a volunteer, the residents became serious. He figured that Slim would probably talk because he liked to listen to himself. "Yo, Slim. Whadaya do when yer wantin' ta use?"

"Uh, well, uh, I turn it over."

"Ya soun' like yer recitin' from a book."

"Nah, man, I really do. I mean, I learnta jus' do what dey say in meetin's. I turn it over ta my Higher Power, and uh, I don' really give a shit what Higher Power means."

The new kid looked totally confused. He was looking around with the standard obvious question on his face, "Can you people be like talking about God and saying shit in the same breath? What's that all about?"

Alex, a white boy with a serious acne problem, looked at the new kid and said, "Listen, man. Don't worry about this Higher Power stuff. The cool thing about N.A. is that you can get clean without gettin' religious." The kid was shaking his head. "No, man, I mean it; ya jes' say, 'I turn this—whatever it is—I turn this over.' That's it. It's gone. You turn it over. You ain' got the problem no more. I mean it man."

The talk went around. The new kid never spoke. But, by the end of the meeting, Roosevelt felt good about his prospects.

* * * * * *

For weeks, Roosevelt had planned and arranged to get the family fishing.

Today, he loaded up Nana's car with the gear. Nana had hummed in the kitchen as she jammed the old picnic basket with fried chicken, cornbread and other goodies. Tad bounced around with excitement. Uncle Theodore arrived, picked up Tad and swung him in the air. Then, he hugged Roosevelt and Nana. Auntie Barbara arrived. Even she was friendly and happy. She also picked up Tad and engulfed him in her large arms. He wiggled like a worm.

They piled into the car. The car squeaked and rumbled eastward. At Beach Street, Roosevelt parked in the usual place near the Halifax River Yacht Club. The family piled out and took their places. Roosevelt helped Tad roll a sloppy little bread ball and slip it onto the hook. Nana hooked the first mullet.

Roosevelt hooked the next one, but deftly switched his pole with Tad before Tad realized there was already a fish. Then he handed his pole to Auntie Barbara, slipped his arms around Tad, held his arms and tugged lightly to set the hook. "Think you got one, son," he said.

The boy squealed gleefully as he snatched the pole back, making the poor fish leap from the water and crash unceremoniously into the wall. "Easy, now, son," Roosevelt said. "Set him back into the water for a second, then we'll pull 'im on up together. There's no need to hurt 'im."

Together, they pulled the fish up, and laid it on the sidewalk. It thrashed around on the sidewalk. Roosevelt freed it from the hook and dropped it into a bucket of water.

As the fishing wound down and Tad began to turn restless, a man exited the yacht club dock and strolled toward them. Roosevelt recognized the stature and the bouncy step of Jude's father, Mr. Armstrong.

He walked straight up to Roosevelt and held out his hand, saying, "Good day, Roosevelt Harris. How are you?"

Roosevelt felt a bit uneasy. He didn't know why. He dealt with rich, white businessmen all the time. But this was Mr. Armstrong. He knew Roosevelt's history. Right now, with his family, Roosevelt didn't feel like the businessman he was. He just felt like little Roosevelt, standing here talking to young Jude Armstrong as kids, worrying that his grandfather disapproved. He introduced Mr. Armstrong around. Nana thanked him for getting Roosevelt out of trouble when he was a troubled teen. Tad paid no attention. Auntie Barbara was uncharacteristically speechless.

"I'm sorry about your mother," Mr. Armstrong said.

"Thank you," Roosevelt and Nana said at the same time.

"Catchin' anything?" Mr. Armstrong asked, glancing into the bucket. He nodded with approval and turned to Tad. "So, I see you're quite a fisherman," he said, smiling.

The boy looked up at his dad, and then put his arms around his leg.

Mr. Armstrong stood for another few awkward moments, and then said, "Roosevelt, when you have the time, I'd like to talk to you."

Roosevelt didn't respond right away. He figured it was about the job offer.

"Well, would you mind talking to me?"

Roosevelt shrugged. "No sir. Course not."

"Would you mind coming over to the Roasted Oak tomorrow or the next day? What's your schedule?"

They worked out a suitable time, Mr. Armstrong said goodbye, and they loaded up and headed home.

* * * * * * *

Roosevelt arrived at the Roasted Oak at the appointed time. Jude emerged from the kitchen, and appeared surprised to see Roosevelt walk in, dressed like a businessman.

"Hey," he said. "Whatchaupto?"

"Hey, bro'," Roosevelt responded. They shook hands, the old, cool way, thumbs up.

"Whatcha doin' here?" Jude asked.

"Meeting your dad," Roosevelt answered.

Jude's eyes lit up. "Oh, so you decided ta take my advice." He smiled.

Jude's Uncle Lee walked in. "Good morning, David," he said and turned and shook hands with Roosevelt. "I'm really pleased to meet you," he said. "Lee Steward. I've heard great, great things about you from Lansing Armstrong." He smiled. "Of course, I'm sure David would support you too." All his dad's friends called him David, just like his dad did.

"Have you eaten here?" Dr. Steward asked.

Roosevelt shook his head no.

"You've got to try the food. David here created this fantastic cooking device that really provides a unique taste."

Roosevelt smiled affably. "I remember the fish he used to smoke as a kid. I'm sure it's great. We go way, way back as far as food preparation goes."

And some other types of cooking too, Jude thought.

Griswold banged the door open and sauntered in. "Doc . . . David," the arrogant son-of-a-bitch said in a monotone. "You must be Roosevelt," he said, extending his hand to Roosevelt, who shook it lamer style.

"Yessir. Glad to meet you . . . uh . . . Mr . . . ?"

"Griswold. Mr. Griswold."

"Armstrong's on the way. Let me show you around." He put his arm around Roosevelt's shoulder and guided him into the kitchen, followed by Dr. Steward, and leaving Jude behind.

Roosevelt was struck by the organization of the work areas. He always honed in on systems and procedures that led to increased efficiency, and he could see that here.

"Who set these tables and support areas up like this?" he asked.

"Huh? What'da ya mean?"

"The system. I imagine you have two workers here pushing these food products through, right?"

"Well, uh, I dunno." Griswold shrugged. "I guess David did it."

"I like it," Roosevelt said, nodding approvingly.

"Wha'. . . well, uh, sure, that's why we're successful." He obviously wanted to bullshit but had no facts at hand.

Dr. Steward added, "Yes, all that set-up design is David's doing."

The three men continued the walk through the kitchen, with Dr. Steward now describing and pointing out products, refrigeration, prep areas and equipment. He seemed to have a better handle on the workings than the hotshot. A couple of workers were prepping in different areas of the kitchen.

Mr. Armstrong breezed through the kitchen door and greeted Roosevelt warmly.

Roosevelt was intrigued by the way the chicken was cooked, being carried on a conveyor belt traveling through the kitchen, out to an outdoor alcove, and back inside again. As part of the process, there was a hot fire, a convection oven, and a smoking device. The food kept traveling through the different areas until it was done.

He smiled at Jude. "So, you still into smoking food, just like in that old refrigerator down by the river."

Jude nodded, grinning. "Things never change. Some a the old ladies who useta buy smoked fish at the yacht club come here to get our partly smoked foods."

Roosevelt already had an idea as to how the contraption could be improved. But he wanted to taste the product.

Mr. Armstrong asked Jude to put together a smorgasbord of all the products they offered. Muttering to himself, Jude returned to the kitchen to create a sample plate, pissed that he wasn't invited to the talks with Roosevelt.

As they ate, Roosevelt said, "The food is good. The cooking technique and preparation are unique. I'm impressed."

"Well, sir," Dr. Steward said, "We hear good things about you, and we would very much like to have you involved in our operation as we improve and expand." He sipped his iced tea and wiped his lips with the back of his hand.

"I appreciate that," Roosevelt said. "I hope you understand that I have a very good and stable position. I'm not sure I should leave such a certain future for the unknown."

"We'd like the opportunity to prove to you that this offers a safe and promising future as well," Mr. Armstrong said. Then he began outlining the areas in which they sought to improve, the details of how the operation was run, the financial performance of the current operation and the future growth plans. He consistently pointed out how Roosevelt could fit into the long-term scheme, and he spoke of stock ownership and stock options.

The meeting ended cordially, although Roosevelt did not commit in any way to even consider the offer seriously. He was not sold yet, although he did see some very positive possibilities.

* * * * * * *

Roosevelt sat at the kitchen table of his apartment, reviewing financials, food purchase records and sales records of the Roasted Oak, crunching numbers and charting possibilities. Considering how many investors were involved, the first restaurant was quite small. The only way it would produce enough to satisfy them all was to grow. But the cooking style and technique were truly unique. There was a lot of promise.

He multiplied the costs and potential income with additional shops and tweaked employee numbers and other overhead. He drew a chart as to how management could best be allocated among several shops. At the end, he nodded with satisfaction. There was a definite opportunity if the money men would step back and let him do his thing.

He needed to go and pick up Tad, who was visiting Tara. It was a nice day, and he could use the fresh air. He decided to walk. Solitude was always refreshing. He headed up the street, through the old neighborhood. The curbs were littered with cigarette butts; the yards in front of the tiny, white, wooden houses still consisted of dirt and no grass. Some were neatly raked. Some would have a tree or two with a white-painted trunk. Little kids played, using sticks for bats. Poverty and desolation were everywhere. He passed the old corner store where so many important issues in his life had occurred, his first high, his first puke, his first buy, his first sale. So many firsts, none of them positive.

He came across Cecil, an acquaintance from school. He hadn't seen or talked to him in many years. Cecil was not right in the head, but he hadn't always been that way. He'd been a nice, normal kid. One day, Cecil had done the wrong combination of drugs, and something had happened to his brain. Roosevelt never knew quite what. But he wasn't right. His face was off center; his mouth slung down on one side. He spoke slowly, with an odd impediment. "Re-y-ed," he said, half smiling with the twisted lips.

"Yo, Cecil. 'S cookin'?" He held a hand up for a slap or a shake. Cecil studied his hand, trying to figure out what to do with it. Finally, he reached up to give a high five, his face studying the necessary move with intensity, his tongue sticking out of his lips.

As the hands slapped together, Roosevelt having helped to make sure contact was met, Cecil smiled broadly and said "Five, man. Fi'. Yeah. Fi'." He was happy as could be.

"So how you doin'?" Roosevelt asked.

Cecil crossed his eyes and scrunched his face. "Doin' . . . uh. Good. Man. Doin' good, Re-y-ed."

"I'm glad ta hear dat, Cece, man. You lookin' good. You lookin' jes' fine."

"Smoke?" Cecil asked.

He wasn't sure whether he was looking for a joint or a cigarette, but he had neither. He shook his head. "No, man. Ain' got none."

"Re-y-ed." He smiled.

"Listen, Cece. I gotta go, man. Gotta get my kid."

"Ki . . . y . . . id. Tha . . . Tha . . . Tha . . . Duh. Duh. Duh. Thad . . . Thadeus. Whoo."

"Whoo. I'll say." Roosevelt smiled and patted Cecil on the shoulder as he continued on his way.

"See ya 'round, Cece."

At Tara's place, she opened the door, smiling. She looked good.

"How ya doin'?"

"Doin' good. Eight months. You?"

"Doin' good." He smiled at her. She was so sweet, so hot, with so much to offer. He was sorry he'd had to escape from her problems. "Tad?" he asked.

"Playin'." She nodded toward the living room with her head. He always worried when Tad wasn't in the same room. But he could hear him making noises like a motor and spinning something on the hard wooden floor.

"Miss you," Tara said, pushing her lips into a little pout.

"Miss you too, Tara," he said.

She moved forward and embraced him. He'd love to enjoy her. But Tad was here, and he had things to do. He embraced her for a minute, took in her smell and essence, kissed her ever-so-lightly and pulled away. "Gotta go," he said.

She looked at him imploringly, but he held strong. "Gotta go."

Back on the street, Tad rumbled along ahead. Roosevelt worried that he'd fall off the curb, or trip over an uneven crack in the sidewalk. Roosevelt struggled not to be over-protective. Let him be a kid. He'll be all right.

After a while, Tad tired, and Roosevelt swung him up to his shoulders, first carrying him like a dead animal around his neck, and then letting him ride his shoulders like a horsey. Roosevelt held his thighs tightly and jumped up and down a bit. Tad yelled, "Whee".

They continued like that until they reached the store, and as they turned the corner, Cecil was there again. "Tha . . . Tha . . . Thadeus," he managed quickly.

Roosevelt figured Tad was smiling. He usually reacted to Cecil like he was another kid, which was kind of true.

* * * * * * *

Jude awoke feeling shaky and weak. He looked over at the clock. Seven. It was late. He had to get to work, to get the fire going, to prep the food. He heard his mom moving around in the kitchen. He lit a cigarette.

His head was pounding. He could hear traffic, dogs barking, and other sounds of morning. He dragged himself from bed, trudged to his mom's bathroom, and then went to the kitchen and made himself a Bloody Mary, with V-8, Worcestershire, Tabasco, plenty of lime, pepper, salt, and of course Smirnoff Vodka. He shook it and poured it into the glass.

His mom staggered in, a cigarette hanging from her lips and a glass in her hand. "Whatcha doin?" she asked. "Ooh. That looks good. Wanna make me one?"

"Okay." He threw a bunch of stuff in the same container and turned it into a double. They stood, swaying, smoking cigarettes and downing the cure.

Duke entered the kitchen, opened the fridge and withdrew a beer. "What time is it?"

"Almost eight. Gotta get to work," Jude said.

* * * * * *

Roosevelt arrived at the Roasted Oak at seven on a Tuesday morning. Mr. Armstrong was waiting at the door and greeted him warmly.

"It's good to see you, Mr. Armstrong," Roosevelt said as he shook hands.

"How are you doing Roosevelt?"

Roosevelt answered. "I'm doing fine, sir, and you?"

"No complaints," the man answered, smiling. "The others should be here in a few minutes. Can I get you some coffee?"

Roosevelt still avoided caffeine, believing it was a drug, and he chose not to defile his body with anything that would alter his feelings. "No thank you, sir."

"Well, I'm going to make some. Come on to the kitchen."

Mr. Armstrong flung around aluminum parts of the large coffee pot and made a batch. Roosevelt looked around one more time at the well-organized kitchen. He marveled at the shiny aluminum prep table, into which Jude had inserted a large, wooden cutting board. A metal hose hung at the side of the cooking area, so everything could be cleaned easily. The tabletop was slanted toward a drain, as was the tile floor. A stack of cedar logs for the smoking contraption stood on a rack just inside the door. He could remember Jude in the kitchen at The Bridge, as the two of them created meals for the residents. Even then, Jude had organized things in efficient ways. Jude wandered in, nodded to them and headed to the kitchen.

He was annoyed to see his father talking to Roosevelt, like two businessmen. Roosevelt exuded a self-assured air.

Mr. Armstrong poured himself a cup of coffee and tapped some artificial creamer into it. Roosevelt turned away. After all these years, it still made him nervous to see powder being sprinkled. It was a good reminder though. He was still an addict and would always be.

Mr. Armstrong led Roosevelt to one of the booths in the customer area.

Griswold rushed through the door and approached abruptly. "Gentlemen," he said, and, ignoring Roosevelt's outstretched hand, collapsed on the hard seat across from him, next to Mr. Armstrong.

Roosevelt knew Mr. Armstrong found Griswold's rude and crude behavior offensive. With his huge belly hanging like a bag of flour over his belt, he struck Roosevelt as a slovenly loser. Jude had told Roosevelt that Dr. Steward had brought him into the business, against Mr. Armstrong's better judgment.

"So, when are you starting?" he asked.

Roosevelt was a bit shocked at the question.

Mr. Armstrong cleared the air. "We're here to talk. He hasn't committed in any way yet. In fact, we're here to convince him. So be on your best behavior."

Mr. Armstrong and Roosevelt smiled, but Griswold didn't seem to get it.

Dr. Steward approached the table, smiling like always. He shook Roosevelt's hand with one hand and put the other hand on his shoulder.

Mr. Armstrong said, "Roosevelt, I take it that you wouldn't be here talking to us again unless you had some interest. Did you find all the information complete?"

"Yessir. I was impressed with the figures. I have some ideas on how the numbers could be improved, and I believe the proposed expansion is a positive move."

"Roosevelt, we believe you are the man to do what we need here. We will offer you the same salary that you are currently earning. We'll give you five percent Class B, non-voting stock now, an additional five percent Class B stock after one year, stock options at favorable prices and on favorable terms, and all other benefits. You would be the District Manager, and your particular area involves expansion. You would be in charge of all decisions involving location, staffing, construction and procedure for the other restaurants, and would also have supervisory authority over this store."

"Sir," Roosevelt said. "That is the one thing that concerns me. You know that Jude . . . er, David is my friend. He's your son. And he created this process. How is it going to go if I'm above him? I'm worried about that, sir. Really, I am." Roosevelt knew he shouldn't refer to Jude as Jude in his dad's presence.

"Don't worry about David. I understand your concerns, but he knows that he's managing a restaurant, and you are doing something completely different. We'll grant him some stock for developing the cooking method."

Griswold plopped his coffee cup on the table and stared at Mr. Armstrong. "What're you talkin' about?"

"David created the unique cooking method," Mr. Armstrong said. "He could've patented it. We had no agreement saying what he created belonged to the corporation."

It seemed that Mr. Armstrong didn't want to discuss this in front of Roosevelt. Roosevelt was concerned about their lack of consensus. The doctor didn't say anything.

"Look," Armstrong said to Griswold, "we can talk about this later." And then, looking at Roosevelt again, he said, "I'm sure you realize you'll be able to control your destiny here. As executive vice president and a director of the corporation, you'll have all the authority you need."

"I understand," Roosevelt said. "I thank the three of you for your vote of confidence."

"Well, what do you think?" Dr. Steward asked, smiling.

Roosevelt sucked in a breath. "I'm still a little concerned about whether the three of you are cohesive in your decisions. I need to know that I'm not going to be subject to the whim of one."

"Whatchu talkin' about?" asked Griswold. "You think I'm gonna just kowtow to these guys?"

Armstrong cringed. Dr. Steward stepped in. "Listen, Roosevelt, we don't always agree, and that's really healthy. But anyway, you will have a binding employment contract, signed by Armstrong as president, attested by me as secretary, backed by a unanimous vote. We all definitely agree that you are the one."

Roosevelt looked at the group. They looked back. Griswold nodded in agreement. He thought back to the time Mr. Armstrong had brought the lawyer, the reverend, and Roosevelt's mother to Louisiana to extricate Roosevelt and Jude from the horrible experience they had gotten themselves into.

Roosevelt had to have one last meeting with Mr. Armstrong, one in which he would lay it out his concerns about Jude, and Griswold, in private. He needed to be able to do something about Jude if he continued to drink and drug. If he was satisfied with that, he would accept.

* * * * * * *

Jude tried to drag himself from the bed again. He tried to recall the details of last evening with an employee named Joyce. He thought she'd kept up with him, drink for drink. He remembered sitting in the car outside a bar at about two a.m., making out. She was letting him touch her everywhere. Then she was on top of him, both still partially clothed, as some people walked by and banged on the hood and roof of the car. "Take it to a motel," a woman with a gruff voice had yelled. He had no memory after that.

He went to the kitchen and made a whiskey and ginger ale. He sipped as he prepared for work, feeling more numb and refreshed with each gulp. Each morning before work, he replenished the whiskey flask.

At work, he hoped not to see his father or the other guys. He wanted to see Joyce, although he was a little concerned about whether he'd behaved. He opened the restaurant, flicked on the lights, and began working his way through the morning pre-checklist.

Before long, Joyce gleefully bounced in. She looked around the kitchen quickly, asked if anybody else was present, and on seeing Jude shake his head, she leapt on him and wrapped her legs around his waist so forcefully and quickly that he almost lost his balance and fell to the ground. She started kissing him forcefully, ramming her tongue into his mouth. Although excited, he was nervous.

"You taste like booze. You drinkin' already?" she asked. He shrugged. She kept kissing him.

Finally, he had to put an end to it. Not that he wanted to. But they had work to do, and he couldn't get caught with her like this. He pried himself away and ordered her to work. But every time one came into close proximity to the other, a touch, a whisper, lips on the neck, would almost derail the effort. At one time, as he stood behind her, she reached back and grabbed his crotch, manipulating him through his pants. He thought he would pass out and stood mesmerized for a little while before breaking away again.

* * * * * * *

Roosevelt and Mr. Armstrong met at the inlet and went out on the sailboat for a private meeting. He'd enjoyed quite a few boat rides with the Armstrongs. He didn't know anybody from the "hood" who'd ever be here. Mr. Armstrong started the engine, freed the lines and steered out of the slip and out of the harbor.

"What do you think, Roosevelt? You know we're ready to have you sign up, and I believe you are ready to sign up with us. Am I wrong?" As they turned around the peninsula and headed out to the ocean, Mr. Armstrong lit a cigarette and reached into the cooler at his feet for a beer. "Wind's coming from the east. We'll hoist the sails in the ocean," he said.

He held out a beer to Roosevelt, who shook his head no. He hadn't discussed this issue with Mr. Armstrong. Perhaps it was time. "Mr. Armstrong, sir, you know I haven't done a drug of any type for a long, long time now. But you gotta understand that I'm not cured. I've got a sickness. Addiction. I can't take anything mind-altering in moderation. It's not in me."

Armstrong was looking at him, perplexed.

"I can't drink alcohol just like I can't do drugs. I even quit caffeine and nicotine." He stopped for a moment. "Mr. Armstrong, I feel very strongly that once an addict, always an addict. It's just one day at a time. I do what I'm supposed to do. I attend A.A. and N.A. meetings. I work with young people who are struggling with the same things. That helps me a lot."

"What's N.A.?"

"Narcotics Anonymous. Just like A.A., but for addicts."

Mr. Armstrong considered his beer can with hesitation.

"It's okay, Mr. Armstrong. It doesn't bother me. Just 'cause I've got a problem doesn't mean you can't have a beer. I'm beyond worrying about that. Honestly, sir, I generally don't even notice anymore. It wasn't always that way, but I'm in pretty good shape now."

"I've never even understood A.A. There was a time when my former wife, David's mother, accused me of being a drunk. It shocked me, because although I like to drink a bit, I never felt that I had a habit. I've never had a problem of any kind related to drinking, as far as I know."

"Sir, even if you did, that wouldn't make you an alcoholic. It's a sickness. An alcoholic will have a craving for a drink that is so overwhelming he'll generally do anything it takes to down a drink. It doesn't matter where or when. It's a need. I don't imagine you've ever felt that."

"No, I suppose not. Sure, after a bad day at work, I've wanted to mellow out a bit, as they say, and alcohol sure helps."

"That's normal, sir. If you were in a bar having drinks, or maybe out to dinner, and somebody ordered an alcoholic drink, and let it just sit there, let's say it's a drink with ice, and the ice is just melting away, spoiling the potency, would that do anything to you?"

"What do you mean? How could it do anything to me?"

"Well, sir, if you had a problem . . . if you were an alcoholic, it would drive you crazy. You just wouldn't be able to bear watching a perfectly good alcohol buzz go to waste. You'd want to pick up the glass and pour it down the man's throat, all the time lecturing him about waste—maybe about how there are poor alcoholics all over the world, and maybe he'd like to share his drink with someone who wouldn't treat it so nonchalantly."

They both laughed. "I suppose I understand."

"If you have to struggle to understand what it's like to crave, you don't have a problem."

They sat quietly, feeling the water lapping gently at the hull, hearing the halyards—a word Roosevelt had learned from Jude—striking the aluminum mast, feeling the wind grab the mainsail, causing the boat to heel to starboard. Roosevelt gazed north along the coast, as the beach curved and veered toward Daytona, dotted with occasional small motels and houses among the palm scrub and sea-oat-carpeted sand dunes. Then he looked to the south where the beach was less inhabited, and watched surfers mounting small, frothy waves.

"Mr. Armstrong," Roosevelt began, feeling his Adam's apple bob involuntarily. "Uh, what I wanted to talk to you was about David."

Armstrong whipped his head around, looking stern. Roosevelt convinced himself to continue. "Sir, I'm afraid that David is drinking too much. I don't think he acknowledges that he shouldn't drink. I'm even concerned he may be doin' more than that."

"What do you mean? You think he's on drugs again?" Roosevelt hated that phrase— "on drugs". It was so lame.

"I don't know sir. I don't think anything needs to be done. In fact, there's really nothing to be done. He's not gonna quit until he's gonna quit, you know?" He looked for understanding. "I mean he's not in a crisis now, so he's not gonna see any problem. But I think he's on a downward spiral, and someday it's gonna affect the business."

Armstrong nodded, dejectedly.

"If it affects the business, I'll have to do something. And if my taking action's gonna be an issue, I can't accept the position."

He paused, trying to hear the light, pleasant sounds of the water and wildlife again, but it all seemed dark and gloomy, tense, awkward.

Armstrong stared down into the cockpit, flexing his jaw muscles, shaking his head. "I understand. It's not an easy thing to face. I think of it as weakness. I can't understand how this came through my genes."

"Sir, don't blame yourself. There's nothing you can do or could have done about David's addictive personality. It just happens to some people. And David's a good person. And a talented person. I just need to be sure we're on the same wavelength. If I see a real, immediate problem, I'll talk to him, but if talking doesn't work, I'll have to do something—for the sake of the Roasted Oak. That would be my duty, sir."

"You're right, Roosevelt. I thank you and I'm more pleased than ever that we chose you. You're going to be a tremendous asset to the future of the Roasted Oak."

A couple of dolphins had joined them. They slid in and out of the white water, being shoved aside as the bow sliced through the ocean water. The two friends sat back and enjoyed the view, the sea smell, and birds swaying in the wind and crashing into the water in search of small fish.

Chapter 19

JUDE HAD MARRIED JOYCE, the former Roasted Oak employee, in a rush of love and foolishness. He rushed through the garage door and into the eat-in kitchen of their tiny home. Joyce didn't acknowledge him. Their daughter, Kim, rushed to him. He lifted her into the air, feet up. Their son, Mark, raised his arms, gooey with baby food, and Jude hugged him. As he approached Joyce, who was serving plates, Kim held his leg and drug along behind. He gave Joyce a peck on the cheek.

She said, "Sit, Kim."

Here he was, like he was supposed to be. They had a deal. Even though he worked in the restaurant industry, he made the effort to escape for an early dinner with his family on two work nights a week. As the manager, he could do that. His restaurant ran like a top. But did she appreciate it? No. Things just kept getting more and more awkward. It made him not want to come home at all. Well, he loved seeing the kids. They were so exuberant and full of unconditional love for him. But she was a cold-assed bitch, and he could just about do without her. Where had it all gone? In five short years, she'd run their fascination for each other into the ground.

He'd downed the end of a rum bottle on his way. He always spent his best quality time in his personal bar—his car. He drove a ten-year-old Chevrolet, and constantly had to listen to the bitch complaining that she was trapped with the kids all day with no car.

He never drank at the restaurant. But when he had the opportunity to get away, he'd stop at 7-Eleven, get a Coke from the soda fountain, pour rum into it, and keep adding rum as he sipped until it was almost pure rum. He loved driving around drinking in his private moving bar. He'd get a mellow buzz going. Then, work would be smooth.

Joyce had forgotten what it was like to work for a living. She just wanted to complain, degrade him, and feel sorry for herself.

They ate in silence, each dealing with the kids' needs and wants. He was numb.

"Daddy," his beautiful daughter asked. "We're goin' to Disney World. Huh, Daddy? Huh, Daddy?" She jumped up and down on the kitchen floor.

It had been quite a while since they'd gone to Disney World. The first thing Jude thought of was how difficult it was to find a drink there. He couldn't very well bring anything sufficient to keep himself normal. The only alcohol available at Disney was a little beer. You had to manage to get into the right restaurant to even do that. Joyce didn't see finding alcohol as important, so she would steer them to a happy little goddamn place for the kids, and he would be dry, with a headache, completely miserable. But he knew his little kiddies loved Disney World. He wanted to take them. He'd just have to try to get himself enough stash on his body to make it through.

"Okay, sweetheart," he said to his daughter, looking at Joyce to try to monitor what was being planned. Her dead-pan face gave away nothing. "I gotta go to work," he said. "We'll talk about going." He hugged his kids, pecked his wife again on her un-giving cheek, and left.

The evening was going all right, until his former friend, now his goddam superior, the high-and-mighty, arrogant son-of-a-bitch Mr. Roosevelt "Uncle Tom" Harris, walked in to spy on Jude and his operation. Roosevelt strolled through the front looking like the snooty, pushy bastard that he was, rubbing his finger along surfaces just like Jude's dad.

Jude ignored him and returned to the rear. A new young girl was cleaning up her area, and he admired her looks for the first time. He'd like to get that ass into the cooler.

But then inspiration-killer Roosevelt came into the back, introduced himself to the girl, "Hi, there. You must be new. I'm Roosevelt Harris, District Supervisor."

"Hey," the girl said, nodding and throwing her hair back. Jude knew Roosevelt was going to write them up because of her waving hair.

"Mr. Armstrong," Roosevelt announced as he reached out to shake hands, lamer style. Jude almost glanced around for his father when it dawned on him that Roosevelt was referring to him.

"Hey," Jude said. "What brings you here?" Jude struggled to appear nonchalant, hoping Roosevelt wouldn't smell the odor of rum. He wasn't pleased with the surprise intrusion.

Roosevelt smelled the booze. He'd known it. Things kept getting worse and worse. In spite of his frank warning to Mr. Armstrong when he'd come on board, he never really expected to have to take action. Jude had run a fairly tight ship and had kept the profits reasonable. But now, the restaurant was sliding, and the reason was obvious. How could this mess of humanity be expected to keep this place running smoothly?

"Just visiting," Roosevelt answered finally, figuring that was better than saying, "Just came here to demote you." He didn't want to say anything negative in front of other employees. He'd just have to wait until after closing time. He watched Jude work, noticed the swagger, noticed all kinds of mannerisms that told him Jude was slipping. He was disappointed, but realistic.

He looked around the kitchen and once more admired the setup. All seven restaurants that Roosevelt had opened followed pretty much the same format that Jude had created. He'd kept the same prep table set up with built-in wooden cutting boards. The cooking contraption differed only in that Roosevelt had developed an innovation in the grease collection and slowed the conveyor belt. He admired Jude's understanding of what would work. Nobody had ever developed anything like it.

Roosevelt would try to keep his salary as high as possible, but he had to remove him as manager of this store. Although the restaurants were still in the growth stage and not throwing off much profit to the shareholders, Mr. Armstrong had created a royalty procedure for Jude to benefit from his creation. And he couldn't leave him here because it would be impossible for Jude to work as an equal with people he used to lead. Why, oh, why had Jude made him have to do this?

Roosevelt went out to the front and observed, helped out and watched the close-down process. He met some other employees. There was a nice-looking black girl at the cash register. He introduced himself. She was fine. But Roosevelt would never dream of having a relationship with an employee of Roasted Oak.

Eventually, the others left. It was time to deal with Jude. He was not looking forward to it. He found Jude in the kitchen cleaning down the conveyor belt. Jude looked up, dread on his face.

Jude knew that something was up. He kept telling himself that he was too valuable to lose—he'd created this system. No matter how he screwed up, that had value, right? And now this pompous black dude, who'd done all the same fucked-up things Jude had and had been brought into this system by special invitation of Jude himself, was about to screw him.

"Jude, we need to talk," Roosevelt said, with the phrase that always sent dread through Jude's veins. Roosevelt waved toward the office, and they entered.

Jude sat in the seat where employees cringed while he read them the riot act. Now he was the one who cringed.

Roosevelt strummed his fingers on the desk, also wishing for a reprieve. "Jude, I've been following your numbers here. This restaurant has declined twenty percent in profitability in six months. Do you have any explanation?"

"Uh, well, yeah. Tourism is down. You know that. This isn't the best time of year. And we've had a lot of turnover."

"I'm sorry, Jude. I've looked at those possibilities. It just doesn't do it. I compared the season's numbers to previous years at the same time. The numbers are still down significantly. And I ran income and expenses, correlating them with turnover. I don't see any correlation. What I do see relates directly to your drinking and maybe drugging."

"Now wait a goddam minute," Jude protested. "You know I've been straight for a long time."

"I'm afraid I don't know that, Jude, and I have serious doubts about your sobriety. I believe you're loaded now. But besides that, the basic numbers are telling."

It wasn't like Jude didn't know his numbers were down. He worried about it. He tried, in his sober moments, to come up with better ways of handling business and marketing the restaurant. He liked to think the problems were caused by reduction in income and liquid funds at the company level, to bureaucracy, to everything other than his just trying to escape life a little. At times he knew he had a problem. But right now, he was indignant that he was being accused of something so fundamentally wrong.

He had founded this place, and now old Red was trying to do him in—probably to put another black in his place. Oh, he was looking forward to telling that bitch Joyce that he'd lost his job, or whatever was about to happen to him. That would be just great. "Red, man, gimme a little time. I'll get the numbers up."

Roosevelt shook his head. "I'm sorry Jude. Please report tomorrow to the Jacksonville store. Jeff Baker is the manager."

Jude nodded. Then he shook his head in despair. This was it. The bottom. He had to admit that drinking had destroyed him. He hadn't done virtually any drugs for a long time.

"Red, goddammit," he said. "You're fuckin' me for no damn reason. I shoulda known you'd just take over—take your power too far." Jude stood and walked out.

Roosevelt sat in the office for some time, second-guessing his decision. He hadn't wanted to hurt Jude. He truly just wanted to reach out and convince him to get it together. He'd almost expected Jude to just fold and admit he had a problem—maybe to ask him to get him into treatment. Yet Jude was belligerent—in denial. Well, Roosevelt had to look out for the best for the Roasted Oak.

Jude drove straight to his current favorite public bar—as opposed to his portable bar—the one near the Y where Roosevelt played. A couple of regulars perched on stools. Harry, an older man who always smelled of B.O., saluted him with a nod.

"Jude," announced the bartender, April. Even though she was slovenly, he thought she was kind of interesting, kind of sexy in an odd way, especially as the evening wore on. She plopped a rich, frosty, foamy mug of Killian's Red down in front of him. He felt the comfort it would bring before even touching it. He wanted to leave the son-of-a-bitch Red behind him now. And he needed to get into shape to go home and talk to his darling wife. The kids would already be asleep anyway. Then he thought that the best thing to do would be to wait until the bitch was asleep too.

So he ordered a hamburger, with the works. He downed several more beers. The other people at the bar talked bullshit. Jude began thinking that April was looking fine, and wishing he could do something with her.

At 11:15 or so, most of the usuals had left. The owner was in the back cleaning up, and April was organizing the bar area. Jude excused himself and went into the bathroom. As he stood in front of the urinal, he heard the woman's room door squeak. It had to be April. Jude finished, washed his hands, and exited, listening for noise in the women's room. He glanced around the corner toward the bar and saw nobody. He stood for a moment, waiting for her to exit. When she did, she was startled for a moment, and then smiled seductively. "Waiting for me?"

She backed into the women's room, and he followed. They embraced and kissed exuberantly before even getting the door closed. He pushed her into the corner. They fumbled with each other's clothes, tugging, reaching, patting, rubbing. They couldn't actually do it here, with old Forbes, the owner, in the back room cleaning up. He'd be yelling for her any minute. But the excitement was too much. Jude thought he would pop through his pants. She looked, smelled, and felt fine at this moment.

They continued for a few more minutes, broke away, went back to it, broke away again, rubbed and kissed a little more, and finally separated and exited, straightening their hair and clothes as they did so. As Jude followed her out, she stopped abruptly, punching her rounded butt into his crotch.

Forbes stood at the door as she exited. "What're you doin' in there?"

"Nothin'," she said, as she popped Jude again, trying to push him back.

"Getcher asses out here," the old man demanded. He pulled April out of the bathroom and pointed at Jude. "You, get the hell out of here. And you," he said, pointing at April, "clean up the goddam bar while I think about if I'm gonna fire you."

Jude drove home slowly and methodically, one eye closed, concentrating on the white line in the middle of Nova Road, a narrow, two-lane road with a steep embankment leading down to a canal. Then he thought of Joyce and was pissed at her nasty attitude. Ughh. The bitch would just love to know about his job problems. He wouldn't tell her that tonight.

He struggled considerably to stay within the lanes, regulate his speed, keep his mind on the mechanics of driving, and avoid arrest.

He pulled into the driveway, got out, lifted the heavy door, maneuvered the car into the garage, and closed the door again. He swayed and caught himself on the car as he tried to make it to the door into the house, which would open into the tiny hall right outside the master bedroom. He turned the knob, attempted to pull the door toward himself quietly, lost his footing and fell into the plethora of brooms, dustpans, ironing board and other noise-producing items behind the door in the garage. He had difficulty moving his numb legs the right way. He clambered back to his feet and made it into the hallway. Rather than entering the room of dread, he moved to his left through the dark kitchen. He thought he walked better in the dark than in the light. He took a leak in the bathroom between the two kids' rooms. He emerged from the bathroom, turned to the right, and watched his beautiful Kim sleeping for a few moments. The room had her gentle aroma and feel, even in the dark. She was at peace. Then he crossed the hall and leaned over the side of Mark's crib for a moment, noticing how this room smelled of baby powder, baby shampoo and other sweet smells. His son's stout little chest moved up and down with his peaceful breathing.

He staggered to the living room, flipped on the TV, lowered the volume, and passed through the channels looking for something. This was how he spent most nights—alone, drunk, usually still drinking, in front of the TV, maybe trying to clear his blurry eyes enough to do some paperwork. He flipped to Johnny Carson, which was already on the last guest. Boring. He stumbled through a few other channels. Black and white re-runs. This was a solitary time. He liked it.

He thought briefly of going into the room and trying to wake Joyce for some activity, but he thought better of it. It was rare that she'd put up with him. He'd go there, lie next to her, try slowly getting closer and touching her, and then be rebuffed rudely. He didn't need that tonight. He wouldn't want to talk to her anyway.

He went back to his car, opened the trunk, got a bottle of rum from the spare tire area, and searched for something to mix it with. Of course, there was no regular Coke. There was only Diet Coke, which he just couldn't tolerate. Finally, he used orange juice to tone it down a bit.

He plopped down in front of the TV, now wanting to go to sleep—wishing the rum would push him down. He needed to get up early to be in Jacksonville by nine. In fact, he wanted to be out the door before seven in order to avoid her altogether.

He downed the drink while watching a rerun of Mr. Ed, the talking horse. "A horse is a horse, of course, of course . . ."

He knew he couldn't sleep. He was too numb, too confused, too shaky. He lit another cigarette and lay on the couch, feeling utter desolation about the state of his life. Here he was, bound by alcohol, just like he'd been bound by drugs in the past. He was completely unable to overcome it.

He suddenly felt like crying, and in fact, tears began to roll down his cheeks. He was sick of this. It was no fun anymore. No fun at all. He couldn't get drunk enough. Couldn't get sober. Just couldn't get to a good place. He clicked off the TV, opened the sliding glass door and went outside. He enjoyed being outside, sitting, watching the stars, listening to the crickets and frogs, thinking, planning his day, usually planning not to drink the next day.

That was it. Tomorrow it would be for real. No drinking. Nothing. He could do it. He had to drive. He had to work in a new place. He had to work under somebody who would and should have been his subordinate. He shook his head in dread.

Barefoot and bare-chested, tugging on a cigarette, he lurched through the dew-dampened grass to the kids' play boat. On top of a real rowboat painted bright blue, he'd constructed a flying bridge out of plywood and attached a steering wheel. The kids could often be found driving, fishing, sitting, or water-skiing, holding a thick rope and being drug through an imaginary sea.

Jude tapped the side quietly, so as not to wake his wife, to be sure that no nest of wasps had taken refuge inside, like they were apt to do. He climbed up, sat on the bench, and steered the boat to nowhere. That's where he'd like to be right now, in a real boat.

He spoke to nobody through a gravelly voice that reminded him of the heroin-dulled voice of old. "Here I sit. Again. Can't sleep. Can't get drunk. Everything is so bad. I need to remember this in the morning. I need to stop. I'm going to die if I don't. I want to die." His voice drug on. "Please. Please. End this. This is no fun anymore." Tears rolled down his face.

A few weeks before, Joyce had found him lying on the floor of his closet, crying. For the first time in a while, she'd acted sweet. She'd tried to hug him. "What's the matter?"

"It's just so bad. I'm depressed. I don't know. I don't know," he'd blubbered, tears rolling down his face, the salty taste in his mouth.

And then he'd broken it off because emotion was not for him, and he didn't want to be a weakling in front of the bitch, even if she was being sweet at the moment.

He rested his head on the hard wood dashboard, looked up at the sky and tried to doze, still swaying, feeling the world fly over his head and himself swoop backward. Oh, that wouldn't do. He sat back up again, exhausted, sad.

When the sun began to lighten the wispy clouds to the east, he went in, showered in the kids' bathroom, used their delicious smelling baby shampoo, an interesting way to carry them with him for the day, and finally crept into the master bedroom.

There, he shaved, snuck to the walk-in closet, closed the door, turned on the light, and dressed.

As he crossed the room in the dim early morning light, he saw Joyce's eyelids shudder in an attempt to look asleep, so he chose to believe that she was in fact asleep. He escaped.

* * * * * * *

Having eaten a healthy breakfast with a sleepy Tad and having dropped him off at school, where he was in the second grade, Roosevelt stopped in the Daytona store to leave specific instructions for the new store manager and each employee. Roosevelt had the habit of organizing everything on white index cards, which he always carried, and pulled out when needed. He'd written the instructions on those cards too. He reviewed the inventory and order sheet, and made changes, shaking his head in dismay. How could Jude have kept this restaurant afloat with the complete lack of order and coherence?

He left by seven a.m. and drove up U.S. 1 to its intersection with I-95. He'd filled two large bottles of refreshing ice water, which he drank methodically on his trip north. He left the radio off because he had to work out plans in his head.

He'd worked through the numbers on the Port Orange store, and calculated salary changes on the Altamonte Springs store. He was fortunate to have a great memory for numbers and the ability to calculate and picture a spreadsheet in his head. He started calculating the possible expansion to Tampa. He had good memories of Florida's west coast, other than the visit from Mama and Jude. He wouldn't mind spending a little time getting the store up and running.

Then his thoughts turned to Jude. What was he going to do with him? He needed him to succeed, but at the same time, he needed him to reach a bottom so he could get clean. But reaching a bottom while working in the Roasted Oak was itself a problem. Roosevelt wondered if he should go meet Joyce and discuss an intervention. This thinking process was neither fun nor fulfilling because he couldn't calculate a certain answer. There were too many unknowns, too much doubt, too many social issues, the insidiousness of addiction, and the inaccuracy of interpersonal relations.

He wondered whether Jude was himself on the road toward Jacksonville and how far along he'd be. He should be close to Roosevelt's location on the route if he was to arrive on time. Of course, he'd probably had a rough night, and even rougher if he'd shared his troubles with his wife. Roosevelt had liked her when they first married. She was fun, and even though she drank a little, she seemed to handle it well. Roosevelt had to remember that not everybody was an addict and alcoholic. Many, many people could drink socially or even drink alone for enjoyment. But he would find himself second-guessing and criticizing if he wasn't careful. Joyce had become somewhat bitter over time, and Roosevelt figured it was the result of Jude's sinking. He probably wasn't a nice boy at home, especially if anybody would interfere with his ability to get high.

Roosevelt had been invited to their tiny home for little Mark's birthday a few months back. It was apparent that Jude had consumed huge amounts of alcohol before the guests arrived, and he had something in his hand the entire time, as he played with the kids, as he cooked hamburgers and hot dogs on the charcoal grill, as he helped Mark open presents, as he held a video camera. His face was pie-like and blubbery, his eyes bloodshot. He'd been putting on weight like a balloon with the empty calories of the alcohol and soft drinks.

At one point in the evening, as Jude grilled hamburgers on the charcoal grill in the back yard, the phone rang. Joyce stared at Jude, giving him the look of hatred, and said, "I'm busy. You get it."

Of course, she wasn't busy at all, and Jude was already flustered over the status of the food, but he looked at her for just a moment and lit out for the phone. He flew right into the closed screen door and tumbled into the room, enmeshed in the destroyed aluminum frame and mesh.

Joyce entered, muttering, "Goddam worthless drunk," as she half kicked and stepped on Jude, who lay crumpled in the metallic net on the floor.

The party guests had stood dumbfounded for a short uncomfortable moment, and then found activities or things to talk about. A few guys, including Roosevelt, helped Jude free himself from the trap and pull the remains of the door out of the house.

As Joyce walked back by, she'd said, "I think he looks good like that." Then she laughed like it was just a big joke. Some of the revelers emitted halfhearted chuckles.

He didn't really blame Joyce for being fed up. But it did make everybody else uncomfortable. The kids had played on, although little Kim and Mark had tossed a few confused and horrified looks toward where the adults stood.

* * * * * * *

As Jude entered the on-ramp to I-95, he adamantly told himself he wouldn't drink today. There was rum in the trunk if he needed it. But this was a new day, and he needed to get straight.

It had been over a year since he was last sober, but that was only for four months. He dreaded this day. He was jittery and off-center. He had to make an impression at the new store. He was the son of one of the owners and the creator of the kitchen.

He was going to have to work and look busy all day long. He wasn't going to be able to sneak a drink. He could get wasted on the way home tonight. He'd definitely do that. He would need to have plenty to face the bitch when he got home tonight.

He was pissed at the bitch and the asshole Roosevelt. He started to think that having a drink now would just polish the edges. It was a necessity, not a choice. And it didn't mean he needed it, like he was hooked on alcohol. He didn't believe you could physically need alcohol anyway. He just needed to smooth himself out after a rough night.

He pulled off the highway at St. Augustine and got a Coke to go at Stuckey's, which he promptly embellished. It burned his lips. Oh, but it was good.

He lit a cigarette, hung back, and sipped his medicine.

* * * * * * *

Roosevelt and Jude arrived in the parking lot of the Jacksonville store at the same time. Jude had just downed the rest of his drink. Flipping his cigarette out the window, he squirted a dose of breath spray into his mouth. He hated meeting new people, but the little bit of drink had mellowed him out. As he got out, he saw Roosevelt.

Roosevelt said, "C'mon. I'll show you around."

They entered through the back door, which led through a tiled hallway that reminded Jude of walking in the back of Old South many years ago, with his then buddy, Red.

Roosevelt felt Jude's trepidation. "Don't worry. The cooking mechanism and workflow area are yours. The setup of rooms and walls was mine, and yes there's some Old South here."

"Jude, I believe you know Jeff Baker," Roosevelt said. They shook hands without a word. Then, Baker strolled through the kitchen, waving this way and that, explaining things that were obvious. "Now, the cooking procedure is unique," he said.

"I'm familiar with it," Jude said.

"Oh, that's right, you already worked in the Daytona store. What'd you do there?"

Jude wanted to say, "I created all this, you idiot," but decided to downplay it. After all, his being here was a demotion. If this guy didn't know that, he'd rather not tell him. "Just about everything."

Jude looked at the part of the cooking conveyor belt that was inside the restaurant. He leaned down and looked at the grease collector, controls, and grates. He walked out the door and looked at the smoking pit. He recognized a variation in the smoke-venting system. He walked back inside and saw that the venting system traveled through the walls. He walked around to the other side of the aluminum cooking machine and examined it. The son-of-a-bitch Roosevelt had altered his artwork.

Baker took him through the rest of the restaurant and introduced him to employees. Jude busied himself, reviewed food order sheets and receipts from the previous day and spent a little time getting to know each employee.

As his alcohol-induced normalcy began to wear off, he needed to get away. After the lunch session and basic cleanup, and just before the dinner session preparation time, he left for a few minutes, drove to a 7-Eleven, got a Coke, poured some rum into the cup and drove around smoking a cigarette, downing the drink and getting mellow. Well, maybe tomorrow he could make it through a day without a drink.

Throughout the day Roosevelt surreptitiously watched the mess that was Jude. He was convinced that Jude was under the influence. Instead of strolling with the confident gait of an assistant manager, he swaggered around like a street dealer. If these people had any idea that Jude was the one who'd created all this, and that he was the heir of a third of the shares of this company, they'd be shocked. He was just another employee now. If Roosevelt let him misbehave, it would cause morale problems with all the employees.

Jude snuck out two more times, right before and right after the dinner period. Roosevelt knew by his walk, by his smell—burnt tobacco on top of sour rum and poorly covered by breath spray. Roosevelt was devastated.

Jude continued drinking on the way home. At ten, he stopped at a bar near his home. The bitch would still be up. He had some good hours ahead of him.

Jude had downed a frothy Killian's when, to his surprise, a dude whom Jude had met on the streets as teenagers, and who'd been thrown out of the Bridge when they were both residents there, drug his heels along the wooden floor and perched next to Jude.

"Hey," Jude said. "Wha's up?"

Bobby shrugged. "Nothin'."

Bobby ordered a beer and lit a cigarette.

They drank in silence for a few minutes. "Got any cash?" Bobby asked.

"Why?"

"Got a line on some coke."

Jude dropped his mug on the bar top. His heart started beating hard. It had been years since he'd done coke. He was already getting high in his mind.

Within twenty minutes they were in an apartment in the projects shooting up with several black guys. His heart took off. He licked his lips, pranced around, feeling millions of tiny pin pricks as a numbness encompassed his body. His hearing faded. Sounds echoed.

Jude lit a cigarette. Everybody became friendlier. They compared notes, introduced themselves, talked about nothing. Talked, talked, talked. And laughed. And bragged.

Half an hour later, Jude convinced himself it was time to do some more. He fixed up and shot. This time he felt like he would blow through the roof. His heart banged in his chest so hard he was afraid he might over-amp and die. He was afraid for his children, and momentarily, even the bitch. He thought of what the newspaper would say, of his father's shock and hurt, and then of his poor *grand-mère*. He wouldn't want her to suffer through another shock from him. He struggled to the sink, his vision and hearing coming and going, petrified.

He paced and sat, waiting for his heart to slow down, at the same time enjoying the zoom of it. Then he stood and paced some more. Then he worried that his heart would explode and sat again.

A half-hour later, his fear had passed, and he shot up again, this time trying to make the dose a little smaller. Again, he paced and sat, paced and sat, worried, thought of his kids, thought again of his father and *grand-mère*. He never thought of his mother. She'd be too loaded herself to be hurt.

Finally, he returned to the bar and drank more to mellow out. At 1:45, as the bar started closing down, he went home. In a few short hours, he'd be up and going again.

He sat in the kid's boat, drinking rum, contemplating his life, his kids' future, and tomorrow at work, as a lowly employee in what should be his empire.

WHITE SUGAR, BROWN SUGAR

At six in the morning, as the sky began reddening to the east, Jude went inside. He showered in the kid's bathroom, fixed up a little stash he'd kept, and sat on the toilet to shoot.

As he finished, the bathroom door opened. He looked up with a start, expecting to see the bitch standing there. But it was his darling daughter, Kim instead. He tried to move his leg to hide the syringe, but she saw it, and her eyes grew wide. She just stood staring for a second, and then looked sad. "I'm sorry Daddy," she said, and his heart broke. She turned and went back to her room.

He hesitated, cleaned his works, and set up a syringe full of the remainder for his trip to Jacksonville. He'd do it shortly before arriving at the Roasted Oak.

Jude dressed and prepared to leave. He stopped in Mark's room briefly; the little tiger was lying flat on his back, his arms above his head, his limbs limp, like a rag doll. Jude leaned over and kissed him on his forehead.

Then he crossed the tiny hall to Kim's room. She lay on her side, facing the wall. He leaned down and kissed her on the cheek. She shivered. Then she turned over quickly and hugged him around his neck. Her cheek was wet. She held on like a vise, whimpering quietly. Neither said a word.

His guilt increased. How could he do this? Here he was, a daddy, a husband, a middle-aged businessman, shooting drugs and drinking, constantly trying to escape—to escape this, the love of a daughter.

"I'm sorry, Daddy," she said again. He felt himself tear up. He didn't want her to realize that. So he kissed her on the cheek and tried nonchalantly to extricate himself from the vise grip. She clung tighter, her breath smelling sour and her tears salty.

That was it. He needed to end this. He had to. He just had to.

* * * * * * *

Roosevelt pulled down the street toward Jude and Joyce's house. Jude would have left already—at least he'd better have if he was going to be in Jacksonville on time. He slowed, hesitating, not wanting to face Joyce. This conversation would not be pleasant, but he had to do it.

Although Joyce wasn't his favorite person, he didn't blame her. Jude couldn't keep his penis in his pants, was always drunk and high, and was an ass.

But Roosevelt still considered himself Jude's friend. They went way back. Jude wasn't a bad guy. He never had been. He just let his addiction control him. Now Jude's habit was truly in control.

Roosevelt pulled into the driveway. The house looked quiet. But she had to be up. She had young kids.

Roosevelt made his way to the front door and detected activity in the eat-in kitchen. He rang the doorbell and heard kids romp and yell with excitement. The door opened and Joyce appeared, haggard, eyes rimmed with dark circles, and pissed. Kim stood beside her with the same dark-rimmed eyes as her mother.

"Hi, Joyce," he said. "How you doin'?"

She stared at him.

"Listen, uh, can we talk?"

She shrugged. She looked around at the street, like she was afraid to bring a black man into her house, then glanced at the kids, who looked up at her expectantly. Kim looked so sad. Joyce backed down the hallway and waved him in.

"Go on in your rooms and play," she said, pointing toward the hallway. She led Roosevelt to the kitchen area. "Would you like some coffee or something?"

"No, thanks." They took a seat at the simple table. "I wanna talk about Jude." She rolled her eyes and looked at the floor. "You know he's got a problem, don't you?"

"He's got lots a problems, and he's caused us lots a problems. I don't got a lot a sympathy for him."

"I know Joyce. I know. And I'm sorry about that. You know I'm not gonna make excuses for him. He's his own man, and he can't hide behind addiction. But he needs help. If he gets clean, he can at least be normal again."

She lit a cigarette. "You know what? I really don't care what he does."

Roosevelt was stumped with that. There wasn't much he could do if she didn't care. "Aren't you concerned about saving the marriage, even for the kids?" he asked, under his breath.

She shook her head. "He pays no attention to us. He just wants to be drunk." Little Kim popped her head around the counter and looked at them through haunted eyes. "Go on, now," her mother said, pointing again. A tear rolled down Kim's cheek.

Roosevelt glanced out the window to see Mr. Armstrong coming up the walkway. Roosevelt had summoned him to come too.

When the doorbell rang, Joyce looked surprised and annoyed. As she stood, she said, "Nobody ever comes to see us." She slunk to the front door, with Roosevelt following nonchalantly, unsure how she would take getting ganged up on. She opened the door and said nothing.

"Hello, Joyce," Mr. Armstrong said. Kim heard his voice and squealed with delight as she skipped and ran to the front door, screaming "Grampa. Grampa."

Roosevelt felt a rumble behind him and turned to find little Mark bounding along, saying "Gwampa. Gwampa."

Mr. Armstrong reached down and lifted both kids in the air, their legs straight out. They hugged his neck, and Roosevelt thought he looked more natural and down to earth than Roosevelt had ever seen him. The delight in his face was vibrant. It was rare that the strict old man even smiled—unless he was in his boat on the water.

Joyce turned, not looking the least bit pleased, and trudged back down the hallway, with everybody following. They returned to the table, and the kids were shuffled off again.

"Joyce, I'm not sure how long I can keep him at work," Roosevelt continued. "I sent him up to Jacksonville instead of letting him go, but it's not really working out there either."

"Jacksonville?"

"Yeah. He didn't tell you."

She shook her head. A pair of tears fell as she lit another cigarette. "He hasn't entered the house while we were up for days. He sneaks in and gets his clothes. He never even comes to sleep. I've got no use for him."

Mr. Armstrong looked pained. He asked, "Have you ever heard of an intervention?"

She shook her head.

"That's where people close to an alcoholic or addict get together and confront him with the problems his abuse is causing. Usually, the person is shocked to see how he's affecting his loved ones, and he'll take action. Sometimes the person is so shocked, he'll agree to go into treatment."

She shook her head again. "Not interested."

"You just wanna let him go?" Roosevelt asked. "What'll ya'll do without a bread winner?"

"I'll go to work. I don't care. It's too late."

"And the children?" Mr. Armstrong asked.

She shot him a look. It was obvious she had a sharp answer for him but chose to swallow it. "Look, I'll make it, and the kids'll make it. Jude hasn't been of any use for a long time. We don't need him."

"Joyce," Mr. Armstrong said, "we were hoping you'd be interested in helping."

"I'm tired. I'm tired of Jude stringing us along. I'm tired of being stuck in this house. I'm tired of you not paying Jude enough to even get me a car. And I'm tired of talking about this." She stood and left the kitchen. "Please see yourselves out," she said as she went to the room of one of the kids and closed the door.

Roosevelt and Mr. Armstrong stood silently. The sounds of muffled sobs echoed from the room. Roosevelt imagined the kids holding and consoling her.

* * * * * * *

Flying along the highway toward Jacksonville, Jude banged his fists on the steering wheel. How could he have been so careless? How could he let Kim see him like that? The fucking bitch could have caught him instead, and although she certainly would have yelled and carried on, it would not have been as devastating as his little girl saying "I'm sorry" for something that was never her fault. He relived the moments from earlier last evening when he'd faced almost certain death, when he zoomed and peaked, declined and shot more, all the while picturing himself not making it through, imagining the newspaper article about his untimely death, imagining the devastated look of loss on the faces of his children. All he pictured was scorn and resentment on his lovely wife's face. It was the children that moved him.

He had one more dose, already set and ready, sitting on the seat next to him. He looked at it, imagined what it would do for him, worried about what it might do to him, wondered whether he would have to have another. He would not have another. He wouldn't have done coke at all if he hadn't been so hooked on alcohol. Maybe it was time to quit drinking.

Now that was a ridiculous thought. It was just a little alcohol. How did that ever hurt anybody? But then he thought of his mother. Was it alcohol that had done her in, or did she just become such a drunk because she was already done in? He just thought of her as weak, slovenly, and miserable. He was strong. He could stop that if he wanted to.

But then again, this was no time to stop. It was almost fall. Fall was full of holidays at which drinking was accepted and expected. It was a good time. He wouldn't stop before that. Then at the beginning of the new year, there were a number of events that he would never dream of engaging in sober. There were speed weeks, when car-racing enthusiasts came to town; bike week, when motorcycle enthusiasts came to town; and spring break, when nubile young college girls (and, well, some boys too, but they didn't count) came to town. All those wild and crazy people coming to town, and during the latter two, all those wild girls, the tattooed, breast-baring, crazy drunken girls of bike week, almost falling off the back of motorcycles, and the fresh-looking, sun-burned, breast-baring, crazy drunken girls of spring break. He wouldn't miss any of that. He had to be ready. Had to have his internal alcohol tolerance just right to slide right into and through that magical time in Daytona Beach. There was no getting sober until at least the end of March. Until then, he would try to cool it a bit and exercise more.

He would not do more drugs. He would not. This was it. This magical little syringe full of power sitting next to him, keeping him company. He wasn't sure how much longer he could wait to do it.

He stopped and got a Coke so he could have a drink. He lit a smoke and looked at the syringe longingly from time to time. Finally, like trying to avoid orgasm once the point of no return had been reached, he could wait no more. Still flying along I-95, he grabbed the syringe with his right hand, held the steering wheel with his left arm, and tapped it into Old Faithful in the crook of his arm. It was beautiful. The last time. The very last time. He could convince himself of that right now.

He poured another drink to mellow out, drew rum into the syringe to clean it, squirted the remnants onto the floor of the car, and made his way off the highway and toward the restaurant, downing the remnants of his drink.

He pulled into the parking lot, flipped his cigarette butt out the window and saw the son-of-a-bitch manager, Baker, glaring at him like a guard waiting to examine credentials. He pushed the bottle under the passenger seat. Fucking Baker opened the passenger side door and sat down. His legs were a bit too long for the seat placement, so he reached down, pulled on the handle, and moved the seat back. The neck of the big bottle, all wrapped tightly in a rumpled brown paper bag, stuck out from under the seat like a dog peering out from under a bed.

Baker said, "What's this, Mr. Armstrong?" as he tapped on the lid of the bottle through the bag. Thank God the syringe wasn't showing. "This car smells like a skid-row liquor joint."

Jude didn't want to talk, knowing he hadn't had time to spruce up his breath much. "I don't remember when I put that there. A while ago."

"Huh? . . . oh . . . sure, Armstrong. Whatever. Listen, you gotta make a phone call inside. Mr. Harris wants to talk to you. You're not staying here today."

That didn't sound good. "Whadaya mean today?"

"Uh . . . well," he stammered, "You're not working here anymore."

Jude could hardly believe what he was hearing. He and his father had founded this chain. He was the master of the cooking method. And here he was being shoved out by somebody who didn't even know or appreciate who he was. The son-of-a-bitch had ratted him out, and the other son-of-a-bitch, Ol' Red, the one who screwed a white girl to death while loaded on every drug known to man, was the one who was going to fuck him up.

They marched inside, Baker flanking him, like a prison guard escorting a dangerous criminal to some important and unpleasant appointment.

Baker motioned to the phone. "Push two."

Jude picked up.

"Jude," began the somber, deep, serious voice that Roosevelt had become. "This Roosevelt."

"I know who you are," Jude snapped.

"Jude, I've got some bad news. We feel that it's not working out up there. I need you to go on home."

Go on home? What the hell did that mean? "You mean I'm not going anywhere to work? Whatdaya mean? I gotta work, Roosevelt. You keep fuckin' with me and fuckin' with me. Where would this place be if not for me?" Fucking Baker stood guard at the door.

"Jude," Roosevelt answered, suffering for having to hurt his friend, and trying not to be too hurtful, "You can't live forever on a past effort. Your dad set you up some stock. One day you'll get dividends on that."

One day. Bullshit. It was all bullshit. He was the brunt of a conspiracy, and his father and the bitch at home were probably in on it. Of course, she had plenty to lose if he couldn't work, but would that stop her from messing with him? Probably not.

"Jude, let's get together. I think we could talk better in person."

"Fuck you, asshole." Jude slammed the receiver down. He'd like to get together with Roosevelt to kick his fucking ass. He could picture himself smashing Ol' Red's pompous head into a brick wall, again and again. Of course, Jude couldn't do a thing to Roosevelt because Roosevelt had built up and become a healthy, athletic man. Jude was a weakened rack of limbs. The son-of-a-bitch. Jude fought to avoid crying. The injustice of it all was getting to him. He was screwed every way he could be.

He wanted to get out of here before Baker saw him crack, but the arrogant fucker was standing right in the middle of the doorway, smirking. Jude started for the door. Baker didn't move, so Jude lowered his shoulder and rammed the little punk out of the way. Baker stumbled backward and nearly lost his footing on the tile floor, but recovered in an awkward way that probably tore his groin. Good.

* * * * * * *

Roosevelt aimlessly calculated figures, charted projections, and did what he did. Jude's haunted, insolent and baffled voice kept floating back to him. He wanted to do something—needed to do something to protect his friend. He knew him all too well. He knew that the zoom of cocaine was there, the rawness of too many cigarettes, and the gravely dullness of alcohol, imbibed today, and retained from all night.

He also knew that Jude would go straight out to drink more and endanger himself by driving drunk and who knew what else. Roosevelt tried to concentrate on his work. He needed to wrap this detail up so he could get on to the Orlando store and deal with a different kind of personnel issue—a cook who'd decided that his own recipes and variations on the menu were better than the tried-and-true recipes and techniques developed by Roasted Oak. The guy didn't understand the value of the mark—the reason people went to Roasted Oak restaurants was the same reason another type of customer went to McDonald's or Burger King. They knew what they were getting, no matter where they were. Sure there could be variations in decor; there could be little unique "special memory enhancers," a term he'd made up to mean that special something that hooked a person to a particular business, like something as simple as a free newspaper, vases with fresh flowers on the tables, a way of treating a person as special, and other variations. But you couldn't use a bunch of spices you'd learned from your grandmother, no matter how good, and call the product the Roasted Oak special, because that would confuse and alienate customers. It had to be the same, everywhere. The food was already delicious, the ingredients the freshest, and while anything in life could be improved, he couldn't have a rogue chef just doing his own thing. He was getting riled up thinking about this next confrontation and broke his pencil tip for the third time since he'd sat down.

Mr. Armstrong, looking haggard, came in and sat in the chair across the desk from him. "How was your talk with Jude?"

Roosevelt shook his head. "Wasn't much of a talk. He was blasted. I mean he was high and drunk. We had to tell him to leave the restaurant." To avoid Armstrong's gaze, he looked down at the papers on the desk.

Armstrong slammed his trembling hand on the desk. He looked like he was about to break into tears. "I can't believe it's come to this." He shook his head.

"He'll come around. He has to. He's got to realize this is all because of his drinking. That should tell him this is a bottom. He won't listen to us, but hopefully he'll get it himself." Roosevelt wasn't sure he believed what he was saying, but it sounded good.

* * * * * * *

Jude found a liquor store, stocked up on more rum, and headed toward the beach. He found a beach approach where he could drive onto the hard sand without too much risk of getting stuck.

An audience had gathered to observe a large ship stuck in the sand. It listed dangerously to one side, battered by waves, as tugboats tugged and shoved it. Jude sat in the car and watched, alternating between rum and beer.

He pictured the bitch exploding when he told her of the newest development in his career. She'd bitched about there not being enough money before. How about none? None. She could whine all she wanted about the high mortgage payment and not having a car. Now they'd lose the house, and the car, and rely on friends and relatives for food. That goddam Roosevelt, making probably twice what Jude had been, on his high Uncle-Tom horse, and pulling the rug out from under Jude.

Jude couldn't kid himself. He wouldn't be in the house with the bitch or the kids. It was all over. She'd tell him to get the hell out. He'd be better off not going home at all. His heart ached at the thought of hurting his kids in any way, of the bitch poisoning them against him, of their having to suffer the injustice that had been done to him.

His father's face fluttered into his mind. He still owned at least a third of the company, at least Jude thought so. He had an equal say on the board. Yet he seemed absent when it came to Jude's future. He'd told Jude once that he abstained on any decision having to do with Jude because of a conflict of interest, whatever in the hell that lawyer talk meant. So he just left Jude to be chewed up by the carnivores and spit out for the vultures.

He was really drunk. It was a combination of everything—a little lack of sleep, a little end-of-the-cocaine highway, a lot of alcohol, and the injustice of it all. He was the downtrodden.

The sun was in his face. The audience still stood and watched the tugs pulling and pushing. The ship seemed ready to tip—ready to go over the edge—just like Jude.

He lurched out of the car and trudged toward the water, behind the crowd. He yanked off his shoes and socks and dropped them in the sand. Then he dropped his wallet on the sand. He checked his pockets for his smokes. He'd left them and his keys in the car.

He wasn't sure exactly what his plan was. Maybe he just wanted to swim; that was logical. Maybe he intended to drown himself. That sounded like an uncomfortable way to go. Maybe he just wanted to stay underwater until his problems went away. Well, that was dumb. He just plain felt sorry for himself and thought the water would help.

He didn't look at the audience or emergency workers nearer the ship. He didn't care about them. They wouldn't care about him. They might think it was a little odd for him to jump into the ocean fully dressed.

He plodded out, being knocked off balance by the same waves that battered the ship, or maybe the liquid inside him. Soon he could touch bottom only occasionally. He swayed through the frothy water, pushing, half swimming, half hopping. He gasped for air while above the water, but inhaled water on the way down. His throat scratched all the way up to his nasal cavity, like the feeling of bile passing through when vomiting.

Then his lungs burned. It hurt like hell. Suddenly it seemed this was not a good idea. It was not an easy way to go. It was not a smart way to get attention. This was being drowned by his sorrows, rather than merely drowning his sorrows. He started reaching up, hoping to grab something, hoping to avoid dying like this. He had the same

MICHAEL A. PYLE 255

thoughts he had every time he came close to over-amping on cocaine: *I am going to die . . . I am not going to die . . . I am going to die.* This wasn't nearly as much fun as dying high. He started jumping higher, trying to get his breath, sometimes gasping air, and sometimes inhaling more water. He thought—he hoped—he was making it back toward shore. God his chest hurt, like the weight of an anvil.

He finally got to a place where he could keep his head above water. He stumbled forward until he lost his footing and fell to his knees, rubbing them severely on the hard sand. He got to his feet again, stumbled a little further, collapsed again, and vomited wildly all over himself. It burned his throat even more. His chest was so tight he thought he'd die right there.

He noticed some people, alarmed, half running in his direction. He didn't want to be saved; he didn't want to talk to anyone; he just wanted to escape. He stood and stumbled again toward shore. His car seemed a mile away up the long beach. He fell. He stood. He puked. He fell again. The world was swirling around him. The voices of the concerned onlookers, who had abandoned the ship, which they couldn't help, for a suicidal drunk who they could perhaps help, but who didn't want their help.

He reached for his shoes, socks and wallet. Two men grabbed his elbows.

"Man, what are you doing?" one asked.

"Leemee lone," he said, struggling to free himself.

"He's loaded," the other one said.

A cop and more men trotted toward him. Now was the time. He had to escape. He leaned down, grabbed his stuff, and came up hard, hitting one in the chin with the back of his head, and knocking the other one to the ground with his elbow. Clutching his belongings to his aching chest, he sprinted like a gazelle shot with tranquilizers.

He reached his car, jumped in, cranked it, jammed it into drive, fishtailed toward the beach approach, lost control, overcompensated, and slid into the soft sand. He revved and rested, rocked forward and back, and quickly mired the car hopelessly.

He jumped out, ripped his shirt off and stuck it under a wheel for traction. The cop tackled him. He fell face-first into the sand. Sand ground into his chin, and his eyes and nose. His lungs hurt even worse. He struggled. He stood halfway up and was thrown roughly onto the hood of his car.

With a loud, hollow, metallic thud, somebody grabbed him by the hair and banged his head onto the hood. His arms were wrenched behind him, and cuffed, pinching his right wrist. The sons-of-bitches had no compassion. The injustice of the world continued.

He was thrown violently into the back of a police car. His head struck the opposite door. He lay on the seat amid a stench. He didn't look up.

In a few minutes, the car spun through the last part of the soft sand. Its tires grabbed as it pulled up the beach approach. Then it whipped this way and that as it made its way toward jail, where injustice to the downtrodden was at its peak.

Jude passed in and out of consciousness and awareness during the ride. His throat, nasal passage, chest, head, arms, and wrist ached. He was alive, for all that was worth, and someday he would see his children again.

Maybe he should call his father. The bitch wouldn't have the money or the desire to bail him out. Then again, maybe he shouldn't call anybody. He'd have time to get his thoughts together. His father was probably in on it anyway. Let his old man see what he'd done. Maybe he'd have a little remorse.

At the jail, after cops brutishly pulled him from the car, dropped him on the ground, dragged him, almost pulling his arms from the shoulder sockets like chicken wings being popped free from the breast, and dropped him in a bundle before some asshole. He chose to be unconscious. It hurt too much to speak or even to think anyway.

"Hey, what's your name?"

"Here's his license," somebody said. He heard the sound of a leather wallet being plopped on wood.

"What's the matter with him?"

"I don't know. Seems drunk, high, or both."

"What did he do?"

"First, he jumped in the ocean fully clothed and disrupted the salvage of the vessel. Don't know if he was trying to kill himself or what. Then he evaded. Then he endangered the lives of a law enforcement officer and other citizens. And he was driving while intoxicated."

"If he's suicidal, we need to contact mental health. Did you do a Breathalyzer? Did you have him walk the line?"

"He was too busy puking to get him to blow, and he hasn't stood up, or been able to stand up since I've had him in custody."

"Hey," somebody yelled into his ear. "You wanna call somebody?" Jude chose to remain silent and still.

"I think he's just loaded. Throw him in the drunk tank and see how he is when he sobers up. I'll charge him with disorderly, DUI, resisting arrest. That's probably enough."

Then Jude was drug along another hallway and deposited behind a creaky metal door onto a rancid, hard, tile floor that sloped down to a large grate in the center of the room, just like the kitchen floor at Roasted Oak. He stayed in that position for a long, long time.

When he awoke, his arm and hip throbbed. His head was killing him. After a considerable struggle, he managed to roll over on his back, looking up at the ceiling. He felt a huge, tender lump on the back of his skull, so he moved his head to the side, and then he realized how much his neck and throat hurt. He gagged from the sour odor effusing from his clothes and hair, and the room itself.

He heard footsteps on the tile floor outside. A voice asked, "You ready to have a little conversation?"

Jude squinted his eyes and made out a big, uniformed figure, standing like a tower above him. Jude didn't respond.

"Hey," the guy said louder, kicking him lightly in the ribs, and causing him to grimace. "You wanna call somebody? You wanna eat somethin'?"

Jude turned away from the man and curled into a ball.

* * * * * * *

After traveling to three of the company stores and resolving various problems, Roosevelt went to Nana's house to retrieve Tad. Auntie Barbara, Uncle Theodore, and Nana sat on the porch admiring Tad as he rode a bicycle in the dirt front yard. Auntie Barbara had mellowed. Maybe she just didn't have any problems to carry on about. Uncle Theodore had been clean and sober, a good Muslim, for a long time. He and Roosevelt understood each other and respected each other's means of kicking their demons.

Roosevelt took Tad to the Y, and they played a little ball. Tad wasn't much of a shooter. He did show speed and dexterity and dribbled well.

Then he took Tad to Tara's and dropped him off. She'd been clean and sober for quite a while.

When Roosevelt had gone to the doctor for a routine checkup, he'd met a nurse named Gloria. They'd ended up on a date so naturally that he wasn't sure whether he'd asked her out or not. That wasn't normal for him. He would have stewed over the invitation, planned exactly when and how to ask, and prepared an agenda on an index card. But it had all just happened.

Their relationship was progressing methodically and in perfect order.

She'd come from Guyana. She had the coolest accent, and light chocolate skin. She was intelligent, outgoing and pleasant. She'd never touched a drug stronger than pot. She was a normal drinker. She'd have a glass of wine or a drink when they went out, but never more than two. Roosevelt couldn't comprehend how a person could limit the number of drinks after drinking one.

On their third date, he'd explained that the reason he didn't drink was that he just couldn't. He'd experienced problems with alcohol and drugs when he was much younger. Had not touched either in many, many years, and hoped never to again. He watched for a response.

"I understand," she'd said. "I've had friends who've been through the same thing. It's okay. Does it bother you if I have a drink?"

He wanted to be honest. "I do worry about it. I'm always afraid the simple smell or taste of it'll set me off. But it's okay. If I'm troubled, I'll tell you."

Tonight, he'd arranged a hopefully romantic meal at the Chart House, a nice restaurant overlooking the small harbor in downtown Daytona. It was only blocks south of where he'd fished so many times with his family. He'd never felt uncomfortable about being Black at the Chart House. Now, in the mid-80s, he shouldn't feel uncomfortable anyplace, but sometimes he just did. He was never sure if people treated him differently, or if it was all in his mind.

This meal would be something to remember. They sat next to a window. Some kids motored by in a small boat. He thought of Jude. They got salads from the salad bar. He ordered a margarita for Gloria and a soft drink for himself. They talked and laughed, and shared stories of their pasts and their families. The food was good, although he hardly thought of it. He could love this woman. He hoped the feeling was mutual. She seemed happy when they were together. She was fine. Just plain fine.

After dinner, they walked around the marina and admired the boats, gently swaying in the still, dark water. They held hands. Sometimes she put an arm around his waist.

Tad was at Tara's for the night. So they went to Roosevelt's apartment. They'd done some serious foreplay before but had not had the opportunity for the play itself. Tonight was the night.

He put on an album of Smoky Robinson and the Miracles. They kissed and went further. He tried to control himself, to be polite, to respect her. She responded sensually. It progressed quickly, and nicely. Her exuberance was sweet and right. They spent a couple of hours in the bedroom, learning all about each other. Finally, they lay entwined, spent and at peace. Roosevelt was sure she was the one.

"You are fine," she exclaimed.

"You are finer," he answered.

He knew better than to say, "I love you and want to spend my life with you." It was too early for that. He wouldn't want to scare her away. But that was what he felt. Take it easy Roosevelt, he told himself. Just relax and go with the flow.

"I need to get on home," she said at last.

"Awe, baby," he said.

"I just don't stay out too late because my mother worries. Yes, I'm a big girl, but she's a worry wart, and she's my mother."

"I understand. Just come back tomorrow."

"You want me to come back tomorrow?"

He hesitated, wanting to answer carefully, not to look too eager. But facts were facts. "I want you to come back every day."

She smiled. "You're sweet. What do you want to do tomorrow?"

He shrugged.

She said, "How about some plain ol' soul food. Down ta Harold Place."

"All right," he said, smiling at her slip to the vernacular. "Sounds good. I'll have Tad with me."

"That's fine. Time I met little Tad. I'm sure he's a gentleman just like his daddy."

* * * * * * *

In the morning, there was a message at the Daytona store for Roosevelt to call Joyce Armstrong. She answered. "This Roosevelt, Joyce. What can I do for you?"

"Well, I shouldn't really say I'm worried about Jude, because I told you I don't give a crap . . . but, I am a little concerned. I haven't heard from him or seen him in two days. Usually, he sneaks in here in the middle of the night. He never comes to bed, but he showers, gets clothes and everything. But he hasn't been here the last two nights, and I haven't heard anything from him. Do you know anything? How did your talk with him go?"

"Hmm. Well, Joyce, the talk did not go well. He left the restaurant. He was loaded the morning we were going to talk to him, and I told him he had to leave. Of course, it was not pleasant. But I have no idea where he went or what he's doing. You call his dad?"

"No, uh-uh. I don't really want him involved. I don't wanna be like I'm tattling or something."

"Well, can I call him, then, 'cause I'm sure he's got connections, and he can check police stations, hospitals and stuff."

"Yeah, okay. Let me know if you find out anything."

He dialed Mr. Armstrong's office—a number he'd learned long ago. No answer. It was early. He opened his briefcase, quickly found an index card, and called the home number. A woman answered and said he'd already left for work. Roosevelt drove the few blocks to Mr. Armstrong's office. He pulled into the parking lot just as Mr. Armstrong strolled toward the back door. "Sir," he said, "I need to talk to you for a minute if you have a moment."

"Sure, what's the matter, Roosevelt?"

"It's Jude; after our discussion the other day, he disappeared. Joyce says he hasn't been home, and she doesn't know where he is."

"Oh." He stood, stewing.

Roosevelt suffered for him. Jude always put him through hell.

"Mr. Armstrong, do you have ways to check with authorities or something?"

"Uh, well, yes. I guess I do."

* * * * * * *

Two hours later, Armstrong called Roosevelt. "Found him. In jail. I'm not sure what exactly happened, but it seems he was intoxicated, became unruly, endangered his life at a beach, tried to escape authorities who were trying to help him, and is now facing serious charges. He has refused to talk, to eat, to request a phone call or anything else. Just this morning, they are preparing to take him to a hospital for treatment."

"Where can I see him then?"

"I don't exactly know. If you want to head up to Jacksonville, call me collect from a payphone at the outskirts of town. I'll try to find out where he'll be."

Roosevelt hurriedly packed up his paperwork, grabbed a drink of juice for the road, and departed. He went straight to the home of a white, long-time A.A. member named Owen. He knew he could count on him for a Twelfth Step. The final step of the A.A. process was to help others find their way to sobriety—to talk to another drunk, just like Bill Wilson and Dr. Bob, the founders of A.A., had done. Roosevelt banged on the door, and Owen opened it.

"Hey, Roosevelt. How are you?" They shook hands white style.

"Good. Listen, Owen. I got a friend in trouble. I know you guys do Twelfth-Step work. I've never done it, and anyway this is a friend of mine. I'm on my way to Jacksonville to see him, either at the jail or the hospital. Not sure where he'll be. And I need somebody to talk to him."

"Drugs or alcohol?"

"He was an old running buddy of mine—a fellow junkie. But now it's alcohol. He might be doing coke too. He works for the same company I do. I had to fire him the other day. He went straight off and got into real trouble. Cops're taking him to the hospital this morning because he's refused to talk, eat and whatever since they busted him."

"Okay, let's go. Usually, two people are required to Twelfth Step. You don't count since he's your friend, but considering he's in custody, we'll be lucky if we can even get in."

On the way, Owen explained how Twelfth Stepping worked. "Mostly, we just talk to the guy. Tell him our stories. It's good that he'd had a couple of days to dry out a bit. He won't listen or won't look like he's listening. He'll prob'ly be negative and annoyed. Don't worry. We just talk. Tell him some stuff. Tell him there's an answer. Don't try to get him to commit to anything."

Roosevelt nodded. "Course he and I went through the same stuff. But I never really went through the alcohol thing like he is."

"Don't worry. I'll tell my story first. Then just tell him how A.A.'s helped you. Tell him how it's worked for you."

Roosevelt knew Owen's story. It had been many years since he'd had a drink, but he could still relay how he'd hit bottom with such realism that everybody was moved. He hoped Jude would listen.

Roosevelt stopped outside a liquor store on the outskirts of Jacksonville and called Mr. Armstrong.

Mr. Armstrong said, "He's at the hospital, probably in emergency," and gave the address. "I don't know if they'll let you talk to him, but please try."

Within a few minutes, Roosevelt and Owen stood in front of a disinterested desk clerk. Owen explained that they'd driven from Daytona Beach, they knew Jude had just arrived, they wanted to talk to him while he was still in crisis, they knew he'd refused to eat or talk, and they believed his apparent suicide attempt was the result of his alcoholism.

"Wouldn't you say," he asked, "he's going to be sitting around for quite a while anyway? It certainly wouldn't hurt to let us talk to him for a little while in private."

The man didn't appear convinced. He acted like he'd never heard of alcoholism or A.A., or at least did not believe in it. "It's against the rules," he said. Then without another breath, he said, "Awe, who cares. Go ahead."

When they arrived at his room, Jude was being held down by two large male orderlies or nurses, one of whom was bound and determined to get a needle into his vein to set up an I.V.

Jude mumbled, "I don't want it. Leave me alone," with a strong enough voice that Roosevelt was heartened to hear that he still had some spunk.

"I don't really give a damn if you want it or not," the man with the needle said, "If you keep struggling, it'll hurt a lot more."

Finally, they succeeded and moved away, tightening straps on his wrists and legs that held him in place.

"Sons a bitches," Jude exclaimed.

Roosevelt moved into the room.

One of the men eyed him suspiciously. "Who are you?"

Owen spoke up. "We have permission from the front desk to meet with Jude here for a few minutes."

The two shrugged and exited.

"Yo, Jude. Whassup?" Roosevelt said, trying to be nonchalant.

"Fuck you, asshole," Jude replied, through dried and chapped lips, the corners of his mouth breaking with the words.

"This is my friend Owen," Roosevelt said, waving his hand toward Owen.

"Fuck you too, sir," Jude said. "I don't know why this son-of-a-bitch brought you here, but I don't wanna talk to anybody, including you. I'm here 'cause this son-of-a-bitch, conspiring with my father, fucked up my whole goddam mother-fuckin' life, and he can kiss my fuckin' ass before I talk to his sorry fuckin' ass."

And Jude meant it. Sure, deep down, he knew that he'd been fired for a reason, and that alcohol was starting to affect his life, but he was sure Roosevelt had it in for him and was just screwing him over for control of the company.

Roosevelt glanced at Owen. He was amused to see that Owen appeared to be enjoying the verbal tirade. His eyes were smiling. The crusty old bastard got off on this.

Owen started. "Jude, if you don't mind, I have a few things I'd like to tell you. You don't have to say or do anything. Just let me tell you a little story."

"I don't wanna listen to your story."

"Jude. This scene is very familiar to me. I myself was arrested for various charges when I was about your age, when I was drunker than usual, and out of my head with despair. Alcohol wasn't working for me anymore. It had calmed me. It had been my lifeblood for many years. I was sure I couldn't live without it. But it had stopped doing what it was supposed to do. For me, it increased the hopelessness rather than helping me. Anyway, I got into a fight in a bar over a drink tab. The tab was right, I'm pretty sure, but I became convinced that the bartender had padded it. So I jumped over the bar, fell on the ground, got up, and pushed him. He could see I was so drunk I would do little to hurt him. So he didn't hit me. He and some others picked me up, each holding an arm and a leg, and carried me face down, like a flying drunken Superman, to the street. They flung me out of the bar, but I didn't fly like Superman."

Roosevelt smiled, and Jude did too. He was listening.

"I collapsed on the hard sidewalk, taking quite a lick to my face, cutting my chin pretty deeply, almost breaking my nose. I tried to get up, but I only managed to get on all fours, like some kind of rabid dog, dripping blood from my chin instead of frothy foam from my mouth. And of course, the St. Louis finest pulled up in front. I tried to get up and look like everything was okay, but I couldn't."

"I don't know exactly when it hit me, but it was right about then, or maybe it was when I got into the jail cell. I said to myself, 'alcohol has beaten you. You've got to stop.' I didn't think I could stop. I really didn't. I hadn't had a day without alcohol since I was seventeen or eighteen. It had progressed and progressed so that it controlled my every move, my every thought. It prevented me from going places and doing things I wanted to do. I had to know that I had enough alcohol on me, or that I could get more, or I wouldn't go anywhere. I wasn't married at the time. I was a merchant marine. Girls didn't put up with my compulsive drinking for too long, even drunk, butt-ugly, skanky ones."

Jude laughed. All three smiled.

"In the jail cell, when I realized what had happened to me, I became despondent. I wouldn't eat, wouldn't cooperate, wouldn't try to help myself get out. They sent me to a nut ward of a hospital for evaluation. These two old geezers popped in to see me. They started telling me this story about themselves and what alcohol had done to them. Sound familiar? At first, I refused to listen. I wasn't as reasonable as you are. But I absorbed some of what they said, against my will. And I became convinced as they spoke that there was a way out. Of course, I didn't acknowledge it to them. On account a they were just a couple of wrinkled, crusty old guys, and I was a young, strong, determined man, who liked to drink a little. What could they know? They were apparently just some weaklings who let alcohol control them. So I had a lot of conflicts in my mind."

Jude was stewing. He too was having internal conflict, like a dupe being swayed by a talented salesman to buy something expensive he couldn't afford. Maybe he could do it. No, this guy was just an old goddam coot. Jude's life was worthless. He didn't even have an alcohol problem. All his problems stemmed from his wife, his father and this big, muscular Black son-of-a-bitch sitting next to the old codger. He started to despise the old guy for making him even think about these things.

But the old guy rambled on. "They left me a book. And I have a copy for you." He placed a paper bag on the bed with a thick, weathered blue-covered book half sticking out. "This is the book that tells how you do it. It describes in detail how it works. It's a prescription to relieve your pain—to get rid of what ails you."

The old guy talked about how A.A. worked for him. Jude turned off completely. It didn't sound the least bit appealing. A bunch of old winos whining about their sorrows. Jude was a successful businessman, at least he'd been until the asshole Red there had done him in. He'd be successful again. He just wouldn't drink. Or he'd go back to just drinking socially—just on weekends. He'd drink like normal people. Because he was normal, wasn't he?

But then he again started to wonder if the old guy was right. Maybe he wasn't normal. Maybe this was really alcoholism.

Jude recalled that once he'd broken down and called the A.A. number in the phone book. He'd been suffering and wondering whether he could actually be alcoholic. A very friendly man answered and asked him a couple of questions. All Jude was worried about was whether it was some kind of sect or church or something. He didn't want a church—didn't want to become a Jesus freak just to get sober. So he'd asked the guy, "Does this program rely on God?"

The guy on the other end had hemmed and hawed and finally babbled something about it not necessarily being God—it was a Higher Power—of your choosing, and some people chose God as their Higher Power. That was enough for Jude. He thanked the guy politely and hung up. The guy seemed genuinely concerned, but helpless. He was losing a big fish on the line, and just couldn't pull him into the little sect.

Now Roosevelt had begun talking. "Jude, you already know my story. It's your story, although I found the answer a little earlier, before I had to get so much into alcohol. But I've learned a lot, and that's what I want to share with you. I've watched people kick drugs and alcohol on their own, without A.A., and they've been miserable. Some have stayed clean and sober for a long time. Some have never slipped, but their lives were not bliss. What A.A. does is to give you a guidebook—a way to live. It removes the urge to drink and to drug. And if an urge ever arises, it gives you tools to deal with it."

Well, that was all fine, but this A.A. was either something or it was nothing. If it was just a bunch of people talking, like a group therapy session, he'd already been through plenty of those and that was just a bunch of horseshit. Half the time he wanted to get high more after sharing experiences than he had without talking to the bunch of braggart ex-druggies. So this had to be some kind of religious experience, something different. Every time he thought of what it must offer, he knew it didn't sound good.

The old man took the stage again, and now seemed to be winding down, throwing the hook. Jude knew a double-team sales itch when he saw one. "Well, yes, Jude, I would call it a spiritual experience, but not a religious experience. Because it is not a church. It is most definitely not a church. All we ask now is that you keep an open mind, take this book, and come to a meeting with us when you're free from here." He picked up the book and held it toward Jude. Jude looked at it but wouldn't actually grasp it.

When they'd gone, Jude was relieved. He relaxed and thought. He did have an interest. But he felt like one who'd been duped into buying some crap from a commercial. He remembered a couple of years ago when he'd been hooked by an advertisement in Family Weekly, the Sunday newspaper supplement. A full-page ad had beckoned him for weeks. A man wrote about how he'd made a million dollars from some vague and elusive business he'd created, and he'd share his technique for the price of his book. Jude read and reread the ad, trying to figure out the secret without shelling out the money for the book. But finally, he bought into it. This was the key to riches. He ordered the book, waited impatiently for a week or so for it to arrive, and read it urgently when it arrived. The first chapters contained only a repeat of the hook—a description of the author's wonderful life. Every now and then there would be a little hint about how he'd done it—by setting up his home business, to handle mail-order offers for companies. Jude kept reading for the answer, but he already had the million dollars in his mind. Every day, he passed a dealership that had two magnificent Lincoln Mark IVs on the showcase, and he would just stop and drool, like a young boy examining forbidden candy, and imagine himself in one. He'd go home and read again, fervently trying to find the answer. Once he understood that it was mail order, and he studied the area on how one finds customers, he began to get disillusioned. But then there was a chapter in which the author explained that anybody could also get rich just by writing something telling others how to get rich. He could publish an ad in the same way the author had, offer some guide on how to do whatever, and the people would just send in money. He'd even contacted Family Weekly to find out how much the ad would be—ten thousand dollars—and had tried to figure out where he could get the money. Then the whole thing had fizzled with the realization that he'd been a sucker and that what he'd spent on the stupid book had helped to buy its author more goodies, but that he hadn't really learned anything at all.

A doctor came in with a nurse. "You're a prisoner from the County jail, aren't you?"

Jude shrugged. "I guess."

"Where's the guard?"

Jude hadn't thought about it. He was strapped down. And even if he wasn't, why would he want to go? After all, he just wanted to be dead. "I dunno."

"Do you have family?" The doctor didn't look like he really gave a shit.

"Yeah."

"Who? Where?"

"Daytona—parents divorced. Wife—two children. My kids are the only ones I miss."

The doctor picked up on that. "I understand people thought you might want to end your life."

Jude shrugged and looked at the floor.

"Where would your children be without you?"

He thought for a long minute. "Well, doc, where are they with me? I'm useless. I have no money. No job. My wife hates me. Won't even let me in the house. So I'm of no use to the kids anyway."

The doctor worked the kid angle for a long time. Jude knew where he was going. As he talked, he examined Jude, looked at his bruises, studied his needle marks and treated his little cuts and abrasions. "I understand you haven't spoken to the police or eaten anything." The doctor stared at him, and he stared back. "You don't seem quite so reclusive to me. You don't seem to me to have any mental illness or physical problem other than that you haven't taken care of yourself, and you need to eat and get better. Am I right? At least you are talking now."

"Watch out or I'll stop," Jude said, laughing. The doctor laughed with him. The nurse didn't. "Listen, I was feeling really bad when they picked me up. I was at the bottom. I just couldn't face anything. I didn't want to. Right now, I'm in a better frame of mind. And I just had a nice conversation with some friends. I think there may be some hope for me."

"That's great David. Listen, why don't we just keep you here for a couple of days. I can say I want to get some food into you slowly and carefully—check your vitals. It'll give you a little chance to get things together in your head."

Jude nodded. "I go by Jude. That'd be nice."

"But David, you also need to deal with the criminal matter. You either need to talk to the public defender or get a lawyer or something. Right now, you have an open jail sentence because you haven't pled guilty or not guilty, or participated in your defense. I don't know anything about the law, but I know you need to take action now."

Jude nodded. "Thanks."

* * * * * * *

Driving home to Daytona, Roosevelt quizzed Owen about whether he saw any hope. He had no benchmark to judge. Jude hadn't seemed to open up at all.

"There's no way to tell for sure," Owen said, "but I think there's a good chance he'll take it. He'll read the book. He's at the bottom. He's as low as they get. That's really ideal. It's much easier to get somebody in the program when they're beaten down like that. He's lost everything, and even though he doesn't want to admit it, he's hurting and he knows it's because of his alcoholism."

"I hope you're right," Roosevelt said. "I hope you're right."

Roosevelt had always done his twelfth-step work by attending meetings inside a facility—a juvenile detention facility, a jail, or a drug and alcohol rehab lock-down. He found those meetings fruitful for the attendees and felt that he offered something useful. Those meetings flowed. He simply stated facts about himself when it was appropriate, and hoped some residents would listen. But that was quite different from meeting one-on-one. This had been much more difficult and was not any easier because Jude was his friend.

"He looked like hell," Roosevelt said. "You think he did all that to himself or he got roughed up?"

"Some of it was probably caused by his falling down. But I'd say he pissed off some cops and they retaliated. Forget about it. He's all right. It's just part of the reason this might be his bottom."

Roosevelt thought it was a shame that police would injure a person who was obviously despondent and at the bottom of his mental-health ladder. But he'd take Owen's advice and forget it.

They arrived at Mr. Armstrong's office and went in. The receptionist, an attractive white girl, smiled. She always lapsed into a half-jive cadence with him. At first, he was almost insulted by the acknowledgment of his race, but she was funny, and she'd grown on him. With her best black accent and intonation, she said "Yo, Rose. What it is?"

He didn't feel like responding with jive talk. He caught Owen looking at him peculiarly. As she dialed the phone, he whispered to Owen, "It's just a little game we play."

"Big Dude waitin' on ya'll. Top a da stairs," she said, mixing the cadence and vocabulary of more than one vernacular. Roosevelt smiled, thinking that she sounded like a street-smart Black mixed with New York Mafia and white farmers of southern Georgia.

They climbed the stairs and found Mr. Armstrong, smiling but concerned. Roosevelt introduced Owen as a long-time A.A. member who specialized in carrying the message to others who were suffering.

Owen said, "Twelfth-Step work is one of the cornerstones of A.A. Dr. Bob and Bill Wilson, the founders of A.A., stayed sober in large part by helping other drunks. It grounded them in their sobriety. Not only does it help the other person, but there's nothing like seeing somebody struggle at the bottom to remind a drunk of where he could be if he picked up again."

Mr. Armstrong nodded, although he didn't seem to get it. That was okay. It was hard to get if you weren't a drunk.

"Jude's all right. Looks a little rough. But also seems like he's ready to come back to the living. He'll start eating now. But he hasn't done anything to get his criminal charges resolved. He's in limbo. The hospital will keep him for a few days and get his health back. But then, he'll probably be released back to the jail. You have a lawyer you can get to help with that?"

Mr. Armstrong nodded. "Sure." He picked up the phone, explained the situation, and put Roosevelt on to tell him where Jude could be found. Roosevelt also explained his layman's view of the charges and the procedure.

The lawyer on the other end said, "Sounds like we might get him off with time served."

"You talk to Joyce?" Roosevelt asked Mr. Armstrong as he set the receiver back in the cradle.

"Yes, she's pretty bitter. She doesn't seem to like me much either. I never realized she blames me for things. I've never really cared for her too much, but right now I wish our relationship were better."

"Maybe this is your opportunity to make it better."

"Maybe. She says she's filing for divorce, but I'm not sure she's convinced. I forced some money on her, to pay the mortgage payment, monthly bills and groceries. We need to get Jude back to work."

Owen piped up. "You'll probably have to help out a little more before he's productive again."

"That's okay." Mr. Armstrong grimaced, shook his head, and looked as though he were on the verge of tears.

* * * * * * *

Jude had plenty of time to think. It was boring as hell sitting around the goddam crazy ward with a bunch of loony wackos. Again. They wandered, sat and played chess, all while their minds were absent. Some were catatonic. He figured they were loaded on Thorazine or something.

He picked up the book the old guy'd given him. He knew it was going to be a bunch of shit, but he was somewhat interested in the snake-oil offer inside. He read the Preface and three Forewords. He was surprised to find that it was good reading. Then he read The Doctor's Opinion. It seemed very logical—scientific. A Doctor Silkworth explained how he believed strongly in A.A. as a program. Then the author stated a number of things that struck home with Jude. One sentence said, "The body of the alcoholic is quite as abnormal as the mind." Yes, he believed that. He had a different chemical makeup than normal people. It explained that the way a chronic alcoholic absorbs alcohol is "a manifestation of an allergy; . . . the phenomenon of craving is limited to this class and never occurs in the average temperate drinker. These allergic types can never safely use alcohol in any form at all . . .." He got that. He knew damn well what a craving was. He'd had them when he was hooked on heroin, and he had them when he was deprived of alcohol.

Then he read Chapter 1, Bill's Story, in which a man told a story about reaching the depths of alcoholism. After describing his plight, he said, "No words can tell the loneliness and despair I found in the bitter morass of self-pity. Quicksand stretched around me in all directions. I had met my match. I had been overwhelmed. Alcohol was my master." Jude started to think that maybe it was his master too.

Jude thought about the last time he'd gotten sober. He'd become fat and blubbery—unhealthy. When he quit, the weight fell off rapidly.

Quitting drinking that time hadn't seemed that hard. Sure, he'd missed it, and felt somewhat out of step, but he just knew he couldn't drink, at least for the time being. He also knew that someday he'd be able to drink again—responsibly—like a normal person—like his father, who could have a beer one day, and maybe another later the same week. Jude wouldn't have to drink all the time.

In the new sober period, he'd spent more time with his kids, gotten along reasonably well with his wife, and had no problems. A few months earlier, they'd gone on a vacation to New England. They'd raced around country roads watching leaves change, picnicking in rest areas and wayside parks, and watching their kids almost change the course of a river or dam a stream by throwing rocks into the channel. The kids were becoming real human beings. They were fun to be around. Jude caught their antics with his video camera. Kim had developed quite a knack for announcing, so he'd put her in front of the camera to explain where they were and what they were doing.

At some point during the trip, they stopped in Boston to visit some old friends of Joyce. Jude thought Boston would be the perfect city to drink in. It just seemed like that. They spent a day in the Faneuil Hall area. In the evening, they ate in Durgin Park, over paper tablecloths, served by a bitchy, gruff woman. He noticed seemingly normal people drinking beer with their meals. It looked cold, frothy, and magical. Of course, he'd thought he was a normal person who just liked to drink a lot. He didn't picture that he really had a problem. His problem had been with drugs. Drugs were physically addictive. Alcohol was not. To think that you could be strung out on alcohol was just a cop-out, or at least that's what he'd thought then. Now, he was beginning to wonder.

They sat around the house one evening with Joyce's friends, a husband and wife a few years older than them, who had kids older than theirs. At some point, Jay, the husband, said, "Would you like a beer?"

Jude's mind lit up like a pinball machine. "Sure," he said without a thought. What could it hurt?

Joyce smiled and said, "You should have a beer. You've been so good for months. You're trim and healthy. You deserve it."

He did deserve it. She was right. His heart raced with the very thought of the beer soothing his insides. Jay stood and went downstairs to the basement. Jude pictured the beer in a frosty mug. He started to wonder why he would be so excited about a beer if he was a normal drinker. But there was no turning back now. Joyce had given her blessing. He'd said yes. He was drinking a goddam beer. Period.

Jay came back empty-handed. Jude was crestfallen. What could have happened? Despair must have appeared on his face because Jay said, "I put it in the freezer to cool it down." Now that was weird, but okay, if it wasn't cold enough, it sure needed to be. He had great trouble concentrating on the banter about family members and people he didn't know. For an interminable time, he waited for the beer.

Finally, Jay stood. But he went into the bathroom. Then he emerged, and descended the creaky stairs again into the basement, to retrieve the elixir. He ascended from the bowels of the home again, with one Old Milwaukee and two frosted glasses. What was that all about? Only one beer? Jay sat, sighed contentedly, poured the beer in equal amounts into the two glasses, and handed Jude one. He couldn't conceive of why they were splitting one, but the glass was cold and the aroma delicious. He took a small sip, trying to conserve it, since there wasn't much. Then he took a large gulp. It soothed his throat. He'd forgotten how wonderful it was. One more gulp and it was gone. He felt cheated. All that anticipation, all that teasing, special permission from his wife, the effort of convincing himself that it was all right, and he got only half a beer.

The three continued to prattle on about so and so, and whoever, and who was marrying, divorcing, screwing, or cheating. Jude was not there. He was concentrating on when he could continue his quest to drink a goddam beer; it wasn't a choice, but a deep need. After what seemed like a long time later, Jay asked, "Another beer Jude?"

Jude nodded, trying not to act too excited. Joyce looked at him with a little concern. He said, "It was only half a beer before." They all looked at him a little oddly, he thought. "Well, it was," he said.

So, Jay began the ritual again, descending to properly chill it, waiting and waiting, and then going to the bathroom, and finally retrieving the half a goddamn beer. Jude managed to sip at least three minutes until the wonderful liquid was gone.

That evening they went to a restaurant—something beyond the type Jude and Joyce were used to.

The waiter asked if anybody would like something from the bar. Wendy ordered a mixed drink, and Joyce ordered a gin and tonic. Jay ordered a draft beer. Jude noticed. The server looked at Jude, as did everyone else. "Rum and Coke," he heard himself saying. He recalled little about the meal other than the drink, and wanting another one, but fighting against it.

Now he was beginning to realize that this whole episode had been very significant. He'd started again down the road to active alcoholism. He'd started counting the hours till he could drink more. He could be patient, so long as there was hope for a drink in the future.

The next day, Jude, Joyce, and the kids struck out across the countryside in search of changing leaves. They marveled that slight differences in altitude, tree type and other factors could make a huge difference in how much the leaves had changed.

When they stopped at a roadside stand, he searched the products for alcohol, figuring he could nonchalantly imbibe something without Joyce realizing it. But there was none.

A couple of long hours later he stopped at a convenience store for gas. He went in to pay and emerged with a bottled Budweiser.

"What are you doing?" she'd asked, half smiling.

"Nothin'. Having a beer."

God, it was good. Too bad she was watching him as he tried to enjoy it. He downed it. But he bowed to perceived pressure and drank nothing else for the next two days. He jogged, exercised, and vowed to stay dry.

Another sentence in the Doctor's Opinion in the Big Book of A.A. had made an impression. It said that alcoholics "drink essentially because they like the effect produced by alcohol. . .. To them, their alcoholic life seems the only normal one. They are restless, irritable and discontented, unless they can again experience the sense of ease and comfort which comes at once by taking a few drinks—drinks which they see others taking with impunity."

After leaving Boston, Joyce wanted to stop at a shop in Newport, Rhode Island. The kids were asleep in the back of the car, so Jude drove around while she shopped. On his first turn, he spotted a market with the doors open, and what he imagined to be cold, cold beer standing inside the refrigerators. That was it. He pulled his car to the curb in a loading zone a half a block down, glanced around at the kids, who were sound asleep, ran to the store, bought a six-pack of Killian Red and ran back to the car. He was relieved to find them still sleeping calmly. He sat, popped the top off a beer, downed the frothy, smoothness, felt the soothing, calming effect, popped a second, and downed it too. Now he felt good. But he also felt guilt, fear, and disgust—disgust with himself for leaving his kids in an open, unlocked car, all for alcohol. But damn, he felt good.

He drove around the block. Joyce hadn't come out, so he drank another one. And he rounded the block again and drank another one. Finally, he was feeling just fine. That was enough. He lit a cigarette and smiled, thinking of a movie of somebody enjoying a smoke after sex. He hid the last two bottles at the bottom of the cooler in the back of the car, picked a space near the door, and waited for Joyce to come out.

* * * * * * *

"Daddy. She pretty," Tad whispered too loudly as they sat on cheap chairs at a small aluminum table in Wimpy's.

Tad and Roosevelt glanced at Gloria. The three of them grinned.

"You are a gentleman," she said.

They ordered fried chicken, collards, corn bread, green beans, corn on the cob. They got a pitcher of lemonade. And then they dug in. It was heaven. Roosevelt generally dipped into the rather unhealthy soul food only at Nana's, but he loved it. He could imagine the fat in the chicken skin and in the ham hocks, pig's feet and fat back depositing in his ass and his gut. But at this moment he didn't care. He was with his favorite two people. Tad's eyes lit up each time he took a bite.

After they ate, he took them to the movies, a rather stupid black take-off on The Wizard of Oz, called The Wiz. A couple of whites inadvertently entered the theater but couldn't take it for long. But the rest of the audience, even his two favorite people, loved it, which made him doubt her intelligence a bit. He found himself drifting, considering work—thinking of Jude.

He decided to try to go to Jacksonville with the lawyer in the morning. He excused himself and went to the payphone bank to call Mr. Armstrong. "Mr. Armstrong, if you think it's okay, I'd like to go with the lawyer tomorrow."

"Okay, that's fine. I'll call him. But you know they'll be talking legal rights. You won't be able to talk about A.A."

"I just wanna kinda be there—maybe to lend support. I don't know."

"All right."

"Anythin' new with Joyce and the children?"

"I called her today, but she wasn't very open."

"How about we go see her tomorrow afternoon?"

Armstrong was silent for a couple of seconds. "I guess. It's kind of awkward. I feel like an intruder."

"I'd like to talk to her, and I don't feel comfortable going alone." Mr. Armstrong agreed.

Roosevelt got some popcorn and drinks and returned to the theater. Gloria looked at him oddly and whispered, "Where you been?"

He took her hand. "Sorry, had to make a call."

She rested her head on his shoulder. Her hair smelled fine.

After the movie, they went to a Dairy Queen and struggled to get it down before it dripped to the asphalt in the intense, sticky, Florida heat. Then Roosevelt drove past the yacht club, the old firehouse, and the baseball stadium, toward the beach. Crossing the bridge, he looked toward Jude's old house, and wondered what had become of Jude's mother. He figured her life was exactly as it was years ago—drinking, smoking, and playing cards.

They drove down onto the beach. Nowadays, he felt comfortable there. Tad jumped around like a jumping bean. They strolled in the shallow water. Tad walked next to his dad, holding hands, as his dad held hands with Gloria. Then Tad abruptly let go of Roosevelt's left hand and ran between him and Gloria, separated their hands and took them into his own. He marched along like that for a couple of minutes, and then apparently thought better of that, looked up first at Gloria and then at Roosevelt. He let go of both hands, turned and joined them again, and zoomed around to the other side of Gloria and took her hand, swinging it as far as his little arms could at the awkward angle necessary to grasp her fingers. Roosevelt and Gloria shared a romantic look, at least that's what Roosevelt thought and hoped.

"You seem quiet tonight," she said to Roosevelt.

"Yeah, I'm sorry. Somethin's on my mind."

"Anythin' I can do?"

"Naw, baby. I got a friend in trouble, and I'm working through what to do about it."

"Is there something you can do?"

He stopped and looked at her. Was he trying to be God? Well, no, he had the ability to help, and a wish and obligation to do so. "Yeah. My friend's got a big addiction problem and," he glanced at Tad to see if he was listening, "and you know I've got a little special knowledge there. Just trying to get my buddy grounded again."

"That's sweet."

"It ain't sweet. It's just plain necessary. But anyway, I'm just not sure whether he's ready for help. We ran together when we were kids. We were in all kinds of trouble together. As you know, I've been in the program for many years, but he never made it, and it's finally catching up with him."

"Daddy," Tad piped up. "What we gonna do tomorrow? She gonna eat dinner wif us?"

Roosevelt smiled at Gloria. "Would you like that, Tad?"

"Yeah," he said, grinning.

"Gloria, Tad's inviting you to dinner tomorrow. Whadaya say?"

"I'd be pleased and honored."

* * * * * * *

For some stupid reason, Jude had been seated in a wheelchair, and had to wait for an orderly to push him out of the hell-hole hospital. At least there were no flowers, bedpans, Styrofoam pitchers or other memorabilia to pack up and wrestle to the curb.

A cop said to the nurse, "This looks really dumb, he's all hand-cuffed, and has to be wheeled out."

She rebuffed him smartly with, "Rules are rules, officer."

Flanked by two cops with hands on the butts of their holstered guns, Jude was surprised to find Roosevelt marching out of the elevator accompanied by a white guy in a suit, carrying a briefcase, looking like a goddam senator or something.

The orderly stopped pushing. The cops seemed to fidget.

Roosevelt said, "Jude, this is Clayton Caldwell. Your father has retained him to represent you."

"Keep moving," a cop said, putting his hand on the wheelchair. To Roosevelt, he said, "Stand back."

Everybody stalled.

The lawyer looked at the cops. "How are you guys? Listen, I'm Mr. Armstrong's lawyer. Unfortunately, there's been no opportunity to meet with him. We didn't know you were taking him now. Could you give us just five minutes? There's no real rush, is there?"

One cop shifted weight from one leg to the other. "We've got an order to deliver the prisoner."

"Understood, but does the order have a time limit?"

The cop eyed him suspiciously. "Well, uh, not really."

"Look," said the lawyer. "The system has been wanting to do something with this guy—not to just keep him in jail. We can get him outta the county's hair if I can just talk to him for a minute?"

The cop said, "Take him back into his room. We'll be at the door. Ten minutes."

Inside, Roosevelt asked, "How you holdin' up buddy?"

"Me. Hell, I'm fine. Just bored as shit with all these fucking nuts. I'd like to hurt myself with those dominoes if they were sharp enough." Jude laughed. The others didn't.

"All right, we don't have much time," the lawyer began. "You've got a bunch of charges on you. Could get you some jail time. But maybe we can play off your apparent mental instability—hell they thought enough of it to send you here—and maybe we can get some sympathy out of the judge and just get you out. He doesn't have to give you jail time. All your actions were really just self-deprecating." Roosevelt had been expecting some legal technique, not just a bunch of soft begging and whining. But he thought back to the time he and Jude had been in jail near New Orleans and the fact that no legal argument had really been made then either. The lawyer was more like a social worker. Help this poor boy. He knew not what he was doing.

Jude was ready to go home. He wanted to lift and hug his kids. Hell, he'd even hug the bitch. She probably wouldn't be too interested in that. But right now, he had a soft spot in his heart, even for her. He'd get back to work. Hopefully, old Clayton here could pull some strings. He looked like he knew his way around the courthouse.

"I might want you to speak, Jude. I just want it clear to the judge that you were despondent. You don't really know what you were thinking. You weren't really trying to kill yourself. But you also weren't trying to be drunk or drive drunk. You just can't even explain it. How's that?"

"It's basically true."

"Okay, and then you can say your stay here has really helped you get your feet back on the ground."

"That's basically true too."

"Okay. Great. Let's go."

Jude held his A.A. *Big Book* to his chest. As he was wheeled out, Roosevelt's hand rested on his shoulder.

Chapter 20

JUDE WAS NERVOUS as he trudged beside Roosevelt through a dirt parking lot toward an old white wooden house for his first A.A. meeting. Roosevelt had told him he'd been coming here for years. Jude didn't know what to expect. The sound of people talking and laughing emanated through the open windows.

Roosevelt, on the other hand, still felt as comfortable here as he ever had. He'd been coming to this same meeting every chance he could. He'd never had a craving, except for a craving to get to a meeting. He believed in the program one hundred percent.

Entering the room, Jude saw aluminum chairs in three sections facing an elevated old desk. Almost every chair was occupied. Most of the people in two sections had cigarettes going. Many drank coffee.

Three people, including a nice-looking, young white girl, hugged Roosevelt. Roosevelt smiled and introduced Jude. Roosevelt moved among the chairs, continuing his greetings and introductions.

Eventually, Roosevelt pointed to a couple of aluminum chairs toward the front of the non-smoking section, since Roosevelt had quit smoking long ago and Jude was now trying to quit. He'd been told not to even try to quit smoking so early in his sobriety, but he just wanted to clean up in general. He felt so weird and out of whack that it just didn't matter. He didn't need the nicotine for energy because he felt like he was speeding all the time anyway. He figured that was because he'd kept himself artificially slowed down for a long, long time.

Jude sat and looked around the room, trying to take it all in. He was overwhelmed. Everybody seemed so normal—so at peace. They smiled, chatted and laughed. The entire room was smooth and relaxed. Roosevelt was the only Black.

An old guy limped to the raised, carpeted platform and somehow managed to get one leg up, followed by the other. He collapsed into an old, creaky, wooden office chair behind a wooden desk. The chair leaned frighteningly backward. He grabbed the desk and slowly pulled himself back up. Jude thought to himself, is this guy in charge?

Roosevelt watched Jude's darting eyes, knowing what he was thinking and what he was feeling. Roosevelt felt comfortable. In some meeting places, holier-than-thous preached their beliefs; in others, well-heeled drunks showed off. They called those meetings "Rolex watch meetings." Their worst complaints were usually financial.

But this meeting was different. The dregs of the earth entered this room. At least several times a week, some poor totally lost soul in utter despair would arrive, scared, shaking, sick, crying. The newcomer would suffer through the meeting, maybe talking, maybe not, and at the end of the meeting, he or she would stagger to the front of the room and take a white poker chip, to indicate surrender. This was the place to be. This was the place every drunk could wind up if he or she didn't stop.

The leader of the meeting announced that it was an open discussion meeting. Then he called on a woman, who walked to the front of the room and began reading aloud. Jude recognized the script as the Steps from Chapter 5 of the *Big Book*.

As she recited the steps, she glanced around the room:

"We admitted we were powerless over alcohol—that our lives had become unmanageable.

Came to believe that a Power greater than ourselves could restore us to sanity."

Jude had no problem with Step One. But he'd felt very uncomfortable with Step Two. It still sounded like a goddam church. But he was desperate, so he was going to try to go with it. The next few steps mentioned God a few times, which bothered him even more. Then he started thinking of the moral inventory that was discussed in the steps, and the confessions. There was a lot of work to be done. Finally, she arrived at Step Twelve:

"Having had a spiritual awakening as the result of these steps, we tried to carry this message to alcoholics and to practice these principles in all our affairs."

Okay, he was feeling hopeful. This was good. There was so much positive energy in this room that it just had to work. Suddenly his gaze fell on two scruffy-looking white males on the front row in the next section and it dawned on him that he knew them. It was Billy and Greg. He was surprised to see that they were even alive. Greg looked hopeful, yet ragged. Billy looked scruffy, but normal. They were smiling and looking relaxed and at home.

If these guys could do this, and would do this, that was all it took for Jude to make up his mind that he was in the right place. Billy turned his head, saw Jude staring, and gave a thumbs up and a huge smile. He elbowed Greg in his still ample rib cage. Greg looked over and signaled too. This was cool—here they were, all over thirty-five years of age, all with features of youth still evident on their faces—all trying to make a new life. What memories—good and bad.

Roosevelt recognized the two across the room. He knew Billy well, because he'd been coming around for a year or so and seemed to have a pretty good program going. But he didn't hold much hope for Greg, who yo-yoed in and out. Of course, you could never say that. There was always hope, and Roosevelt reminded himself that it was not his call. He was just another addict. If a person was ready, he could get clean and sober. That's what A.A. was all about.

The chair announced that he was ready for volunteers, and Greg Dexter raised his hand. "Greg. Addict and alcoholic," he said.

"Hi Greg," the crowd responded.

He cleared his throat, just like he always had, the phlegmy crap gurgling, flicked a long ash into an empty Styrofoam cup and said, "I'm kinda on edge today. You know I've been in and outta this place so many times it ain't funny. I'm really trying. Really tryin'. But I just don't have it. I don't have the urge to stay sober. I can't see any sense in it today. I just wanna get fucked up." He hesitated. Nobody talked. They watched him in utter silence. Jude wanted to jump up and make a speech, but what did he know?

Several hands popped up. An old codger said, "Greg, my man. You seem to be on the right track when you're here, but you aren't gettin' it. You heard the Twelve Steps. You gotta decide if you're following 'em. You know I ain't gonna question you. The key to sobriety is followin' the Steps."

A young woman, not bad looking, in a rough, nightclub kind of way, raised her hand. "Julie," the chair said.

She introduced herself and then said, "Hey, Greg. You know I love ya, man. You come in here and talk good. Then you go on out and try to write another chapter. Every time you think it's gonna be different, Greg, it's not gonna be different. Ever. Every time it's gonna be worse. That's the nature of this disease."

Greg nodded. "I know," he said.

"Do the steps. Start at Step One. Don't go to Step Two until you got Step One down pat. And then don't go on to Step Three till you got Step Two down pat. Okay, Greg? Every sucker in the world can get clean and sober on this program. It's simple. Just follow it."

Greg nodded, head hung low.

Others slammed on Greg. Jude seemed in shock. Roosevelt decided it had gone on long enough. The lesson was learned. It was time for him to turn the course of the river. He raised his hand and was called on.

"Hello, I'm Roosevelt, an addict and alcoholic," he said. The crowd greeted him. "Listen, Greg. I for one, and I know I'm not alone, believe you're exactly where you're supposed to be. And when you come back in and tell us that life's no better when you're using than it was when you're clean, that's good for all of us. It's like sending a scout out to report back to a military unit. The rest of the unit's safe, waiting for the reconnaissance. That's important. Thank you, and thank you for sharing. Now, I brought a newcomer today, and I'd like him to introduce himself."

Jude thought he would faint. His heart pounded in his chest. He wasn't sure if he should speak, but he didn't.

"Jude here and I have known each other since we were little kids. We got into serious, serious trouble together." Everybody laughed, which confused Jude.

"Anyway, Jude's been in some trouble, and decided to give this a try. I thought maybe somebody here might have some advice for a newcomer." Roosevelt leaned over. "Just say your name and what you are."

Jude shivered. "Hey, uh, I'm Jude. I, uh, guess I'm an alcoholic." He was almost afraid to say the word "addict", but that's what he was. "And an addict too."

"Hi, Jude," the crowd said.

A young woman raised her hand. "I'm Debra, alcoholic. Jude. Welcome. You're in the right place. I've been coming here for about a year now, actually, a year today." People clapped. Jude thought she looked kind of cool. Her hair floated around her face in an interesting, hot way. "This place and these people saved my life. Just do what they tell you. Just come here every day. Just give up to your Higher Power, and you will be amazed. I promise."

After several people shared positive thoughts, Jude was floating. The final one was Billy, who said "Jude. I can't tell ya how happy I am to see you here. We go way, way back, even before you knew Roosevelt. Anyway, I just wanna say that you can do this. Yes, it's easy, but you still gotta work it. Read the Big Book. Come to these meetings. Later, give of your time. It's all a miracle. I'm tellin' you."

The chair called a huge biker-looking dude up to the front. The biker held up colored poker chips and explained that they gave out medallions and chips to help recognize steps in sobriety. "But it's all one day at a time," he said.

Then, he held up a white chip between two fingers, looking at it like it was the host for communion. "If it's your first time, or if you're coming back from further experimentation, then we have this white chip for you."

Jude's heart banged. "Is there anybody who would like a white chip?" He looked directly at Jude, who found himself standing on wobbling legs and stumbling toward the front of the room. As he reached for the chip, the man pulled him in and squeezed. Jude was surprised and alarmed, but it felt good. As the crowd clapped loudly, he floated back to his seat and collapsed. He looked at the white poker chip like it was a magnificent jewel.

The man continued explaining the time frames for different colored chips. Then the guy said, "And this is a special day because we've got a one-year anniversary today. Debra," he shouted, "get on up here and pick up a solid gold, brass medallion with a beautiful roman numeral one emblazoned thereon." The crowd clapped loudly.

At the end of the meeting, everybody stood and began clasping hands. It took Jude a moment to realize that a huge circle was being formed. Roosevelt grabbed one hand and a man to his right grasped the other. The crowd began reciting the Lord's Prayer aloud. Jude felt something like a tremendous electrical type of energy flowing through the hands and revitalizing him. At the end of the prayer, everybody pulsed the collective hands two times and said, "It works if you work it."

They let go. Some people left. Some hugged or talked with others. Jude felt spent. Roosevelt hugged him, which threw him off. He wasn't accustomed to being hugged by men. Billy and Greg came over and did the same, which also threw him. They talked to him for a while.

Jude felt exhilarated. He had tremendous hope that the answer had been given to him. There was an answer. He was not alone. He was completely amazed that he'd missed this opportunity for so many years. To see people he knew, who he didn't expect to be alive, much less straight, sitting in a room with a bunch of recovering drunks and addicts, at peace with themselves and the world, flabbergasted him.

Roosevelt was elated. There were good meetings, and not-so-good meetings. This had been a good one, and a good first meeting for Jude. This was one of those days that everybody said the right thing at the right time—there was no controversy—the benefits of A.A. came through. And he would have paid money to have Billy and Greg sitting on the front row sharing their experience, strength, and hope. But he hadn't had to. It had just happened. That's how it works. He smiled to himself.

* * * * * * *

Roosevelt was nervous as a cat. There had been no day—no moment—as hair-raising as this. He'd even thought about the magic of chemical escape. A fleeting thought, and a disturbing one. This was the prelude to the most exciting and fulfilling time of his life. Why would he want to escape? He would not. He closed his eyes, and mentally turned his will over to his Higher Power. He didn't understand the concept at all. But it always worked for him. A calmness would come over him and he would be at peace. He took a deep breath, relaxed, started the car, and drove the last block to Gloria's house.

He'd been here many times before; he liked her family and they seemed to like him well enough. But this occasion was so momentous that things could change. Everything and everybody could be and act differently after today.

He again took a breath, and again turned it over. He didn't want to take too long getting out of the car. They might be watching. He pushed the ring box into his pants pocket. Then he decided he didn't need it now, so he placed it into the glove compartment. He floated toward the door, feeling like he was not himself.

At the door, he raised his hand to knock, but it opened before he did. Little Carver, Gloria's young nephew, opened the door, smiling. He had much darker skin than the others, and of course no foreign accent. "How's my man?" Roosevelt asked, holding out a hand to be fived.

"Good." He retreated so Roosevelt could enter.

He bent down to Gloria's tiny mother for a kiss on the cheek. Gloria appeared, radiant. They made small talk for a few moments. On the way to the car, Gloria said, "You seem wired up this evening. What's up?"

He hadn't thought it was that obvious. "Nothin'."

"Nothin' my eye," she said, giggling.

He changed the subject and they drove off to dinner. He managed to talk about her work and his for a while, and made it through dinner.

Afterward, he drove over the bridge, rehearsing, second-guessing, and panicking.

"Roosevelt, is somethin' up?"

"Huh? Naw. Uh-uh, baby." He clenched the wheel.

The tide was high, so he parked in a motel parking lot. They walked across the pool area and down onto the beach. They strolled in the soft sand, hand-in-hand. They walked along the shore; warm water lapped at their feet.

He realized he'd left the ring in the glove compartment. He tried to figure out how he'd arrange to get the ring and present it. He couldn't pop the question outside or inside a car. This was too hard.

They strolled for a while, talked, stopped, kissed, groped, and walked some more. She playfully kicked water on him, and he chased her and grabbed her around the waist. It was love. He knew it was.

Eventually, they returned to the pool area. This had to be it. "Uh, let's sit here for a while," he said.

"Huh? Well, all right. Where you wanna sit, Roosevelt?"

"Uh, how about over here," he said, pointing.

As she began to sit, he got the power, and said, "Uh, I'll be right back. Need to get somethin'."

"Whatchu talkin' about?" she asked, smiling.

"I be right back, baby."

He floated toward the parking lot and the car, snatched the ring box, jammed it into his pants pocket, and returned to where she sat, looking at him quizzically.

"Don't see you got anything," she said, still smiling.

He didn't answer—didn't know what to say. He took a seat on the lounge chair opposite her and took her hands in his.

"You're actin' so weird," she said.

"Baby, I love being with you."

"I love being with you too." She looked puzzled.

"Well, uh, uh, I really want to spend more time with you."

"Well, that's a relief. I thought you were about to break up with me."

"Naw, baby. Uh, well, uh, I wanna spend the rest a my life with you."

"Huh?"

"Baby, uh, well, uh, would you marry me?" he asked, reaching into his pocket. His pocket was too tight to get the box out. He stood, grasped it, went down to his knee and opened the box in front of her.

He knelt with the open box, his heart racing, his mind racing, watching tears streaming down her face, knowing she would say "no," and waited.

"Roosevelt, my sweet Roosevelt."

This wasn't good. This was a no.

"You been actin' so weird I thought you were gonna dump me. Now you went and did this."

His mouth was dry. Why wouldn't she answer?

"Roosevelt, I'd love to marry you, and I will marry you."

He almost collapsed. He jumped back onto the lounge chair. They kissed passionately; he marveled at the tenderness of his fiancée's lips.

* * * * * * *

Jude finished up the afternoon preparations for the evening meal at the Daytona Roasted Oak, where he'd been manager prior to his downfall. Roosevelt had allowed him to be assistant manager but watched him like a hawk.

A five-o'clock meeting was just a few blocks away. While Jude preferred Roosevelt's group, it didn't suit Jude's schedule. The Five O'clocker was a smaller group. The attendees, who were mostly older, were serious about their sobriety. They went around the room and made everybody speak. He liked being forced to speak.

He'd started keeping a detailed journal of his accomplishments and failures of the day, how he'd avoided temptation, if any, whether he'd harmed anybody, and what he'd done about it. It helped him. At least he thought it did.

Walking to the meeting, in the pleasant air, he reflected on the day. He'd been a little short with a customer who kept asking for a food combination that didn't exist. He'd tried to explain rationally, but the customer had been insistent and had raised his voice, to which Jude had responded curtly. Now he regretted it and wished and hoped he'd have the opportunity to make amends. Of course, the guy probably wouldn't return, because all he would remember was the brash employee behind the line being rude to him. Jude analyzed it from all angles. Even though he was technically right, he could have handled it better. Roosevelt would have.

Jude enjoyed the meeting. There were no real topics at these meetings. Everybody just shared what was going on with them. The people were nice and open. After the meeting, he felt great. He strolled back to the restaurant, grateful that he'd given up smoking so he could appreciate the fresh air in his lungs.

After the evening shift, he rushed through the closing procedure, so he could get home in time to see his kids. They should have gone to bed earlier, but they just had to see their new daddy. That's the way he felt, like a new daddy. His love for them, his ability to spend time and play with them, and everything else in his life was new. It was a lame saying, but it was accurate—his new view of life was like he was wearing a new pair of glasses.

He got out of the car to raise the heavy wooden garage door. As it came up, his two exuberant children raced through the garage and into his arms. He lifted them and kissed them multiple times on their cheeks. Joyce opened the door, smiled and waved. It was nice to see her smile, something he'd missed during his downward spiral. He approached, kissed her on the lips, delivered the squirming children, and pulled the car into the garage. He'd eaten at the restaurant so that eating wouldn't interfere with his quality time.

They all sat on the living room couch and chatted about kiddie nonsense. The kids snuggled tightly between them. Joyce asked him about his day. "Great," he replied, smiling.

They made plans for a trip to Disney World. This time it sounded like fun. He didn't have to worry about getting a drink. Thinking of the rides and activities for young kids, he was as excited as they were.

As their eyes started to droop, he read them a story, with Joyce at his side, and then carried them to bed. It was a joyous time. They fixed a couple of glasses of sparkling water and went outside. The air was pleasant. The stars shone brightly. They sat on the rear seat of the little blue boat that the kids enjoyed so much and talked about nothing and everything.

Eventually, they went inside, to the bedroom, and enjoyed a wonderful union—as they did regularly now.

* * * * * * *

A few months later, Roosevelt's life was complicated with wedding and honeymoon plans. It wouldn't be a huge wedding. Neither had a large family. Their list of friends was modest. Their budgets were modest. Tad and Gloria were tight. Roosevelt rode a new high, on top of the world. Things flowed smoothly.

One day, Mr. Armstrong called in the late afternoon. His voice seemed to shake a bit. "You have time to meet in the morning?"

"Sure, Mr. Armstrong. Where? What time?"

"Uh, how about the restaurant at say, uh seven."

"All right. Is there an agenda?" Roosevelt always used an agenda.

"No, and I'll get the others there. I've gotta go. Bye."

Roosevelt was concerned. What could be the matter? Was he unhappy about something? Was something happening with Jude? What could it be?

Before he'd gotten back to anything, the phone rang again. It was the nurse who'd taken blood as part of his life insurance application.

"Uh, Mr. Harris," she said, "one item from your blood test raises a red flag. Your liver enzymes are elevated. You indicated that you do not drink alcohol. And you've never had hepatitis to your knowledge. Is that right?"

"Yes ma'am. I do not drink a single molecule of alcohol."

"Whenever liver enzymes are elevated, an additional test is required. We have to determine whether you have liver damage, hepatitis or liver disease."

Roosevelt swallowed deeply. He couldn't imagine what it could be. He was the healthiest person he knew. He worked out regularly. He didn't smoke or drink. He was very careful with his diet. He felt fine. It was probably a false positive.

He returned to his work.

* * * * * * *

Jude sat in the living room sipping coffee and reading the paper. He had the sliding glass door open so he could enjoy the early morning air.

His little girl emerged from her bedroom, ran over and sat next to him. "Hi Daddy," she said.

"Hi Baby."

"Can I watch cartoons?"

"Of course."

She smelled good, like a little girl.

A few minutes later, his other little one wandered out, dragging his blanket behind. He didn't speak, just climbed up and plopped himself on Jude's lap, obscuring the paper, sucking his thumb and holding the blanket under his nose. "How's my boy?" Jude asked.

He fixed Joyce some coffee, made scrambled eggs and toast, took a tray into the bedroom so the kids could join her, kissed them all goodbye, and left for work.

His father had called an early meeting at the restaurant.

He drove down to the office along the river, a narrow, winding road with a low-speed limit. He'd learned to use the route to the office from his father, who'd said one day, "It's the closest I can get to being on the water during the workday."

Jude felt that way too. Things were running smoothly in his life. The water was flowing smoothly too, with only a very light chop. A light chop was good to keep things real.

Jude arrived at the office to find Roosevelt sitting at a table rewriting his index cards. "Hey bro," Jude said. "How are the wedding plans?"

Roosevelt laughed and shook his head. "A lot of things to worry about." He pulled a short stack of index cards from his front right pants pocket. "This is the data on that project." They both laughed.

Dr. Steward arrived, smiling like always. He shook hands with the two of them. Plopping himself down in the booth, he said, "How you guys doing? Anybody know why we're here?"

They shook their heads. Roosevelt was dwelling on the blood test he was going to take right after this meeting.

He wondered why Mr. Armstrong was unhappy. He didn't think he was ready to retire. He still worked full-time in his law office. Roosevelt couldn't imagine him retiring.

Mr. Armstrong strolled in, looking serious. They all shook hands. He pulled himself into the booth. "I told Griswold to show up later because I wanted to talk to you three first. Maybe I should have talked to my real son first, alone, but I thought I'd talk to my real son, my other son, and my closest friend, who's like a brother.

"Okay," the old man sighed. "Here it is. I've got terminal cancer, and I won't see Christmas."

The three sat stunned.

Finally, Dr. Steward spoke up. "Lansing, can you give more details?"

"Started in the colon. Already in the liver. I've had a second and third opinion. That's it. They can put me on chemo, but it'll make me sick and probably won't give me more than a few months. I may try the chemo, but I haven't decided."

Jude didn't know what to say. He felt like crying, like yelling, like undoing the morning, canceling the meeting, getting back in bed with Joyce. He thought of his young kids and how they'd never known their grandfather well. He'd always been distant. That was just his nature. "I'm sorry, Dad," he managed finally. "Whatever I can do."

"We're with you, Mr. Armstrong," said Roosevelt reaching across the table and grasping his forearm.

Jude's dad looked into Roosevelt's eyes, and Jude felt a little pang.

* * * * * *

The night before his wedding, Roosevelt received a phone call from the nurse who'd done the blood test.

"Mr. Harris," she said. "I'm afraid there's some bad news. Your second blood test shows that you have a chronic illness known as hepatitis C. It's an infection in the liver."

Roosevelt's mouth was dry. He looked at Tad conversing with the other family members. He pulled the phone as far as he could stretch it.

"I've heard of hepatitis," he said. "But I thought there were two types, serum and infectious."

"Those terms were changed to Hepatitis B and A. C used to be called non-A, non-B, because they knew it was different from those two but were unable to identify it. It's a long-term, chronic infection. It's becoming a bit of an epidemic. The people who have it are medical personnel, people who've had transfusions, and people who used drugs with shared needles. Many people your age used drugs with needles when they were young—they've felt fine— they find out they have it just like you did. You need to see a doctor—a specialist called a gastroenterologist."

Roosevelt returned to the table in a fog. "What's the matta Roosevelt?" Nana asked.

"Huh? Oh, uh, nothin', Nana."

They looked at him. He looked at the table, waiting for a break, and finally said, "Can you watch Tad for a bit? I need to go talk to Gloria."

Roosevelt went straight to Gloria's. She came into the front room drying her hands on a kitchen towel. "Hey, honey. I wasn't expecting to see you. What's up?"

They kissed lightly on the lips. "Can we go out for a bit?"

"Honey. I thought we agreed to spend the last unmarried evening with our own families."

"Yeh, I know. I need to talk to you."

"Is something the matter?"

"Naw. I just need ta talk to you."

"Okay. Just a moment." She looked at him with concern.

As they strolled, Roosevelt said, "Gloria. Something has come up that perhaps should result in a change in our wedding plans."

She stopped abruptly and glared at him. "What're you trying to say?"

"No, Gloria, I'm, uh, I'm not explaining myself well. I just learned that I have a medical issue. I don't know how serious it is. I don't know if I'll have to go through treatment. I don't know if I'll die. I don't know if I could pass it to you. I don't know what to think, and I don't have time between now and tomorrow morning to find out anything about it."

"Honey, what is it?" They stood face to face.

"I got a blood test in order to buy life insurance, for the company and for you."

As he cleared his throat, she asked, "Liver enzymes high?"

"How'd you know?"

"I'm a nurse, remember?"

He nodded. "Well of course there's more to the story. I had to get another blood test, and they say I have hepatitis C."

"I'm sorry, baby." She hugged him and kissed him lightly on the cheek.

"You don't seem all that surprised, or shocked or anything."

"Roosevelt. I love you. I intend to marry you. I know quite a bit about this illness. This is one of the areas of practice of the office where I work. I'll get you in to see Dr. Goldstein."

"You still want to marry me?"

"Of course I do. You could be pretty sick, even though you don't feel it. But you probably aren't. Many victims of hep C die of old age. It probably won't kill you, especially considering your healthy lifestyle. There are some drugs that can help, but they don't work for a lot of people. And they make you feel a bit bad, but not nearly as bad as the kind of chemo given to cancer patients. Don't worry."

They hugged again. "Thanks Gloria."

"Thank you for thinking of me. We'll get through this. Don't you even give it another thought until our wedding and little honeymoon are behind us. Okay?"

* * * * * * *

Jude borrowed his father's speedboat to take his wife and children to Disappearing Island, the huge sandbar at the mouth of Ponce Inlet, surrounded by rivers leading to New Smyrna and the Daytona Beach area. At low tide it was huge, with wispy, white sand in the center, and rippled, compact sand at the edges. Tidal pools, varying in temperature by the depth, trapped fish, starfish, hermit crabs, sand dollars and other water life. If the fish were lucky, the pool wouldn't dry up before the tide came in again. Seagulls pecked in the sand and tidal pools.

As they approached shore, Jude turned the stern so he could back in. He bounded up to the bow and dropped the anchor. Before the hull touched bottom, he hopped out in the shallow water and took an anchor to shore. The kids bounced with excitement. He dropped Mark into waist-deep water. He splashed and ran, tripped and fell, and popped up laughing. Jude swung Kim around in the air twice and set her into the water.

She hopped daintily toward shore, saying, "It's cold, Daddy."

He helped Joyce down the stairs off the stern, and took chairs, picnic items and toys to shore. Mark dug up whatever he could and dropped mud into the ocean. Kim swam, lay in the water, sunbathed and acted girlish.

Joyce sat beside him, sipping a soft drink. She'd given up all alcohol too, for him. "You're mighty quiet," she said, rubbing his arm lightly.

"Huh, oh, sorry. I guess being here made me think of my dad. How he loved this place—well, I guess he still does. But now he's too sick to boat."

"He hasn't lost much weight. Is he feeling bad?"

"It's hard on him." Jude wasn't sure what he felt. Maybe guilt—for never being close to his dad—for getting into trouble and causing him heartache.

Mark had spied a group of seagulls pecking at the sand. A plan formed on his face, and he sprinted lithely toward them, but the birds escaped.

Joyce said, "Did you say Roosevelt is sick too?"

"Well, he doesn't feel bad or anything. But he's got something. I don't really know."

A boat pulled up, with four thirty-something-year-old, long-haired white guys. One hopped off, staggered and fell in the water. As he pulled the boat in, two guys stood swaying like bowling pins about to topple. Jude watched the loud and stupid troupe, picturing himself not too long ago. One fell off.

The last guy stood up from behind the windshield, looked over, and said, "Hey Jude. What's happ'nin', dude?"

It registered. The huge hunk of flab was Greg Dexter, not sober today. "All right," Jude answered, disgusted.

Greg climbed onto the transom and collapsed into the water, sending a tidal wave toward shore, almost swamping Mark, who played in the shallow water. Greg trudged in the deeper water toward Jude.

"Who's he?" Joyce asked.

"Greg. I've known him since we were kids."

"What a nightmare."

"You got it. Remember the story about the chick who died on Roosevelt? His sister."

Greg arrived, puffing heavily. "Yo, dude," he announced thrusting a hand outward, thumb up.

Jude shook with him. Greg looked down at the beer can. "Hey, yeah, I know. Just drinking a little beer for a day or so."

Jude nodded.

"Hey, I'm Greg," he said to Joyce.

"Hey, I'm Joyce," Joyce responded, laughing.

"Kid don't look like you, Jude, and that's a good thing," he roared with his raspy, phlegmy, smoker's voice.

Joyce kept the half-amused face on.

"Me and this guy," he said, pointing a thumb at Jude, "we go way back. Way, way back."

Jude didn't know what to do with the awkward silence. Joyce smiled politely.

"Well, anyway, that was back when Jude was friendly. Looks like he's become much better than the rest of us now," he said as he lumbered away.

"I can't believe he's drinking," Jude said.

"Is he in A.A.?"

"Yeah, he was an inspiration to me," Jude answered, feeling guilt at violating his anonymity.

* * * * * * *

Roosevelt stood in front of the church waiting for his bride to enter. He looked at the crowd. The crowd, mostly black, watched the door. The whites sat huddled together like scared refugees. Jude and Joyce held hands. Mark and Kim slid all over the pew. Jude's dad was pale as chalk.

Pearl Mae, who'd worked for the Armstrongs and was a good friend of the Harris family, sat with Nana, Uncle Theodore, and Auntie Barbara. When they'd entered, she'd given Jude's dad a big hug, and gave Jude a look, trying to ask what had happened to make him look so weak.

Roosevelt whispered the Serenity Prayer to himself for the hundredth time, hoping he wouldn't faint dead away and collapse to the floor. He'd seen a groomsman do that once. He reflected on how great sobriety was. The memory of being drunk was always with him, as the result of attending meetings.

Tad walked in like a little man, dressed in a mini tuxedo, carrying a little pillow with rings. Beautiful Gloria followed, her hand on the crook of her father's arm.

Jude admired Roosevelt, strong and resolute, standing proudly in front of the crowd. It was hard to remember where he'd come from and what they'd put themselves through.

Kim and Mark fidgeted. Little Tad marched down the aisle, smiling, eyes gleaming. Mark giggled at Tad. Tad glared back sternly, like a little man ready to scold a child.

Joyce rubbed Jude's hand. "Roosevelt looks so calm," she said.

"He's about to jump out of his skin," Jude whispered.

The crowd stood and turned to watch Gloria float down the aisle. Her light brown skin glowed. Joy exuded from her.

Roosevelt stood at the front, palms pouring sweat, saying the Serenity Prayer in his head again. His handsome son reached him, and looked up, smiling. Then Gloria was in front of him, glowing. He could smell her delicious skin. He was mentally entwined in her soul.

Jude remembered how drunk and high he'd been at his wedding—numb, but not with love. He'd only hoped to stay on his feet and not crash to the floor until the ceremony was complete.

Chapter 21

AT THE END OF ROOSEVELT'S third week of treatment to combat hepatitis C, he met with his gastroenterologist. The doctor kept saying, "We know very little". Roosevelt had the impression that all treatment was complete speculation. A drug known as Interferon was available, but it had to be injected intramuscularly every other day. Sticking a needle into himself was weird—he felt the same way looking at it as he did when he saw the contents of a sugar substitute bag—but then there was no rush.

Besides the needle issue, another problem was that the drug only worked for some people. It might work and it might not. If it didn't, there was another drug to be used as dual therapy, but it was experimental.

Before taking every shot, he took Tylenol to combat the flu-like feeling the medicine caused. But it still made him feel like he had the flu. Still, he kept working like normal.

His health insurance wouldn't pay the huge cost, but the manufacturer had a program available to help.

Roosevelt was scared at the beginning, but after all the blood tests, and liver biopsy, the doctor said it had progressed so slowly over the past twenty years that it was not likely to kill him. He had no cirrhosis and no liver cancer.

Roosevelt told Jude he should get tested.

"I've never heard of it," Jude said. "Anyway, I already had hep. I lived through it."

"Well, what you had may have been a different strain, because supposedly people normally don't have symptoms from C. You probably had B, what they used to call serum."

Jude had just shrugged. "Yeah, that was it."

* * * * * * *

Jude ate dinner while his kids hovered. They were clean and ready for bed. But they'd waited up for him. Joyce's cooking seemed to have improved since he'd sobered up. Her attitude had too.

He spent some time wrestling with Mark, who was full of boyish energy. When he thought he had Mark under control, Kim would fly onto his back and knock him to the ground. Before long, Mark was worn out and tucked in bed.

Jude regularly read classics, rewritten for children, with Kim. They'd started reading Moby Dick on the weekend. They were lying in bed reading about Queeg's wild activities. Kim had one hand on Jude's forearm, while the fingers of her other hand quickly rubbed back and forth over the little balls on her blanket, like the hand of a blind person reading Braille. Suddenly Kim stopped, sat up, and looked straight into his eyes.

"Rum," she said, and looked at him. "Queequeg drank way too much rum."

"Uh huh," Jude answered, remembering himself.

"You used to love rum, Daddy."

He hadn't realized she'd been old enough to know. "Yeah," he said, not sure where to go from here.

"You loved rum so much you coulda married it."

That was it. Jude felt his eyes well up. She was absolutely right. What a pitiful thought. She knew. She'd figured it all out.

* * * * * * *

Roosevelt again told Jude he should get tested for hep C as they entered the A.A. club where they'd both gotten sober.

Jude repeated his usual argument. "What's the point? So, I find out I have it, I start jabbing myself in the thigh or stomach with something that's no fun at all, and probably doesn't even work. And, as you've explained, if the drug doesn't work, you do nothing, and then you still probably don't die from it. Is that it?"

Roosevelt laughed. "You make it sound pretty stupid."

"Well, it sounds to me like a disease that's really some kind of joke. I've got hep C. So what. It has no symptoms, no effect, and it doesn't even kill you."

"Okay. Okay. Listen, some get cirrhosis and even liver cancer quite early. A lot of hep C patients need liver transplants and die when they can't get them." Roosevelt shrugged, and said, "Well, I'm gonna keep doing the Interferon to see if it works."

After the meeting began, a tall, lanky, long-haired biker, perpetually dressed in leathers, raised his hand. "Bulldog. Addict."

"Hey, Bulldog," the crowd responded.

"Got a problem. Not sure what to do. I found out I got hep C. Kinda severe. Guess I might not be around long." He stopped, trying to compose himself.

Silence fell on the room.

Finally, Bulldog got it together. "You know. It was so stupid. So sick." He paused, looked around, and said, "The first thing that came to mind was to use. To just fuck myself up and forget about it. Now how's that? That's what my liver needs, right? But the thought consumed me. And I did it. Gave up a year and got high because I'm gonna die from a disease caused by gettin' high. Probably took a few days off the old liver right then." He laughed out loud. Nobody else did.

Eventually, a hand went up. The chair recognized Percy, a short, wiry forty-something loner who didn't speak often. "Percy. Alcoholic. Addict."

"Hi, Percy."

"I got it too. Maybe not as bad as Bulldog. But I got it, and cirrhosis." He looked over at Bulldog. "Listen man. I know about those feelings. I got on the pity pot when I found out. Started thinking of just gettin' loaded. Almost did. Decided not to. Trying to get and stay healthy, extend my life. I've heard, and I believe, that if you really watch out, you can carry on for quite a while."

It was true confessions day in the old A.A. room. Two more spoke up. Roosevelt was on the edge of his seat, wondering whether or not to speak.

Jude quietly calculated the high incidence of the disease in this room. Maybe he did have it. Why not? He'd shared needles so many times it wasn't funny.

He decided to get tested.

* * * * * * *

Jude's dad hadn't been around Roasted Oak. The chemo was getting to him. Roosevelt went to his house for a visit.

Climbing out of the car, Roosevelt felt weak and heavy, like he was loaded with lead, from his weaker chemo that was supposed to eliminate the hep C. But his problems were nothing compared to those of his good friend and surrogate father, Mr. Armstrong.

He was greeted at the door by Claire, a calm and gentle lady he'd met before. Her relationship with Mr. Armstrong was a bit mysterious, but she seemed to take good care of him.

"How's he doin'?"

298 WHITE SUGAR, BROWN SUGAR

"Not great. Seeing you will cheer him up. You're one of his favorites." She smiled.

"How's the chemo affecting him?"

"It's worse than the sickness itself. Go on in now and see him. That's the best medicine."

She smiled and steered him toward the stairs with a hand on his forearm. He climbed the stairs and found Mr. Armstrong in a cushioned chair facing the sliding glass door and the river.

"Hey old buddy," Roosevelt said, approaching and extending a hand.

Armstrong turned and looked up, smiling. He held out a hand and they shook. "It's good to see you, Roosevelt."

"How you doin', sir?"

"Fine."

"Fine? I don't think so."

"Well, I'm doing all right. As well as can be expected. Chemo is rough."

Roosevelt nodded. He wasn't sure what to say. "Are you in good spirits?"

Mr. Armstrong was silent for a couple of minutes. Finally, he answered. "You know. I'm kind of bitter, and I'm embarrassed to admit that. I'd prefer to simply accept the end of my life like a man. To acknowledge that I had a good life—it's nobody's fault—the doctors didn't miss anything—well, that it's just okay." He shook his head sorrowfully.

"I guess it's normal to feel cheated."

"I don't really feel that way." He cleared his throat. "At least most of the time. I'm just sorry that I worked all my life to be able to retire and really enjoy life. But before I had a chance to do it, the possibility was snatched away." He smiled ruefully and gazed out the window at the lightly chopped, dark water.

Roosevelt knew Mr. Armstrong had enjoyed life and loved to be outdoors. The old man hadn't missed much. Still, you couldn't blame him for not wanting it to end.

Roosevelt didn't want to think about his own illness. But he didn't want to end up regretting his life when the end was near.

He was sure Mr. Armstrong had some regrets about his family life. Trying to spend time with Jude when he'd been using was useless. Mr. Armstrong seemed content not to have remarried. Roosevelt pictured Jude's mom sitting at the table in the Florida room surrounded by the living dead.

They looked out the window as a sailboat slowly made its way down the choppy river. Roosevelt struggled to find something to say. At the same time, he was comfortable in silence. It was okay to sit and enjoy the water.

Roosevelt stayed for a while. More boats crossed the window.

"My boy, David, has trouble communicating with his old man," Armstrong said.

"What do you mean?"

"He and I have never talked much—we've always had a rather awkward relationship. It's not his fault. It's as much mine as anybody's. I came from a family that was like that. And I apparently passed it on. That's why his mother divorced me."

Roosevelt waited as he paused and cleared his throat.

"I want to see him, WITH Joyce, Mark, and Kim. I have even more regrets there. I've never been a father-in-law to her, or a grandfather to them. I'm not sure I knew how." He shook his head. "But it's my fault, not theirs. Now, just like so many who are ready to die, now is when I want to develop some kind of relationship before I go." He put his face in his hands for a few moments. He shuddered. Roosevelt wondered whether he was crying. "Do you think that's wrong, Roosevelt? Is it unfair to the kids to develop a relationship now that I'm going to die? Am I just being selfish, at their expense? Will my death be harder on them?"

"Sir, I think they'd be honored to know you better. I saw how they adore you. Don't be hard on yourself. I'm sure they don't even think that you've been inattentive." And he meant it. It was time for Mr. Armstrong to get closer to them, for all their sakes. After all, kids adapted easily. If he made an effort, they'd probably appreciate it.

"I hope you're right. See if you can get David to bring them for a visit. Maybe I should take them out to dinner."

"Sir, they're kids. They don't need dinner. Just let them be kids. Invite them to go to the pool or the river."

"You know, Roosevelt, we've had an interesting history, but I think of you as a son. I really appreciate you. I wish I could talk so frankly to my actual son."

"Yes, sir." Roosevelt was starting to feel ill again. Sometimes it just hit him like a ton of sandbags. He needed to escape before his face gave it away. And he did.

* * * * * * *

Within two weeks, Jude found himself injecting Interferon, just like Roosevelt, to try to combat his own hep C.

Roosevelt dragged himself into the office late one evening after the restaurant had closed. Jude sat at the desk trying to reconcile the evening receipts.

"Yo, bro', whassup?" Roosevelt slapped Jude on the back.

"You suck," Jude said.

"What?"

"I felt fine. I thought I was fine. Now I feel like shit. My house and your house are a couple of shooting galleries."

"Sorry, Jude. But you can't get better unless you do the chemicals. One person sticking a needle into his belly or thigh three times a week and not even getting high hardly qualifies as a shooting gallery."

"Oh sure. Nobody even knows if it works."

Roosevelt shrugged, opened a file cabinet drawer and rifled through some papers. He looked the same. He didn't seem to have lost any weight or anything.

"How you feeling now, Roosevelt? Any better as time goes on?"

"A little. It grows on you. Just keep on taking it. Keep going to meetings. Listen, I got another meeting for you to attend." Jude looked at him. "A hep C support group. It's a little like an A.A. meeting, but not really. It's an information session, put on by the doctor's office and pharmaceutical company. But it's kind of nice learning how other people react to the illness and the medicine." He hesitated. "Tomorrow night at seven?"

Jude nodded. Roosevelt left the office and poured a glass of water. He walked through the restaurant inspecting equipment and food.

Roosevelt returned. "Jude, I saw your father this afternoon. He asked me to have you, Joyce and the kids go for a visit."

* * * * * * *

After a month on Interferon, Jude's blood tests were inconclusive. For the most part, he felt okay, in spite of his headaches and fatigue.

Jude was surprised to see people he knew at the hep C support meeting. Bobby was across the room.

Warner, a guy Jude knew from dealing days, arrived with a group of men and a halfway-house counselor. His eyes and skin had a yellow cast. Jude tried to remember whether they'd ever shared a needle. Jude shook his hand. Warner didn't smile. The counselor watched.

"You remember me?" Jude asked.

"Yeah," Warner answered without emotion.

Roosevelt talked to some people who didn't look like former drug users. Jude had read pamphlets that said in addition to drug abusers, hep C attacked people who'd had a blood transfusion, and medical professionals who'd accidentally pricked themselves with infected needles.

Jude approached a fortyish white man he recognized from A.A. They shook hands, and Jude asked, "How ya doin' Henry?"

"This is my wife, Donna," he said, indicating her with his head.

She eyed Jude and said, "I was there when you celebrated your first six months sober."

"Oh, yeah," Jude said.

She walked away, leaving Jude and Henry standing silently. "It's quite an A.A. contingent," Jude said, laughing.

"I didn't get it the way the rest of you did. I may have been a drunk, but I never injected a drug. I got it from being a paramedic. Donna's pretty bitter about all you guys who gave it to innocent people."

"Oh," Jude said, not sure where to go from here. "Sorry, I guess. Is that the way the other straights, I mean the ones who didn't get it from drugs, feel?"

Henry just shrugged, stone-faced, and walked away. He and Donna sat on the opposite side of the circle of chairs, next to the non-druggies.

Jude felt uncomfortable. He wasn't a druggie anymore, but that's what he felt like. He whispered to Roosevelt, "Is it always us versus them at these meetings?"

"As you see," Roosevelt answered with his hand shielding his mouth, "I talk to everybody. You don't look like a junkie anymore, so they won't be rude to you. But there is a tension between the straights and the users."

Jude guessed he knew how the straights felt. They hadn't abused their bodies; they hadn't been careless with their own health, and they hadn't sold plasma for money, endangering innocent people. They'd suffered an illness or injury and needed blood. The blood had been tainted by mercenary junkies who hadn't cared enough to stop selling blood when they'd become infected. Of course, on the other hand, the junkies had all been completely unaware they were sick until twenty or more years after they'd injected the virus. It wasn't intentional, but it was reckless. Jude had sold his own plasma in the drug days, and now felt guilt over having done so.

The spirit of an A.A. meeting was not present. This meeting was more of a presentation by medical professionals and pharmaceutical representatives. Jude grasped more about the disease and the treatment.

After the presentation, the facilitator opened the meeting for questions. One of the straight women complained bitterly about how her life had been altered because of the treatment. She didn't really ask a question. Jude felt that she looked toward the druggie side of the room too often. Others stepped in to offer helpful advice, but she kept telling them they didn't understand her plight.

Several druggies offered techniques for reducing the discomfort, and a debate broke out about how much stronger the new, experimental dual treatment was than the Interferon itself.

Then the topic turned to money. Some had to pay, and others didn't.

Warner raised his hand. "The treatment's a bunch of crap anyway," he said. "Has this treatment worked for anybody in this room?"

Some had already indicated their numbers had declined with the drug. But nobody raised a hand.

"Now I'm on the way out, man. They put me on the transplant list, but you know I'm not gonna get a liver." He shook his head in disgust.

A woman with the drug company spoke up. "Warner, I'm sorry the drug didn't work for you. It's true that many people don't respond. But the drug does work well for some people." She focused on Warner. "Warner, we'll do whatever we can to assist you. Please talk to us after the meeting."

He looked at her suspiciously. She kept her gaze on him. Finally, he nodded.

Nobody seemed to know what to say then. Roosevelt felt the urge and spoke up. "I was wondering if there's any news on whether the new dual treatment is better than the Interferon alone."

"It's expected to be released soon. It is stronger, so it will likely make patients feel worse. There is evidence that it will work for patients who were partial responders to the Interferon treatment. It will likely not help patients who were complete non-responders to

Interferon alone. The dual therapy is a new drug used WITH Interferon.

Henry Black spoke up. "I was on Interferon for six months. I've been on the new treatment for four months. I tell you what. I feel beat. I don' know if it's worth it, man. I'm just drained."

"How are your numbers?" somebody asked.

"Better."

* * * * * * *

As requested, Jude arrived at his father's house with Joyce, Mark, and Kim. The kids bounded from the back seat of the car, dressed in swimsuits and dragging water toys. Joyce seemed uptight. She'd never been close to Jude's dad. Jude was uncomfortable too. His father had rarely invited them over. He hadn't played kiddie games with Jude when he was young, and he hadn't with Kim and Mark. Now, he wouldn't be able to even if he wanted to.

Mysterious Claire opened the door. They trudged up the stairs to the bedroom, with the kids dragging their plastic pool toys behind.

They found Jude's dad sitting in his chair admiring the river. Jude approached, feeling awkward. "How are you?" he asked. Neither touched the other.

Joyce leaned down and gave him a peck on the cheek.

Kim and Mark stood to the left of the chair, looking at their grandfather uneasily. He smiled at them, and said, "There are my grandchildren."

They looked shell-shocked.

"You guys look all ready to swim."

They nodded enthusiastically.

"Just give me a few minutes, and you can go right to it." He gazed at Jude, like a little kid seeking approval. Looking back to the kids, he said, "Would you two mind sitting here on the chair with me? There's plenty of room."

Glancing at their parents, they climbed on.

"This is my favorite view in the world, and I wanted to share it with the two of you. Isn't it beautiful? The river is rich. The water comes and goes. It's always there. Soothing." He smiled. He looked up at Jude. "It all made a lot of sense in my head before. Now I don't really know what I mean."

"It's okay, Dad. We're here to visit." Jude tentatively set a hand on his father's shoulder.

"What's that?" little Mark asked, pointing to a patch on his grandpa's stomach.

"Medicine."

"Does it make you feel all better?"

His eyes seemed to glaze a bit. "Sure, Mark. It makes me feel all better. Do you like my view?"

Kim said, "I like the boat. You used to take us sometimes on a big boat." She looked at her daddy for confirmation. "We went on a big boat with him, didn't we Daddy?"

"Uh-huh. Yeah. A few times baby."

"I wanna swim, Mommy," Mark said, looking up at her, and grabbing her blouse.

"You know what," Jude's dad said. "I haven't been out of this room for a long time. A very long time. Let's all go down to the pool." He struggled to move toward the front of the large chair, and the kids hopped off.

Jude helped his weak, almost-weightless dad to his feet. Looking apprehensive, Joyce stood still for a moment, and then took his other arm. They guided him to the stairs and down, following Kim and Mark, who bounded down the stairs ahead of them.

"Walk please," Jude said. "You guys aren't used to stairs."

Outside, they helped the fragile man to a seat with a perfect view of the river beyond the pool. Joyce took a seat on the main steps in the shallow end, where the children romped in the clear blue water.

"You've done well, David. The two of you, that is. Your children are well-behaved—I mean—they're nice children."

"Not barbarians?"

His father raised his eyebrows and then caught it. He laughed. "No, they're not barbarians."

* * * * * * *

Jude and Roosevelt entered the A.A. club on a Saturday afternoon. It was the third time this month they'd been to a memorial service at the club. The first was a girl named Beth who'd been coming around for a few months and had died in a car wreck. Nobody seemed to know of any family who cared, so they'd had the memorial with the people who loved her.

Then it was Warner, the first they'd known who'd actually died of hep C. But he'd been regularly running all kinds of things through his poor diseased liver. Jude and Roosevelt had done all they could to keep their livers healthy. Still, it was hard to believe that Warner could be sizzled so quickly.

They said he'd been found with blue toenails and lips. Paramedics had gotten a weak pulse, taken him to the hospital, hooked him up and tried to bring him back. But there was no hope. All the organs had failed. It could happen. It could happen to anybody.

Today the service was for Greg Dexter, who'd died of an overdose, just like his sister, Linda.

Reverend Rogers made an unusual, surprise visit to the club to say some words for him. He hugged Roosevelt and Jude, saying "You two have come far since that disaster in New Orleans."

The meeting was opened as a free-for-all. The chair read something written by Greg's girlfriend, who didn't want to speak. His parents and brother sat on the front row of the non-smoking section, looking out of place among the unshaven, scruffy members of the club. Greg's mother walked to Jude, shock on her chubby face. "First my Linda, and now my Greg. You boys never learned, did you?"

Jude didn't answer. He'd learned a lot, but it hadn't helped Greg.

"Fun, fun, fun. That's all you ever wanted. Now my second one is gone." Then she saw Roosevelt, the black man her naked daughter had died on top of. She shivered and turned away, crying. Various people spoke, saying good things, making excuses for why Greg had to use, saying how much they'd all loved him. That anybody would say they loved Greg surprised Jude. Reverend Rogers spoke some words.

As the members continued to share, Jude felt uncomfortable. The way A.A. members joked and laughed seemed out of place with Greg's unhappy family sitting stone-faced. Jude thought he should say something nice, but he couldn't put his thoughts together. As soon as the meeting ended, he escaped.

Chapter 22

ROOSEVELT AND JUDE boarded a Greyhound bus for West Palm Beach. Roosevelt thought it was funny that the two of them were riding a bus. Jude was the only white person, dressed in his neat shorts and button-up shirt and carrying a colored duffel bag. Roosevelt might not be dressed like he was unemployed, but at least he was black.

Across the aisle, a man drank a malt liquor tall boy in a turned-down, rumpled paper bag. He glanced at Jude without expression.

As the bus moved slowly across the asphalt parking lot and turned south on U.S.1, Jude looked out the window at the drab, orange-bricked building. "How long you think it'll take to get there?"

Roosevelt laughed. "In a private car, about four hours. In this bus, probably seven."

"I guess your dad's already at the boat," he said, looking out the window at a scuzzy prostitute.

"Yeah. I guess he's looking forward to the trip, but it must be really frightening for him, knowing the end is near."

"He seems to have gotten closer to God."

"I imagine a lot of people getting ready to die suddenly start to worry and wonder about that."

"I think he's sincere," Roosevelt said. "God doesn't hold grudges against people just because they didn't choose to believe in him or to trust in him before the final crisis. Do you think he's been in much pain?"

"I don't know. He doesn't talk about it much. Last week when I saw him in the hospital, he obviously wasn't feeling well. But I wasn't sure if it was the cancer or whatever they did to him. He's pretty secretive." Jude felt so helpless with the whole situation. The inability to communicate between him and his dad hadn't really improved. They were like a couple of social misfits. "He's turned humble in his dying. He's become almost likable." Many people liked his dad—in fact, loved him—but Jude had always found him so gruff and demanding. Now, he was more human.

"That's the spirituality at work too," said Roosevelt.

Jude cringed. "Red, you know I can't stand that God talk."

"Watch your father—you'll see the evidence." Roosevelt looked out the window. He was no holy roller. But he knew the origin of the world and his place in it.

After numerous stops and oh-so-lethargic resumptions, they pulled into the parking bay at West Palm Beach at ten-thirty at night. They took a taxi to the marina, hefted their canvas bags and walked down the sturdy, wooden docks, echoing beneath their footsteps. Lights showed through the windows of the boat, a sixty-foot shrimp boat converted into a yacht. Its name was Caprice. The boat moved slightly when they boarded.

The wooden door into the indoor pilot station / living room / kitchen was ajar, and Roosevelt slid it open, whispering, "Hello."

Dr. Lee Steward and Mr. Armstrong sat at the kitchen table studying charts. They all shook hands.

Jude asked, "How long'll it take to get there?"

"Four to six hours," Uncle Lee responded.

"How's the weather?" Roosevelt asked.

"Should be good. Might rain a little in the morning. But should be fine."

The four sat at the table drinking water and chatting. Jude was amused that they were drinking water. At one time this table would have been the scene of the most serious of alcohol consumption. He thought back to the time Uncle Lee made a spectacle of himself trying to pick up an old wench of a barmaid in St. Augustine. Jude had never found out when, why or how he'd quit drinking. But a peace effused from him.

"Have we got plenty of ballyhoo in case we decide to troll on the way over?" Jude's dad asked.

"All set," Uncle Lee responded.

"I guess I'd better get on to bed," Jude's dad said, and left.

The other three sat silently for a few minutes, all studying the table. Then Uncle Lee stepped into his physician role. "I think he's nearing the end," he whispered. "He knows it."

Jude swallowed hard. "How long?"

"Don't know. May finish this cruise. May not. May live for months. Don't know. But the cancer is very advanced."

Roosevelt felt sadder than he'd ever been. He'd never been closer to anybody, other than Nana. Mr. Armstrong had been like the father Roosevelt had never had. A white man. A very proper soldier-like businessman. And he and Roosevelt had developed a special bond—still had it—until the end. He was honored to be able to attend this final cruise.

Roosevelt worried about the state of the business. They'd tried to leave everything so the individual store managers wouldn't need to talk to Griswold. That man was a menace. But he was an owner, and he was in town while the rest of the upper echelon cruised across the Gulf Stream and to the Bahamas.

Jude worried. He looked at Dr. Steward. "Did you bring something in case he's in pain?"

"He's got a little oral opiate. Not much, and not enough for a serious crisis, but enough for an emergency. If it gets worse, we'll have to get more. I've got arrangements in the Bahamas, and I've got arrangements to deliver even by helicopter if we need it."

"You've been working hard." Jude was impressed. But this was the way Uncle Lee operated. He and Roosevelt were planners.

"David, how's your mother?" Uncle Lee asked.

"The same."

"The same?"

"All she does is drink. Duke's out, but now she's got some new guy. A married guy. He's there all day. I don't like going there. I hate having to eat there. It's dirty. The Chihuahua and the cats hang out on the table. All she and her friends do is drink, play cards, and smoke."

"I'm sorry to hear that. Has anybody ever tried to help her?"

"Actually, yes. I dragged her to an A.A. meeting at a time that she was down. But she rebelled. Just like me, she never liked hearing that God stuff. I introduced her to A.A. women her age, who contacted her quite a few times, but she resisted."

"Does she know about Lansing?"

"Do you really think she'd care?"

Jude felt a little antsy. Boating sober was still new to him. Being on a friggin' yacht like this called for some kind of serious alcohol. Oh, that was a bad thought. A very bad thought. That was the first thought he'd had of imbibing for a long time. And it was totally out of the blue. "What time is it?"

"Almost twelve."

310 WHITE SUGAR, BROWN SUGAR

"Don't guess there's a chance of finding a midnight meeting," he almost whispered to Roosevelt. Roosevelt wasn't sure what to say in front of Dr. Steward.

Uncle Lee looked back and forth at the two of them, who looked at each other, and then said, "God, grant me the serenity to accept the things I cannot change, courage to change the things I can, and the wisdom to know the difference." The other two joined in after a few words.

He looked at Jude. "Listen, David. I know you remember what I used to be like. I'm sure you also realize that I have serenity. Do I have to say why?"

It dawned on Jude. Uncle Lee arose and went below for a moment, emerging with a Big Book. Jude felt the anxiety melt away. Uncle Lee opened directly to "How It Works" and began reading:

"Rarely have we seen a person fail who has thoroughly followed our path. Those who do not recover are people who cannot or will not completely give themselves to this simple program, usually men and women who are constitutionally incapable of being honest with themselves. There are such unfortunates. They are not at fault; they seem to have been born that way. They are naturally incapable of grasping and developing a manner of living which demands rigorous honesty. Their chances are less than average.

"There are those, too, who suffer from grave emotional and mental disorders, but many of them do recover if they have the capacity to be honest.

"Our stories disclose in a general way what we used to be like, what happened, and what we are like now. If you have decided you want what we have and are willing to go to any length to get it— then you are ready to take certain steps.

"At some of these we balked. We thought we could find an easier, softer way. But we could not. With all the earnestness at our command, we beg of you to be fearless and thorough from the very start. Some of us have tried to hold on to our old ideas and the result was nil until we let go absolutely.

"Remember that we deal with alcohol—cunning, baffling, powerful! Without help it is too much for us. But there is One who has all power—that One is God. May you find Him now!

"Half measures availed us nothing. We stood at the turning point. We asked His protection and care with complete abandon.

"Here are the steps we took, which are suggested as a program of recovery:

1. We admitted we were powerless over alcohol, that our lives had become unmanageable.

2. Came to believe that a Power greater than ourselves could restore us to sanity.

3. Made a decision to turn our will and our lives over to the care of God as we understood Him.

4. Made a searching and fearless moral inventory of ourselves.

5. Admitted to God, to ourselves, and to another human being the exact nature of our wrongs.

6. Were entirely ready to have God remove all these defects of character.

7. Humbly asked Him to remove our shortcomings.

8. Made a list of all persons we had harmed and became willing to make amends to them all.

9. Made direct amends to such people wherever possible, except when to do so would injure them or others.

10. Continued to take personal inventory and when we were wrong promptly admitted it.

11. Sought through prayer and meditation to improve our conscious contact with God as we understood Him, praying only for knowledge of His will for us and the power to carry that out.

12. Having had a spiritual awakening as the result of these steps, we tried to carry this message to alcoholics, and to practice these principles in all our affairs."

At the conclusion of the reading, Lee said, "It's rough going through what Lansing's going through. And it's rough for the two of you to watch and be with him. But you have to be strong for him. So you have to have a good foundation in your sobriety."

The two nodded. Roosevelt said, "I feel strong. I haven't had any threat to my sobriety for a long time."

Jude hesitated. He hadn't really had any threat to his sobriety, but was suffering from so many emotions, all things he'd never faced before, and sobriety was still new to him. "I feel—I don't know—anxious. I don't have serenity. I don't. My gut is wrenched."

Uncle Lee asked, "Have you thought of using?"

"No, I haven't."

They talked of techniques, of prayer, of turning it over to the Higher Power, of the fact that death was as much a part of the cycle of life as birth, and of the feeling of being cheated when death comes early. They talked of the need to reflect a good attitude for Jude's father, in order to make this trip a final joyous occasion for him, as well as for themselves. Then they spoke of the details of the trip and of fishing. Finally, they closed with the Lord's Prayer.

Roosevelt and Jude each popped a couple of Tylenol, fixed up their Interferon shots, and injected, Roosevelt in the thigh and Jude in a pinched piece of belly. Jude said, "This stuff's no good. I don' feel nothin'."

The two men laughed.

* * * * * * *

Like they'd done as residents of The Bridge when they were nineteen, Jude and Roosevelt fixed a magnificent breakfast. The sun tried to shine through heavy, dark clouds. Uncle Lee had stocked the galley as Roosevelt had instructed. He'd also supplied pots, pans and cooking utensils that would rival the restaurant.

"I wouldn't admit to anybody else how excited this well-organized kitchen makes me," Jude said.

"Homo," Roosevelt said, laughing.

"Admit it. This is great."

"All right, I'll admit it."

Roosevelt made a batch of pancake batter and threw bacon on a griddle. Jude cut fruit and made omelets. They worked in concert, never intruding on each other's procedures. The coffee perked loudly in the little pot, infusing the air with its aroma.

Jude's dad climbed the stairs from the forward, master bedroom. He wore shorts and a button-up shirt with sailfish flying through the air. He looked as healthy as ever. "The coffee smells great." He approached the two cooks, put his arms on their shoulders and admired their handiwork. "You guys are pros. You should have a restaurant or something."

They all laughed. Uncle Lee took a cup of coffee. "I'm concerned about the weather. The rain seems to be moving to the south of us. The reports indicate there are three-foot seas. That's really of no great consequence. I don't know."

After they'd eaten and Jude's dad had reviewed documentation and electronic devices, Uncle Lee rose and cranked the engines. Jude and Roosevelt cleaned and stored everything. They attached bungee cords to secure cabinets, drawers, and the refrigerator. Then, they cast off and idled along the glassy marina water.

As they sped up, Jude climbed to the flying bridge and found Uncle Lee at the wheel in the light wind and salt air. His dad stood on the forward deck, facing the bow, hair blowing back, sipping coffee. The sun peeked out of the clouds, revealing blue sky in the distant north. But to the south and behind, the sky was dark. Ahead, to the east, on their route, the sky was splotchy, with dark, ominous clouds, but light, grey clouds as well.

Roosevelt joined Mr. Armstrong on the deck. "How you feelin' sir?" He held the railing for stability.

Mr. Armstrong jumped and turned to him. "Roosevelt. You startled me." He smiled. "Glad you joined me. I was just trying to have a connection with my Higher Power, to use the lingo you use."

"There's no place better. This is where you can be the closest. There's nothing like nature. You feelin' okay?"

"I feel great." The old man swayed on sturdy but flexible sea legs.

Choppy waves, crisscrossing with the large swells typical of an inlet, knocked the boat left and right.

"Think it's gonna get calmer when we get out?" Jude asked Uncle Lee.

"I hope so. I'm not sure." He shook his head. "If it doesn't, we'll turn back."

"Think we oughta go inside?" Roosevelt asked Mr. Armstrong.

"I like it like this. You know you're alive if the waves knock you around a little." He grasped the rail again and swayed. "Listen, Roosevelt, I wanted to talk to you."

Roosevelt looked up at Jude and Dr. Steward, rocking on the flying bridge. He was starting to feel a little queasy. He wasn't sure he belonged here. "What would you like to talk about, sir?"

"The future of Roasted Oak." He breathed in deeply. "I don't think it's any secret, Roosevelt, that I believe taking Griswold as a partner was a mistake. He offers nothing and undermines everything. If I had a way to get him out, I would. I've created a trust and conveyed my shares to it. The trustees will be you and Lee. It will give the two of you an effective majority, so you can outvote Griswold. I believe you know my lawyer, Luis Morales."

"Sure. I admire that man." Luis Morales had escaped Cuba and created a law firm in Miami. Mr. Armstrong had helped him free his family. Morales had represented Roasted Oak when it bought property for a restaurant in Miami.

"Well, contact him when I'm gone."

Roosevelt nodded. "What about Jude? He's not a trustee?"

"That was the hardest part. I'd like to give him control too, but I'm not sure he's ready. Yes, yes, I know about one day at a time. You or Lee could go off at any time, but I don't think so. I made you and David the beneficiaries of the trust. But I gave David a larger percentage than you. After all, he is my blood son. There's a detailed description about how and when shares are released to beneficiaries, and there's control so if he's drinking or doing drugs, you trustees can withhold. So, there you go. In fact, there's similar protection if you slip up too."

"Sounds well thought out." Roosevelt's stomach continued to swim. He was impressed with the logic behind Mr. Armstrong's plan.

Mr. Armstrong grabbed Roosevelt for stability as the boat took a hard jolt from a large wave.

"I guess we should go inside before we end up in the drink." He escorted Roosevelt into the living area.

On the bridge, Lee observed, "The sky seems to be clearing. Do you think the sea is rougher?"

Jude shrugged. "A little. We're an hour out now. If it's not gonna get any worse, I guess we go on."

It didn't improve. Within another hour, the boat was being tossed up and down and in all directions like a cork. Lee had to decrease the speed. He fought the wheel on every wave. Sometimes he'd aim straight up a wave. Sometimes he'd try a slanted course. It didn't really matter. Waves attacked from all sides. As they rode down one swell like a surfer riding the pipeline, it broke and dumped a heavy, frothy head of water on Jude and Uncle Lee. Jude lost his footing and fell, smacking his hip, and banging his head. He grasped the stand of the captain's chair.

"Christ," Uncle Lee said, using a word stronger than Jude had ever heard him say. "This isn't letting up, is it?"

"Uh-uh," Jude groaned from the floor.

"Guess we'd better try to get inside. Probably should have climbed down sooner. You all right?"

"Yeah." Jude pulled himself up, and held on for dear life, as the boat rocked strongly from side to side.

"You need to go down first. Then you take the wheel down there. Honk the horn so I know you got it, and I'll come down."

"Shit, here comes the rain," Jude said, noticing a large sheet of rain slamming toward them.

"Get on down now."

Still lying prone and hanging on, Jude slid his legs around and off the edge of the bridge. He knocked his nuts as he reached his feet into the air, angling down to find a rung on the stairs. He suffered that pain in silence. He held the stairs and dangled over the water as the boat climbed straight up a large wave bow first. Then the boat took a jolt from the port, and he swung to one side, banging his knee and losing the grip on the ladder. He reached wildly and found a railing. Then the boat swung to the other side, and he did too, hitting his chin on the ledge. "Goddamn it," he said. He mustered the energy and stability, hurriedly took control and descended, losing his footing on the last rung, and crashing on his back onto the hard, wet, deck surface. "Fuck," he exclaimed aloud, though nobody could hear.

He scooted toward the door like a soldier trying to stay below flying bullets. Still lying on the deck, he pulled the heavy sliding door as far as he could, and pulled himself part way in. His father pulled the door further and helped him in. He lay on the floor wishing for peace.

Roosevelt was standing against the control cabinet near the inside wheelhouse. "Your chin's bleeding."

"No shit," Jude said. He didn't think swearing in front of his father was out of place now.

His father stood without needing support, swaying like a spring. "Did Lee decide to continue on?"

"We're two hours out now. I think he figures it doesn't make sense to turn back now. It's only supposed to be a four or five-hour trip."

Roosevelt asked, "Is he coming down?"

"Oh, yeah. You're supposed to grab the wheel and then honk the horn."

Jude's father shot him a dirty look for not saying it as soon as he came in, turned quickly to the wheel, gave it a tug left and right, turned on the windshield wipers, and tooted the horn. Waves crashed on the windshield like slaps of hard rain. "Roosevelt, can you help Lee down? Carefully."

Roosevelt thought again about what a black city dweller like him was doing in the middle of the ocean in a horrendous storm like this. He pushed the door open far enough to exit, held onto the interior and exterior rails and rolled his way toward the stern and the ladder leading to the bridge. As he turned, he found Lee already halfway down the stairs, holding on as the boat took a bump. Roosevelt kept a hand on a rail and reached for Lee's leg. "Hey, you all right?" He asked. "Hold on. Let me get below you." He moved around, grasping both sides of the ladder rails, and said, "Come on." Lee dropped like a fireman sliding down a pole but was protected by the web Roosevelt had formed.

Roosevelt grabbed his arm and the outside rail. He helped Lee get his hand over to the inside rail, and they moved together slowly back toward safety.

Jude was embarrassed to admit that his stomach was turning. This would be the second time in his life to be seasick. A flood of water-like fluid arrived in his mouth, a sign that vomit was not too far behind. He slouched on a couch with his feet on the floor, reliving many drunken evenings. There was no porcelain bowl to hug, so he calculated how many steps he needed to get to the door to puke on the deck.

The boat continued to rock, climb and fall, abruptly changing, never repeating a movement. Roosevelt lay on the floor, leaning on one arm, watching Mr. Armstrong deftly guide her through the rough seas. Dr. Steward leaned against the wall, with no color in his face.

The boat crashed down a wave and suddenly banged to port. It started up again, and immediately crashed down again. A cabinet door opened, and cans and bottles crashed to the floor, along with boxed goods. An unbroken bottle of wine and one of whiskey rolled back and forth on the floor. The boat rocked again, and the two bottles converged and crashed. Jude wondered momentarily why they hadn't continued rolling in the same direction and never met. The mixture of red wine and liquor created a unique and strong aroma of alcohol. It flowed toward him and then away, raising further ruckus in his gut.

Roosevelt lay on his stomach, his cheek on the floor, and his hands folded over his head. Dr. Steward had crawled to the refrigerator, unstrapped it, and pulled the door open, still on his knees. "Whatchu lookin for?" Jude asked.

"Water. Gotta have water."

The alcohol mixture flowed toward Jude. He tried to evade it but lost his balance and fell back. The bow rose and food began falling from the refrigerator, beginning with an open cardboard milk container, which sloshed creamy, bubbly, white milk into the red and tan liquid swirling around on the floor. Jude heard more glass breaking as he crawled to the door and unloaded on the deck.

* * * * * * *

Roosevelt didn't know how many hours had passed since he'd collapsed. He'd puked on himself. His bladder was distended with pee. But he couldn't get up. It wasn't safe to try over the side and couldn't make it down the stairs. He felt completely helpless. Mr. Armstrong continued steering.

"Sir, is there any relief in sight?"

"Nope."

Crashed bottles of pickles, mayonnaise, mustard, olives, anchovies, Coca-Cola and other unknown fluids and solids had joined the mixture and swirled to and fro. Dr. Steward puked into the concoction, tried to rise, slipped and fell into the mess, cutting his arm on the broken glass. "Dammit," he exclaimed.

"You all right?" Roosevelt asked.

"I wish it'd kill me, but it won't."

"What time is it?"

"Four fifteen."

"I thought it was a three or four-hour trip," said Jude.

"Not in this weather."

"Dammit," Mr. Armstrong exclaimed.

"What?" Roosevelt asked, face down.

"We lost the skiff."

"What?" Jude asked.

"The skiff. It got loose. I just saw it off to starboard." Mr. Armstrong sounded like a young man, with no illness, standing on solid ground.

"You sure it was ours?" Dr. Steward asked, as meekly as a pitiful dying child.

"I'm coming around."

The boat was assaulted from several new directions at once as Mr. Armstrong swung the wheel.

"Oh, man," Roosevelt said.

Jude and Lee groaned.

"Somebody's got to get the skiff," Mr. Armstrong said.

Nobody moved. The boat roared up a wave, and down the other side. Water sloshed in through the partially open door.

"There it is," Jude's dad hollered, pointing. "David, we need to recapture the skiff. Come on, boy."

Jude didn't like being called "boy" at his age. And he didn't like lying around in vomit, being assaulted by the smell of a concoction of wine, whiskey, milk, and pickle juice. He pulled himself up. There was nothing left to vomit.

"You can't go out alone. Somebody else needs to help. To tie you down."

Roosevelt groaned again, but got to his feet, wobbling back and forth. Vomit covered the entire front of his shirt and pants.

"You fucking reek," Jude said under his breath.

"Fuck you," Roosevelt whispered back.

They half trudged, half slid toward the bow, being tossed to and fro. The skiff appeared on top of a swell two waves away, and then disappeared as the positions of the boats and waves changed, like a ghost ship coming into and out of view. Jude's dad chased it down and had it within a wave. Jude looped a rope around his waist, tied the middle to a cleat, and tied the other end to Roosevelt. Water poured on them in buckets. They slipped and jerked with the movement of the boat.

"This is nuts," Roosevelt yelled.

Jude didn't answer. He watched how his father attempted to reduce the distance between the two boats. Suddenly the skiff was right there just over the crest of a wave. Jude lunged toward the side and leaned over to try to reach it, banging his hip on the rail, but it suddenly moved away. He and Roosevelt tried to regroup, and suddenly it was there again, this time closer. Jude trounced again, reached over, touched the gunwale, and squeezed two fingers over it, but couldn't maintain.

Roosevelt sat on the little raised roof over the master bedroom, trying not to move. The boats converged again, and Jude ran again. As he went to grab it, the boats met violently, wood on wood, almost catching his arm.

"Goddam it." He didn't feel sick at the moment. He just wanted to catch the damn thing.

The skiff sat atop a wave quite a few yards away again, taunting him. His dad started the slow approach again. The skiff came within two yards, moved away, approached, and started retreating. Jude made a decision, put a foot on the top of the railing, and leapt toward the skiff, praying that it would stay put for a few seconds, that he wouldn't fall into the sea, that it wouldn't crush him into the hull, and that he wouldn't run into any frightening sea life. He told himself that sharks and other frightening things were far below, avoiding this weather mess. He crashed head-first onto the bottom of the skiff and again smashed his frail nuts. He struggled to right himself, worrying that his legs might hit the boat. He didn't know how far away he was. He felt a tug on the belt around his waist.

Roosevelt had managed to stand, had secured the rope around his own waist with less slack, and began pulling Jude toward the boat, skiff and all. He motioned to Mr. Armstrong to hold still for a moment, and while the boat couldn't quite stay still, he managed to pull the skiff gently in. Jude knelt in the bow preparing to brace if necessary. Of course, that was a bad idea.

The boat rocked and the skiff slammed against the hull. Jude pulled his arm out of the way just in time and was thrown down into the bottom again. The skiff came alongside, so Jude hurriedly got to his feet and grabbed on. His dad steered broadside of the waves.

When they'd secured the skiff, Jude flopped onto the deck of Caprice. Roosevelt collapsed next to him.

Uncle Lee stuck his head out. "You guys all right?"

"Yeah, all is secured."

"Okay, we're heading back into the waves again."

Jude yelled, "Couldn't we just stay on this course and maybe go to Bermuda or something?"

The boat changed direction and immediately they were assaulted with jolts, twists, and buckets of water. The cool salty water splashing and pouring on them felt good, but the gut-twisting movement of the boat did not. They both held onto the base of a fishing chair, being flung and bounced back and forth along the hard floor.

"Will we ever arrive?" Roosevelt asked.

"The sun's almost down."

"Guys," yelled Uncle Lee. "Hurry. I need you in here." He sounded a bit frantic, so the two climbed to their feet, and struggled to the interior on wobbly legs.

They found Jude's dad lying on his back on the floor, as Uncle Lee stood spread-legged and fought with the steering wheel. Roosevelt knelt by Mr. Armstrong and held his arm. "Did you hurt anything?"

"I'm fine," he answered, struggling to sit up.

Jude took the wheel, and Uncle Lee attended to his fallen friend. After quizzing him for a few minutes, the doctor cleaned and bandaged a bruised and cut area of his shin.

As Roosevelt and the doctor helped him up, Mr. Armstrong winced.

"Did you bang a rib too?" the doctor asked, reaching for it.

"I'm fine."

The two were moving him toward the couch when he hesitated. "No, I want to resume my position at the wheel."

Jude thought it was a funny statement—just like something his father would say. But they took him at his word and returned him to his position. Jude stepped aside and moved to the couch to stabilize himself.

Shortly before midnight, they limped on calm waters toward lights sparkling above the marina, peaceful docks and swaying boats. Jude's dad maneuvered the gears and backed cleanly into a slip.

Chapter 23

MOVEMENT STARTED SLOWLY the next morning. Jude's dad took it easy. The doctor treated his leg with ointment, bandages and ice. Then he examined his ribs and wrapped him. Roosevelt and Jude both held their breath and fought back nausea as they crawled on the floor cleaning up broken glass and curdled and grungy, dried sediment of the awful concoction that had swirled around the kitchen floor for hours the previous afternoon and evening. The odor of alcohol still gave Jude an uncomfortable feeling, despite the number of other unpleasant odors mixed with it. When the kitchen was presentable enough, they fixed coffee and breakfast.

Jude went out to clean up the skiff that had roamed separately around the ocean. As he began bailing, he was assaulted by strong gasoline vapors. Jude thought of the many times he and a gas can had sat alone in his garage as he reached another level of hallucination and insanity. He tried holding his breath. He needed to avoid getting high like that. But he couldn't escape it. He struggled to clean it, but before long, decided it was no good. He leapt out of the boat, spit several times into the water, and walked to the bow of the big boat, where he sat and put his hands between his knees.

Uncle Lee came out and dumped a bucket of dirty water over the side. "Hey, what's up? How's the skiff?"

"Sorry. I couldn't clean it."

"What do you mean?"

Jude thought there was a bit of an edge to his voice. "The skiff's full of gas. It was setting me off. I couldn't stay there. Really. It was too much."

Uncle Lee regarded him for a time. He looked a little unhappy, but Jude thought maybe it was just fatigue.

"I'm sorry," Jude said.

"Don't worry about it. You're right. You made the right decision. You're too close to it to subject yourself to that danger."

* * * * * * *

"We're invited to a cookout this evening," Uncle Lee said upon returning from a medical clinic with Jude's dad. "We need to keep an eye on his leg."

Jude didn't quite get it. Sure, he had a nasty bruise, but how did that compare to terminal cancer? "What'd they say?"

"We're concerned about blood clots," Uncle Lee replied. "His ribs are just bruised."

At first, Jude thought it was odd he'd say, "We're concerned," but then he remembered Uncle Lee was a doctor.

"Should Dad go to the cookout?"

"I'd like to go, Lee," his dad responded.

"All right. But I don't want you walking. We'll have to get you there in a wheelchair. I don't think we can use crutches on the docks and the sand."

* * * * * * *

In the evening, Uncle Lee got a wheelchair and loaded up his patient. They walked along uneven boards of the dock, Roosevelt pushing the wheelchair. The aroma of roasting, island-seasoned pork and chicken permeated the air. Thick gray smoke rose from a huge horizontal metal barrel, around which stood two busy chefs. Long wooden picnic tables stood on the dirt. A wooden platform held a band setup, and black men with colorful shirts prepared to play.

The food was unique and delicious. Jude admired the spicy sweet seasonings on the pork and chicken. He even tasted a succulent sausage. There were several vegetables that he couldn't identify, but the seasoning and cooking technique made them sweet and powerful.

Jude noticed a few natives and a number of Americans ordering beer, wine and mixed drinks at a bar. That was okay. He didn't do that. He had all the tools. Two cute American girls, about twenty years old, leaned on the bar. He admired their nubile bodies, but then considered the fact that he had a family at home.

After they ate, Roosevelt stood and said, "I'm ready to turn in. You ready to go back to the boat, Cap'n?"

Jude's dad looked at him. "No. I want to stay and absorb the culture for a bit. Does anybody want to stay a little bit?" He looked at Lee and Jude.

They both nodded. "Sure," Lee said. "We'll enjoy some music, and maybe a Junkanoo."

"What's that?" Jude asked.

"A parade of drunks dancing around to music like a conga line, all holding on to each other," Uncle Lee answered, laughing.

"Can I join in my wheelchair," Jude's dad asked, grinning. They all laughed.

Jude sat at the table for some time, his dad sitting next to him tapping to the music, which swelled with drums, bells, and unusual string instruments. One musician stood and began tooting on some kind of horn, a sing-song rendition of nothing Jude could identify.

The two young blondes had gotten drinks again and were walking toward Jude's table. He admired the walk, a little short of a stagger. One had a cute face, and wore short, low-cut jean shorts, and a chest-hugging T-shirt. The girls spoke to each other as they approached, never looking at Jude or anybody at his table. The cute one caught the toes of her bare feet in the sand, stumbled, and dumped her entire drink onto Jude. He knew immediately that it was rum—a little sweeter and more Caribbean in aroma than he was used to—but it was rum, and he was a rummy, just like his daughter had pointed out. The girl stuck her drunken face into his and said, "Shorry."

He shrugged. "'S okay."

She reeked of alcohol. She wasn't so cute up close. Her face had the puffy lack of definition of a drunk. She stood back, and tripped again, being grasped and steadied by her friend. As the girls staggered away, two American guys joined them. Jude suddenly felt depressed, old, and out of place—unable to enjoy single life or alcohol. The girls had begun dancing with the boys across the dirt lot.

"I'm about ready for a ride back to the boat," his father said.

Uncle Lee stood up.

"I'll come in a few minutes," Jude said. "I like the music." He wasn't sure that was why he wanted to stay, but he did.

Uncle Lee pushed the old man in his wheelchair back toward the boat.

Jude felt like a spectator watching an event from afar. He wasn't part of it. He couldn't be. He was a family man. He was a recovering drunk and addict. He was older than the young people and younger than the old ones. But the music was unusual, and he enjoyed watching the people dancing, including the two blondes, who now were falling all over each other in the middle of the sand lot.

The music increased in intensity. The man with the horn was joined by another with a trombone. The drummer picked up a portable tom-tom and another player began beating on a cowbell. The crowd moved toward the front of the stage. Even sedentary members of the audience stood, attracted to the front like metal filings pulled by a powerful magnet.

The musicians hopped off the stage and started half-dancing, half-marching, tooting horns and whistles, and banging on their instruments. People began joining the impromptu parade, hands on the gyrating hips of the stranger in front of them. The line grew and grew like a gigantic serpent slowly winding this way and that around the lot, toward the water, away from the water, around trees. A few times it seemed like the thing might head in Jude's direction, and he tried to decide what to do. He didn't feel comfortable joining in.

He sat, feeling strange. Wanting to party. Wanting not to be there. Knowing he shouldn't be there. Enjoying the music. Worrying about his feelings. The two blondes stood out, bouncing in the line. The tall, thin, marching black man with a horn at his lips veered in Jude's direction. Jude hoped he'd veer away again. He wasn't sure whether to move or just sit.

Suddenly it seemed there was no escape. The huge reptile headed by four black musicians was aiming straight for him. As it approached, he looked around and realized he was the only person in sight not pulled into the snake's inner being. He looked away, trying to act like he wasn't really there. Just a lost soul having a little evening meditation session, as though he had no idea a serpent was approaching. The leader passed closely, too closely. The bell ringer freed a hand to grab Jude's shoulder and tried to pull him up and in. Then somebody else grabbed his arm and pulled him part-way off his seat. Several more hands grabbed him, and suddenly he was up and enfolded into the mass. He was swaying and moving against his will. Suddenly hands went from his hips and wrapped around his stomach, and he felt breasts in his back, a crotch humping his behind, and a beer breath nibble on his ear. He hoped it was the blonde, but he wasn't sure.

He was now getting rocked from side to side by the pelvis and breasts implanted in his back. It felt good. The serpent wove toward the bar, and the bartender handed plastic glasses full of beer to anybody who held out a hand. Jude did not, but his rear appendage did. She released the hold with one hand to do so, and to take a swig or so. Soon, the serpent took a sudden jog, and she dumped beer on his shoulder. It smelled good, and felt cool, dripping down the inside of his shirt. "Shorry," she said, erupting a slight burp into his ear.

Jude decided he was not supposed to be here. Everything about it was dangerous and contrary to all he had learned and believed in. He tried to extricate himself from her grip. After failing twice, he dropped down and slipped away. She seemed to forget him the moment he was out of her hands. He marched briskly away, toward the dock. The musicians at the front of the line swerved and played on.

Jude shuffled along the dock trying to reconnect. He pulled off onto a side finger dock and sat down, dangling his legs over the side and admiring some large boats standing proudly on the still water. Several river bugs scurried around on the dock. How could he have even thought of enjoying that?

Suddenly he found himself mired in a muddy bog of self-pity. He was here because his father was dying. Being sober seemed completely out of place and time in this atmosphere. His wife and children were at home. The business could be going down the tubes with Griswold running the show in the absence of all the true businessmen. A drunken loose woman had poured alcohol on him, humped his ass, and belched in and nibbled on his ear.

Suddenly, to his horror, he realized that the rambling human serpent had made its way onto the dock and was approaching. He determined that it wouldn't turn down the finger dock where he sat, because it was a narrow dead end, but it was going to come too close for comfort, and he didn't want anybody to come and snatch him away. So he moved to the end of the finger dock and huddled against a piling, trying to become invisible.

The boisterous group grew ever closer, hooting, tooting, laughing, singing, and making noise and merriment. He felt as though he were from another world, dropped onto earth to observe as a terrible mistake. Now the dock thumped and bounced with the multiple feet of the swooning centipede. It took a very long time to pass by. He watched the humping crowd, and picked out the two blondes, one of whom was now attached to another man's ass.

Finally, it was gone. He was alone with his thoughts. He didn't really want to be alone with his thoughts either. He stood and made his way toward the boat.

* * * * * * *

Roosevelt had little experience with deep-sea fishing tackle, but he pitched in to prepare for tomorrow morning's fishing expedition.

Only Mr. Armstrong would be fishing. Dr. Steward had located medium-strength poles that were light enough for him. Roosevelt carefully wrapped thin wire around the nose of a small beak-nosed fish called a ballyhoo, attaching it firmly to a hook.

Roosevelt brooded over Jude's whereabouts. He hoped Jude was strong enough to get past the island-party atmosphere, and particularly Jude's weakness, rum. Besides that, he wasn't sure about Jude's ability to resist a loose woman. In the past, Jude had seemed very loose himself. Roosevelt knew that falling to temptation in the sex or romance area could lead right down other treacherous paths, just like a dieter who slips just a bit with a little sugar, and then makes a decision to go all the way.

Dr. Steward asked Roosevelt, "What do you think of Jude being out there?"

"It's a test. That's all. He knows what to do. He's got the tools. And then again, if he slips, he slips. Nothing we can do about it."

Dr. Steward handed Roosevelt some lures to thread. "I agree completely. I'm just concerned. I don't want to think we threw him to the wolves. He's going through a lot right now, and I'm not sure he even realizes it."

Roosevelt thought for a moment. "We didn't do anything. If he makes it, it's because he used the tools."

* * * * * *

Jude felt alone and lonely. It was the vague, unexplainable, desperate, utterly hopeless feeling that often was the precursor of using. He had a tight, empty feeling in the gut. He wanted to cry, but he hadn't done that in many, many years. He thought again of his dad's impending death. How awful would it be? How long would it take? What would it be like? He felt an empty sadness at his failure to be closer to his dad. But then he thought that he just acted the same way his dad did. It wasn't that they didn't love each other. They just weren't used to showing it.

The goddam Junkanoo kept wandering hither and yon, the music and revelry sparkling the night sky, coupled with the dulled sense of increasing drunkenness of the participants. He could hear the waves breaking at the beach across the road from the marina. He stood and walked off the dock and back across the parking lot toward the public phones. He had some difficulty communicating with the operator, but finally got connected with his home.

"Hey," he said to his wife. "How's everything?"

"Okay. Mark's sick. Just a cold, I guess. How are things there?"

"All right. The trip over was a complete nightmare. I don't remember ever being so sick."

"How's your dad?"

"Happy. I guess that's why we're here. He's smiling. I don't think he's thinking about dying. He's where he wants to be."

He asked if the kids were up. She said they were in bed, but she brought Kim to the phone for a short, sleepy conversation. Soon he was off the phone, standing there, listening to the crowd wandering around in the dark.

He felt an urge to talk to his A.A. sponsor and tried to reach him. There was no answer. He tried two more numbers, but everybody was out, probably at meetings. He remembered that there was a ready-made meeting right at the boat, but he just wasn't in the mood for that. So he wandered down to the beach, strolled, sat, thought, strolled some more, kicked the water, and eventually returned to the boat.

The boat was dark except for a single lamp burning in the living room. He sat on the couch, facing the kitchen. He could hear the party continuing, with island-style music echoing through the night sky. He thought again about how left out he felt, how much he'd wanted to join in the fun—to really join in. He'd been such a fuddy-duddy.

Suddenly he focused on a bottle of rum in a basket on the floor in the kitchen. A full liter of Jamaican rum. Where the hell had that come from? Who'd left it out to taunt him? The only person on the boat who could drink was his father, and it probably wouldn't be wise for him to drink either. He listened for any sound from the main cabin where his father slept. How would they know if he had a crisis?

A moment later he felt the rum bottle pulling him into its realm like an evil spirit. Oh shit. This was too much. Just too much. Look at the fucking bottle standing proudly, reflecting the light brown, powerful, fluid within. His mouth watered. He remembered many good effects—good memories. No, no, no. Remember the negative effects. Remember the nightmare in Jacksonville when he'd wound up in a nut ward. That one seemed rather funny right now. Remember how close he came to losing his family. Nothing. Remember how he would sit outside at night, driving his kids' toy boat to nowhere, so desperate, so sad, so suicidal. Give him time and he could rationalize all those bad times away. It wasn't working.

He began to sweat. He recalled the short phone call he'd had with his wife and Kim. He thought of his efforts to find an A.A. person by phone. He remembered that he had two A.A. members sleeping right downstairs. He didn't want to bother them, and he didn't want to confess that he was concerned about his sobriety.

He lay back on the couch, closed his eyes, tried to ignore the wild, thumping island music, and tried to think of good things. He relived running along next to his kids as he taught them to ride bicycles. He considered the promising improvement of his relationship with Joyce. He dwelled on issues at work.

After a while, he decided it was time to go to sleep. He sat up, swung his legs off the couch, and came eye to eye with the bottle of Appleton Rum. Instantly he felt the taste, remembering how tart it was, how different from other rums, how intriguing. His father had first introduced him to it. Of course, his father could drink with impunity. The bottle beckoned to him again. He saw himself get up, move across the room, pour some of the beautiful fluid into a glass, take it down, feel the burning, numbing in his gut, and collapse again. What would he do? Go to the beach, lie down with the bottle, make proper drinks with ice? Whatever he would do, he became convinced that it had become inevitable. He was destined to drink now, and nothing would stop him. He'd felt this feeling many times. He'd experienced it when he'd been destined to do heroin, and he'd experienced it many times when he'd awakened in the morning, bound and determined not to drink, all to no avail. The goddam bottle wouldn't leave him alone. It was unfair.

He stood with the intention of approaching it but hesitated and sat again. He had to have it, but he couldn't. He knew it wouldn't work, but he felt powerless to resist. God, he didn't want to go down this road. And then he remembered, when all else fails, he was taught in A.A. to pray. He still had the same fear of religion and praying. But at this point, it didn't matter. He was desperate.

Jude fell to his knees for the first time since he was a small child, bowed his head on the couch, and began. He didn't know quite what to say, so he just started with, "God, thank you for this day of sobriety and for all the days you have given me. Uh, I pray for your strength and guidance in all things. I pray that you'll help me to uh, I pray that you will remove this desire to drink from me. Um, I turn this over to you, and I thank you, and I pray that you will help me. Please remove the desire to drink. Thank you. Um, Amen."

He continued to rest his head on the couch, almost afraid to look behind him. But, to his great surprise, he felt completely different. He felt great hope that when he turned around the rum was going to be nothing to him. He pushed himself to a standing position, turned toward the kitchen, and saw the bottle as nothing more than a simple bottle. It had caused him great pain and anxiety, but no more. He marched toward it, grasped the neck, took it down to his father's room, and stuck it in the closet. His father snored quietly.

He was relieved. He was free. He was exhilarated. He sat at the wheel looking out over the bow. He couldn't believe it. He'd never felt so free. He threw his arms up in the air in a show of victory, gave a mostly silent hoot, and whispered aloud to himself, "I just fuckin' prayed, and it worked. I can't believe it."

There was no way he could sleep now. He decided to go and walk the beach, to be closer to nature, maybe even to be closer to God. He had a whole new appreciation for life, sobriety, and spirituality. The air outside was warm and fresh. He walked on clouds, exhilarated. He strolled down the soft sand to the beachfront, kicking soft sand and cool water on the slanted shoreline. Stars sparkled in the dark sky. The slight waves slapped the shore, reverberating in the still air. He was one with nature. He was sober. He'd beaten the craving. He could do it again, one day at a time.

* * * * * * *

At daybreak, Roosevelt was alarmed not to find Jude in his bunk. He threw on some shorts and climbed the stairs. Nobody was in the living room. Shit. He should have followed Jude around the evening before. He'd let him down by going to sleep, not caring about his friend's fragile situation. He stepped out onto the deck into the warm early morning air. "Yo, bro," Jude said from his perch on the bow.

Roosevelt was still alarmed. He must be loaded to be sitting out here at this time of the morning acting so cheerful with no caffeine. He approached. "'S up?"

"Man, I can't describe the night I've had."

"Try."

"I got this incredible urge to drink. An uncontrollable craving. I tell you the goddam rum bottle was put in my face as a test. It was beckoning to me. That's the only way I can describe it. It was fuckin' sayin' 'come here and drink me; I can make it all better'."

He didn't really look drunk. He looked like he was doing speed. "And?"

"And the first time in so long, I fell to my knees, and I prayed, and the craving was removed from me. I mean it. It was removed. I've never even imagined such an experience."

Roosevelt smiled. "Why did I doubt you?"

Jude looked at his feet. "You had every reason to doubt. I was in trouble."

"Then I should have been with you."

"Fuck it, man. This was the best thing that could a happened to me. It showed me that I had the tools."

Roosevelt remembered his Uncle Theodore saying something similar about Mama long ago. He'd said her time in jail was necessary. It was the only way she could come to terms with her addiction and get clean. Unfortunately, it hadn't worked for her. But Roosevelt believed that one had to reach the bottom. He knew that was true. Jude hit his bottom that last time. This trial had shown him that there was a way. The tools really were there.

"Let's go fix breakfast," Roosevelt said and ushered him toward the cabin.

They did their magic in the galley. The other two were inside preparing to depart. Jude's dad removed fishing gear and took it to the stern. Uncle Lee fired up the engines. The cooks presented omelets, loaded with cheese, ham, bacon, and other great things, laid on sautéed onions and peppers. They served orange juice and coffee and called the two guests to the table.

"I'll eat at the wheel," said Lee. "Let's cast off so we can head on out."

They dropped two fishing lines off the stern before they'd even cleared the bay. Jude's dad sat in the stern watching the lines pop in the still, bright-blue water.

"How you feeling?" Roosevelt asked.

"Actually, I feel fine, Roosevelt. I really do. Since I stopped the chemo. It's odd how this cancer works. I know it's killing me, but only because the doctors say so. Last week I went back to my oncologist and told him there must be a mistake. He said 'no'. There was no mistake." He shook his head. "I really appreciate your being here on this trip."

An hour later Jude's dad yelled "strike," snatched the starboard pole, and yanked it backward. Roosevelt stood at his side but didn't interfere. Lee throttled down. The line squealed, and then the dying man ground the gears and pulled in for a few minutes. He let it slack off, dropped the tip of the pole down and let the fish pull out for a bit. Then he tightened the drag again, pulled back and began reeling in again.

Jude came out and watched. His dad grimaced when working hard but smiled as well. "You doing okay?" he asked.

His dad nodded and continued working. Jude worried but knew better than to question. Eventually, a tired Mr. Armstrong brought a jack to the side. Jude gaffed it and brought it aboard. The old man was pale, his wispy white hair ruffled and dancing in the breeze. "That was the best fight I've ever had. Now, I need to go rest a few minutes." He rose and made his way to his cabin.

Chapter 24

THE FOLLOWING MORNING, Jude and Roosevelt made their ritualistic breakfast and together carried a tray down the stairs to the main cabin. Jude's dad didn't look right. His eyes beseeched them for help. Breathing rapidly through an open mouth formed like a plastic mold, he seemed to be struggling for breath, and hyperventilating. The sight stopped Jude and Roosevelt; they stood, eyes wide, looking at a drawn, pushed-back face, eyes staring out hard.

"This can't be good," Roosevelt whispered.

"Dad. Are you all right?" Jude asked, approaching the bed. Fearful eyes looked up at him, pleading. "Oh, God. Are you feeling any pain?"

His dad shook his head no. Roosevelt shot up the stairs to look for Dr. Steward.

They removed the food from the room and brought in some crushed ice for his lips. Lee confirmed in whispered words that this was the dying process. Then he left to call the mainland and report the news and call for help.

Jude didn't know what to do. Roosevelt whispered, "Did anybody do an obituary?"

Jude hadn't thought of that. He shrugged. "I dunno." "We need to do it."

Roosevelt sat by Mr. Armstrong's side and put a hand on his arm. "You all right?" Of course, there was no answer, although Mr. Armstrong did look his way. "We just want you comfortable. I know you're prepared for the end. I know you've made peace with your God." He squeezed his arm.

Mr. Armstrong stared at him. The rapid breathing through the plastic-looking lips was disconcerting.

* * * * * *

Reinforcements arrived in the afternoon in the form of the Reverend Rogers and a middle-aged black woman dressed in a white nurse's uniform. The Reverend went straight to Lansing's bedside, sat, held his hand, and said a little prayer. Then he stood, and hugged Jude and Roosevelt together. "I'm so pleased to see the two of you, looking so good."

The black woman approached Roosevelt and inquired about logistics. She opened a small cooler and removed a pill bottle. She placed syringes inside a drawer in the corner table. Roosevelt took the cooler to the galley to place the liquid drugs in the refrigerator.

She looked at Jude. "You must be the son."

He nodded.

"What's your name?"

"Jude."

She extended her hand. "I'm Eve. I'm a hospice nurse."

"What's that?"

"We help people die with dignity and free of pain."

Okay, so her job was helping people die. Whatever. "I thought you were a nurse."

"Well, I am," she whispered, "but the goal is different when somebody is dying. Rather than trying to help him get well, I am here to make him comfortable. It's okay. You just be here with your father. Spend time with him. I'll take care of the rest."

She was efficient. She figured out where everything was, who was who and what needed to be done.

When they'd finished working on an obituary, Jude left the boat and walked to the phones to call his sister. She answered the phone.

"Jen. It's Jude."

"I know it's bad news if you're calling."

"Yeah. Dad's dying. Can you come? We're in the Bahamas. We're gonna keep him here on the boat. Maybe we'll boat back to Florida. Don't know yet."

"What? Why aren't you taking him to a hospital?"

"Jenny. He doesn't want to be in a hospital. There's nothing to be done but to keep him comfortable. You know what hospice is?"

"Uh-uh."

"It's an organization. They provide medical professionals that help people deal with death. They know how to keep him comfortable. His doctor . . . oh, you know, Uncle Lee . . . he's here too. He ordered a hospice worker to come here. Reverend Rogers is here too."

"How do you know there's nothing to do?" She started blubbering.

"His oncologist—you know, a cancer doctor—told him he had a short time. That's why we came on this trip. He's accepted that. He understands it. He doesn't want to prolong his life. There's no point in it. He's ready."

"Tell me how to get there."

He told her and hung up.

Then he called his dad's lawyer, Luis Morales, the Cuban refugee his dad had met at a seminar at the Fontainebleau in Miami. "Mr. Morales," he said. "This is David Armstrong." Since Jude's dad always called him David, he figured Mr. Morales wouldn't know him by Jude.

"Ah. I'm sorry to hear your voice, because I know what it means."

"Yes sir. He's had a good few days here, fishing, relaxing."

"Is he gone yet?"

"No. He's in the dying process. I've never seen anything like it, but there's a nurse from hospice, and Uncle Lee, and they say this is normal."

"David, spend your time with him. We'll talk next week. Give him my regards, and my love, even if you think he can't hear. He can."

* * * * * * *

In the evening, Jude's dad started to squirm and grimace. "Jude," Eve said. "Please get the morphine from the fridge and bring it here."

The word "morphine" momentarily stunned him. He shot a glance at Roosevelt, who also recognized the effect that word would have on Jude.

Uncle Lee was not present. "Okay," Jude said, rising and climbing the stairs to the galley. Damn, what he could do with some injectable morphine. How could he even think that? His father needed the drug. It was not for recreation. Yet, the scheming had already begun in Jude's mind. He opened the refrigerator and took in the view of endless ecstasy. He stood in front of it, stunned, remembering the night before last when a rum bottle had tried to get to him. He grabbed one container of morphine and returned to the cabin, handing it to Eve.

Roosevelt kept an eye on Jude, who stared while Eve drew the clear liquid into a syringe. He knew what Jude was thinking. It had been a good test for him. Eve injected Mr. Armstrong intramuscularly, and soon he seemed to relax a bit.

This was just about too much for Jude. He felt sorry for himself for losing his father, sorry for his father, craving an escape, having touched morphine. Too much. He went outside and sat on the deck, passing the refrigerator again on the way. He looked out over the water, said a little prayer, and felt better.

Lansing Armstrong appeared to float in and out of consciousness and pain. He was where he wanted to be, on the gently rocking boat. He got Roosevelt's attention and called him over with his eyes, maybe grunting a little. Roosevelt leaned down and looked into his face. He was trying to say something, but Roosevelt couldn't make it out. Mr. Armstrong moved his head from side to side, looking, and then looked toward the port hole.

Finally, Roosevelt got it. "You want a view?"

Mr. Armstrong nodded.

"Sure, Mr. Armstrong. Anything else?"

The old man looked again, trying to make head motions that would deliver the idea.

Eventually, he just guessed. "Would you like to go out to sea?"

The dying man nodded and made a vocal sound.

"All right. I'll tell Lee."

It took a while for the crew to remove the dying man from his bed and place him on a couch, move the bed up to the living area, and carry him to it. They put his feet toward the bow so, when inclined, he could look forward. They opened all doors and windows so the sea smell and salt air would come to him. The move seemed to have worn him out, so he rested for a while, still doing the rapid breathing.

Jude's sister Jenny boarded the boat and came to the door. Jude saw her alarmed face. She looked a little plumper, her face a bit puffy.

Jude approached, and they did a half hug. "Hey, glad you made it."

"How is he?"

"He's alert right now. Can't really talk, but he'll know you're here."

She went to the bed and leaned over. "Dad?"

He opened his eyes. She appeared horrified at his grotesque face and mechanical breathing. He managed to say quite clearly, "Jennifer."

Everybody stopped and looked. Jenny sat on the bed and took his hand. Lansing seemed happy to see her. She'd left home after high school and worked in Tampa. She didn't come home often. He hadn't seen her in more than a year.

Roosevelt said, "Captain, Mr. Armstrong would like to enjoy a final boat ride rather than sitting at the dock. I believe we have all the personnel, equipment and medicine right here to keep him comfortable and head back to Daytona."

Lansing opened his eyes, looking alarmed.

"Don't worry. We will not take you to a hospital. We won't take you off the boat. But I bet you'd like the view and the ride."

Lansing nodded and closed his eyes.

Shortly, the boat pulled out of the marina. Jude asked Uncle Lee, "I take it that you're sure about the weather and the seas?"

Uncle Lee nodded.

Jenny went to the refrigerator and snooped around.

"Hungry?" Roosevelt asked.

"No, uh-uh. Looking for beer."

"Sorry. There isn't any."

"What're you all drinkin'?"

Roosevelt looked around at the others. "Jenny. Nobody here drinks alcohol."

"Come on!" She pointed at her brother with a turn of her head. "Never known this guy to pass up a beer or something more."

Jude shook his head and said, "Had to quit. I've had enough . . . in my life".

"Well, why didn't you tell me this place was dry? I'd a brought my own supply."

Jude said, "Listen, if you've got to have alcohol, make yourself a rum and Coke. There's Appleton Rum in the cabinet over there. Just please pour it, drink it, don't leave it around for me to smell, and don't leave the bottle out, okay?"

"Whatever you say, brother."

The boat crept along the dark water all evening and all night. As Lee steered through the darkness, the entire crew sat on the bed or the couch. Roosevelt and Jude took their Tylenol, fixed up their syringes, stepped out of view of Jude's dad, and injected their medicine.

Eve noticed what they were doing. "That's Interferon, right? You both got hep C?"

The boys nodded.

"Had biopsies?"

"Yeah", Jude said, "neither of us have very severe infection, and neither has any significant damage to the liver."

"Have your numbers gone down?"

"A little. My doctor's not that impressed."

"Mine isn't either," Roosevelt said.

"You know about the combination treatment? You don't have to shoot up every day."

Jude said, "My doctor doesn't believe the new treatment will help me since I'm only a partial responder to the Interferon."

At some point during the night, Jude sat next to his father and put a hand on his. His father stirred slightly. For the first time, Jude felt tears welling up. He was a little embarrassed getting choked up with all these people around, but everybody else had said goodbye and Eve had told him more than once to say goodbye. He couldn't remember ever having said he'd loved his father, or his father saying it to him, but right now, it seemed the appropriate time. He felt a sob escape as he said it, but he managed to say, "I love you." It was awkward. He wasn't sure if he'd enunciated clearly. So, he said it again. He was embarrassed. He felt his father's hand tremble, he thought. He looked at his face, like something from an old painting he recalled of men with mouths open and haunted eyes staring. His father looked at him, still breathing like he never even got a breath all the way in before it escaped.

* * * * * * *

The sun was rising behind them as they approached the Ponce de Leon Inlet, where the old red lighthouse stood guard, which joined the Intracoastal Waterway that would lead to the yacht club in Daytona. During the night, Lansing Armstrong's breath had slowed to a shallow whisper. Despite the open-mouthed look, he seemed at peace. The breath began to whistle as it entered and exited, like a slow-speed Lamaze technique. His body looked so diminished. Bones showed through nearly transparent skin.

Uncle Lee and Jude sat on the bed. Lee periodically checked Jude's dad's pulse. Eve sat watching, her job done. Jenny sat in the corner sobbing. Roosevelt steered. Reverend Rogers said one prayer after another. Lee called everybody around the bed, including Roosevelt, who slowed the boat and put it on autopilot for a few minutes. Lee held out his hands to form a circle. Jude and Roosevelt on either side of Lansing, included him in the circle. Lee said, "Whose Father?", an A.A. means of commencing the Lord's Prayer, and the crowd said the prayer. Energy flowed through the circle.

At ten after nine, as the boat entered the channel of the Halifax River, turned north and inched past Disappearing Island, Lansing Armstrong lay in silence, a shrunken remnant of the man. Dr. Lee Steward announced, "He's gone."

Eve, standing at his side, nodded agreement. Roosevelt set the autopilot again and approached the foot of the bed. Reverend Rogers extended his arms and drew everybody in. They said the Lord's Prayer again. Then, Reverend Rogers recited the 23rd Psalm.

The ride to the yacht club was somber. The former lieutenant colonel lay in state. Jude remembered good and bad adventures with his father. Most of the good ones had been on a boat, in the same waters where they now floated.

Roosevelt thought of Lansing Armstrong as his surrogate father. He'd never known another person like him, before or since. He was so honored to know and work with this gentleman, who'd rescued him and freed him from the stupid moves of his former life. He hadn't offered any help after Linda had died on him, but he had brought all the people to New Orleans who could help him and Jude both.

Uncle Lee got on the radio and announced to somebody that Lansing Armstrong had died, and his body would be arriving at the yacht club in a couple of hours. "I feel like just cruising at this speed. It wouldn't be appropriate to go any faster. Agreed?"

Everybody nodded.

* * * * * * *

At eleven fifteen, the Caprice approached the South Bridge and turned into the channel that led to the yacht club, past where Jude had practiced little league so unhappily, had ridden his bike so many times to and from his house and the yacht club, past the ballfield where he and Roosevelt had had an uncomfortable encounter long ago, and finally, toward their dock at the yacht club, where Jude's father had scolded him as Roosevelt and his family fished on the wall across the water.

A number of people stood on the docks looking toward the boat. Jude tried to discern their faces. As they drew closer, Jude recognized family, friends, yacht club regulars and employees, staff from the law office, and others. Jude's dad lay on the elevated bed in the living area, but the doors were closed so his privacy could be maintained in death.

As the Caprice came around the large boats to its slip, Roosevelt and Jude, standing side by side, each with an arm around the other's shoulder, almost cried to see the groups of people standing on the dock—Jude's wife, Joyce, holding the hands of Mark and Kim; Roosevelt's wife, Gloria, holding the hand of his son, Tad; Pearl Mae; Roosevelt's grandmother; Uncle Theodore and Auntie Barbara; Billy Howell and his mother; A.A. members; and friends of Lansing who Jude knew from the yacht club and other places.

Jude and Roosevelt jumped off the boat and tied lines to the cleats, as Jenny, Reverend Rogers and Uncle Lee climbed down and were greeted by people on the docks.

Jude's and Roosevelt's wives and children embraced them. And then they were greeted by so many people it was difficult to keep track. Somebody in the crowd started a chorus of "Amazing Grace" and the entire crowd joined in. The two friends, brothers in many ways, had chills as they embraced each other, their families, friends, sobriety and life.

EPILOGUE

Ten years later, as Jude and Roosevelt approach the age of fifty, they both have years of sobriety. Both have stayed close to A.A. and utilized its tools.

Both remain happily married and enjoy their children. Roosevelt and Gloria have a nine-year-old girl as well.

Roosevelt is completely free of all evidence of hep C, continues to work out, play basketball, and maintain a healthy lifestyle. While Jude still has no symptoms, and is quite healthy, he has been advised by his doctors to continue to monitor his condition and not to try additional treatment for the immediate future.

Although they might still jump if they see a small white mint, white or brown powder, or a sign saying "Drugs" —or even just saying "Rugs"— both men live in peace and tranquility, having left their pasts far behind, like many others of their generation.

END